*It takes him about three heartbeats to go running past me, realizing I'm there when he's three strides down the hall. As he slides to a stop and spins around, I step out of the doorway and turn to face him.*

*"You aren't looking for me, now are you?"*

*The absurd amount of adrenaline flowing through me forces my brain to switch to the 'smart-assed' Whitney. I simply can't help it.*

*"Конечно ищу, вы, нахалка!" (Of course, I am, you insolent female) he replies, testing me perhaps.*

*"Well, I suppose I am a bit on the 'insolent' side, but let's discuss the issues at hand. And let's do it in English — my Russian still needs work."*

*"As you wish. I want the 'item' that Elena has given you."*

*He takes a step toward me, and I know I can't allow him to get any closer. Distance — Howard, and the Marines who trained us, always emphasized that until you are mentally ready, keep distance between you and your opponent.*

*"I can hear just fine from where you are — let's keep the distance, shall we?"*

*He stops and continues staring at me, a rather sinister grin covering his face.*

*"Now, assuming I actually have an 'item' — and I'm not saying I do — what in God's name makes you think I'm simply going to hand it over to you?"*

*Again, the smartass. So much for playing dumb, I suppose. I'm definitely in it up to my ass now.*

*"Well now, Miss Nelson, you certainly are bold for one who is on her first assignment. If you choose to defy me, I suppose I will be forced to take it from you — which I should point out, will not be a pleasant experience."*

*"Okay, now that I'm scared..."*

# SOLUTION SQUARED

## *Important Acknowledgments*

Thanks to the following people for their understanding and willing assistance in keeping me straight and ensuring that the languages other than English, found throughout the story, were properly translated:

Mr. Cemre Güngör of Ankara, Turkey, for his assistance with the English to Turkish translations.

Ms. Maria Kuruskina of Moscow, Russian Federation, for her assistance with the English to Russian translations.

Mr. Haggen Kennedy of Salvador, Bahia, Brazil for his assistance with the English to Greek translation.

Mr. Ron Basedow of Tampa, Florida for his assistance with the English to German translation.

Ms. Louise Lewis of Gatineau, Quebec, Canada for her assistance with the English to French translations.

I tip my hat to these five individuals as well as every person on earth who has put forth the effort required to become bi- or multi-lingual!

Finally, I'd like to send a very special THANKS to Mrs. Heather Young of Oregon, Wisconsin, for her inadvertent assistance. She unwittingly gave me a really good idea. And while you will find several 'images' throughout the book, Heather is solely responsible for the only piece of 'artwork'!

*Mike*

Main Entry: **so·lu·tion**

Pronunciation: sə'lüshən *also* səl'yü-

Function: *noun*

Inflected Form(s): **-s**

Etymology: Middle English, from Middle French, from Latin *solution-, solutio* act of loosening, solving, from *solutus* (past participle of *solvere* to loosen, solve, dissolve) + *-ion-, -io* -ion

**1 b :** an answer to or means of answering a problem : a clearing up : ***EXPLANATION, DENOUEMENT*** <**your solution to the problem**> c : (1) : a set of values of the variables of an equation that satisfies the equation

Main Entry: **square**

Pronunciation: 'skwa(a)][(ə)r, -we], ]ə

Function: *verb*

Inflected Form(s): **-ed/-ing/-s**

Etymology: Middle English *squaren,* modification (influenced by Middle French *esquarre* square) of Middle French *escarrer* to square, from (assumed) Vulgar Latin *exquadrare* -- *transitive verb*

**3 a :** to multiply (a number or **quantity**) by itself : ***RAISE TO THE SECOND POWER...***

*Quoted From:*

*Webster's Third New International Dictionary, Unabridged.*

Merriam-Webster, 2002

http://unabridged.merriam-webster.com

"There is no such thing as chance; and what seems to us merest accident, springs from the deepest source of destiny."

Friedrich Schiller
German Poet and Philosopher
1759 – 1805

# 1

I remember... stepping through the main door and onto the sidewalk in front of the hotel.

I remember... being grabbed from behind.

I remember... turning to find two huge guys behind me.

I remember... turning and looking at Daria and seeing her collapsing into the arms of another guy.

I remember... being stabbed in the lower back.

I remember... being in the back seat of a speeding car.

And... I remember the stench of alcohol and cigarettes.

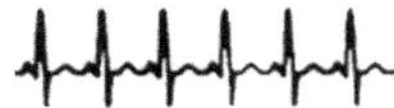

# 2

I'm dreaming... I must be...

I'm on a plane... a small plane... going somewhere...

My head is lying against a window, and as I look out it through still blurry eyes, I see water. Lots of water.

We are close to the water. Maybe just a few feet above it. I know I'm drugged, so the few feet must be more.

I move my head, and feel someone grab my arm... it's a guy... the same guy who grabbed me... back in Rabat. He's got a syringe... and he's sticking it into my arm... I try to move it... but it just lays there. I hear moaning behind me... but I can't move my head enough to look.

I hear voices... guys talking.

It's in front of me... I try to make my eyes focus. It's all blurry... That's right... I remember... I'm dreaming...

I try to make myself listen to the voices... Russian voices...

Yes... that's it... they're speaking Russian...

I catch a few words... 'Daria', and 'money'...

Now... the dream is fading...

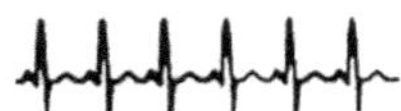

# 3

"Mrs. Whitman, there are some guys from the DoD here to see you. They don't have an appointment," I hear from the intercom on my desk.

"Okay, Angie, I have a minute. Send them in."

"Yes ma'am."

Two seconds later, my office door opens, and Mikey and my brother walk in. They stand quietly and wait until my secretary closes the door behind them.

"Good morning, Sis," Rhyan says, looking perplexed.

"So, Court, whose birthday..." Mike starts to say but is interrupted when the door again opens.

When I see Howard standing there, I damn near faint.

"Hello, Courtney," he says, closing the door behind him. "Seems I'm not the only one invited to this party."

It's been slightly more than five years since I've seen or spoken to Howard. Two years after we 'lost' Whitney, he chose to retire and has since been working in the private sector. I figure seeing me is too hard for him, because to him, to his eyes, I *am* my sister.

Hazards of being 'identical'.

Now, his apparent requested presence along with Rhyan and Mikey 'turning up', raises all kinds of red flags. When the door to my office opens a third time, without a knock, 'the other shoe drops' as they say, and there stands Alice Williamson, Director, Central Intelligence.

"Absolutely no calls, no visitors, no interruptions of any kind, until I tell you otherwise," she pretty much orders my secretary, who is standing behind her.

"Yes ma'am!" Angie replies, closing the door.

Alice walks directly over to my desk, hands me a stack of photos that are in her left hand, then turns and takes a seat in one of the chairs across from my desk.

"Those were taken approximately one week ago."

The photos are in color and were taken with a wide lens, close up. All are of the same two females. Dark tans, very black hair, toned bodies, and expensively dressed. There's one of them getting out of a black Benz limo, one of them exiting what appears to be a high-end department store, and one of them in an upscale restaurant. All total there are nine photographs. The last image is of them exiting what appears to be a large office building.

"So, who are they?" I ask, laying the photos on my desk.

Without answering my question, she leans forward and hands me a second stack.

"Those were taken three hours ago."

I'm holding three 8x10, high-resolution, color photos. They are very grainy and the first two are a bit out of focus, telling me they were taken by hand, from a distance, with a long lens, and in a hurry. It appears I'm looking at the process of a female being abducted, by at least three males, and those doing the abducting aren't being at all careful about their task. In the second photo, there's what appears to be blood visible on the woman's forehead.

The last one, makes me zone out the moment I look at it. I *know* my heart rate increases, and I even stop breathing.

"Courtney?" someone says, I have no idea who.

I sit motionless, slowly running out of oxygen, my eyes locked on the photograph in my hands, and I somehow know what's happening.

Even with the subtle changes, and as weird as it will sound, I *definitely* recognize the face, and because I know who it is, I know where this conversation is going as well.

Alice is apparently expecting just this reaction.

"Yes, Courtney, it's her, as difficult as that is going to be for you to understand."

Her voice snaps me out of my momentary daze, and my lungs finally force my brain to acknowledge that I need oxygen. I finally suck in a deep breath, concentrating on the photograph to the exclusion of all else. Graininess and poor quality aside, I am definitely holding a photograph of *Daria Ladenko. A recent photograph.*

My heart now racing, I stare at the photo, realizing that if my sister survived that 'explosion', by whatever bizarre means, her nemesis must have survived it too.

Then another revelation. The covert message Whitney left at the daycare center, years ago, was very well planned. Either Alice has perfected her acting techniques or, based on what's currently happening, she actually doesn't know what Whitney did. Either, I know, is quite possible.

"Courtney?" Alice prompts me.

"Uh, Alice... I'm seriously confused. She's dead unless, like me, she has an identical twin." I know I have to play this out, lest I give away what my sister did.

Alice again leans forward and hands me yet another photograph. It was taken in a manner to allow for clear identification as if the photographer carefully stabilized the camera against something. Even though it was taken from a distance and with a long lens, the face is in almost perfect focus. It's a second female, putting up a decent fight as she too, is being forced into a car. Although she doesn't look like my sister physically, I somehow know it is. Perhaps it's the bright red ponytail, being held in place with a yellow scrunchie. I have to consciously force myself not to laugh – it's without a doubt, her favorite alias – *Alexandra Jaeger.*

Howard steps up behind me and looks over my shoulder, at the photograph in my hands. When I glance up at him and see the look on his face, I know he recognizes the disguise, but his confusion is quite apparent.

"You've been out of circulation for a long time, Howard, but this has a huge bearing on you which is why I've asked you to come."

In a single heartbeat, based on what Alice just said, and the photo he is staring at over my shoulder, Howard's proverbial light bulb goes on.

"*Holy shit, Alice!* You staged it? The whole damn thing was staged?" he blurts out as he takes the photo from me.

Once a spy, forever a spy, as Whitney always liked to say. Apparently, 'spy blood' still flows through Howard's veins, retired or not, and in true spy fashion, his first comment is about the 'op' rather than the fact the only woman he ever truly loved, is still alive.

Mike walks over to my desk, picks up the rest of the photos, and has Rhyan looking over his shoulder at them as well. Mikey too catches on, the moment he recognizes Daria.

"*No fucking way!*"

"Yes, Sergeant Major, there is a way. She is, and always was," Alice replies to Mike's outburst, "*our asset.*" When she finishes the sentence, she's looking right at me.

The moment she says it, I understand, and again, my heart rate increases. In a single moment of absolute clarity, the 'why' of what my sister has done, makes perfect sense.

Fourteen years earlier, Alice used us, the entire detail, as a means to get Daria clear of the Russians, without getting her killed. I flashback to Alice's comment in Howard's office on the day we first started planning the operation – *'The catch to all this is, I won't give up any of our assets to do it. I've made that clear to the Director.'*

She couldn't lose any assets because that would cause a situation that would need an explanation, something those in power don't like to do. Alice always planned to 'kill' Daria, in order to retrieve her. Our little operation in Istanbul, the one that made Daria 'public', gave her the perfect means to pull it off. And, at some point during the process, knowing she would never get an opportunity so perfect, Alice offered my crazy-ass sister the chance to play in Daria's world. One of ultra-deep cover, black operations. The type that only God knows about. Whitney is the type of spy that only comes along once in a career, or in Alice's case, twice. She already had Daria. If she could somehow recruit Whitney, and team them up...

I have to block the thought and force back the smile I know is about to break on my face. The last thing I need is Alice asking me questions I don't want to answer.

Knowing Whitney like I do, if Alice made an even slightly enticing offer, no way would my sister have been able to turn her down. From the day we started our little 'adventure', deep in my heart I always had a bizarre, but intense feeling, that of the two of us, my sister would become the ultimate 'spy'.

Alice also knew that recruiting Whitney in the middle of the Crete operation gave her an ace in the hole. Someone on both teams.

How damn convenient was that?

Alice Williamson is scarily efficient at her profession.

"Oh... my... God..." I mumble, giving Alice reason to believe I realize who the female in the second photo is.

"Yes, Courtney, it's her. They've been together since Crete. And, if you choose to do what I'm about to ask you to do," she turns and looks at Rhyan and Mike, "ask all four of you to do, I will give you a full accounting."

I let go, and the tears come. In my head, I flashback to the daycare center and know that all of this is about to finally come to an end. My sister is going to have to go back to being just Whitney. She won't have a choice. This, *whatever this is,* is going to end up being the ultimate 'compromise'.

"Yes, Howard, it was staged. It was necessary. I couldn't afford to lose her to the Russians after you," Alice says, pointing right at me, "pulled her into the open in Istanbul. Turning them into a team seemed to be a natural evolution. You should all know this – *she chose to do it*. All I did was make an offer."

She pauses for a moment as if waiting for a response. When none of us says anything, she continues.

"Once you see what they've managed to accomplish over the last decade, I can only hope you'll understand."

Finally, Rhyan speaks up.

"Okay, so am I the only one in the dark here? *They?* Who are these people?"

"It's hard to explain, Senior Chief..." Alice says, just before I stop her.

"Alice, please, give me some time. I need to talk to him, and to these guys also," I say, pointing at Howard and Mike.

"Fair enough. My office in thirty minutes, and plan to be there for a while. You two," she says, pointing at Mike and my brother, "are, for the time being, TDY to this office. You can call your Commanders and verify if you like."

She stands up, turns, and disappears out the door.

I take the photos from Mike, pull one from the pile, lay it on the desk in front of my brother, and then spin it around, orienting it so that he can see it.

"That," I say, tapping on the female in the photograph, "is Daria Ladenko, an employee of the Sluzhba Vneshney Razvedki, killed in a gun battle on Crete, almost fifteen years ago."

"This is about Whitney's death?" Rhyan asks.

"Brace yourself, Rhyan," Michael says, putting a hand on his shoulder, as he watches Howard hand me the photo of Whitney, which I lay on top of the first photo.

"And that," I look right into my brother's eyes, tapping on the face in the second photo, "is our goddamned sister. You know, *the dead one?*"

Although my younger brother was never one for being emotional, the look on his face is priceless and I will never forget it. When I turn and look again at Howard, for a second, I wonder if he's going to lose it. I stand up, step around my desk, wrap an arm around him, and we stand watching, as my little brother picks up the photo, and carefully examines it. After a couple of seconds of quiet contemplation, and without looking at us he says, "Doesn't much look like her, but she's undeniably behaving like my sister would – being a general pain in the ass."

Mike, Howard, and I, laugh at the same time.

"Are you okay with this, Rhyan?" I ask, stepping over, and taking one of his hands.

He shrugs, then after a few more seconds of thought, lifts his head, and looks right at me.

"Nothing the two of you ever got into surprised me, Sis – why start now?" he replies, a devious little smirk covering his face. "But, actually seeing her, after believing she was dead for almost fifteen years, that's going to be, seriously weird."

I allow myself to relax and silently thank God for making my younger brother, the awesome man he's become.

"I couldn't have phrased it any better, Rhyan," Howard adds, laughing.

"Let's go talk to Alice, shall we?" I ask.

"Yeah," Howard replies, "I don't know about the rest of you, but I can hardly wait to hear the rest of *this* fucking story."

Each of them starts toward the door, but Mike hesitates. When I pass him, he reaches out, tugs on my sleeve, and when I stop, he leans over, and at barely an audible whisper, says, "I bet you never expected it to end like this, did ya, Court?"

As weird as this will sound, when I turn to look at him, that same sinister little smirk is on his face – the same one he had eight years ago, at the daycare center, when Misty described the woman who drew on my daughter's hand, and gave her the Sharpie.

*"Kiss my ass, Michael!"* I whisper as I turn to follow the others out the door and into the hall.

All the way to Alice's office, I'm forcing back the tears.

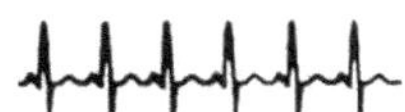

# 4

"They're *deep cover*. With the exception of the last Director, Melinda Aston, and me, *no one* knows about them. They've been doing things... things that we can't legally do ourselves."

"Black Ops?" Howard asks as he thumbs through one of the numerous volumes, all of which are stamped 'TS/SCI/ISOP' in bright red letters, of data stacked on Alice's desk.

"Among other little tasks," Alice replies.

"So, my *'dead'* sister spent the last decade killing people for the CIA?" Rhyan asks.

"Yes, she has," Alice replies, in a cold, calculated voice. "She and Daria have terminated at least twelve high-profile targets that *your bosses* said they couldn't legally take care of. The DoD came to us on a number of targets."

"Imad al-Din Qaderi and Abdul-Aziz Barad," Mike says, looking right at Williamson.

"Among others," she replies in the same cold, impassive voice.

"My sister is an *assassin?*"

"Yes, Courtney, that's part of what she's done for us. But the two of them have done far more than 'kill some people', so don't isolate their existence to only that."

"*No shit!*" Howard blurts out as he's reading, causing us to turn and look over at him.

"The incident on the Zaliv America," he says, looking right at Alice.

"Yes. Based on excellent intelligence, but unbeknownst to the Russians, Daria and Whitney were placed on board, and the hijacking never occurred. To this day, no one has identified the people who thwarted the attempt," she replies. "Whitney and Daria also 'acquired' enough info during the operation, that they selectively removed several high-ranking individuals from 'Al Mueed' after the fact. You should also recall that, for the most part, their organization completely collapsed shortly after that incident."

"Shit," I reply, still turning pages in the thick folder on my lap. "The CIA has certainly gotten their money's worth out of my sister."

"Yes, we have, which is why I want them back. Alive. We owe them. Both of them. I'm not going to let it end like this. I'm officially making it your," she pauses and her eyes lock to mine, "responsibility to recover them. If anyone can be compelled to complete such a task, it will be the four of you."

"Where did it happen?"

"Outside a hotel in Rabat. To complicate things further, we have no damn idea why they were there."

"They weren't on assignment?" Howard asks.

"No. They were working on a project at the compound in Marsá al Burayqah, with Melinda…"

*"The compound?* The same one that…"

"Yes, Courtney, *that* compound. Well, it's *our* compound, actually. We managed to 'appropriate' a certain Greek shipping line amid all the chaos that followed the operation on Crete as well. The Greek government, however, still doesn't realize we have our hands in it."

"Who the hell has been running all this?"

"That's not important. Getting Whitney and Daria back is. As I was saying, they were at the compound and when Melinda went looking for them the following morning, they were gone. After she did some investigating, she discovered they flew to Rabat in the middle of the night, for reasons unknown."

"Okay, the big question. Who has them?" Michael asks.

"The answer is, we don't know."

"Okay," I stand and face the others in the room, "let's go get my screwy sister and her 'partner' away from the bad guys, shall we?"

"Where do you want Melinda?" Alice asks.

"It stands to reason we can't function freely in Libya, so..."

"Melinda is mobile, and can set up wherever you want her."

"Tell her to call me in an hour. I need to research something before we start this. I assume someone in Signals knows what's going on?"

"Yes. They also know that you have Level Five access now. On this one, Courtney, anything I know, you know."

Howard's surprise is not only visible but instantaneous as well. Unlike my brother and Mike, Howard fully understands what Alice's comment means.

Five minutes later, I'm once again, standing in a secure room in the basement of CIA headquarters, staring at giant wall monitors.

Déjà vu... for sure.

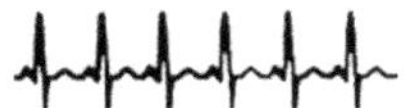

# 5

"Okay, I'm here. What are your other two wishes?"

Mike, Rhyan, and Howard are quick to turn toward the voice, but I know exactly who it is. When I too turn around, I find Miss Cassandra Cartwright grinning at me.

"CASSIE! Holy shit!" I yell. Then, as if we are a couple of high school kids seeing each other after summer vacation, I run across the room and throw my arms around her.

Cassie is now the Station Chief at the Istanbul embassy. When Carl retired five years earlier, as the most senior agent remaining, Cassie stepped right into the job. Even though we talk occasionally, and swap emails constantly, I haven't *seen* her since she became Station Chief.

"What the hell are you doing here?"

"Rumor has it you're about to 'start some shit' as they say. I figure you can probably use someone good with a handgun," she replies, referring to our 'loading dock' incident years ago.

"Well, I tend to use people that *'don't fucking miss'*."

"I definitely qualify. You know *I never miss, Courtney,*" she replies with a wink.

I hug her a second time and whisper, "It's really good to see you again, Cass."

With a smile, she takes a step back. "Willie wants in too if you need him. He's in 'hot standby' back in Turkey, and can be anywhere we want him in a couple of hours. Melissa says to tell you 'HEY', that she still has your sunglasses, and that she isn't giving them back. And of course, she too, is ready to play, if you need her."

"Do you guys know what's going on?" I ask, glancing at Howard.

"Doesn't matter, Court. We're all in, regardless. If it's important enough to draw Courtney Whitman out from behind a desk and back into the field..."

I hear snickering behind me.

"Yeah, yeah..." I give Cassie a dirty look. "But there is one thing I need to do really quick. Wait here."

I turn, walk into one of the empty offices, close the door, and pick up a phone.

Seconds later, Alice Williamson is on the line.

"Whatever it takes, Courtney. Period. I will deal with any questions from higher up than me, understood? I owe your sister something, a debt of sorts, and now is my chance to clear the books. If anyone asks for authorization for anything from this point forward, use the authorization GAIA."

I laugh, I can't help it.

"Gaia. As in the mother of the Titans?"

"Yes. It's a nickname they gave me on the Hill after I took over the Agency. Anyone who might have reason to question anything you do will recognize it."

"And personnel use is at my discretion?"

"Absolutely. Whoever you need, wherever they are."

"And funding? How are we going to explain that?"

"Think back for a moment, Courtney, and I bet you can answer that one yourself," she replies, letting the thought hang.

It takes a few seconds, but I eventually grasp her meaning.

"*Oh, crap!* You still have that?" I blurt out.

"The fact is, Melinda and Whitney turned it into about six times the original amount. One of your sister's hidden talents seems to be 'investments'."

I do some quick mental math, and then damn near faint.

"*My God, Alice*! Do you know what that works out to?"

I hear her laugh.

"Yes, Courtney, I do. It's the single source of funding for everything the three of them have been doing for the last fourteen years. I was being *literal* when I told you *no one* knows about them. *Not even this country's Commander in Chief.* We, the three of them and myself, have operated in the 'black' all along. Now, do you understand?"

"Yes ma'am, I guess I do."

"Just get them back, Courtney. That's the single thing that will make my tenure as Director of this organization matter."

"I have one more question."

"And that is?"

"My parents. Although they will accept all the secrecy, I would like to give them some kind of a reason, when I ask them to take care of my kids."

"More importantly, you want to tell them your sister is still alive," she replies, following it with a muffled laugh. "Do whatever you have to, but do it quickly."

"Yes ma'am. I'll make sure everything goes across your desk. I'll talk to you again soon. Goodbye."

"Goodbye, and good luck as well!"

I hang up the phone and stand a moment, thinking. She's being too congenial, too agreeable. Basically, Alice is making this way too easy. The thing is, Alice Williamson is *never* easy. *Everyone* who's ever worked with, or for her, knows that. My mind is already analyzing, as I reach out and open the door next to me, making everyone in the Signals room turn to look at me. I walk over to the table where I laid the photographs Alice gave me, pull two of them out, and then walk directly over to Cassie, who is now sitting with Rhyan and Mike, staring at one of the wall monitors.

"Look familiar?" I hand her the photo of Daria.

"*FUCK!* That's not possible!" She looks at me, confusion covering her face. "Courtney, *we saw her die!* For God's sake, we were there. No one could have survived it."

I hand her the second photo, which shows the face of the other female as she's trying to fight off two guys.

"Care to guess who that," I tap on the face, "is?".

She too, recognizes the disguise, and for a second, I think she may faint.

"Jeezzz, Courtney," she mumbles. Still staring at the photo, she adds, "It doesn't even look like her."

"That's the 'shit' you just volunteered to get into, Cass. We're going to retrieve them, and at this point, we don't even know who has them. Your career has moved so far past this kind of crap, that you, and you too," I point at Howard, "are going to have to decide just how far into this screwed-up mess you are willing to get. We – all of us standing here – know that based on the history of the situation, at some point, there will inevitably be gunplay."

Howard laughs, shakes his head, then flips me off, making both my brother and Mike break up laughing.

"I was getting shot at when your *mother* was a rookie," Howard says, looking me right in the eyes. "And you damn well know it wasn't bullets that made me retire, Courtney."

"I know Howard, I know."

"Howard's 'universal sign language' pretty much covers it for me too," Cassie blurts out, trying to lighten things up again.

"Okay then. I need to make another call. Howard, you and Cass can get with Keith," I point at a guy sitting at the largest console in the room, "and get every intercept they have from Morocco in the last seventy-two hours. You two," I turn and point at Rhyan and Mike, "need to get your stuff ready to deploy. We're going to Spain."

"We're ready, Sis. I mean come on, what do we do for a living?" my smart-ass little brother responds.

"You guys need to go by military aircraft, based solely on all your damn toys. Get to the terminal at Langley and I will make sure you're on the next aircraft to Morón. Once I know where we will be, I'll get word to you. Okay?"

"We're gone. See you on the other side, Sis," my brother responds.

"*Slowly*, Courtney. Plan carefully. Think..." Mike offers, gently tapping on my forehead. "Got it?"

"I promise, Mikey, I promise," I reply, smiling at him.

He knows my adrenaline levels are completely out of control, and once again, he's looking out for me. I know I have to move quickly, yet very, very, carefully.

Seconds later they're gone. The moment the door closes, I reach down and pick up the nearest phone. I need help from one very specific person.

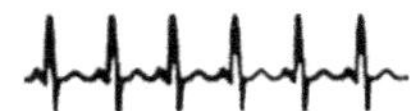

"United States Embassy, London. How can I direct your call?" the female voice says.

"Extension 6100 please."

"Yes ma'am. One moment."

After several clicks and circuit changes, I finally hear the secure line ringing. It's after 4:00 pm in England, so I figure all the circuit changes mean the call is being forwarded to her cell. She answers on the third ring.

"Masterson."

"How's my favorite Russian today?"

Dead silence.

"Hummm. Dead apparently."

"Is it actually you?" Joey asks, in a whisper.

"Who else calls you their favorite Russian?"

"Damn. I'm not sure what to say."

"It's a secure connection, say whatever you want."

"Time hasn't changed you much."

I think I hear the smallest of laughs.

"You're going to get a chance to find out, first hand. Clear your calendar, book a flight to Gibraltar – *as Veronika* – and meet me in the airport restaurant tomorrow for breakfast at, say, 7:00 am local time."

"I'll be there."

The speed of her response surprises me.

"Good. And can you keep it between us for now?"

"If I'm coming as *Veronika*, I most certainly can."

"Excellent. I'll explain tomorrow."

"Done. See you then."

"Bye."

I hang up and sit for a moment, reflecting.

After Whitney's 'death', Joey pretty much avoided me. Howard told me at one point, that she was being consumed by the belief that *she* should have been in the van that day, and not my sister. Once Chuck came and put me back on a straight path, I went to find Joey in England, to set things straight. Although she feigned agreement, I knew in my heart that she would always blame herself – just as I'd been trying to do. It was blatantly apparent that every time she looked at me, she saw Whitney. However, I also realized I didn't know what, if anything, could be done about it. With the multitude of harsh realities in Joey's life, this was yet another. No matter how hard I tried, I couldn't make myself imagine what it must be like to be inside her head.

I made five trips to see her over those first three years – to try to get through to her. Eventually, I decided to let it be. Both Chuck and I invited her to visit, but she very politely begged off each time. Since she became Station Chief in London, we've had a bit more contact over various projects and missions, but it's all very businesslike. In my heart, she's still my friend, but I can't seem to make her see that. Eventually, I had to accept things as they were.

Now I wonder, how badly the truth will screw her up?

Howard's voice brings me back to reality.

"Jezzz, Courtney, you need to see this."

Cassie is standing next to Keith, reading something over his shoulder while he's typing away. Seconds later, some message traffic pops up on one of the wall monitors. It appears to be a transcript of some kind, and it's in Russian.

"That's nice guys. I can't read Cyrillic. Neither can you."

"But I can," comes from a male voice behind me, which I immediately recognize as my husband's.

"Hey, babe. What are you...?" I start to ask.

"Duh? What the hell do you think I'm doing here? At times, my dear wife, I really do worry about you." He shakes his head as he walks over and hugs me.

Everyone laughs, including me. Chuck stands quietly for a second, staring at the monitor, mentally translating.

"Where did it come from?" I ask Keith.

"Our guys in the embassy in Tripoli captured it, in the clear no less. It originated from a cell phone there, and ended up on a land-based line in Rabat."

"I want to know the physical location of that number."

"The Russian Consulate, Mrs. Whitman. The cell phone had a number originating in Turkey. The call originated on a tower about two blocks from our embassy."

"So, what the hell is going on?" Cassie mumbles, still looking over Keith's shoulder.

"Someone made Daria, that's what. The conversation is about the fact she isn't dead and is actually alive and living in a compound in Marsá al something or other, using the name Allison Paddison," Chuck offers, still diligently staring at the wall monitor. "Whoever was at the receiving end was Russian, his diction and language use tell me that. The originator wasn't. The receiver said he would need confirmation before acting. Then the call was terminated."

"Jesus! Are you telling me that Alice ran a scam on the Russians and now, after over a decade, they've figured it out?" Howard asks, looking dumbfounded.

In a single instant, the answer magically materializes.

*The money!*

"Oh God! If they've taken them, and they believe they know anything about that money..." My heart is racing.

"Easy, Court. Slowly, and by the book," Cassie says.

"She's right, Court. Slowly and carefully if we are going to give them a chance. We rush into this, everyone gets screwed," Howard offers.

I collapse into the nearest chair, and Chuck is next to me immediately, holding one of my hands. Mentally, I'm back in that warehouse in Odessa. Then, as quickly as my mind drifts, my husband grounds me again – just as he did once before.

"Court? Courtney? Are you listening to me?"

When I don't respond, he suddenly shakes the crap out of me, almost pulling me out of my chair.

*"Damnit, Courtney Whitman, pay attention!"* he yells at me, in front of everyone in the room. "Don't you dare freak out on us now! Do you hear me!"

I blink my eyes, glance around the room, then say, "Yes dear, we all hear you."

After a simultaneous sigh of relief, everyone laughs.

"This is what you do babe. You are the best damn analyst this agency has, and if that is who you think it is, she's in the best hands she could be, at this exact moment. Now, quit with all the 'oh God' bullshit, and do what the hell it is you do, okay?"

"Yeah," Howard says, "let's do this!"

"Uh-huh," Cassie adds.

I stand, look at each of them, and then with a forced smile say, "Refresh my memory, Cassie, why in the hell do we keep doing this?"

Again laughter, which is a good thing. I know that if I focus too narrowly, I'll lose it.

Five minutes later, I'm back in Alice's office.

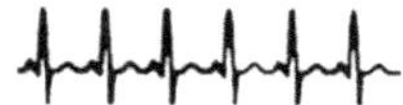

# 7

"You believe the Russians are involved? After all this time? Damn. I better make some calls. What else?" she asks, as she starts scribbling notes.

"I'm calling in a favor, and to collect on it I need to be in Gibraltar in," I turn my wrist and check my watch, "twenty-one hours. Also, we've decided to set up in…"

I'm interrupted by a knock on the door, and without hesitation, Alice yells "COME IN". When the door opens, there staring back at me is Melinda Aston, Asset Specialist. The scary part is, she looks *exactly* like she did the last time I saw her, although that was close to ten years ago. I watch quietly, as she walks over and stops in front of Alice's desk.

"If this is going to work, Alice, I'm going to need a couple of minutes alone with Courtney."

Without a word, Alice stands and leaves her own office, and closes the door behind her. Melinda quickly takes a seat and starts talking.

"Okay, so you must know by now that I was a major part of what happened on Crete. If you're willing to listen, I want to explain some stuff."

"Why?"

Melinda is confused and unprepared for my question. I lean forward in the overstuffed chair I'm in and look directly into her eyes.

"Melinda, a very good friend of mine once gave me the best definition of our lives, and about what it is we've chosen to do. I was upset about the fact the Agency blatantly used the two of us, and in her own weird little way, she made me understand. Her explanation was '...*it's what they do... what we do, what we agreed to when we signed up. It's all very convoluted, but then it has to be if it's going to work.*'"

Melinda stares at me as if I've blown her entire speech.

"Hey, you guys – you and Alice – didn't force this on my sister. She made a choice. A choice that at the time, seemed to her to be the right one. I don't need to know the 'why' of it all, honest. But, right now, I am going to need your help to get her and Daria back."

"And you don't have a problem with that? The Daria part I mean."

"I'm not in a position to have a problem with it, Melinda. You say she's on our side, I take you at your word. Simple as that. Even if my sister wasn't involved, and you told me Daria was ours and wanted her back, I'd be in it with both feet in a heartbeat, because *that's what we do.*"

"Okay. What do you need from me, Courtney?" She goes right back to 'spy', in the blink of an eye.

"The first issue is to set up somewhere. Some place close to where we think they are. Howard and Cassie are working on a location now."

Melinda laughs.

"Courtney, my dear, we are completely mobile. Tell me where and twenty-four hours later you will have a complete operations center up and running. Anything else?"

"The next request might fall under 'impossible', but I'm still going to ask. I need to be in the airport restaurant on Gibraltar in less than twenty hours, for a meeting."

"First, let's clarify. There's no 'not possible' or 'it can't be done' during this op. If you need it, I *will* make it happen or get it. Clear?"

"Yes ma'am."

"Next, I've put Covert's non-designated Gulfstream at your disposal. It can easily cross the Atlantic and can get you anywhere you need to go in Europe, quickly. Give me a departure time and I will have it on the tarmac ready to leave. Will Howard and Cassie be going with you?"

"Yes. And so will Keith, although he doesn't know it yet."

She laughs and says "Very good choice on that one, Courtney. He's probably the best we have. But, be gentle with him, he's never been in the field before."

"We all need to be in Spain, and from there I'll let you know what site we choose. I'd rather go commercial to Gibraltar. That will draw less attention than arriving in a high-dollar, private jet with no markings."

"I'll make the arrangements. The Gulfstream can get you to Morón, and we'll get you a helicopter ride to the airport at Seville. Based on your time constraints, I suggest you're all on the plane in four hours. Also, I got in touch with my contact at the DoD, and your boys – and all their toys – are already in the air, and should be in Morón in twelve hours."

"Still your disgustingly efficient self, I see."

With a laugh, she says, "I do try, Courtney. Now this," she pulls a new cell phone, still sealed in plastic, from a pocket in her sweater, "is your new phone. My number is auto-dial #1, Alice's is #2, and *yours* will *always get through* even if ours are in use. The rest of them will all have the same phone, with you listed as #1. Do you know where you will need to go after your meeting?"

"Not yet, but once I do, you'll be the first to know. Right now, however, I'm going to go pack some stuff and make sure the rest of this team knows what's going on. And, I'll need two extra phones."

"Now?"

"No. One to take with me, and the other I want you to give to Chuck. He knows what to do with it. I'll need both numbers."

She smiles, stands up, pulls something from the same pocket of her sweater, and after a moment of contemplation, hands two items to me.

"That's who you're looking for, Courtney. I went through their stuff, and those are the duplicates of the only missing passports. I'm assuming those are the identities they're currently using."

I'm holding two British passports, which are, of course, forged, but only a very well trained eyed will know that.

"The strange thing is, even though she looked like Christie Monroe when..."

*"Who?"* I ask, interrupting her midsentence.

"Oh, sorry," she replies with a grin. "Christie is her take on Alexandra. The same visually, but a different persona. She's from Texas."

"Okay," I reply.

"Anyhow, I don't understand why she'd leave made up as Christie, and not take Christie's passport. Doesn't make any sense, unless she plans to change at some point."

I flip open one of the passports, read the name, Alexis Paddison, and instantly understand Melinda's confusion. The image in the passport is one of the two women Alice gave me photos of earlier. When I open the second one and read the name, Allison Paddison, I laugh. I can't help it. I also notice it's the second female from the photographs.

"She couldn't live without a sister. Go figure."

Not knowing how else to respond, Melinda only smiles at me.

"So..." I say, trying to ease the moment.

"Chuck will have a phone by the end of the day, and the other one will be on the plane, along with a list of all the numbers your team will be using. Good luck, Courtney, and God's speed."

"Somehow, I get the feeling we'll be depending on HIM a lot during this one. Talk to you soon, Melinda."

I reach out, shake her hand, and then go out the door. I find Alice sitting in a chair, across from her secretary, in the outer office.

"Are we good?"

"Yes ma'am. And on track as well. We're going to see if I can pull off the biggest op of my career. How do you want me to report back?"

"As you see the need, Courtney. This is on you, and over the years, I have learned to trust your judgment. I want to know what's going on, but don't feel that you have to continually report."

She stops talking, stands, walks over and closes the main door to her office, then turns back to face me. She nods at Amanda, who reaches under her desk and pushes a button which I know is a signal scrambler, so that whatever she's about to say can only be heard by those present.

"Off the record, Courtney, and pay very close attention. The people responsible for all this? They die. *No exceptions.* Are we completely clear on that?"

Mike and Rhyan's presence makes sense. My operation just became what we refer to in our business as 'dirty', and I'm a bit freaked out.

"Yes, ma'am, crystal clear. In the open or covertly?" I force myself to ask.

"I don't care, Courtney. I do know that there will be none of that 'diplomatic immunity' bullshit. No turning anyone over to anyone. The mastermind, the four bastards in the photos, and whoever else may have been even slightly involved, end up in boxes. Period. If you don't feel you can deal with that, tell me now, so I can find other means to facilitate it."

I look at Melinda and Amanda, both of whom look shocked, not so much at what they heard, but by the fact that Alice said it in front of them. I'm pretty sure the goosebumps, cover every inch of me.

"Alice, if that's the order you are giving, off or on the record, that's what will happen. Period. Even if I have to 'facilitate' it myself."

"That's the answer I wanted to hear. Get to it, lady. Keep me apprised."

She walks past Melinda, into her office, and closes the door.

Melinda turns, glances at me, and says, "I'll be manning the compound, Courtney. Call me when you need me, okay? If you decide you need me on site, I can be anywhere in Europe in a matter of hours."

"Copy that lady. As my little brother likes to say, 'see you on the other side'"

She disappears out the door and I'm right behind her.

I'm going to find my husband.

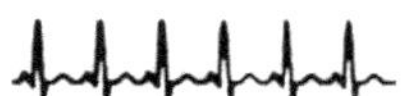

"What will not woman, gentle woman, dare; when strong affection stirs her spirit up?"

Robert Southey
English Poet
1774–1843

"Why are you so damn calm?" I ask my husband, as I go about packing my bag.

"One of us has to be, Court," he replies.

I stop what I'm doing, turn, and wrap my arms around my husband, the rock of my life. My sister's 'death' fourteen years ago defined my path through life, but Chuck always seems to be able to keep me on it.

"I do, and will always, love you with everything that I am Charles Whitman."

After he kisses me, he steps back and with a smile says, "My children would like to meet their aunt – so what say you and Howard go get her?"

"Yes sir. First, I have to go tell my parents what's going on. This should be fun."

"Yeah, good luck with that dear. I'll tell the kids Mom had to go to work again."

I zip my small bag shut, and after another kiss, I head for my car.

Twenty minutes later, I'm sitting in my parent's driveway, scared to death. When I see my father look out the window at me, I know I have to go do it, so into the house I go.

"Hi, Dad!" I wipe my shoes and close the door.

"Is it good, or bad, Courtney?"

"Am I that damn predictable, Dad?" I ask, as my mother comes around the corner.

"You were the first, Courtney – and ever since the first time I held you, and looked into those beautiful green eyes, I knew you'd be 'daddy's girl'. So yeah, to me, you're that predictable."

"What's going on, Courtney?" my mother asks.

"I need to tell the two of you something – and it's going to sound bizarre."

They laugh at me, making me realize just how ridiculous that statement is. Realistically speaking, most of my 'adult life' can be classified as 'bizarre'.

I walk into the dining room and stop at the table. I pull the photo of my sister fighting with the two guys out of my pocket, unfold it, and lay it on the table. Then, I look right at my mother and say, "You – sit down right now." She immediately does, and my father takes a spot right behind her, with a hand on her shoulder. Then, I freak them both out.

"This was taken less than six hours ago, and that," I lay a finger on Whitney's head, "is..."

"You," my mother says, lifting her head, and looking at me. "You left here one day, over fifteen years ago, looking just like this." After a moment, she returns her gaze to the photo.

I can't believe it. My mother remembers the day I had to change into Alexandra, down the hall, in her guest bathroom. I have to stop and absorb that one. After thirty seconds of total silence, she prompts me.

"Courtney?"

"It's not me, Mom. It's actually... well..."

My hesitation gives it away, and even though I haven't said it yet, when she looks back at me, her eyes tell me she knows.

"It's your *other* daughter. You know, *the dead one*."

Silence. Complete and total silence, from both of them.

"And, as if that little revelation isn't enough insanity for one day, here's the kicker. I'm assembling a team, which includes Howard, to go and retrieve her."

Still no response. They continue to stare at the photo.

"I'm not sure how long this will take, but if Chuck needs help with the kids, you'll be there, right Mom?"

"Of course," my mother responds, never taking her eyes off the photograph. "Tell him that their grandfather will pick them up at the bus stop this afternoon, and they can stay with us until this is over. That will free him up too."

My mother's ability to feign calmness, although 'calm' isn't even a vague consideration, is at times, very spooky.

"Howard and I are on a plane in about an hour. Alice gave me permission to keep you up to speed during the operation, and later today, Chuck will be dropping off a secure phone. There's no telling when I might call, so keep it where you can get to it at all times, and for crying out loud, keep it charged. I'll call you when I can, okay?"

"That will work," my father finally says.

"Well, I need to get going. Say a prayer, will ya guys?"

They both look at me, and Mom says, "For God's sake, Courtney, be careful. If it *is* your sister, I want her back as much as you do, but you have other things in life now, to consider. You know exactly what I mean."

"Yes ma'am, I do. And, I have Howard to make sure I will be."

"Good luck, Courtney – to all of you," my father offers. Then, as an afterthought, he says, "And once you get her back, tell her that her father says she's done with all the silly bullshit."

"Yes sir," I reply, winking at him.

Forty minutes later, I'm following Howard up the stairs of a jet-black Gulfstream G550, that's standing by at Langley Air Force Base. Five minutes after they close the door, we're airborne.

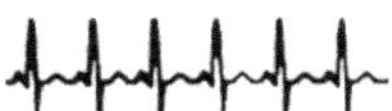

# 9

The first thing I see when I board is Keith sitting alone, at the back of the plane. I momentarily flash back to the first time I was in a field environment and know what needs to be done. Involve him immediately.

"Keith, you're up here with the rest of us," I tap on a seat next to Cassie. "That's why we call it a 'team'".

Howard smiles and whispers, "I taught you well, lady."

Keith responds with a nervous-sounding, "Yes ma'am, Mrs. Whitman," which makes Cassie snicker.

"Okay, Keith, let's get straight on this 'formality' thing right off, shall we?"

Cassie and Howard laugh, and Keith just looks confused.

"I'm 'Mrs. Whitman' in the building because of protocol. I've learned to live with that. But out here where things can get..."

"Insane," Cassie offers.

"Formality has no place in a daily environment that can involve death and bullets," Howard interjects.

"So, henceforth, I'm Courtney, this is Howard, and the gorgeous older woman is Cassie. Are we clear on this?"

"*'Henceforth'*? Jezzz, Court! Age and a desk have made you even weirder than you used to be," Cassie says, shaking her head.

Everyone laughs, and it seems that Keith might be a bit more relaxed. I settle in and spend most of the flight next to Howard, reading.

And reading. And reading some more.

Cassie spends a couple of hours, explaining what's going on, and what we're about to attempt to Keith – in general terms. She neglects to tell him it's my 'dead' sister we're after. He listens to and absorbs every word. The guy is totally into the whole situation, and it shows. For just a moment, I see me and my sister reflecting in his eyes.

The more I read, the greater my understanding of what Alice has accomplished becomes. My sister and her new 'associate' have been very busy girls since they 'died'. They 'neutralized' (that just sounds better than 'terminated') several very bad individuals, and, at least two very, very bad ones. Knowing who the targets were, I realize they fall into the category of 'people who need to be killed', lest they cause the deaths of many others.

The termination of the attempted hijacking of a Russian oil tanker was genius, and I *know* my sister planned it. Even as I read the Op Plan, I see 'Whitney' all over it. I couldn't have done it any better.

Howard is astonished by the 'apparent suicide' of one Abdul-Aziz Barad, leader of a very radical movement that attempted a coup of the Syrian government. Even though Syria's current regime isn't on our 'buddy list', they're far preferable to having this fanatic in power. Howard's only comment after he reads the report is, "Do you realize *how close* to someone you have to get, to make their death this personal?"

In addition to the high-profile incidents, the two of them pulled off several smaller, less noticeable operations. In one instance, they sabotaged a stolen Russian nuclear warhead beyond repair, which in turn caused a huge rift between the buyer and seller. The 'deal gone bad' resulted in a gun battle inside a warehouse in Paris, that concluded with an absurdly high body count. The truly amusing part is that each side placed the blame on the other, yet neither knew about Whitney and Daria's participation. This one makes me laugh.

Next, the liberation of hostages from a hijacked German train, and nine dead terrorists. Again, no one could say for certain, what happened, not even the hostages. The last terrorist made a strangely bizarre dying declaration – 'CIA' – which no one understood. Alice had to assure the German Chancellor, and the head of their intelligence service, that the CIA was not even remotely involved. Strangely enough though, on the list of hostages are two names I recognize from my conversation with Melinda. *Two sisters...*

Alexis and Allison Paddison. British citizens, on holiday.

Howard comes up with the best story of the bunch. A large hijacked shipment of weapons headed for Afghanistan.

According to civilian reports, for some unexplained reason, the entire shipment went up in a tremendous explosion (which caused readings on seismographic equipment three hundred miles away, at Kabul University), destroying the weapons, and the terrorist encampment they were delivered to. I laugh when I see the small annotation indicating that the truck carrying the weapons was delayed briefly, due to a 'mechanical failure'.

Based on the lack of a plausible explanation, the Afghan government was quick to claim responsibility, telling the press how they 'acted swiftly to defeat the terrorist scourge infecting their country'.

It seems that Whitney and Daria have become the ultimate black ops team, in the world of espionage.

As I close my eyes, lean my seat back, and let my mind wander, it occurs to me that perhaps, it's Alice Williamson who is the real intelligence genius. After all, this entire thing is her doing and the results are nothing short of astonishing.

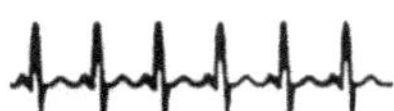

# 10

I spot Joey instantly. She's still short, still quite blonde. However, time is taking its toll, and the lines on her face seem to be deeper than I remember. I walk up behind her, gently touch her shoulder, and then, without saying a word, take the chair across from her.

We sit quietly for a good thirty seconds, and she never once looks at me but instead keeps staring at the 'something on the rocks' that fills the glass on the table in front of her.

"Kind of early for that," I say, breaking the silence, and pointing at the untouched drink on the table, "isn't it?"

She lifts her head, and when she makes eye contact with me, I see the tears. I reach across the table, touch her hand, and can feel her trembling.

"I'm sorry. Honest to God I am..." she says, looking more 'through' me than 'at' me.

When the waitress walks up, I turn and look at her.

"Breakfast. The biggest one you have. One for me, and one for her," I point at Joey. "I've been on a plane for close to ten hours and I'm starving, and she," I again pause, and point at Joey, "needs to get something into her stomach if she's going to be drinking this damn early in the day."

The girl smiles and is quick to reply, in a thoroughly British fashion.

"That's the first one I brought her ma'am, close to an hour ago. As you can see, she hasn't touched it yet. So, are you having a British breakfast, or perhaps the American version?"

Even before she quits talking, I turn back to face Joey, who is now looking me right in the eyes.

"British, of course," Joey replies, tears trickling down her cheeks.

"Ma'am?"

'That works," I reply, never breaking eye contact with Joey. "And coffee too, please."

"Very well. I'll be back in a moment with the coffee."

Once she's out of earshot, Joey wipes her cheeks, glances at the glass on the table, then looks at me.

"I was going to drink five or six of them..."

"I'm Courtney. *Not Whitney*. Why can't you see that?" I ask, and then immediately realize the stupidity of the statement. "Fifteen years. I think it's time to stop punishing yourself, for something you weren't responsible for."

"I guess you'd have to be me, to understand," she replies, still staring at the glass.

I pull Daria's photo out of my pocket, carefully unfold it, lay it on the table, and slide it over in front of her. Then, I pick up her drink, which turns out to be a very good scotch, and take a sip. It takes less than ten seconds for the response I expect.

"NO FUCKING WAY!"

Every head in the restaurant turns to look at us, which in turn, makes me laugh, as I take another sip from the glass.

"Have your attention, do I?" Glancing at the people two tables over, I add, "She excites rather easily."

Joey reaches out, and without a word, takes the drink from my hand, and finishes it in a single gulp.

After contemplating the photo that she's holding for a few seconds, she finally says, "If I need a reason to drink this early, *this* would be it."

I laugh as I watch the look in her eyes and her demeanor, change, as she slowly reverts to the deadly spy she's always been. In only a matter of seconds, *Veronika Sadikov* is across the table from me.

"When?"

"It was taken about twenty-four hours ago, your time."

"Where?"

"Outside a hotel in Rabat."

"Have you verified..."

"Yes. I'm 'abso-damn-lutely' certain," I reply, following it with a laugh. The waitress returns and goes about filling our cups with coffee.

Once the waitress is gone, Joey lifts her head and looks at me.

"But... how? No one could have survi..."

She stops midsentence, as her mind puts two and two together. The look on her face tells me she knows what's next. She takes a deep breath, glances at the photo again, then lays it on the table.

"Is..."

I don't wait for her to finish her question. Instead, I pull out a copy of the photo I left with my parents, unfold it, and then look her right in the eyes as I lay it down on the table.

"No outburst this time, okay?"

"Uh-huh."

I slide it over, lift my fingers off it, and watch as she picks it up and closely examines it.

"Care to guess who *that* is?"

She glances at me, then back at the photo, and after a few moments of quiet thought, when our eyes meet again, I see that the tears have returned.

"*Oh my God...*" she whispers, turning her attention back to the photo and running her fingers over the face.

"Yeah, no shit. That's what I said when Alice showed me the photos. Needless to say, Mom and Dad are a bit miffed too."

About that time, the waitress brings our breakfast and goes about putting things on the table. Joey, however, can't seem to tear her eyes away from the second photo. The one of my sister.

"So, Miss Masterson," I say, as I watch the girl refill my coffee cup, then turn and leave, "I do believe I've outdone *your revelation* in that conference room in Istanbul, sixteen years ago."

She finally laughs. A deep, honest laugh.

"Jesus, Courtney, *you think so?*" she glances down, and nods at the two photographs, now lying in the middle of the table.

We sit quietly, each lost in our own thoughts, as we eat. After about five minutes of silence, Joey pauses and again makes eye contact with me. What I see in hers, is a plea for some kind of an explanation. Something that will help her understand.

"It's a long, convoluted story, Joey," I say between bites, "but right now, I'll tell you this. I have a team in place to *retrieve both of them,* as screwy as that will sound. I need to know if you are in."

After a few seconds of silence, and a few more bites, I pause and look at her. She too, stops eating and returns my stare.

"More than anything, Joey, anything in my life at this exact moment, *I need you to be in.*"

She looks down at the photos again for a couple of seconds, puts another bite of food in her mouth, and then looks me directly in the eyes. She swallows what's in her mouth, and with a sinister little smirk on her face, and the remnants of a few tears still covering her cheeks, she says, "I'll need a gun..."

I finish the coffee in my cup, and after I wipe my face with my napkin, I ask, "Are you telling me that the London Station Chief left her damn gun at home?"

When we start laughing, the waitress, who is passing our table, shakes her head, and mumbles "Spies... I swear..." as she continues off toward the kitchen.

⌁⌁⌁⌁⌁⌁

　　　　　　　*Solution Squared: Recalculation*

# 11

As we watch the Army Huey set down on the tarmac in front of us, my phone rings.

"Whitman."

"I have a trial, Courtney. Can I make a suggestion this early in the op?"

"M, you can suggest your little butt off at any time you please. What are we doing?"

"With your permission, I want to set up the mobile unit at the safe house on Crete."

My entire world falls silent. No rotor noise from the helicopter, no jet engines, and no voices around me. Only total silence. My eyes close, and within seconds, I'm back on that street, watching it all happen again.

Joey sees me fading and tries to bring me back.

"Court, what's the matter?"

Hearing her voice, I force my eyelids open, ending the movie running behind them. I shake my head from side to side a couple of times, then stare blankly at the phone in my hand, unable to make my brain reengage. Joey reaches out, takes the phone from me, and sits me down on a nearby bench. Although I hear her side of the conversation, it isn't registering. My brain is elsewhere. When Melinda mentions the safe house, my mind takes me back to that street in Kato Galatás.

"Masterson. Who is this? Not sure. She just sort of went somewhere. What the hell were you guys talking about? She brought me in on her op, Melinda, so how about you fill me in on what's going on? Yes. She gave it to me a few moments ago. Fair enough. You needn't explain. Following protocol is always the best route. I just turned it on. Yeah, make it ten minutes and give me a chance to get her straight again."

I hear her flip the phone closed, and then feel the bench move as she sits down next to me.

"Damn it, Courtney. I'm joining your op, not running it. What the hell freaked you out?"

When I don't respond, she tries again.

*"Courtney!"*

As she's yelling, a guy in an Army flight suit walks up.

"Is one of you Ms. Whitman?"

"She is. Can you give me just a minute, Major?"

"Yes ma'am, of course. Come get on board when you're ready. Should I leave the engines spun up?"

"Yes sir. We'll be aboard in two minutes."

Realizing she needs help, Joey scrolls through the list of numbers on my phone. She finds the one she wants, pushes the #3 speed dial button, and waits. She starts talking the moment she hears his voice...

"Howard, it's Joey. Mindy said something to Courtney, and now she's in space somewhere. What do I do?"

"Someone needs to talk to you Court..." I feel her put the phone in my hand, and raise it to my ear.

The instant I hear his voice, my entire world comes back.

"Damn it, Courtney. What the hell is going on?"

When I don't respond, he hammers me.

*"Okay, so fuck it? We go home and forget your sister, or what?"*

He gets me. It seems Howard can still push my buttons.

"LIKE HELL!" I respond, and with a couple of blinks of my eyes, I'm back and realize what happened. "Thank you, butthead, I needed that. I'll see you in a bit, okay?"

"Yes ma'am. We're waiting on you."

I disconnect the call, take a couple of really deep breaths, and then punch #1 to call Melinda back. It only rings once.

"Aston."

"So, back to Crete, huh? You have a reason I assume?"

I turn and give Joey the best 'pitiful' look I can muster.

"Yes, I do. Striking distance. They, *whoever they are,* are probably still in the Med somewhere. Almost everywhere is a short jump from the island. You give me the word, and I will have the place up, and running before you get there."

"Go for it, M. You think these Army guys will fly us there instead of back to the air base at Morón?"

Melinda laughs and says, "Not a chance, Court. Not in the Huey. I have a better idea. Can you hang out a while?"

"Sure. I can use another cup of coffee, and it'll give me time to apologize to Joey, as well."

"Okay, I'll call you back in a few. Tell the Major to go home, as the plan has changed. I'll info his HQ."

"Gotcha. Bye."

"Come on, Miss Sadikov. Melinda has just changed our plans, and we need to cut the Major loose."

"Okay, but would you do me a favor?"

I laugh and reply, "I promise to hang around from now on. No more mental vacations."

"Cool..."

She follows me across the tarmac, toward the helicopter.

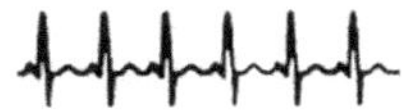

# 12

We're sitting on the patio of the airport bar when my phone, which is lying on the table, rings again. As I set my coffee down, I pick it up and answer it.

"Whitman."

"Can you talk, or only listen?" Melinda asks. I know she's questioning the privacy of my location.

"I'm cool. What do you have for us?"

"A Lear 40 with corporate markings will land there in forty minutes. It'll draw less attention than the Gulfstream."

"Okay, and then?"

"Howard, Keith, and Cassie are on it. It will take you to Heraklion. I'll have a couple of rentals standing by, one in Joey's name and one in Keith's. I'm trying to keep this low-key if I can, so I avoided using the Director of Intelligence's name on anything."

I laugh. "I take it you have a plan to get a couple of tons of equipment onto the island in a low-key manner as well?"

"Of course. Four Greek Army communications techs and their truck will get it on-site and assembled. Keith is the best operator we have at the moment, so you're in good hands."

"I have one more question, M."

"Yes?"

"What can you do there, that can't be done on-site?"

"Damn! I was *so* hoping you'd ask me that," she replies sounding enthusiastic and excited. I know her response is based on her need to feel 'hands-on' in getting her deep-cover people back.

"Will you get there before, or after we do?"

"Depends."

"On?"

"What the boss tells me to do."

"The boss expects to find you typing away at a terminal when she gets there."

"Done. See you there, Courtney."

"Uh-huh. Bye."

"She has a trail of some kind, and we are setting up on Crete," I say, taking my last gulp of coffee. Joey sits staring at me.

"Hey, you okay with that?" I ask, wiping my face with a napkin, and tossing it onto the table.

"Are you?"

"Gotta be dear. I want my sister back."

"Yeah, me too. But I do have a few questions for Daria."

I laugh. "You *are* gonna be nice, right?"

As weird as it will sound, that's all it takes to vent our stress. We spend the next few minutes laughing like fools and making everyone on the patio think we were nuts.

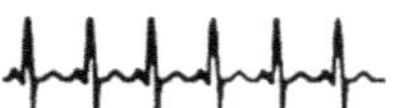

# 13

I start laughing, when I see the emblem on the Learjet, as it rolls to a stop in front of us.

*'Erasmus Shipping'*.

My mind flashes back to the comment Alice made during our second meeting: *'We also appropriated a certain Greek shipping line'*. I find myself wondering just how far into that company, Daria was.

Someone inside drops the stairs, we quickly climb them, and the plane is taxiing again before the door closes.

Before I sit down, I stick my head into the cockpit, and in the sole interest of being a smartass say, "Captain, you do realize you only have about 6000 feet of runway, right?"

He and the co-pilot laugh at the same time.

"A passenger that knows something about the aircraft? That's a first, isn't it, Bob?"

"Uh-huh," replies the co-pilot.

"Not to worry, Mrs. Whitman. We have been flying this thing for so long, that, if necessary, we can land and take off on a sidewalk."

"And not hit any pedestrians," the co-pilot adds.

I laugh, pat them on the shoulders, and go to find a seat.

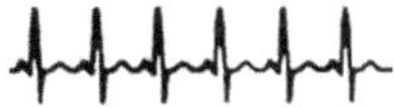

# 14

My eyes pop open when I feel the wheels touchdown, and the engines reverse. As I look around, I realize Keith is the only one who doesn't appear to have slept the entire three and a half hours. He also still looks nervous.

"Keith, you're on one of the cars. Don't ask questions, just smile, be polite, and sign where they tell you to."

"Yes ma'am," he replies, forcing a smile.

"And you are gonna have to loosen up too. The next time you call me anything other than 'Courtney', you and I will be rolling around on the floor. Are you catching my drift here?"

His eyes get really big, and a stunned stare covers his face. Then I hear Howard, Cassie, and Joey crack up.

"*Oh please,* do it again. I want to see that," Cassie says.

Again, laughter fills the plane.

"Seriously, Keith," Cassie offers, "if you call her 'ma'am' or 'Director' within earshot of the bad guys, you instantly make her the target. Not something you want to get in the habit of doing."

"Understood," he quickly replies, nodding at me.

We exit the Lear and find two SUVs waiting for us on the tarmac, and a polite Greek girl with the rental agreements. She says all I need to do is sign, as the vehicles are under contract to Erasmus Shipping. Again, I feel a smirk on my face.

"I'm going with Keith here," I lay a hand on his shoulder and feel him shudder. "You guys follow us."

I watch the three of them get into the second vehicle, realizing that Joey hasn't said much since we left Gibraltar, which makes me wonder. When I see Keith's nervous face staring at me as if unsure what to do, I slip back into reality. Time to fix the 'nervous' thing I figure. I walk up to him and get right in his face.

"Why the hell do I make you so damn nervous?"

"Uh... well, you're the boss?" he forces himself to say.

"I'm just a girl, Keith. The only difference between us is time. I've been doing this longer. That's all. Assuming you stick with it, one day, you'll be me. Melinda says you're the best we have, so do us all a favor and stop sweating me, and get into a space that will allow you to do, what it is you do, okay?"

He stands for a few seconds, looking at me.

"Did Mindy really say that, or are you jerking my chain?" he asks. As a grin forms on his face, as he offers me the keys to the truck.

"You're driving, I'm navigating. And yes, she did. And," I open the door on the passenger's side of the truck, "if you can call her 'Mindy', you can damn sure use my first name!"

"Yes ma'am! You'll have to live with that. It's habit. Mom used to smack the crap out of us if 'sir' or 'ma'am' wasn't part of every sentence out of our mouths."

"Fair enough. Let's get to work, shall we?"

"Point the way..." he says, climbing in behind the wheel.

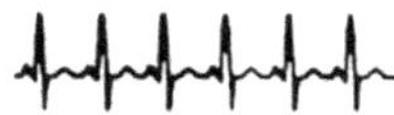

# 15

The rush I experience when we pass the café is so intense, that even Keith senses it. When he sees me tense up, he reaches over and gives me his hand to squeeze – which I am sure must have hurt like hell. My heart is racing as I once again flashback, but I make myself get through it. I also find myself wondering how Joey is handling it.

We arrive at the house, fifteen minutes later, and find four guys unloading a truck that's backed into the driveway. Most of the small houses in the neighborhood are vacation homes and aren't currently occupied, so people unloading a truck doesn't usually draw any attention. The side of the truck is covered by a large emblem and the words 'Erasmus Shipping', which tells anyone watching, that it's probably another rich person moving in.

The second Keith sees some of the stuff stacked in the living room, he turns into a kid on Christmas. The last thing we hear as we walk through the front door of the house is "damn, she wasn't kidding when she said *'totally mobile'*"

I find Melinda exactly where she said she'd be, tapping on a keyboard. It's attached to a large laptop with a bunch of cables coming out of it, that run out through the dining room window. I walk up behind her, with Joey on my heels, and we watch over her shoulder. Howard and Cassie go and look out the open window.

*"Jeezz!"* Cassie blurts out, her face awash with disbelief.

"Mindy, you're one scary female," Howard adds.

Melinda doesn't miss a beat. As she's typing away, and without looking away from her keyboard, she says, "Mobile means *'mobile'*, okay? Get over it."

Just then, Keith comes bouncing into the room, wound so tight, it's possible he's going to fly apart at any second.

"Hey, Mindy! You brought everything didn't ya?"

"Yep. Start setting up the processors. They're stacked in the back room. I'll get the receivers up and running as soon as I am done here."

"Okay. I'm on it."

"And what, exactly, are you doing here?" I ask.

"The two Mercedes were rentals."

She instantly gets Howard and Cassie's attention with that one. They cross the room and stop on either side of me.

"So, will all this technology tell us who rented them?" Howard asks.

"You aren't gonna like the answer," Melinda replies as a copy of the rental agreement pops up on her monitor.

*"The Russian Consulate?* Seriously?" Cassie says.

"I'm sorry guys, but that's just too damn convenient."

I turn and look at Joey, who made the last comment, realizing she's right. The Russians are as professional about what we do, as we are.

"Let me help Keith get the rest of this online," Melinda offers, turning to face us, "and I'll be able to tell you more."

"When did you and your team eat last?" I ask. When she stands there looking at me, I shake my head. "I figured as much." I turn to Cassie, and with a smile say, "Dinner duty, girl. Let's go."

We leave Howard and Joey to help as much as they can and go to find some food.

# 16

We reach the end of the two-mile road leading from Galatás to the coast and are sitting motionless at the stop sign, as I stare at the building in front of us, lost in thought.

"Court?" Cassie finally says, her voice full of concern.

I turn, look at her, and with a devious smile ask, "What are the chances, Cass?"

I drive straight across the intersecting road and pull into the parking lot of the small neighborhood restaurant that we'd gotten into a fight in, almost fifteen years ago.

Even with the astronomical odds, the face that greets us at the door is very familiar. The instant we make eye contact, I'm fairly certain she gets the same rush of goosebumps that I do.

"*Εσύ είσαι...*" (*It is you...*) the woman, who half a lifetime earlier, loaned me her bike, all but whispers. Her tone gives me yet another rush of goosebumps and makes me shudder.

"I'm sorry," I quickly reply, "we don't speak Greek."

"It is I, who am sorry," she forces out. "It is just that you look very much like someone who was here many years ago." She lets the sentence fade into the tension of the moment, and after a few more seconds of staring at me, her gaze shifts to Cassie. "You too, look quite familiar."

"Well, as strange as it may seem, this is my first time on your beautiful island, so I'm quite sure it wasn't me you saw before."

"Same for me," Cassie adds, smiling at her.

It's obvious she forces herself back into the moment, and I feel a definite cringe, knowing I have no choice but to lie to her.

"So, a table for two perhaps?" she asks, a smile returning to her face.

"Well actually…"

With her help, it takes us about twenty minutes to get an order together, large enough to feed all nine of us. Once I give her an address to deliver the food and throw in an absurdly large tip, she assures us the food will be there in an hour.

I'm not sure what makes me do it, but when I pull out of the parking lot, instead of making the left that will take us back to the house, I make the half-mile drive into Kato Galatás. At the edge of town, I find a spot to park the truck, and after a glance at Cassie, get out, walk to the edge of the road, and stand there, letting it all sink in.

After a few seconds, Cassie walks up next to me but never says a word. I turn to look at her, and with a big smile, say "Come on," and start toward the main street.

Being back isn't as weird or tense as I had anticipated. I figure it's because I know Whitney didn't actually die that day. Even the buildings that were repaired now looked quite weathered. On the corner outside the Minoa Palace Resort, they erected a memorial monument to the couple who were killed in the initial explosion. After reading the inscription, which is in Greek and English, I continue down the street, stopping at the entrance to the alley where the van had been parked. I stand listening to all the sounds around me, lost in thoughts of what *actually* happened that day.

A hand on my shoulder brings me back.

"How are you doing, Courtney?"

"I'm cool, honest," I reply, turning and smiling at Cassie. "It's all very strange. I was thinking about how I would be reacting if I still thought they'd been killed, that's all."

"Yeah, me too. I'm pretty much covered in goosebumps."

"Let's see if we can beat the food back to the house."

"Okay."

It takes us thirty minutes to get back to the truck, and another ten to get to the house. The woman from the café is delivering the food at the back door when we get there. It seems Howard didn't feel a need to let her see what we are up to *inside* the house. I experience a small pang of guilt each time I see the questioning look in her eyes, knowing she's right, but being unable to confirm it to her. Once she's done, Howard slips her yet another tip. With a smile, she turns and leaves.

I have to pry Keith away from what he's doing to get him to eat. He's wound up and ready to play. The closer they get to being fully functional, the antsier Melinda becomes too. When I get up from the table after eating, I glance out the still-open dining room window and see what garnered the earlier outburst from Howard and Cassie. Standing on tripods, out in the middle of the backyard, are two very powerful satellite transmitters and three smaller receivers, as well as a really big 45KW Onan generator mounted on a trailer, that isn't yet running. Apparently, what Melinda wants, Melinda gets.

After everyone finishes eating, Joey, and I pick up the mess and watch as Melinda supervises the installation of four sixty-inch plasma monitors onto one wall in the living room. At the same time, Keith is hooking up four smaller monitors, keyboards included, on the now empty dining room table.

Finally, only minutes before sunset, Melinda speaks to one of the Greek guys, and he immediately disappears out the back door. Seconds later we hear the generator start up and Keith starts his system checks. Forty minutes later he smiles at me and says, "You are fully operational, *Courtney.*"

Melinda signs a check drawn on the shipping company and hands it to one of the Greeks, he thanks her, and the three of them go out the door. Seconds later, we hear the big truck start and drive off.

I walk over to Keith, who is diligently typing away, and say, "Tell me something I need to know."

"Gimme a few, I'm locating those Benz's."

"I'm getting some enhanced photos," Melinda adds.

I glance around and realize Cassie, Joey, and Howard have disappeared. Now curious, I leave Melinda and Keith to their tasks and wander toward the back end of the house, only to find the three of them asleep in two different rooms. I smile and find my way back to the living room.

"They were all pretty burnt," Keith offers.

"You're looking kind of rough yourself," Melinda adds. "How long have you been at this?"

"Since we arrived at Moron – about 2:00 this morning."

"You need to go catch some sleep. A catnap at least."

"And what about the two of you?"

Keith stops what he is doing, and spins around in his chair, stopping when he's face to face with me.

"This is what we do Courtney. What *we* are good at. You guys are probably going to be doing the whole 'bullets and bad guys' thing at some point, so you can't afford fatigue. How about you let us do our thing, and you go join the others so that when the time comes, you're ready to do your thing."

First, I laugh, then lean over and kiss him – right on the lips. He turns so red, that Melinda lets out a good laugh of her own.

"Okay, *Boss*. You guys find out anything, *you will* wake me up, right?"

"Yeah, Court, I promise."

"Okay, see you in a few."

There are three bedrooms, but I don't want to wake up alone later, so I crawl onto a queen-sized bed with Howard, kick off my shoes, and pull the light blanket up over me.

I'm dreaming the moment my head hits the pillow.

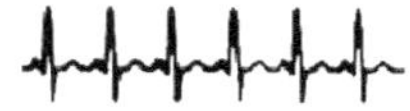

　　　　　　　*Solution Squared: Recalculation*

# 17

"I've got one of the rentals!"

It's 9:30 pm. The four of us manage about four hours of sleep, and I'm standing in the kitchen pouring coffee when I hear Keith.

"Where?" Howard asks as I wander into the living room.

"Tangier. At the airport. It appeared in the return lot two and a half hours after the incident in Rabat."

"Damn," Cassie says, typing away. "That means it went directly from Rabat to Tangier, probably without stopping."

"A sat sweep of the airport, maybe?" Keith suggests.

"I'm on it," Melinda replies as I walk back into what was, at one time, the dining room. "Let's see who came and went during that period."

Fifteen seconds later the four large screens combined to act as one and a huge image of Tangier fills it. Carefully and diligently, Melinda zooms and adjusts the image, until we have a screen full of the International Airport in Tangier. We watch quietly, as the image updates every few seconds.

"Is this real-time?" Howard asks, breaking the silence.

"No sir," Keith replies. "I'm getting a feed from thirty minutes before, and thirty after, the car was discovered."

"'Discovered'?" Joey asks.

"Yeah," replies Melinda. "It was dropped off. Automatic Return Account. The barcode is scanned at the gate and the information is sent to a computer that automatically bills the customer's account."

"So, no video from the counter. Nice."

"That tells us that whoever they are, they damn sure aren't amateurs," I add, laying a hand on Joey's shoulder.

When my phone rings seconds later, I pull it from my pocket, flip it open, and after a glance at the Caller ID, answer it.

"Whitman. Yes, ma'am. You're certain? Crap. Okay. We do have a trail of sorts, so I'll get back to you as things progress."

I flip the phone closed and stick it back in my pocket, then share with the rest of the team.

"The Russians are copping to it possibly being some of theirs. The credit card used for the cars belongs to one of their field assets assigned to the embassy in Casablanca. He and a second guy have disappeared. Alice says that Sokolski has assets out searching for them and that all their accesses have been terminated. If they try to use any part of the Russian's system, for whatever they're up to, he will freely give the info to Alice."

"Damn," Howard blurts out. "Why is it the Russians have so much trouble keeping track of their people?"

"Who is the asset in question?" Joey asks.

"Alice says his name is Vadym Kovalenko."

A look of 'knowing' sweeps over Joey's face, as she turns to a terminal and starts typing. Seconds later, she spins back around in her chair and says, "You need to get Alice back. There's a new issue here."

"Keith – make it happen. Alice on the big screen. Now."

I watch as Joey starts typing again, pauses, and types some more. Finally, a photograph pops up on her monitor.

"And he is?"

"Vadym Nikolayevich Kovalenko. Their missing asset. He isn't the issue," she replies as the video connection to Alice is completed and she pops up on the main monitor.

"What's up, Courtney?"

"Joey says there are additional issues with our missing Russian. I'll let her explain."

Just as I finish talking, a new face – a female – pops up on a second monitor.

"Can these images be ported to Alice's monitors? Joey asks.

"Done," Keith calls out and immediately begins typing.

"And who are these cute individuals?" Alice asks.

"Vadym Kovalenko, our missing Russian. He's not the issue. The female is. When I met her, she was Vera Ivanova Nekrasov, a 'secretary' at the embassy in Budapest."

"Oh really?" I blurt out without thinking, although my brain is now running a mile a minute.

"Shortly after I was posted to Istanbul, I went to see Crystal in Budapest, which is when I first met Daria. Care to guess what the relationship between Daria and Vera was?"

"Holy shit!" Cassie blurts out.

"Nicely done, Josephina. Is there some other relevance here?" Alice asks.

"Yes ma'am. While there, I was invited to a wedding. An old school, Russian wedding."

"Are you fucking serious?" Howard asks, having figured out where she's going.

"That pretty much reaffirms Cassie's 'holy shit', doesn't it? I bet you'd like me to ask poor old Yakiv if he has any damn idea where *she* is, right?"

"Do you think they would be so dumb as to snatch the two of them thinking they could get to the money?" Howard asks, looking completely dumbfounded.

"Although Daria closely controlled it, Vera knew exactly what she was doing, and by default, how much money was involved. She probably kept quiet so as not to get entangled in the ensuing mess. If she stumbled across and recognized Daria, all she had to do was tell her *husband*."

"Stand by and keep this connection open. I want you all to hear this," Alice says.

While everyone watches Alice dialing on a secure phone, I turn my attention to the one person in the room who seems lost in what he's doing. Keith. I walk over behind him and stand quietly.

He's replaying, repeatedly, a series of satellite photos of the airport in Tangier. Every so often, he stops, enhances, and then closely examines a specific area. Although I'm now intrigued, when Alice starts talking, I turn my attention back to her.

We listen as Alice queries Yakiv Sokolski – the current head of Russia's Foreign Intelligence Service, or SVR – as to the whereabouts of Vera Kovalenko. He compliments her on her knowledge of his agency's business and assures her that he knows exactly where she is. When we see Alice shaking her head, we realize she doesn't believe him. The Russians have yet another disaster brewing, and aren't ready yet, to admit it. After they swapped feigned pleasantries, Alice excuses herself and hangs up.

"There you have it, guys. He's blowing smoke up my ass. He is definitely concerned that we know about her, and has no damn clue where she is."

"I'll find her," Joey says.

"I have no doubt you will, Josephina. Keep me up to date guys. If Yakiv becomes more forthcoming, I'll get the info to you ASAP."

Then, Melinda comes to life, and boy is she excited.

"Sorry Alice, we need that monitor."

In the blink of an eye, Alice is gone and a zoomed photo of a hangar at the Tangier airport covers the main monitor.

"Keith, you're a damn genius, I swear to God," Melinda says, as she starts manipulating photos on the monitor.

Everyone immediately turns their attention to Melinda, and we find ourselves watching a video of a small plane being rolled out of a hangar, but the building itself obscures most of the plane. In each successive frame, we can make out someone prepping the plane for use. Then, in the last frame that comes up, a car appears. Well, part of a car. Just enough you can tell it's a car. As everyone else quietly watches Melinda manipulate the picture on the monitor, I turn and see that Keith is already diligently working on something else. They appear to be high-resolution photos of the airport's main runway. I find myself torn between watching Keith and watching Melinda. After a few more seconds, Melinda wins.

I'm concentrating totally on her, as she quite deftly directs her software to remove a portion of the building and then extrapolate the rest of the car. When it's done, we're rewarded with a crisp image of a black Mercedes C-350, the same vehicle that was rented in Rabat and returned to the airport.

"Let's see who dropped off that car, shall we?" Melinda says aloud, to no one in particular, and then starts typing.

"I want that plane," I say, walking up to the monitors.

"Here you go, Boss," Keith instantly replies.

I watch as the photo Melinda is working on minimizes to the lower left-hand corner, and the rest of the screen is filled with the image of a small twin-engine plane as it's leaving the runway. The camera is apparently, strategically placed, to capture every aircraft ID number as they take off. How the hell Keith tapped their system, I have no idea. However, by the third frame, it's easy to read – RF 23 760Q.

"And here's our bad guy," Melinda says, posting a new photo to the lower right-hand corner of the main monitor. It's a guy walking away from our Benz, in the drop-off lot. It only takes her a few seconds to clear it up enough to make the face.

"Who the hell is that?" I ask.

"It must be the second guy. It isn't Kovalenko."

"Hey! Hang on a damn second..."

"What, Court?" Howard quickly asks.

"The shadows. Look at the shadows..."

The shadow of the departing plane stretches out *directly behind* it, while the one of the guy that drops off the car is at almost a forty-degree angle to his left, and isn't much longer than he is tall.

"The runway in Tangier is east-west if I'm not mistaken."

"It is," Mindy replies.

"So, based on that knowledge, what time would you say that plane is taking off?"

It takes them all a second, but they finally catch on.

"No shit…" Keith mumbles.

"And, if they dropped off the car at…" I ask, turning to face Melinda.

"11:22, Courtney."

"What the hell were they doing for the five or six hours between then, and the plane leaving? *And,* if they had time to kill, why the fast drive?"

"Jesus," Howard mumbles, as he shakes his head. "Only in Courtney's brain, I swear to God."

"Damn!  Nice catch, Boss," I hear Keith say.  "The plane's tires left the ground five hours and thirty-three minutes after they dropped off the car."

"Very damn interesting," I mumble, still staring at the plasma.

"Uh, Courtney, this just got even more convoluted," I hear Cassie say behind me.

"Jesus, now what," Howard asks walking up behind her.

"The plane. It's registered to the Russian government."

Now, I'm getting a headache. The look on Howard's face when he turns to look at me, tells me he's getting the same one. I rub my temples and walk over to the huge monitor, my eyes going from image to image. The plane… the guy… the car… the hanger.

*What* is going on? I need to think, *to concentrate.* And standing here staring at these monitors isn't helping. I know there's some kind of logic to it all, but I'm having trouble formulating.

"It's a Piper Seneca, Courtney," comes from Keith, who is again, diligently typing away. "Max range is 825 nautical miles give or take. I'm guessing 'take' if it's fully loaded. It seats six, so figure pilot and at least one person to watch their 'captives', and the captives themselves. That will put them in the ballpark of a full load. The other issue is that the damn thing can stay aloft at 70 knots, down to a hundred feet easy, which means below radar if they want."

"Wouldn't make sense," comes from Joey. "They won't hide *in the plane;* they will hide *after* the plane. Flying under radar would only draw attention."

"Okay, Joey, give me destinations."

"I have a better idea, Boss," our resident genius offers.

He again begins typing, and as the image on the monitor again changes, Howard, shaking his head in disbelief, asks, "Where in the hell did you find this guy?"

Everyone laughs at once.

The next image that fills the big monitor is a list of alphanumeric strings. We wait silently to see what our little genius is going to come up with next.

"Unfortunate for them but fortunate for us, their ICAO address goes wherever they go."

"Their what?" Cassie and Howard ask at the same time.

"Transponders guys. All aircraft have them, and built into the transponders is the ICAO address. When a plane is built, the address becomes a permanent part of the aircraft's Certificate of Registration. Mode S transponders have made the ADSB and ACAS systems functional."

"Speak English, Keith," Howard says, jabbing his arm.

"The Automatic Dependent Surveillance-Broadcast and Airborne Collision Avoidance are aviation safety systems," he replies, as he changes terminals. "Mode S transponders are mandatory in controlled airspace above most countries. They also require all commercial aircraft be equipped with Mode S, even in uncontrolled airspace above their borders."

He's typing at blazing speeds, and the images on the screen are changing almost as fast as his fingers are moving.

"Mode S transponders broadcast information about the aircraft to the Secondary Surveillance Radar System, which is now pretty much worldwide, to ADS-B, as well as to TCAS receivers on board other aircraft. They transmit the call sign of the aircraft, the transponder's permanent ICAO address, and the latitude and longitude at the time of broadcast. The damn thing will start broadcasting when the transponder is switched on.”

“So, unless the plane is still operating how, exactly, does this help us?” Joey finally asks.

“Generally speaking, it doesn’t. But keep in mind, we *are* spies.”

“AeroSat. Damn it, Keith, you’re making me look bad,” Melinda says, laughing. “Which one are you accessing?”

“Six – it’s over the Med. Fifteen seconds.”

Keith stops typing, and after a brief delay, what he’s doing appears on the main screen:

```
REQUEST PROCESSING… … …
ICAO REGISTRATION: RF 23 7b0Q
ICAO HEX ADDRESS: XC52EC
LOCATION: LATITUDE 36.2310 LONGITUDE 4.2572
LOG TIME: 16:28.55 UTC
```

I realize the time indicated is twenty minutes after the plane left the ground. I walk over, with Howard right behind me, and lay a hand on Keith’s shoulder.

“How the hell are you doing this, Keith?”

“I know stuff, Boss,” he replies with a rather sinister laugh, as he rolls back to his original terminal.

“Right after 9/11 the FAA put them in orbit, Court – they track and record every single damn Mode S transponder on the freaking planet. If a plane is up and the transponder is on, the satellites are recording every time they transmit,” Melinda said.

“No shit,” Joey mumbles. “Big Brother is watching.”

“We can see who queried them, and what their response was, as well as all the pertinent time-stamp information,” Melinda adds, walking over and stopping next to me.

“I see what you mean about him,” I say, winking at her.

“I’m sending an info-specific query, to two satellites and they should only return what I am asking for.”

```
REQUEST PROCESSING… … …
ICAO REGISTRATION: RF 23 7b0Q
```

```
ICAO HEX ADDRESS: XC52EC
LOCATION: LATITUDE 37.6251 LONGITUDE 0.5109
LOG TIME: 17:38.15 UTC
```

"Joey, find those coordinates, please."

Her fingers are instantly typing.

"Over water, just off of Cartagena, Spain."

"Where the hell are they going?" I mumble.

"More like, where are they *right now,*" Keith says.

```
REQUEST PROCESSING… … …
ICAO REGISTRATION: RF 23 760Q
ICAO HEX ADDRESS: XC52EC
LOCATION: LATITUDE 38.8749 LONGITUDE 1.3654
LST LOG TIME: 18:44.15 UTC
```

I turn my wrist, glance at my watch, and do some quick math. They took close to eight hours to make the flight. Why haul ass to the airport, then wait five hours before making a casual flight to...

"Those coordinates are at the southwestern end of the runway at Ibiza, next to the water, near some hangers," Joey says, answering my question before I ask it.

"Let's have a look," Melinda says, taking her seat again and pulling a keyboard over in front of her.

Seconds later Keith's numbers disappear, and Melinda fills the main monitor with a satellite image of the airport in Ibiza. The second I see it, I understand.

"It's dark, damn it," I blurt out, my eyes on the monitor. "They were making sure it was dark when they got there."

This time it's Joey, who is standing next to me, who has a comment.

"You are beginning to freak me out, Courtney."

Melinda types in the coordinates, and lets the computer system automatically center the image on them. Howard looks at me and again shakes his head in disbelief. When she zooms in the final time, the screen is filled with a hangar at the end of one of the access roads, with a big yellow X right in front of the doors.

"They secured the transponder *after* they were parked. Good for us, bad for them," Keith says.

"Is that satellite stationary, Melinda?" Joey asks.

"Nope. Sun-synchronous orbit. I'm checking to see if there are any on different orbits that might have been taking pictures."

I turn to the nearest keyboard, punch up a map of the same area on one of the smaller monitors, and then sit down in front of it. I zoom the view out and let my mind wander. Why Ibiza? Where are they taking them? And, why are they being so damn casual about it all? Money. They probably want the money. I need to talk to Alice.

"I'll be back. Keep doing whatever the hell it is we're doing," I say, standing up and heading for the kitchen. The response to my comment is joint laughter.

I walk through the kitchen and out onto the patio on the side of the house where the driveway ends. I pull my phone out, hit the #2 on the autodial, and wait.

"Willamson."

"It's me, Alice. I need some info, assuming of course you are in a position to share."

"What do you need to know?"

"The money. Do Whitney and Daria have *direct* access to it?"

"To some of it. It's spread out in a lot of different places."

"Stands to reason."

I stand silently for a few seconds, visualizing how my sister would handle that situation. Access to *a lot* of money.

"Courtney?"

"Oh, yes ma'am. Sorry. My brain is in about six places at the moment. Has anyone claimed to have them yet?"

Even as I'm talking, my brain is still cycling. My sister and Daria are *very* experienced field assets, and they'd have money where they can get to it, in a hurry if necessary. A stash. Would they tell Alice about it?

"Not a word. The Russians are still feigning they don't know what's going on, and they aren't willing to give up Kovalenko, although they insist, they know where she is. Sokolski assures me he'll pass on any info they get from her."

"Do me a favor, Alice. Ask him about a Piper Seneca aircraft with the registration number RF 23 760Q would you? I'd like to know who in the Russian government has control over it."

"Immediately. Anything else?"

"They took them to Ibiza on that aircraft, and it's still there. That's it so far. I'll get back to you. Call me about the plane."

"As quickly as possible, Courtney."

Once I hear the click telling me she hung up, I close my phone and stand staring at the roofs of the other houses, thinking. After a few seconds, I walk around the house, sit down on the grass, cross my feet under me, and turn my mind loose.

What would I do in Whitney's position? Knowing that at any moment I might need it, I find a way to strategically place an amount of money that will easily get me out of almost any situation. They have access to far more than enough to do that. I have to be able to get to it quickly, and it will have to be substantial – less than a million dollars will be useless in a negotiation. No, I won't tell Alice I've done it, but she's smart enough to know I *will* do it, so in reality I don't have to tell her. She'll also understand why I did it. Next – access. I have to believe, under the circumstances, Daria and Whit are close now, as close as she and I always were. Daria will have to be able to get to it too.

At the same moment, I sense that someone is behind me, my Courtney/Whitney switch flips, and I know exactly what the hell the two of them will do! It's what my sister and I would do if I was involved.

"Hey, Courtney, you okay?" Joey asks, sitting down next to me.

"Yeah," Cassie, who turns up on the opposite side, adds, "Are you?"

"Yep, I am. I think I know what they've done. What do you two think this whole fiasco is about?"

"Hard to say. But it appears we once again have Russian assets operating unsanctioned."

"Exactly, Joey. Why?"

"Must be something substantial in it for them, Court," Cassie interjects. "They wouldn't take a chance of incurring the wrath of the SVR, and perhaps the FSB as well, unless it's *very* worth it."

"The missing money," Joey offers.

"Bingo. Let's look at the players. Daria's secretary, her husband, and another guy who works with the husband. She knows guys. Kovalenko knows about the money. Someone discovers Daria isn't dead, and they are able to locate her."

"They snatch her and not realizing who Whitney is, take her too. They offer to trade their lives for the money. Sounds reasonable, Courtney."

"Like I always used to say," a male voice behind us says, "I'm damn sure glad the two of them are on our side."

We turn to find Howard walking up behind us.

"You're on her wavelength again, aren't you, Courtney?"

"Maybe, Howard, just maybe. But we need to get ahead of them instead of trying to catch up. I believe, and these two seem to agree, this is probably about the money."

"And?" Howard asks.

I look at Cassie first, then Joey, then back at Howard.

"I think they, Whit and Daria, have something stashed. I think they preplanned for this eventuality. "

They're all concentrating totally on me.

"And more importantly, I believe they've set it up so that it will take *both of them* to get it."

"No shit," Cassie says.

"Because that's how *you and Whitney* would do it. You two are still scary, Courtney," Joey, who's grinning and shaking her head, is quick to add.

"It would have to be a pretty large sum," Howard offers. "Where does one put that kind of money, for no-questions, instant access?"

Cassie and I look at each other, then I look at Joey, who still has a smirk on her face, and simultaneously the three of us turn to look at Howard and say, *"Swiss bank!"*

I jump up and rush back into the house with Howard, Cassie, and Joey, right behind me.

Finally, it seems, we have a chance to get ahead of the bad guys!

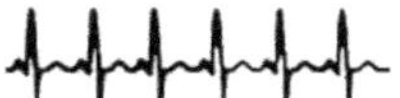

# 18

"Look at this, Courtney."

I turn and find a bizarre-looking image that I know is an infrared shot of something, filling the main monitor.

"What is it, Melinda?" I ask as I count all the visible heat sources.

"It's a 'hot shot' of the hangar area taken twelve minutes after the plane landed."

"Well, the lighter area has to be water, and you can pick out the buildings. Why am I looking at it?"

"This is why," she says, zooming out a little further with each click of her mouse, until a spot so bright it washes out the image, comes into view.

"What the hell?"

"It's in the damn water," Joey offers.

"It's a boat," we hear Howard say.

"Based on the ranges of the heat signatures, the engines were running when this was taken," Keith offers.

When Melinda overlays an earlier shot of the same area, I realize our suspected 'boat' is beached less than fifty yards from the hanger they parked the plane in!

"How in the hell..."

"Ask him," Melinda replies, pointing at Keith.

"It gets better, Boss," Keith says, as he continues typing. "This," a new photograph appears in one corner of the wall, "was taken seventy-three minutes after the other one.

"Taken by whom?" I ask, turning to face him.

"The automatic cameras on the ISS."

"The Space Station?" Cassie blurts out. "You're tapped into the damn *Space Station*, Keith?"

He and Melinda erupt in laughter.

"No, not technically, Melinda replies with a laugh. We just know where to look. It's a continuous automated system that takes photos with six cameras mounted on its exterior, as it orbits. Two of the cameras just happen to be infrared. All the countries involved have access to them. It's all non-classified stuff."

Then as Keith zooms the new image, I see what he means about it 'getting better'. The damn boat is *gone!*

"Holy crap!"

"I agree, Cass. *'Holy crap'*. Keith, you just got a raise."

Even as he is laughing, Howard has a question.

"Decent sized boat. What do you figure the range is?"

"Who cares? Wouldn't you rather know *where it is?*"

"Damn it, Courtney, I will ask this again. *Where* in God's name did you find this guy?" Howard offers as he shakes his head in disbelief.

A few seconds pass before a new image fills the screen, and although noticeably less intense, the heat signature is identical to the one in the previous image. It appears the boat is now beached next to a rather nice villa, somewhere. The villa is bright red as well.

*"So, where are they?"* Cassie asks, sounding too eager.

As Keith zooms the image out and overlays a topographical map on it, we can see it's the northern end of the island of Formentera, less than ten miles from where they started. Then, to the surprise of everyone, he overlays it a second time with a real-time image, and there are instant gasps of understanding.

I pull my phone from my pocket and hit the autodial for the Air Base at Morón. 1q

"Base Operations. How can I direct your call?"

"Colonel Wright, please."

"May I ask who is calling?"

"Courtney Whitman."

"One moment, Ms. Whitman."

I hear three or four clicks, telling me she's switched the call to a secure line, and then hear the Colonel.

"Wright."

"Colonel, this is Courtney Whitman, CIA Director of..."

The Colonel interrupts me mid-sentence.

"I was briefed, Mrs. Whitman, and told what you need, you get."

"Well, Colonel, this is a 'mission critical' issue," I reply, trying not to laugh. "I'm told you can put me in touch with Sergeant Major Osborne, quickly."

"Yes, ma'am I can. If it involves him, I can understand the 'mission critical' tag. Can I have him call you?"

"Yes sir. Securely. My number is 202-884-3112."

"Two minutes, Mrs. Whitman."

"Thank you, Colonel. I appreciate the assist."

"Are you sending the guys in?" Howard asks from behind me.

"That's what I'm thinking," I reply, turning to face him, and disconnecting the call at the same time.

"How do we know they're still there?"

He's making me slow down, and think. I quickly turn to Keith.

"The image showing the boat at the villa was taken slightly more than twelve hours after they took them – about 21:30 GMT. The last image was taken about twenty minutes ago. All I can tell you for certain is, the boat has been there for at least sixteen hours."

"You must be certain of what you're doing Courtney, *before* you start cycling your assets."

I smile, look at him, and say, "Thank you, Howard."

I turn back to the monitors and say, "Keith…" which is as far as I get.

"I'm already there, Boss. On the big screen."

A photo of the same area comes up on the big monitor, and Keith immediately zooms it. What we end up with is a very nice photo, of a very nice boat, on a beach next to a very nice villa. I let out a heavy sigh.

"Time on this, Keith?" Howard asks.

"Real time, sir. As it's happening."

Then my phone, which is still in my hand, starts ringing, and I quickly answer it.

"Whitman."

"Do we have a target?"

"Truthfully, I'm not sure Sergeant Major. If we do, I'm not sure how long it will be stationary. We know where they took them. That's all I have. What's 'too far' for a recon?"

"You say 'go' Director; we go. Simple as that. Distance is only a concern where time is an issue. Can you send the info to the base Communications Unit securely, so we can have a look at it?"

"Let's ask."

I walk over to Melinda, put a hand on her shoulder, and ask, "How do you get that photo," I point at the monitor, "to the guys?"

"Tell Sergeant Osborne to speak with Chief Sanchez," Melinda replies. "He runs their Signals Intelligence Group."

"A Chief Sanchez at SIG will have the target info. Once you see it, call me back."

"We're on our way. It's a short walk. Shouldn't be more than ten minutes."

"Okay. Bye."

"What did you send him?" I ask Melinda.

"The boat, the villa, and the coordinates."
"Now, we wait and see what their assessment is..."

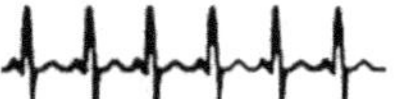

"Honesty is for the most part less profitable than dishonesty."

Plato
Greek Philosopher
424 – 348 BC

# 19

Am I dreaming again, or am I actually waking up?

The first thing I'm aware of is just how badly my head is pounding. Dreams don't usually generate pain, so I figure I must be waking up.

Next, I realize that I'm lying on a bed, and I'm freezing. I also notice my hands are no longer bound.

I concentrate on breathing and the pain in my head for a few seconds, and as the fog begins to clear, I understand why I'm cold. I'm nude. No clothing at all.

I force my eyes open, only to find more darkness. I blink my eyes and try to find something to focus on. The darkness makes it difficult.

I'm in a small room, a bedroom perhaps. There's a small window at the foot of the bed, that appears to be boarded up, yet a small amount of light is visible through the cracks. I turn my head and discover a door right next to the bed, the shiny handle inches from me. I concentrate on it, forcing my eyes to focus.

I feel around the bed, and find I am lying on a blanket, which I decide I need to put to use, not because I'm vain, but because I'm freezing! I carefully roll onto my side, pull the blanket out from under me, and then over me. It has an old, musty smell to it.

As my eyes adjust, I scan the room for information. What can I see that might tell me something... anything.

The room is very small. The bed barely fits into it. No closet. No other furniture. Maybe this is a closet? No wait… A closet wouldn't have a window. There is no light coming under or around the door, which seems odd. If it is daylight outside, as would be indicated by the slivers of light coming from the window, why isn't there any light on the other side of the door?

A basement perhaps?

I close my eyes and try to make my memory function… to remember what happened.

They snatched us… in Rabat… at the hotel.

Why?

Am I still in Rabat?

No… think, Whitney. Concentrate! There's a plane and a boat…

I'm being carried. One guy on each arm. I force my eyes open and see two guys carrying Daria ahead of me. We're on a beach, and light is coming from behind us… headlights I think… from vehicles.

What has become of Daria? Think damn it!

They are discussing money… They want money… They know who Daria is. Something about a villa… on the beach… hour and a half… plane in hanger…

It's all a jumbled mess in my still-pounding head. I keep trying to sort it all out and battle the pain at the same time.

More voices… male voices… speaking Russian. "Они обе всё ещё без сознания." (Both are still unconscious.) Then… a second one… "Я бы был не прочь переспать вон с той…" (I would like to get that one in bed…).

I reach up, rub my throbbing temples, and attempt to push the confusion aside.

Now I remember. Someone wanted to have sex with me. Is that why I am nude? I force myself not to laugh. I wonder? I reach down and gently touch my vaginal area. Seems normal. I lift my butt and feel under it. Dry. Apparently, they haven't raped me.

So, why am I nude?

I am quietly contemplating how someone could possibly find sex with an unconscious partner in any way satisfying, a blood-curdling scream rips through the building.

A female scream.

And, it's close.

I momentarily try to imagine the level of pain required to make someone scream like that.

My heart is racing, and I realize that I need a plan. It's apparent they, whoever *they* are, aren't shy about using pain to get what they want. For only a second, I wonder if it was Daria who screamed.

I hear a door close in the distance, followed by footsteps getting closer and closer, then slowing. What to do next? Start a fight, and hope for the best? Element of surprise – whoever it is doesn't know I am awake, but there were at least two of them on the boat. I might be able to take one, two if I'm fast and really lucky, but if there are more...

Key in the lock. Better think quickly.

I hear the handle turn and then the hinges squeak as the door opens, and a female, based on the smell of her perfume, steps into the room, and stops next to the bed.

"Hello 'Alexis', although we know that isn't your name."

She waits a few seconds for a response, and getting none, she continues.

"I know you are conscious. The motion detector told me. Besides, I doubt you covered yourself while unconscious."

A split second, before I am about to make a move, I smell something different. Although the scent is very weak, I know exactly what it is.

Cologne. *Men's* cologne.

I take a deep breath, then simply open my eyes and stare at the female next to me.

"Good choice. I only want to talk," she says, reaching over and turning on the lights. "If you behave, your clothes will be returned to you. The answer to your first question is no, neither

Sergei nor Pasha touched you while you were unconscious. I am the one who undressed you."

"Because?"

"I had to be certain there were no tracking or listening devices contained in your clothing, of course."

I frown, shake my head, and then ask, "May I sit up?"

"Of course."

As I do, I push the blanket off and hang my legs over the edge of the bed. After the renewed pounding in my head subsides a bit, I again look at the woman.

"What time is it?"

"It is approximately 9:30."

"am or pm?"

"pm."

"On what day?"

"You were abducted thirty-six hours ago. You have been here for about twenty-four hours.

"What did you find in my clothes?"

"Nothing."

"And now that we know I'm not 'bugged', what's next?" I ask, fairly sure they didn't discover the items – Melinda's little gizmo, *and* the tube of shampoo – concealed in the soles of my sneakers.

"We know that your 'sister' isn't your sister, as well as not being 'Allison Paddison'. Based on that, we must assume you too, are using an alias, although so far, we have been unable to determine who you actually are."

"And who, exactly, is it that you think my sister is?"

"Her name is Daria Ladenko, and she is an ex-operative of the Sluzhba Vneshney Razvedki. According to official reports, she was killed in an operation fourteen years ago, on Crete."

"Interesting. And what the hell is the Sluzhba Vneshney Razvedki?" I reply, thrashing my Russian as much as I can.

"Nicely played," she replies, ignoring my question. "We believe you to be the other person 'killed' in that incident. Your fingerprints, however, do not confirm that."

"So, you've disproved your own theory?"

"That one particular theory, perhaps. However, in the interest of keeping this simple, I am in hopes you will tell me what is going on."

"And if I don't, or if perhaps I tell you the truth, and you choose not to believe me, do I end up screaming too?"

She laughs.

"I told him it would work. The scream was Daria, but because I told her to under threat of something undesirable. I, of course, told her you were still unconscious."

"How come I don't believe you?"

"Based on your responses thus far, I would guess that it is because you are a woman of above-average intelligence?" she replies, a rather devious grin covering her face.

"Why?"

"Being Daria's '*sister*', I would expect you know why."

"May I ask who you are?"

"My name is Vera Kovalenko, and I am a past associate of Daria's. At one time we worked together."

I try to think... Vera... worked with Daria. Unfortunately, I can't make the association. It's been well over a decade, and the truth is, we don't spend much time discussing the past.

"Okay, you say my sister is this Daria person. Can we just cut to the chase and you tell me what it is you think makes us valuable enough to kidnap?"

"When she was 'killed' I happen to know for a fact she had very close to sixty million U.S. dollars stashed in various accounts."

"*My God!* You can't be serious?" I blurt out, doing my best to feign both ignorance and shock.

"Quite serious. I was her 'accountant' we will say. It took less than twelve hours for all of the 'funds' we acquired, to vanish. I spent years trying to track all that money."

"Where is my sister?"

"*Daria* is in another room."

"Can I talk to her?"

"To what end?"

"So that I can see she is still alive. I'd also like to ask her about all this silly bullshit you are feeding me."

She stands looking at me for a few moments and finally turns toward the door. "Sergei, bring her clothes," she says to someone I can't see. She turns back to me and says, "You may want to cover yourself with the blanket."

"Why?" I ask, again rubbing my temples, "Hasn't he seen a naked woman before?"

She starts laughing as a guy comes in with my clothes in a neatly folded pile. I immediately make a mental note of the gun in a holster under his left arm. *Right handed.*

"Thank you," I say, standing and taking my clothes.

"Dress and Sergei will bring you upstairs. We will talk further. While I will not be so brazen as to ask for your promise to cooperate, I will say that any attempt to escape will be met with force. Do we understand each other?"

"Completely."

"Very well, I will see you upstairs."

I watch her turn, go out the door, and down a short hall leading to a set of stairs, and then I go about dressing under the close scrutiny of Sergei.

"Я вижу, у вас есть пулевые ранения," Sergei offers, a chiseled stone look on his face.

"In English?" I reply, opting not to use Russian.

"The scars. Are they bullet wounds?" he replies, in damn near perfect English, which tells me he *was* testing me.

I button my blouse, turn, and look him directly in the eyes and with a deviously coy smile, softly say, "Perhaps..."

Ten minutes later, I'm sitting at a small table, in a cozy kitchen, across from my 'sister', drinking coffee.

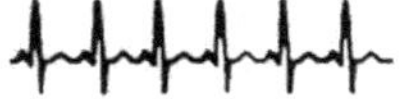

# 20

I'm staring out the window, at all Melinda's 'stuff' in the backyard, when a new thought forces its way into my mind.

"Keith."

"Yes ma'am?"

"This one may not be within your abilities but, we need to find out if either of our girls has a bank account in Switzerland."

"Hummm," I hear him reply from behind me.

When I turn to look at him, he's looking at Melinda.

"We can't watch every bank. We need to know ahead of time which one they're going to."

"I can do that, Courtney," comes from Joey, who's been sitting at a console since we came back inside.

Everyone turns to look at her as she finishes her sentence.

"Don't ask. Just say 'Okay, Joey, do it.'"

She spins around and pulls out a keyboard.

Howard and I say, *"Okay Joey, do it!"*

Again, everyone laughs. I watch as Keith stands, crosses the room, and stops behind Joey, as she begins typing.

"Can I watch?" he asks.

She laughs, and says, "Sometimes, Keith, it's more about *who* you know, than what you know."

Seconds later, she's talking with someone, somewhere in the world, using a secure encrypted 'chat' program. We watch over her shoulder as she types away. I bite my cheek to keep from laughing when I see their screen names.

```
Athena: I need a huge favor, and while it's
'official', it's also kind of personal.
Odysseus: You ask, I respond. Pretty simple.
We both know you wouldn't ask me to do
anything if it wasn't necessary.
Athena: Thanks. I need to know if an account
exists - anywhere in the Swiss system.
Odysseus: Name?
```

Joey turns to look at me.

"Uh, Paddison I think. One sec…" I start looking for the passports Melinda gave me earlier.

"Alexis or Allison Paddison," Melinda offers from across the room. "If they did what you are thinking, they used the 'rich girl' identities. Would make for fewer questions."

Joey turns back to her keyboard and starts typing again.

```
Athena: One of two - Alexis or Allison
Paddison - British citizenship.
Odysseus: Info required?
```

Joey turns and looks at me again.

"All we need to know is which bank."

She turns and once again begins to type.

```
Athena: Location.
Odysseus: That's it?
Athena: Yes. I owe you big on this one.
Odysseus: Give me thirty and I'll get back
to you. Leave this open. And, you don't -
and never will - owe me anything lady.
```

When my phone rings again, it startles everyone.

"Whitman."

"The close-up image indicates the target is isolated," I hear Mike say. "No neighbors. The best way to approach will be from across the peninsula, preferably after dark. You just want a 'recon'?"

"I'm leaving that decision to you guys. We still have no idea who has them, or what their manning is. We aren't even sure at this point, that they are still there. The order I'm giving you is, if you see an opportunity and are good with it, take it."

Everyone is now watching and listening to me.

"I've brought two others onboard – both Navy SEALs. I trust both implicitly. The Colonel has his U-28A on standby for us. We expect to be on the ground at San Javier in about an hour. The Marines are loaning us one of the Black Hawks off the USS Iwo Jima, along with the pilots, one of whom I have worked with in the past. It will be waiting for us in San Javier. With full fuel tanks, we will have a one-hour ride to target. We feel it will be better to do this while they're asleep, and if you tell us to proceed, anticipate being on target at around zero-thirty hours. Once we complete a recon, I'll call in via sat-phone."

"You have a *'go'* Sergeant Major, but keep two things in mind. First, if you see any op, take it. Don't worry about calling me first. I trust your judgment. Second, keep an eye on the Senior Chief. Don't let him get out of control, if you are getting my meaning."

"Copy both instructions. We'll talk again in a few hours."

I hear the series of clicks indicating the call has been terminated, close my phone, and take a huge breath. Now the waiting begins.

"Hey, Boss," I hear Keith yell from his seat across the room. "I have an idea."

Melinda and I walk over to his terminal, stopping behind him.

"And that would be?"

"Well, a lack of direct ground access will make getting assets in covertly to watch the villa pretty much impossible. I'm thinking I'll bootleg a couple of geo-sats and keep a constant watch on the place from here..."

Halfway through his comment *every single one of us* spins and looks at the image that's still on the big monitor. Melinda takes her seat and begins manipulating the image, and as she zooms closer and closer, the realization that Keith is right slaps us in the face. *No access other than by water.* The scary part is, *no one other than Keith noticed.*

It's becoming apparent that my need to get Whitney back has begun to cloud my judgment. My earlier comment to Mike, about my brother, now applies to me as well.

"Damn it," I mutter.

"Ditto," Howard, who grasps what I'm thinking, offers.

"Keith. You and me, in the yard, now."

He turns and looks at me, panic all over his face, then without a single word, he stands up and heads for the back door. He's finally beginning to understand the concept of 'team'. Once we're outside, I turn, close the door, and then face him, finding the same look of panic on his face.

"I'm about to drop a huge responsibility on you, Keith, so if you can't handle it, I need to know now."

"Huh?" he replies, the panic changing to confusion.

"Did you notice what just happened in there?"

"What do you mean, Boss?"

"None of us noticed, Keith. None of us caught the 'water access only' thing. We're all too deep into this. You are the only one here who sees it as just another operation. Do you get what I'm saying?"

"Uh, no ma'am, I'm sorry, I don't."

The look of total confusion on his face makes my 'oh duh' light go on almost instantly, and I realize that the poor guy has no clue about what's really going on, or who the players actually are!

"What's your assessment of what we're doing here, Keith?"

"Based on what I have seen and heard so far, I'd say we're trying to retrieve some assets," is his matter-of-fact reply. I know he's trying to hide his nervousness.

"Okay. What, if anything, do you know about my past?"

His nervousness gets the better of him. His eyes get big, he begins shifting his weight, and he breaks eye contact with me.

"Uh, well, I... uhh..." he says, looking down at the grass.

"Enough, Keith. Look at me!"

I wait the few seconds it takes him to again raise his head and make eye contact with me.

"It's probably not fair to drop you into the middle of shit like this, but I have no choice. This has gone way past easing you into it. You know about my sister, right?"

"Uh, yes ma'am, I do."

"Okay, pay attention. Howard, the civilian inside..."

"Is the retired London Station Chief, and was very... uh... 'attached' to your sister."

"Exactly," I reply. "What do you know about the others?"

"Not much. I know they're Station Chiefs. One in Turkey, the other in England."

"Joey was the 'bait' for the op my sister lost her life in. Cassie was standing next to me when it happened."

I watch as his shocked expression grows exponentially.

"The Sergeant Major – remember him?"

"Yes ma'am."

"He grew up with my sister and me. We've known him all our lives. He was there as well when Whitney was killed."

I think in that instant, he realizes he's in it up to his ass, and that there's no way for him to escape.

"And the SEAL – the Senior Chief?"

"Yes ma'am?" he replies, again close to panic.

"That would be my little brother. Rhyan."

I stop talking and watch his eyes for a few seconds. Then, being the overly intelligent guy, I've already figured out he is, his brain flips his 'oh shit' switch.  In a moment of clarity, all of the conversations he's heard make sense.

*"Holy crap, Boss!"* he suddenly blurts out.

I pull the two photos I've been keeping with me, out of the back pocket of my Levis, unfold them, and put one in each of Keith's hands.

"In your left hand is Daria Ladenko, ex-SVR operative, killed by the Russians on Crete. In your right hand is Whitney Bergstrom, CIA field asset, killed at the same time."

He looks first at me, then diligently at the photos, then back at me, once again, totally confused. The look on his face also tells me that every one of his 'analytical' gears is turning at full speed.

"Oh man, this is so far past anything I ever expected to be involved in, Courtney," he finally says, staring diligently at the two photos.

"Okay, but do you get it now? Do you understand what I meant earlier?"

"Yes, I do. Should I point out everything?"

"Yes. You see it, and ten seconds later I haven't, you tell me. You have the only unbiased pair of eyes here. We need you more than you might understand right now."

"What about Min... I mean Miss Aston?"

I laugh, and at the same time, hear the door open behind me. I turn to find Melinda standing there.

"Speak of the devil..."

"Oh crap," I hear Keith blurt out behind me.

I glance at him and find he's white as a ghost.

"For crying out loud Keith, would you please ease up?"

"Yeah. What she said!" Melinda yells.

"What's up, M?"

"Joey's pal is back, with way more info than we asked for. You need to come see this."

"Lead the way. Are you coming, Keith?" I laugh and head into the house.

The instant we enter the living room, I'm greeted by scrolling text on the giant monitor on the wall.

```
Odysseus: You still here?
Athena: Waiting patiently.
Odysseus: You have some wealthy friends,
lady.
```

```
Athena: Found them did you?

Odysseus: Uh-huh. Even though you wouldn't
ask, I knew you'd want to know it all, so
here you go.
ACCOUNT IDENTIFIER: A39U22O1TY
FACILITY: LB(Swiss) Private Bank Ltd.
ACCOUNT HOLDER(S): Alexis Paddison AND
Allison Paddison
COUNTRY OF CITIZENSHIP: Great Britain
TRANSACTION AUTHORITY: Alexis Paddison AND
Allison Paddison
LAST ACCESS DATE: UNKNOWN
```

When the scrolling text stops, I turn and look at Keith, but he's already typing away at another terminal. I lay a hand on Joey's shoulder, and wait until she turns to look at me.

"Can we ask your source questions?"

"Sure. If he doesn't know, he'll say so."

"What does the 'unknown' mean?"

```
Athena: 'UNKNOWN'?

Odysseus: Banking code. Means no activity
for over eight years. Between five and eight
years, it would have said 'UNDETERMINED'.
```

"I have the bank. Börsenstrasse 16, Zürich."

"Nicely done, Keith. Get a map on one of the monitors."

"I'm on it."

"Damn, I like him!" Howard says as he sits down next to Joey. "Can you ask your 'friend' what the process is when they go to access the money?"

```
Athena: Still with me?

Odysseus: Yes ma'am.

Athena: What's the process to access the
money?

Odysseus: Depends.

Athena: On?

Odysseus: All at once? In cash? Transfer to
a different account? Endless parameters
lady.
```

Joey looks at me first, then at Howard.

"Not going to be cash. Too damn conspicuous," Howard says.

"Yep. And a cashier's check will draw the same attention, especially if it's not in the account holder's name."

We turn and look at Cassie, who is sitting quietly behind us.

"Guys, come on. We know there are at least six of them, maybe even seven, right?"

Joey goes back to typing.

```
Athena: Which method draws the least amount
of attention?
Odysseus: Are we talking about the entire
amount here?
Athena: Let's assume we are.
Odysseus: No matter what you do with it, red
flags will fly at the bank. The account
holderS will both have to be there,
physically.
```

Everyone notices the bold capital 'S' in his statement. I turn, look at Howard, and with a smirk say, "I told you damn it! It will take both of them to do it, so they can't kill either of them."

```
Athena: Okay damn it, you got me. Give me a
figure so I can quit wondering.
Odysseus: You held out far longer than I
anticipated. You sitting down?
Athena: No you knucklehead, I always type
standing up. Jezzz. Yes, I'm sitting down.
```

Everyone starts laughing.

```
Odysseus: $12,211,997 and change.
```

"Just enough to buy their way out of a bad situation."

"No shit," I add, looking at Howard. "Tell him thanks, Joey."

```
Athena: Thanks O - you were more help than I
could have hoped for.
Odysseus: My pleasure lady. You know how to
find me. Laters.
```

Suddenly the screen goes black and is just as quickly filled by a satellite shot of Zürich. Then down in the bottom right-hand corner, a road map appears.

"There's your bank, Court," comes from Melinda.

"Print that. Hopefully, however much I doubt it, the guys will solve our problem in a few hours and we won't need it."

I sit down in the nearest chair, close my eyes, and start rubbing my temples. Cassie walks up behind me and places both her hands on my shoulders.

"Come on girl. Let's take a break, and power your brain down for a little while. Your world is pretty much on hold for now anyhow."

"Yeah," comes from Joey, who's rubbing her eyes as well, "good damn idea." She stands and turns to look at me, just as I open my eyes. "It's a nice night, let's take a walk."

"I'll keep an eye on these two," Howard says, indicating Keith and Melinda. Then with a snicker that makes everyone laugh, he adds, "Especially *that* guy," and points directly at Keith.

Then as if by magic, but actually 'by Keith', the satellite image of the villa pops up on the big monitor again.

"I'm gonna keep an eye on that boat myself," he says, leaning back and putting his feet up on the console. Then, in the bottom corner of the main screen, a chess game appears, and pieces start moving. When we look at Keith, he laughs.

"What? I gotta keep my brain busy, don't I?"

We're shaking our heads and laughing as Cassie, Joey and I disappear through the kitchen, and within seconds, are outside, walking down the middle of the small road leading to the highway.

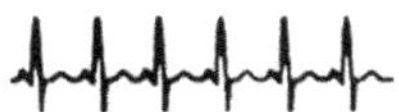

# 21

"We've been here for almost two days. Why?"

"You will be told what you need to know when you need to know it. The delay is necessary."

"Yeah, right," Daria says. "Do you think I am an idiot? *If* I *am* who you think, you must know what my 'profession' was. It is apparent you have lost control of your operation."

I immediately notice she isn't using her British accent.

"Think what you wish. You do not have any option, other than to do what you are told, Daria."

"Are you certain, Vera?"

"We could kill you both, right now."

"I seriously doubt that. You *think* we have that money, you greedy little bitch."

I quietly listen to Daria's rant, wondering where she is going, and what she may, or may not, have already told these people. I also wonder if this woman is the ringleader, or if there's someone else pulling the strings.

"You truly have no clue what you've done, do you?" I ask, using a heavy British accent, and laughing ever so slightly. A quick glance at Daria tells me what I need to know. She wants me to play the card I'm dangling.

"In reality, the mastermind behind this operation isn't very bright."

If looks could kill, the one Vera gave me after my last comment would have done me in, instantly. However, it also tells me that she isn't at the top of the food chain on this one.

"Assuming for a moment that she," I pause, and point at Daria, "*is* Daria Ladenko, and that I am working with her, do you *really* believe that the two of us could have set up *and* executed what happened on Crete, *alone?*"

Silence. She never utters a word.

"Do you even know what happened on Crete?"

She sits, a look of suspicion covering her face, and stares at me. It takes thirty seconds before she finally speaks again.

"So, you are now ready to admit that she is Daria Ladenko?" She points at Daria, without looking at her.

"Oh, come on, we're way past that. You want to know who I am, don't you? The suspense of it all is driving you bonkers, isn't it?"

We sit, our eyes locked, in a standoff of wills.

"My fingerprints are not in any system you've checked – are they? Neither is my face. Quite confusing, isn't it?"

Still, her stone-faced stare is her only response.

"And, the confusion is compounded if she," I grin and point at Daria, "is actually *Daria Ladenko.*"

Again, total silence.

"You are in so far over your head, Vera, that by the time you figure it out, your life will be worthless," Daria adds.

That gets her attention. For the first time, I see what I think is a sliver of doubt in her eyes. Seconds later, a new guy walks in. Daria's body language and first comment tell me she knows him.

"Well damn, I wondered when your silly ass would turn up, Vadym," Daria says, following it with a laugh. "Alexis, meet *Mr. Kovalenko...*"

"Вы, несомненно, смелы для той, которая вот-вот умрет." (You are certainly bold for one who is about to die.)

"Возможно," I reply to his comment, "но вы двое тогда вскоре отправитесь вслед за мной." (Perhaps, but the two of you will soon follow.)

Their heads snap in my direction. 'Confusion' would be a gross understatement of their response to my use of fluent Russian.

"А вы. Вы можете позволить себе быть смелой, поскольку я все еще даже не знаю кто вы такая." (And you. You can afford to be bold for I still do not know who you are.)

"I am the person who will be your downfall, Vadym. I assure you, that when death finds you, I'll still be a mystery."

"Perhaps then, it would be beneficial to me to simply kill you now, and thus change my future?"

"Make a note, Sis," I say, looking across the table at Daria, "this is a perfect example of jumping into the pool before you check to see if it has water in it."

"Perhaps," Vera replies, sitting up in her chair, "you might point out the many errors we seem to have made?"

"First one, *Mrs. Kovalenko*, is that you have no damn idea *who* you have kidnapped. That is what will ultimately screw you."

Daria smiles and winks at me, which I assume means I should keep talking.

"So," Vadym says, "enlighten us."

"What happened on Crete?"

"Daria and a CIA asset were allegedly killed," Vera replies.

"Who killed them?"

They sit quietly staring at me, trying I assume, to figure out where I'm going with my line of questions. After a few seconds, Vadym answers me.

"Popkovich ordered it. You are smart enough to know that. They feared what might happen if Daria fell into CIA hands."

Then as anticipated, Vera's light bulb goes on.

"Oh my God. You *were* in the van with Daria. YOU are the CIA asset that was killed."

"She has always been the smarter one of the pair," Daria mumbles.

"Any idea what the key part of your sentence is, Vera?" I ask a very devious smirk covering my face.

I'm watching her eyes as realization floods into her when without warning, Daria and I find our situation complicated even further.

"Вы неплохо выглядите – для мертвой женщины, Дарья." (You look very good – for dead woman, Daria.)

The comment comes from a deep male voice behind me, and even before I turn to look at him, Daria's face tells me our problems just grew exponentially.

"I should have known," Daria says, looking at me and shaking her head. "They were waiting for your treacherous self to arrive."

"Yes, they were. And now that I am here, our 'operation' can proceed."

I turn and find the last thing I want to, standing behind me, smiling.

*Leonid Tarasov*

"Did she do as you told her?"

"She did," Vera responds.

"Good. Once our transportation arrives, we will depart."

I turn and lock eyes with Daria, and what I see, confuses me. I'm about to say something when she raises her eyebrows and gently shakes her head. It's a signal she wants me to be quiet.

Considering I have not a damn clue as to what's really going on, I don't seem to have much of a choice...

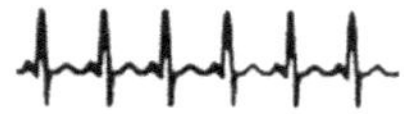

 Solution Squared: Recalculation

# 22

I open my ringing phone and answer it.

"Whitman."

"Get back here, Courtney. All of you, right now."

"Huh?" I reply, the stress in Howard's voice evident.

"Keith found something that you, and the girls, need to see. ASAP."

"We're on the way. Twenty minutes," I reply.

"What's up?" Cassie asks.

She and Joey reverse direction at the same moment I do.

"New issue apparently, and Howard feels we need to see it. He used the term 'ASAP'."

"That can't be good," Joey says, as we increase our pace.

It takes twenty minutes to find myself back in front of the plasma, staring at four images of the same person.

"What's up, Melinda?" I cross the room and stop next to her.

"It's not fucking good, Courtney."

With the exception of a couple of 'hell's and 'damn's, it's the first time I've heard the woman curse since I met her fourteen years earlier.

"He," she says, pointing at Keith without looking at him, "keeps complicating things for us."

I turn to look in his direction and find him typing away.

"We have a new player," Howard says but is interrupted midsentence as Cassie and Joey come in from the kitchen, coffee cups in hand, and in a single heartbeat, recognize the face on the monitors.

"*Oh God*, please tell me that son-of-a-bitch isn't involved in this," Cassie blurts out.

"*Oh my God,*" is Joey's only comment.

"So, why is this idiot filling all my monitors?"

Keith stands, walks over to the monitors, and explains.

"This," he points at a photo of Leonid Tarasov getting into a limo, on the upper left-hand monitor, "was taken three days ago outside the Russian Embassy in Rabat."

"The day *before* they were snatched? Oh shit…"

"Yeah. Now you know why I called you back," Howard says.

"It gets worse," comes from Melinda.

"This," Keith continues, his finger on the upper right-hand monitor, "was taken eighteen hours later at the airport in Tangier. Care to guess what he is doing?"

"*Checking to make sure the damn plane is there*. That sorry bastard masterminded this! Howard, get Chuck on the phone, tell him to get copies of the recorded phone call, and Tarasov's voice, and get his little twidgets to compare them. I'll bet you *he* was on the receiving end of that damn phone call."

Keith's finger slides to the lower left monitor, filled with an image of Tarasov exiting a Russian diplomatic aircraft next to a small hanger somewhere, "This one was taken about nine hours ago. And yes, Court, it was taken right where you think it was."

I'm on the verge of crying when I turn to look at Howard.

"God help us, Howard. What if…?"

"Okay guys," Melinda says, turning to look at me, "would you mind filling me in here?"

"If he already knows, or figures out, *who my sister is*, it will all come crashing down," I say, to no one in particular.

"You'd better call Alice," Howard suggests.

Once again, I lose it. I feel all the air and energy surge out of me and let myself drop into the nearest chair. The tears come. I can't stop them. The situation just became so precarious, it's possible I could actually lose my sister this time. For good.

"Courtney, don't do this. Focus girl," Howard says as he stands up and lays a hand on my shoulder.

"It's getting too hard, Howard. I can't live through it twice. I can't..."

"Well then damn it, let's get them back!" comes from a very irritated sounding Melinda. "We don't give the sorry bastards the opportunity to kill them."

"We have to move now, Boss. Quickly. This one," Keith says, his hand on the last photo, which was taken on the corner of a poorly lit street, next to a hotel entrance, "was taken about two hours ago. He's on the damn island."

Something about the sound of Keith's voice, a strength, and determination I feel from it, makes me look over at him. When we make eye contact, he walks over and squats down in front of me, using my knees to balance himself.

"Courtney, I have the utmost respect for you and your abilities. A lot of us, the minions in your basement at home, have talked amongst ourselves more than once, about how intense it would be, to be able to watch you work, and now, here I am. Right smack in the middle of the shit. You know as well as I do – even with my limited experience – that there is more than enough expertise in this room to pull this off, but we need a leader and whether you like it or not, you get the job. So, lead, Boss. Fire this thing up and let's get the hell on with it, okay?"

*"Well fuck me to tears!"* Cassie blurts out, which again fills the room with laughter. "I love this kid!"

"Yeah," Joey adds, "The bastard has screwed with us for the very last damn time. I'm tired of it. No more bullshit, Court, it's time to kick his ass. *And...*"

Joey's treacherous tone, makes every head turns and looks at her.

"*...Tarasov's ass is mine.* And yes, it is personal."

"You are the scariest bunch of women I have ever met. No wonder I retired," Howard says, disappearing into the kitchen.

"I need a goddamned beer!" we hear him yell.

"Thank you, Keith," I say, wiping the tears from my eyes, and then leaning over and gently kissing him.

"Oh shit! Please don't tell your husband you did that," he blurts out, grinning as he does.

"Your butt is mine now," Mindy says, again prompting laughter.

Suddenly, all the monitors go blank and when they come back, I'm looking at Alice.

"What's up, Courtney?"

"We believe Tarasov has her, Alice. Should we assume you know what he is up to?"

"He planned all this?"

I immediately notice her sidestep around my question.

"All of what we've discovered so far points to him. Once Chuck does some voice analysis for me, we can confirm it. We believe he was at the receiving end of the original call."

"Do you believe he's focused on the money, Courtney?"

"Perhaps. But you must realize that if he figures out who Whitney is, *and* her relationship to Daria, you and the entire 'operation' will be completely compromised."

She sits blankly staring at us as if her mind is elsewhere. I'm about to ask 'what if' when Melinda damn near explodes.

*"HOLY CRAP!"*

Keith, who just sat down, again comes out of his chair. I think Cassie and Joey are, out of habit, reaching for weapons they don't have, while Howard comes running back into the room, beer in hand.

"Jesus, Melinda, what else can go wrong at this point?"

"Not wrong. Quite the opposite actually."

Keith is furiously typing, and in only seconds, an image appears in the lower left corner of the large monitor. It's a satellite image of the island of Formentera, with a blinking red dot at the top, right where the villa is.

*"What the hell..."* I start and am instantly interrupted.

*"Whitney's damn sneaker!* That's what! And, you have to know *how* to activate it. It can't happen by accident."

"I have to go Alice. I have some analyzing to do. Sorry."

The image of Alice is gone before I finish the sentence. I walk over and stare at the blinking red dot, then look at my watch. Midnight. I flip open my phone and hit the speed dial number I want.

"Osborne."

"The target is on site, Mike. Copy?"

"Yes. Is that confirmed?"

"Yes. Melinda had her bugged by some means that can't be accidentally activated. Only she knows how to light it."

"When was this verified?"

"How about thirty seconds ago?"

"We're airborne. ETA to target is forty minutes."

I hear the howl of the Black Hawk's jet engines through the phone, as well as the 'whoop-whoop' of the rotors.

"Copy that. My position is the same. If you see a window, take it. *Do not* compromise yourselves if not necessary. We believe that we know where they're going and are planning accordingly. Be careful Mike, and for God's sake, keep my bother out of trouble."

"Will do. Keep a line open, okay?"

"Yes. Use this one. Good luck to all of you."

Then I hear the clicking circuits as we're disconnected.

"Nicely done, Courtney," Howard says, smiling at me.

I force a smile of my own and say, "I'll be back in a minute. It's time I report in to someone," then turn and walk into the kitchen, dialing as I go. The call is answered on the first ring.

"Courtney?"

"Yes, Mom, it's me. I found her. The intrusion team is going to attempt retrieval. I wanted you and Dad to know."

Silence.

"Mom?"

"Yes, Courtney, I'm here. How long?"

"An hour and we'll know one way or the other. I wanted to tell you now, so you could sweat with me."

"Now *that* is something your sister would have done!" she says with a laugh. "Call us back when you know. I love you, young lady."

"Two hours at the most. Love you too, Mom. Bye."

As I close the phone, I feel myself smile, and know that my mother's comment, *'something your damn sister would have done'*, caused it.

I'm lost in one thought when my damn overactive brain begins forming another one, based on something Keith said earlier. Sometimes, my mind's aptitude for migrating between issues so quickly scares the shit out of me. I turn and hurry back into the living room, stopping directly behind Keith.

"Hey Motivation Guy..."

"Yes ma'am?" Keith replies, amidst the muffled snickers.

"The photos of Tarasov. Put the last one back up."

It takes five seconds for him to fill all four monitors with the photo.

"Interesting."

"What, Court?" Cassie asks.

"We know there isn't an airport on that island, and he's *in town* – probably La Savina – based on the ferry terminal in the photo."

"No shit," Joey says. "Once again, her brain is at work."

"And, if a second boat hasn't turned up at the villa, how in the hell did he get there, guys?"

"Let's find out, shall we? We know he landed at the airport in Ibiza. From there..." Mindy is quickly interrupted.

"...he chartered a helicopter. You guys want to see it?"

Once again, every head turns to look at Keith. With a grin, he fills the monitors with an overhead image of a helicopter that is sitting on a small pad at the end of a dock, at the end of a narrow street.

"It belongs to Ibiza Air Tours," Keith says.

"Get this, Courtney," Mindy adds a few seconds later, "the silly bastard used his embassy credit card to hire it!"

"How do you think I found it?" Keith asks, laughing.

A few seconds of silence pass, and once again, everyone's attention focuses on me. Howard is the first to realize that I'm analyzing.

"What Courtney?"

"Keith split the monitors and put up the first daylight image of the villa for me."

I walk toward the monitors, and the moment he finishes his task, I see what I knew I was going to do. I laugh and lay a finger on each boat – the one beached at the villa, and, *the one tied to the pier, next to the helicopter.*

*"No shit!"* Cassie blurts out.

Without me asking, Keith separates the images, putting each on its own monitor, and filling a third with a real-time image of the villa.

"It's back, and beached in another spot," Howard mumbles.

*"He's at the villa..."* comes from Joey almost whispers.

When Howard and I look directly at each other, the look in his eyes tells me he too understands. The rest of them realize we know something.

"What?" Joey and Cassie blurt out simultaneously. The other two turn and look at us as well.

"Come on ladies!" I reply, following it with a laugh, as I turn and walk up to Cassie. "Think about what they – *all of them* – are doing. It should be blatantly obvious."

Howard and I watch as the two of them walk right up to the monitors and stand looking at them. After a second, Joey sits down at a terminal and starts typing. Things pop up on a small monitor in front of her, she types some more, and the images change. Cassie is right there for every keystroke. After a few seconds, Keith and Melinda step over together and watch as well. Howard walks over next to me and places a hand on my shoulder.

"Nicely done, *Miss Bergstrom*."

No one has called me that in close to fifteen years, and it makes me turn and look right at him. I find myself face to face with a big smile and a pair of twinkling eyes.

"Just once, I'd like to get inside that blonde head and watch that brain work. What was it?"

"The boat, of course. They left the damn thing in plain sight on the beach, and then, right next to the helo? Can't get more blatant than that," I reply, laying my head on his shoulder for a second.

"You never stopped learning, girl. Now, you've become me. You're the teacher, and it's very cool watching you pass it all on."

"They're leaving blatant trails, *everywhere*," Cassie says.

"With what seems like total disregard," Joey adds.

"Even I get this one, Boss," Keith, who is standing right behind the two of them, offers.

"So tell us, computer geek," Cassie says, poking him in the ribs.

"They have no clue they are being watched or tracked."

"Which means?" I ask, prompting him. I can tell by the looks on their faces, that Cassie, Joey, and Melinda have all figured it out.

Keith hesitates for a couple of seconds, his mental gears turning, then turns to look in the direction of Howard and me.

"Either, they don't care – which isn't realistic. Or..."

"Go with it," Melinda offers. "Follow your thought process, Keith."

"Or they have no reason to suspect anyone is watching them, which would make more sense."

"Because?" Joey asks.

Finally, Keith's proverbial 'light bulb' comes on and it illuminates the entire room.

"Oh, crap! *They have no idea they work for us!* They don't realize the two of them are *CIA assets*! Holy shit! They think the two of them are rouge, stole the money, and are now out there living the high life, *without any backup!*"

"Bingo cutie," Joey says, as she kisses him gently on his cheek.

"Oh shit! Now it makes sense. Why didn't I think of this sooner? It's so blatant..."

Blushing like a little kid from Joey's kiss, he jumps over a chair, slips between Melinda and some equipment, and slides right back into his chair. He's typing furiously before his butt comes to rest. At first, we girls are busy giggling, but when Howard queries him, we once again turn our attention to Keith.

"Whacha got, kid?" Howard asks.

"Something I saw earlier, but it didn't make sense at the time. Now, it does. One sec."

He fills all four monitors with the same photograph of the helicopter but expands it out a distance past the end of the dock. Anchored a hundred yards offshore is a yacht, which Joey and Melinda recognize immediately.

"Okay, damn it, this is getting ridiculous."

"What the hell?" I blurt out.

Melinda freaks. She turns and looks right at me.

"Everyone out, now. The Director and I need the room, please."

Looking befuddled, they do as requested. Once they're all gone, Melinda turns to me and says, "Only four people can issue orders to move that boat, Courtney. The bad guys have two of them, and I didn't do it." She turns, starts typing, and fifteen seconds later Alice is once again on the monitors. "What's going on, Alice?" she demands, with no reserve.

"Meaning?"

"The yacht is tied up in Formentera, and I didn't send it there."

"What?" Alice replies and instantly starts typing. Within seconds, sounding surprised, she blurts out, "Damn! *Daria* wrote the orders and sent them directly to Captain Bell by secure satellite bounce."

"How the hell did she..." is as far as I get before Melinda's voice interrupts me.

"Jezzz! The back door. I'm so damn stupid! She used our secret access to get to the satellite."

I turn and watch her typing like a mad person, and when she pauses and lifts her head, with a little smirk, she adds, "Okay, so I panicked. I'm seriously sorry guys."

I again glance at the big monitor, and with a smile, Alice says, "Don't look at me, Courtney, I'm in the dark room with you at this point. I have someone waiting on me, so do I have permission to continue running the Agency?"

Melinda and I laugh, and without warning, Alice's image disappears. I walk up behind Melinda who's still standing, and slide a chair under her, forcing her to sit down. I watch the small monitor over her shoulder as she types.

"Can I let the guys back in yet?"

"Yeah, and I will explain why I did that later, okay?"

"I know why you did it, Melinda. Protocol. Move on."

I turn and walk to the kitchen door, and stick my head through it.

"Back to work you slackers," I say, making them turn to look at me. Being the professionals they are, not a single one of them questions being asked to leave. They just file past me back into the living room.

Melinda speaks the moment Keith's chair moves.

"Keith, there's an incoming alert on the scrambled sat system. See what it is please."

Keith rolls to the next terminal over and starts typing. Almost immediately, a very strange image appears on the main monitors. All of us, except Melinda, turn to look at it.

"Oh, man! How bizarre!" Keith says, still typing.

"Infrared," comes from Howard. "Must be your team, Court."

When the image becomes sharper, I think I recognize my little brother's silhouette. I feel my heart rate quicken.

"Keith, can you do something for me?" Melinda asks.

"Sure, whacha need?"

"I'm trying to backtrace a satellite communication, and I need to know approximately when that yacht showed up."

"No prob. One sec..."

Even though I can hear Keith's fingers blazing across his keyboard, my eyes, like everyone else's, are glued to what's happening inside the Black Hawk.

"I have it in a frame from about nine hours ago, Mindy. Looks to be about a mile offshore, inbound."

"Okay, thanks."

Keith rolls his chair next to Melinda's and sits watching her.

"I don't want to get into stuff I shouldn't Mindy, but..."

"Christ, Keith, there isn't anything we're doing that you shouldn't be right in the middle of. You got an idea, let's hear it."

"I can see what you guys set up. I assume it was from a civilian point of origin?"

"It has to be. They had her by then. I know she's trying to tell us something. I'm certain of it."

"Based on the type of message and its required security level, there is only one way it got there."

"And?" she asks, looking up at him over her shoulder.

"AUGUR."

"Keith, God is the only entity I know that has direct, non-DoD, access to that piece of equipment."

"Yeah, and HE gave me his access code."

The look on Melinda's face is totally priceless, and I wish so badly I had a camera. I take three steps over to where they are and lay a hand on Keith's shoulder.

"Melinda, would you please close your mouth, and blink your eyes a few times? I'm concerned that they may get stuck like that."

She looks up at me, then back at Keith, apparently lost in a suspended state of shock.

"You gonna let him do what it is we are paying him for?" I ask, letting myself smile just a little as I do.

Melinda slowly stands up, and lets Keith push her chair aside, and roll up to her console. Keith immediately begins typing, as Melinda turns, makes direct eye contact with me, and whispers, "He isn't who he claims to be, Court…"

"Yeah, I am, but there's a bit more to it than you've been told. And," the lower right-hand corner of the monitor is suddenly filled with a jumble of incomprehensible, scrolling information, "the uplink originated on a civilian computer, using a civilian satellite internet company with a transmitter on Formentera. She used the 'civilian' URL for IKON ONE which read the classification header, forwarded it to AUGUR, which scanned it and sent it directly to the captain."

Now, everyone is staring at him.

"You want a hard copy?"

"Just who the hell are you?" Howard asks.

Keith spins his chair around to face us, the look on his face telling me he expected this kind of response. Melinda's right. He *isn't* what he purports to be.

"Do we need to talk, Keith?"

"I'd love to, but Mindy seems to have a direction here, so what say we help her pursue it first?"

"Fair enough. You need a hard copy, Melinda?"

Now it's her turn to freak and fade. I smile and gently poke her in the side.

"Yoo-hoo?? Anyone home?"

Cassie and Joey start laughing, and Howard still looks kind of spooked. Keith – well, he's just sitting there with a smirk on his face. Melinda looks at me as if to ask *'what do I do?'*.

"No matter who he is, he seems to be on our side, Mindy."

"Yeah," she says, turning to look again at Keith. "I'm fairly certain she moved the boat to send us a message. She did it the hard way, she could have simply *called* the captain on a secure circuit. Why bother with bootlegging a message via that satellite?"

"She's using the *message* to tell us something?"

"Uh-huh, and I know where to look for it in the text."

While she's talking, Keith spins back around, types a few lines, and in seconds the printer behind me spits out three pages. As I turn to pick them up, I hear Howard.

"They're on the ground, Courtney."

Every pair of eyes in the room, except one, turns toward the big monitor. I, however, am still diligently staring at Keith.

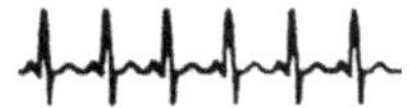

# 23

From the moment we took control of the yacht, eleven years earlier, we set it up for every conceivable emergency. The crew, while all civilians, (with the exception of the captain and the radioman) are loyal to us. Captain Bell was Navy intelligence, and he jumped at the chance to come work for us. Jamie, the communications expert, was Air Force intelligence and is one of only four females on the crew.

I had no idea the yacht was here – it was apparently Daria's doing, for unknown reasons. I'm fairly certain, she *did* intend for me to end up on it alone – again for reasons unknown.

We never get a chance to 'talk' before they separate us, but we know what their ploy is going to be. Cooperate or the other one dies – which would make sense, save for the fact it will take *both of us* being physically present, to get to the money.

That's a little secret we aren't ready to share just yet.

The moment I realize they intend to put me aboard the yacht, I know it's time. I have to gamble – gamble that they didn't find Melinda's little gizmo while searching my clothes and that they aren't monitoring the house.

While I wait for my 'escort', under the kitchen table, I lay my left shoe over my right, bringing Melinda's tiny transmitter into close proximity with the weak magnet that will activate its power source, then instantly pull it away. I repeat the motion twice more, and after the third pass, I feel the short vibration from the sole of my shoe, telling me the device is active, and more importantly, is transmitting.

The question is – how long will it take Mindy to hear it?

Twenty minutes later, I find myself being locked in the captain's cabin, along with Jamie and Mr. Bell, with no idea what has become of Daria – or Leonid Tarasov. I watch Jamie flip a small hidden switch to scramble any 'signals' that might be present, so we can talk freely. Vera seemed rather jumpy when she put us aboard, so who knows what she may have planted where.

"Finally!"

"Are you okay, Alexis?" Jamie asks, taking a seat next to me.

"Of course. These idiots are far too focused on money."

"And do we understand Allison's anal need for redundant planning now?" the captain asks, looking right at me.

"Yes, Skipper, we damn sure do!" I reply, smiling at him.

He rolls his eyes and returns my smile.

"How the hell did they take the ship, Captain?"

"Food delivery. I thought they were here to stock us. Foolish mistake, considering."

"Hell, Russ, they get the best of us every so often. And, come to think about it, you are here because?"

"Automated satellite dispatch, routed through AUGER. Figured one of you sent it – knew it had to be something hot."

"Wasn't me," I reply, frowning.

"Considering I've never been directly tasked by the *'others'*, I'm leaning towards Allison being the culprit."

"Interesting..."

I smile at his reference to Alice and Mindy – as they're the only other people who can give the captain orders of any kind.

"Any indication of where she plans to go?"

"No ma'am. I received a location and time to show up, along with a latitude and longitude that are nowhere near the location."

"Meaning?"

"I'm clueless. If we had the message, I was thinking you'd know what it meant..."

"I can tell you where we *are* going" Jamie volunteers.

"Oh yeah?"

"Yeah – I was watching the jerk who stuck the gun against my head, while he was typing at the Nav station. They've plotted a course to Genoa."

"Genoa? As in Italy?"

"Yes ma'am. And the only place to tie this thing up around there is going to be some deep draft piers just north of the airport, in Multedo."

"Industrial piers," the captain adds. "A boat this size, in that environment, isn't going to draw any attention."

"How many bad guys did you count?"

Before the Captain can answer, we hear a key in the door and Jamie immediately resets her hidden switch. When the door opens, I'm once again face to face with Vera Kovalenko, and one of her henchmen – who incidentally, is armed with an MP5.

"Can we keep this civil?" she asks.

"You're the one who brought the guns, Vera."

"In the interest of keeping the peace, of course."

I shake my head, turn, and take a seat next to the Captain.

"Piracy is a crime in most countries, you do realize that, right?"

"Oh please, Captain, be realistic. *Miss Paddison* owns this ship."

"No ma'am. *Erasmus Shipping* owns this vessel."

"Yes, of course they do, Captain, but let us move on to more important things. Miss Paddison, you do realize why we have chosen to separate you and your 'sister', do you not?"

"Let's assume I don't, and you can tell me."

"This," she says holding up what appears to be a small PDA of some kind, "is what keeps Daria alive. Leonid has a second one that is keeping you alive. We each send a message at specific intervals. Miss one, and someone dies. See how that works?"

I have to bite my cheek to keep from laughing. They truly have no clue – which is somewhat odd considering Leonid Tarasov is involved. I also feel quite uneasy about his choice to take Daria with him and send me with Vera. This can be a bad thing on several levels. I'm fairly certain Daria, by some means, manipulated him into doing it.  The question is – why?

"At some point, Vera, reality will set in and you're going to understand just how much shit Tarasov has gotten you into – and more importantly, that there isn't any way out of it either."

"Well, I suppose we will see. I have eleven armed men aboard, so you will concede to behaving yourselves, will you not?"

"Yes."

"Captain?"

"I will follow Miss Paddison's orders, as always."

"Well then, you may feel free to leave this cabin. Do not go to the engine room or the communications suite. Do we understand each other?"

I nod in response to her question.

"We have approximately twenty-four hours before we arrive at our destination. Once there, I will inform you of the next step in our operation."

With that, Vera and the guy with the gun turn, and leave, without closing the door. Jamie stands up, carefully peeks into the passageway, and then closes the door.

"Well, I'm thinking my earlier comment has been verified," the captain comments looking directly at me.

"Meaning?"

"If they know she *is Daria*, you two are probably in a world of shit – which explains her use of AUGER to dispatch me..."

I smile at him, and then shake my head in disbelief.

"You damn sure don't miss much, Russ."

"Question is... what do we do now?"

"We have to play along. Daria did this for a reason – all we can do is wait, and see how it plays out."

"Okay then, what say we go find some food?"

"Cool! I'm starving," Jamie blurts out, turning and opening the door.

I shrug my compliance, and ten minutes later, the three of us are rummaging around in the galley.

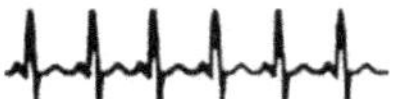

# 24

We're all locked onto what's happening on the big monitors. In the lower-left corner, we watch the Black Hawk drop to water level, compliments of a DoD infrared satellite. In the upper left corner is a close-up infrared image of the villa itself. The rest of the screen is displaying the feeds from the small cameras each of the incursion team is wearing.

We can see the movements of at least five heat signatures inside the villa, while at the same time, are watching the guys move through the palm trees, and across the small peninsula toward the house. The Black Hawk moves offshore, and hovers just above the water.

I hear someone on a keyboard behind me, and suddenly there's audio. When I hear the sound of my brother's voice, my heart races.

"Hold. I have visual on the house."

"Copy. Stand by," comes from Mike.

"I have movement on the back deck," comes from a voice I don't recognize.

Then from Keith, who's standing behind us, we hear, "Oh jezzz! How damn freaky is this? I have a new feed, Boss – you wanna see it?"

"Put it up," I reply.

The moment the image opens in the lower right corner, I know exactly what it is.

"Infrared from the Sergeant Major's scope," Howard says. "Isn't technology cool?"

"And scary as hell," Keith replies.

As I glance around the room, I notice that Joey and Cassie, while being excessively quiet, are also watching quite intently. Their stress levels show on their faces.

"Listen up!" we hear Mike say. "Hostile Target count."

"Go," comes from each member of the team.

"I've got six. One, you have two of them at the front of the house. Sitting it appears. Three, you have one on the deck in the open, smoking. I have two upstairs, prone. Probably lying down. The last one appears to be sitting on the toilet."

We hear them laugh.

"I don't see our 'friendlies'. Could be below ground level. The east end of the building is 'hot' – probably a basement."

"Copy," each of them responds.

Then, my phone rings.

"Whitman."

"We're on site," Mike says.

"We're watching. Assessment?"

"I'd like to enter – with your permission."

"At your discretion, Sergeant. But there is a caveat."

"Issued by?"

"It comes from the top of the food chain."

"Understood. This is confirmed?"

"Yes. Verbally, and directly to me, by the Director. Stand by for secondary confirmation."

I turn and look at Melinda, who nods, walks over, and takes the phone when I hold it out to her.

"Sergeant Major, this is Melinda Aston. My tag is Sierra, Sierra, Charlie, Seven, Nine, Victor. Copy?"

"Yes ma'am, that authenticates," Mike replies.

"The confirmation for Mrs. Whitman's caveat is G-A-I-A. Copy?"

"Yes ma'am. Thank you."

When Melinda hands the phone back to me, I realize everyone is looking at *us* and not at the monitors.

"I'm releasing control to you, Sergeant. Good luck."

"Courtney..." Howard starts to say but stops when I raise my hand to him, accompanied by my best 'pathetic' look.

"Listen up," we hear Mike say, his voice echoing through the room. "Priority change. This op is now Tango Oscar Sierra. Copy?"

With no hesitation, they each respond with a firm "Copy." Then, Mike changes frequencies and speaks to the Black Hawk pilot.

"Bravo Hotel – Team Leader."

"Go Leader."

"We have been issued a caveat, repeat a caveat. Copy?"

"Copy that. Will you be hot?"

"Affirmative. Request extraction point be modified."

"Give me a holler, Mike, and light the beacon. We'll be there in a heartbeat. Copy."

"Copy that. Stand by."

"Okay guys, let's do this. Remember – there are supposed to be two friendlies on-site. Verify your targets."

Then, as if meant to break the tension, I hear Rhyan's voice.

"Copy that. Is that your polite way of telling me not to shoot any other family members, Sarge?"

Everyone – at both ends of the connection – breaks up in laughter. Then, we – those of us watching the monitors – hold our collective breath, and watch as the intrusion team advances toward the house. In only seconds the sounds of suppressed weapons fill the room.

First, the figure on the back deck falls off it, landing in a heap. Next, we watch both the sitting figures collapse at the same instant. The one who was 'sitting on the toilet' is now moving quickly toward the back of the house.

Then, one of the computers behind me starts screeching. Keith immediately turns to look at it and damn near freaks out.

"Shit! *She's exceeded the perimeter!*"

"What the hell?" Melinda blurts out as she starts typing.

Keith jumps back to his terminal and starts typing as well.

My attention is drawn back to the monitors by the sound of an automatic weapon but is just as quickly drawn back to an over-excited Mindy.

*"They aren't on site, Courtney!* The transmitter is *outside* of the one-mile perimeter! Tell them – *everyone at the site is hostile!"*

"Yeah, and they have guns too," Howard mumbles, making Joey and Cassie snicker.

"Jesus Christ," I blurt out, putting my phone back to my ear.

"Team Leader! Do you copy? Michael!"

"I'm just a bit busy, Courtney."

The circuit is again filled with the muffled snickers of his team.

*"They're all hostile, Michael!* The original targets are not on site – repeat – original targets have been removed! Protect yourselves!"

"Done deal. Did you guys copy that?"

"Copy," they each repeat in order.

Then more automatic weapons fire.

"Jezzzz! A couple of them have AK's, Sarge."

"I show them confined to one room. Steve, drop one of your big rounds in there, please. Let's finish this and get the hell out of here."

"Copy that, Sergeant."

A distinctive 'fooomph' is heard, as a grenade leaves the barrel of someone's weapon, and two blinks of an eye later, the entire southeast corner of the house simply disappears. The ensuing silence, tells us what we need to know.

"Chief – you and Steve recon the wreckage. Pete, you and I are around front. Bravo Hotel – come get us. Beach side in ninety seconds. Just follow the fire."

"Copy that. Things get out of hand, did they?"

"We're just returning fire, Major, that's all."

*"The damn yacht is underway!"* Keith yells, typing away.

"Shrink the villa and show me," I reply.

"They must be on board it – or at least Whitney's sneaker is," Melinda adds. "Assuming Whitney activated it inside the house, I'll bet they exceeded the device's perimeter the moment they started moving."

As she's talking, yet another satellite image fills one corner of the main monitor. I watch as Melinda suddenly stops what she's doing, turns around, walks to Keith's desk, and searches for something. After she rummages for a few seconds, she pulls out a single page.

"Should they," Howard points at the monitor with Mike's team on it, "take the yacht?"

"NO! DON'T DO THAT!" Melinda screams. "Oh my God. She's a damn genius... the woman is a genius!"

"Team Leader," I say into my phone, which is still to my ear.

"Go ahead."

"Is the site sterile?"

"We have one survivor – Russian passport says his name is Kovalenko. Instructions?" I hear him reply, as the sound of the Black Hawk's rotor begins to fill the circuit.

I quickly look at Melinda who shrugs at me, then at Cassie and Joey. Both remain silent. It's Howard, who finally speaks.

"Follow the thought process, Court." He has a devious little grin on his face, telling me he's thinking the same thing I am.

"You think?" I ask, knowing he understands the question.

"Do you?"

"Sergeant – what's his condition?"

"He's pretty fucked up, but we can keep him alive."

"Take him with you and go home. Copy?"

"Yes ma'am," he replies, as the chopper's rotor noise all but washes out the call.

"I'll call you later, Sergeant. And well done!" I pretty much yell.

"She's got another damn plan," Cassie says.

"Cool," replies Joey.

"Okay, Melinda, you ready to explain yet?" I ask, causing everyone to turn and look at her.

"Uh, yeah, but what about…" she starts to ask, referring to what I just did.

"You first?"

"Yes ma'am," she replies, seeming a bit 'guilty' for lack of a better word. "Daria is setting them up – they just don't know it yet. The auto-activation code she used – it's a 'duress' code. *The captain knows something is up.* He moved the ship to the *location* specified in the message. Look closely," she says, handing me the message. "Notice anything?"

It only takes a heartbeat to figure it out. The latitude and longitude in the message don't coincide with the location. The coordinates are way too far north.

"That tricky little bitch," I mumble.

"Yes she is," Keith adds. "Do you want to see where the coordinates are?"

"Sure."

Four clicks of his mouse later, there's a map of Italy covering all four monitors, with a blinking red dot over Genoa. It's as if we all 'get it' at the same time. Joey and Cassie are the first to verbalize it.

"Switzerland. They're headed for the damn bank," they say simultaneously.

"Melinda, we need to be in Zürich, ASAP."

"I'm on it."

I turn and find the rest of them in a group across the room, staring at me. I slowly cross the room and join them.

"You guys are *sure* you want to be in the middle of this, right?"

"You couldn't *make* us leave at this point," Cassie says.

"Look," Joey adds, as she steps over next to me and gently puts a hand on my arm, "we have two advantages here. First, they don't know we're coming, and second, and even more importantly, we have you. So, just like fifteen years ago, you plan, we execute."

"Sounds like a hell of an idea to me," Howard says, smiling at me. "Been years since I dodged any bullets."

Then, out of nowhere, Cassie hands me an open phone.

"Hello?" I say, after putting it to my ear.

"Say the word and I'm there, Courtney. I want to help," I hear a deep, male voice at the other end say.

"Holy shit! Willie?"

"Yes ma'am."

"Okay, if you're sure. I keep saying this, but it's inevitable that at some point…"

Then, to my surprise, *everyone* has the same comment.

*"Someone is going to be shooting at us!"* they say in unison.

I hear Willie laugh through the phone as he asks, "Where do you want me?"

"Meet us in…" I turn to look at Melinda.

"Dübendorf. It's the nearest nondescript airport that has enough runway for the Gulfstream. Twenty-four hours."

"…some place called Dübendorf. It's near Zürich. We'll be there tomorrow in the 'corporate' jet."

"See you then."

When I hear the click indicating he hung up, I look at the others and say, "Hell, he hung up. I guess he knows where he's going, huh?" Everyone responds with a laugh.

"Okay boys and girls, time to take this show on the road."

After a few muffled 'about time's', and one 'finally', I turn and look at Melinda.

"The plan at this point is, to get a few hours of sleep, some food, and you getting us to Switzerland before Willie – and the bad guys."

Cassie, Joey, Howard, and Keith are headed for beds, even before the last word leaves my lips. I, however, go out into the backyard and, standing beneath one of Melinda's huge dishes, call my parents for the second time.

I decide, as I'm dialing, that the next time I call them, I will have my sister – one way or another.

When I finish the call, I go back into the house, walk past Mindy who smiles at me, and flop onto the couch, and close my eyes.

Once again, I have to fight a mental battle to get my brain to slow down and idle. Fortunately, the fatigue wins out and, although it seems like forever, I'm asleep within minutes.

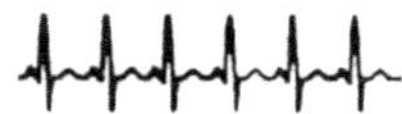

# 25

I'm washing some dishes for lack of anything else to do, when Jamie walks up behind me, and gently lays a hand on my shoulder.

"So, should I send our duress signal yet?"

"Huh?"

"The satellite duress ping. Should I send it?"

"You lost me, Jamie."

"Oh. Sorry. It's a security thing. If the boat is hijacked – like now – I can send a ping to a satellite and it will tell them what's going on. The captain said to ask you if I should send it."

Instantly my brain engages.

"How? You can't get to the radio room."

"Jezzz, Alex, we're spies, remember? You don't think we have a plan for this eventuality?" she asks with a laugh.

"You guys – I swear to God," I reply, as I finish putting the dishes away. "What's in this 'ping' of yours, anything specific?"

"Well, it's a binary message to the satellite that tells it we are hijacked. In response, the satellite will send an initiation signal to activate a passive laser transmitter here on the ship, which in turn sends a signal back to the satellite every sixty seconds. That's how they track us."

"Hummm..."

"Whacha thinkin', Boss?"

"Can we modify it at all?"

"Without getting caught? Probably, but the message will be seriously limited. And, the satellite won't be able to respond and activate the tracking laser."

"How limited?"

She pulls a pencil out of her pocket and does some math on a napkin, then looks at me and says, "Twenty-one characters max."

I walk over and stand looking out the galley porthole at the open water now between us and the shoreline of Formentera, letting my mind wander for a few seconds.

We don't need to be tracked by the satellite. Melinda – and most likely my sister as well – will already be doing that. What I need to do is let them know that the bad guys separated us. I'm about to ask a question, when the entire skyline in front of me, lights up a bright orange.

"*Oh my God!* What the hell was that?" Jamie blurts out, stepping up next to me and staring out the porthole at the huge fireball now rising into the night sky.

"That…" I reply, watching the remnants of the fireball dissipate, while at the same time, a small smirk spreads across my face, "was the good guys. Courtney is all over this one, apparently."

"You think they stormed the villa looking for you guys?"

"*Absolutely.* Once my sister gets a hair up her butt…"

"What about… well… what about Daria? You sure she wasn't in there?"

"They left before Vera brought me here, Jamie. She's fine – definitely up to something, but fine," I say, turning to face her. "So, can this satellite of yours forward the info once it gets it?"

"Depends," she replies, still staring out the porthole.

"On?"

"Who you want to send it to."

Grabbing her shoulders, I spin her around to face me, and ask, "Seriously?"

"Sure. In binary, I can give it a relay code in four characters. Do I want to know who we are sending it to?"

I laugh because, over the years, Jamie has become a fairly decent spy, by doing nothing more than listening.

"To Mindy, of course. I'll bet the mortgage that wherever she is, so is my sister."

"But what can you tell her in only seventeen characters?"

"Mindy? Nothing that will make any sense. But Courtney – more than we need to. Where's the Captain?"

"That woman let him onto the bridge to ensure they weren't screwing up his boat. In reality, he figures that if they're watching him, they aren't paying that close of attention to us."

"Can we change things without telling him?"

"His last words to me were, 'she's the boss'"

"Okay. Here's what we need to do..."

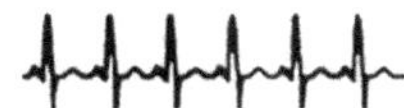

# 26

We head for Chania – about ten miles away – as it's the nearest place with a restaurant that is open all night. As luck would have it, when we reach the stop sign at the end of the road, I notice lights on in our local restaurant. Although it's absurdly early by business standards, I figure it can't hurt to ask, and quickly drive around to the back of the building.

I'm locked in a losing battle with the cook, when the same girl I spoke to the day before, walks around the corner. After allowing me to plead my case, she readily agrees to feed us again – even though they don't open for three hours.

She seats us, takes our orders, and is on her way to the kitchen when I jump up and follow her. We reach the swinging door at the same time, I put a hand on her shoulder, and she spins around to face me.

"Yes ma'am? Was there something else?"

Although she's smiling, that same small pang of guilt is steadily jabbing my gut, and I know I have to do the right thing.

"You're right. We did meet before. Unfortunately, that's all I can tell you..."

I watch as her smile grows even bigger, a twinkle develops in her eyes, and her chest heaves as she takes a really deep breath.

"For that, I thank you. And... I do understand."

She winks at me, turns, and disappears through the door.

An hour later, we've finished breakfast, and it seems, have all relaxed – even if only slightly. The big issues – *who, what, why, and where* – have been resolved.

Now, we just need a plan, which is what everyone at the table is discussing. I, however, am once again lost in thought.

We have to take them at the bank – that much I'm certain of. Logic would dictate that in addition to the money, Tarasov intends to extract a little revenge as well. Howard agrees that neither of them will live long once they give up the money – especially once the bad guys realize it's only $12 million, and not the $60 million that was originally missing. I'm completely lost in thought when Melinda's phone rings, and I only partially notice her pull it out and answer it. When she raises her hand for silence, she gets everyone's attention.

"From where? No kidding? How? Damn! Genius... total genius! Of course not, you knucklehead – it's Sierra, Sierra, Charlie, Seven, Nine, Victor. I'll wait."

I immediately realized she gave someone – presumably Keith – her encryption password. This is the second time he's given me reason to wonder. Why call Melinda, and not me? He knows I have a password, and that my clearance easily exceeds hers.

"Melinda?"

"One sec, Courtney."

"Uh-huh, okay. We'll be there shortly. Bye."

"Care to share?" Howard asks.

She turns, looks right at me, and says "A long time ago I said your sister was born to do this, remember?"

"Yes, I remember the conversation, at her funeral," I reply. "I was good at it; she was born for it."

"Well, she once again – as she has so many times over the years – reaffirmed my statement. The girl is a genius, I swear to God. She had Jamie modify the duress transmitter on the yacht. Daria is good at some stuff, but your sister thinks like you do. The message had to come from her."

"They sent a message?" Joey asks, now giving Melinda her full attention. "Using the activation ping of the duress transponder? Jezzz. You're right, that had to be Whitney."

"It gets better. She had Jamie override the transponder signal and use the sixty-four-bit binary space to send the message. She knows there's no need to activate the ship's laser position indicator. Somehow, Whitney *realizes we're tracking the damn ship!* She used the single outgoing transmission to route a message to my encryption point on the satellite, which in turn routed it to where it knows I am, even if it makes no sense."

My heart is racing. Whitney knows we're on her. I find myself wondering if perhaps, after all this time, she actually 'felt' me.

"What was the message?" Cassie finally asks.

"'Smiley Face'. They were seriously limited on space."

"Oh shit," I mumble, as my mind once again shifts gears.

"Mean something does it, Courtney?" Howard asks.

"Yes, it does. It means only Whitney is on the ship. They've separated them. She wants us to know they've separated them."

It suddenly gets eerily quiet at our table.

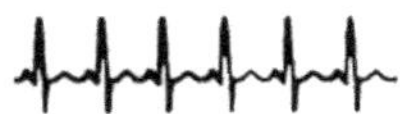

# 27

I'm sitting on a nylon recliner, on the aft deck, staring up at the star-filled night sky, when Vera walks up and sits down next to me. I remain silent, and purposely wait for her to start the conversation.

"Мы поняли, что вы не та, за кого себя выдаете, и хотите, чтобы мы в это поверили." (We have determined you are not who you would have us believe you are.)

I immediately detect the 'nervous' and 'uncertain' tones in her voice – something that over the years I've become quite adept at. She's fishing... question is, for what?

"Хорошо, кто же я тогда на самом деле?" (Well then, who, exactly, am I?)

"Я надеялась, что вы мне просто скажете это" (I was hoping you would simply tell me.)

"I've told you several times – my name is Alexis Paddison."

"And why does a quite wealthy, British citizen, speak such fluent Russian?"

"Ich spreche fließend Deutsch aber ich bin deshalb kein Deutscher." (I speak German fluently as well. It doesn't make me German.)

"I do not speak German, so you win that one."

"No matter what my sister gives you – money or anything else – you will unfortunately not live to enjoy it. You have no idea what you have done," I say, without looking at her.

I give her a few seconds to respond, and when she remains quiet, I finish my thought.

"You must decide if you fear Tarasov enough to follow him with this folly."

When I finally turn my head and look at her, I find myself looking into eyes full of uncertainty – which tells me my tactics are working.

"Without knowing *who* I am, I think that you have figured out *what I am*. People – the people you should fear – are as we speak, tracking this vessel. You have no clue because Tarasov has no clue. His greed has blinded him."

She sits silently, staring at me.

It's very apparent – as evidenced by the explosion we saw earlier – that Alice and Mindy are all over this, whatever 'this' is. And, based solely on how fast they found the villa, I have to believe Courtney is involved as well.

It turns out, activating the transmitter while still in the house, was a good move. It's designed to initiate the perimeter warning from the point of activation – and within minutes of getting underway, we exceeded the one-mile limit. I'm guessing it was just about the time we saw the villa explode...

Acting on the assumption that Vera too, saw the explosion, I decide to try a bluff, to see if she will call it openly or shrug it off and excuse herself to look into it privately.

"Vera, we both know you are smart enough to figure out what that explosion was earlier. I'll bet that if you check, you will find that your husband, and the others left behind at the villa, are now out of contact."

"Yes, Miss Paddison, I believe I do know *what* you are," she replies, trying to ignore my comment. "And yes, I believe you are perhaps correct in assuming Tarasov does not know who his opponents truly are – because *he* was not told."

When she turns to face me, her eyes give her away. She knows *exactly* what happened – even if she isn't ready to admit it.

"Now, if you will excuse me, I need to go check in with *my captain.*"

I watch as she climbs a nearby ladder to the upper deck, and disappears in the direction of the bridge.

Somehow, I know I have her. I'll bet she is dialing before she is out of sight. She also confirms – in an indirect manner – that Tarasov *isn't* in charge of what's happening.

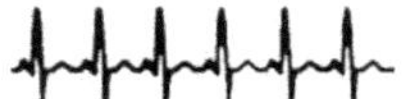

# 28

*"NO, DAMN IT!* There isn't going to be any 'at least we can get Whitney' bullshit! *Are we clear on that?"*

My outburst is in response to an honest comment, made by Melinda, as we walk back into the living room of the safe house. Although I get everyone's attention, I may have scared the shit out of Keith. I also notice a little smirk on Howard's face.

"This isn't – *and never was* – about 'Courtney getting her sister back'. This, *goddamnit,* is and always has been, about recovering *two of our deep cover assets.* Clear?"

"Yes ma'am, quite clear on both counts actually. I apologize for my comment," Mindy replies, smiling.

"Computer geek – you still with me?"

"Yes ma'am!" Keith responds, rather loudly.

"I need to know where that chopper went. Sometime between when we first noticed it, and when the yacht left, it left too. Find it."

"Yes ma'am."

"Joey."

"Yeah, Court?"

"The chopper's reach is limited. Find me another Russian jet within its operating radius."

"I'm on it."

"Melinda, move the 'boys' – and their toys – to Dübendorf. And get the military to buzz that damn yacht – with something that's *armed* – but not to attempt to stop it."

"They'll be moving that way, as soon as they land at Morón, and I'll have the Marine Detachment at Rota get some aircraft on the yacht immediately."

"Cassie, call Alice and fill her in – please."

"I'm on it."

"Howard, I need to talk to you outside."

Howard turns and heads for the door, and Cassie is dialing just as quickly. Having followed Howard out the door, I pull it closed behind me and turn toward the road. Although the sun has barely breached the horizon, it's already apparent it's going to be another hot, humid, Mediterranean day.

"Walk with me, Howard?"

"Of course, Courtney. What's up?"

He takes my hand, and together we walk out to the small road, make a left and continue up the middle of it, following the same course the girls and I had earlier. For the first half-mile, I don't say anything.

"Verbalize it, Courtney. It might help," Howard finally offers.

"I can get inside Whitney's head, Howard..."

"But you're concerned about Daria's position?"

"Yeah, but not in the manner you're thinking."

"So? Talk to me Court. Don't make me guess."

"Too many 'what if's' – which forces me to believe Daria must have another agenda. The question is, whose agenda? The assumptions at this point are that Tarasov left in the chopper at some point before the yacht moved and our guys landed. Whitney is on the yacht, based on the message she sent us. Because she wasn't one of the bodies left at the villa, we have to assume Daria is with Tarasov. We know it's about the money and thus know where they're going and why. We're assuming it will take both of them to do what Tarasov wants, but don't know if Tarasov knows this."

I stop talking, letting my thought processes continue to run, as we wander up the road. Howard remains quiet.

"Why? Why is Whitney on the yacht, and why is Daria with Tarasov?"

"You tell me."

"She did it purposely, Howard. I believe Daria is trying to shield Whitney and limit her exposure to Tarasov – like I said, she has an agenda. There are two possible scenarios to explain this. The first, and most obvious, would be that Daria is in on the whole thing, and is Tarasov's 'accomplice' rather than his prisoner. The second – which I'm leaning towards – would be, even though they know who Daria is, they can't identify my sister. Thus, they have no idea the two of them are tied to us... to the CIA. Yet. I believe Daria, for reasons unknown, is trying to keep it that way. My issue is trying to figure her angle. Why? What the hell is she up to?"

"Here's a nudge. Ask yourself how Tarasov will respond to the knowledge that Whitney *is active CIA.*"

We stop at a bus bench along the side of the road, and as we sit down, my phone rings. Figuring it's another unforeseen disaster, I quickly flip it open and answer it.

"Whitman."

"I have a Colonel on another line, asking me what to do with the 'nearly dead guy' that your team brought back with them."

"Get a number, and I'll call him back right now."

"34 978 548 611 is direct to his desk."

"Thanks."

I hang up and dial the number. It rings twice before I hear a voice at the other end.

"Coats."

"It's Courtney Whitman again, Colonel. I'm responsible for the 'nearly dead guy' you have at your base."

"I see..." he offers, with a little laugh. "And what, exactly, would you like me to do with him, Mrs. Whitman?"

"The Sergeant Major wasn't specific about his condition."

"He'll survive, Director. They have him isolated in the base hospital. He probably won't be conscious for a while."

"Good. I need to talk to him. I can be there in twelve hours. Should I have our flight plan sent to you?"

"I take it that means you have your own transportation?"

"Yes sir. A black Gulfstream 550."

"Oh yeah… that one," he says, a muffled laugh escaping as he does. "I'm guessing that the absence of any markings on it means it probably belongs to our favorite people – *'spooks'*."

I laugh.

"Well now, Colonel, in this instance, you could say I'm the 'head spook'."

This time he can't hide his laugh.

"Send me your transponder code, and I'll see if I can't keep Spanish Air Traffic Control off your butt. My Deputy will meet your plane and take you to the hospital. If you need something that requires my input, feel free to call me."

"Yes sir. And thank you."

"No problem, Ms. Whitman, and good luck with whatever it is you're in the middle of."

I disconnect the call, and then redial Melinda.

"Aston."

"How fast can you get the Gulfstream here?"

"It's on its way. It'll be on the ground here in about an hour, and ready to fly again in two."

"Good. Change of plans. I have to go to Morón."

"You do realize the Gulfstream will draw attention, right?"

"It's a military installation M, and the CO already knows about the silly thing. Besides, we aren't dealing with another intelligence agency here – they're renegades. Because they don't know we're on to them yet, they aren't watching airports. Everyone else who sees the Gulfstream, anywhere it lands, is going to assume it's just more rich people. Are the Swiss going to let an undesignated aircraft land at Dübendorf?"

"The military controls that base, so yeah, they'll let us. They won't be happy with only a transponder code, but they'll play."

"Set it up. Howard and I will be back shortly."

"I'm on it."

I close the phone and ask Howard, "Where were we?"

"You were about to tell me what Tarasov will do if he discovers Whitney's identity."

"Depends on what the two of them do. No cooperation will undoubtedly get them killed. He wants that money."

"Come on, Courtney, think past all that..."

I sit quietly, staring into the distance at an awesome sunrise unfolding in front of me, thinking. Howard is trying to lead me somewhere, but my mind is so cluttered I can't find the path. I start thinking 'out loud', because sometimes, just as Howard said, it works for me.

"Tarasov is the mastermind. Someone recognizes Daria and calls him. He confirms it, lures her out of Libya, and abducts her. I have to believe he didn't expect anyone to be with her."

"No 'assumptions', Courtney. Think. See it all again..."

I force my severely cluttered mind to go back to the photos of my sister being abducted. Black cars... guys in black suits. Then it hits me. *Plural.* Car**S**. Guy**S**.

"*Shit!* They *knew* Whitney was with her. They brought *two vehicles,* which tells us they sent *two teams,* at least six people. Blatantly excessive if they were going to covertly abduct a *single* female."

"Keep going girl."

"He makes the snatch and tells them it's their lives for the money. Straight trade. They, of course, don't have any options. They realize they need to protect Whit's identity, or perhaps their *affiliation with us.* That's where it gets convoluted. If Tarasov discovers they're *CIA assets,* regardless of who they are, and he realizes *he's up against us* and not some rogues, wouldn't he bail?"

"That's the right direction, but you still have it cropped to a snapshot. Pull back and look at the entire picture, Courtney."

I close my eyes, clear my head of everything, and let myself go back to the beginning. Then, I let my mind run...

The trail began with the cars, rented by Kovalenko using an embassy credit card. At the time, the Russians couldn't account for him. After a full sixty seconds of silent contemplation, I go right back to 'thinking out loud'.

"We discovered Nekrasov – or Mrs. Kovalenko if you prefer – who according to the Russians, is 'accounted for'. Next, the damn plane, which also belongs to the Russians, but has been 'appropriated' by..." I stop and look at Howard.

"That's still an unknown, Courtney, but keep going."

"Oh shit."

"What?"

"We never determined *who owns the villa,* Howard. When that damn transponder was activated, I got so excited, I lost my focus."

"*And?*" he says, prompting me to continue.

"We discover Tarasov is the mastermind. First, the photos of him in Rabat – when he shouldn't have been, and then he turns up in Tangier. Then a photo of him in Ibiza..."

Although part of my mind is following the steps, a different part has already jumped right to the point that Howard is subtly guiding me toward. A point my subconscious decided to ignore... because it was easier *not* to deal with it.

As I turn to look at him again, I feel my heart begin to race.

"*Oh God, Howard,* we were here once before – you and I. I freaked, and blocked it all out because the possibility scared the shit out of me..."

Howard smiles at me and gives my hand – which he's never let go of – a gentle squeeze.

"No one else sees it either, Courtney. I know it tears you up, but you have to realistically consider this particular 'what if'. The only reason I saw it immediately, is because I don't even trust my own mother anymore. Now go back, and tell me where the ramifications of what you said earlier, lead you."

"If *they* already know what we did, the bastards certainly are being excessively sneaky about it all."

I sit quietly for a full minute, lost in thought. When Howard doesn't say anything, I realize he's waiting on me.

"Why wouldn't Sokolski simply tell us they want their traitor and money back?" I ask, turning to face him.

He stares at me, grinning, as he waits for me to continue.

"IF they know, Sokolski will be in a position to hang Alice and the entire Agency out to dry. Alice will crash and burn. The fact that Whitney and Daria are *still* together will tell him what she did, as well as give him a damn good idea of how she did it."

"What about your boy? What about Tarasov?" Howard asks.

My brain again clicks.

"Hard to say. They could be using him, but I don't have enough info to say for certain. If he is being used and knows it, I wonder if he would cross them – for a few million."

"Sixty million could be very tempting, Courtney, and that's the figure he has in his head."

"And, at the moment, Tarasov has the only person who can effectively answer that question. I think Daria knows what's going on. She knows whose agenda we're following – who our 'manipulator' is. I can only hope she's still on *our* side."

Even as the words leave my mouth, the answer hits me, as if it's a large brick.

*"Well, shit!"* I blurt out, turning to look at Howard. "You silly old bastard, you knew I'd decipher it, didn't you?"

His only response is to smile at me.

"Her actions *are* her answer, damn it. She's 'black ops', for God's sake. Everything she's done so far has been with reason and direction. I don't need to know whose agenda it is; I just need to keep up with Daria. I bet we can not only get our people back alive but can also put this mess right back in Sokolski's lap. And, if I'm really lucky, I may even find a way to dispose of Leonid Tarasov as well."

A look of apprehension sweeps over Howard's face after my last sentence, leaving me with a need to justify my feelings.

"I'm sorry Howard – but the bastard *needs* killing. And, like it or not, it's what we do."

"I think the speed with which you are willing to do it, is what astonishes me, Courtney. Don't mind me, I'm a civilian, remember?"

He stands, holds out a hand to me, and when I take it, pulls me to my feet. As we start our walk back to the house, I find myself giving serious thought to what he just said.

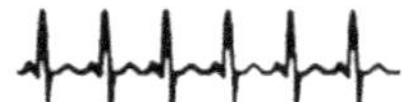

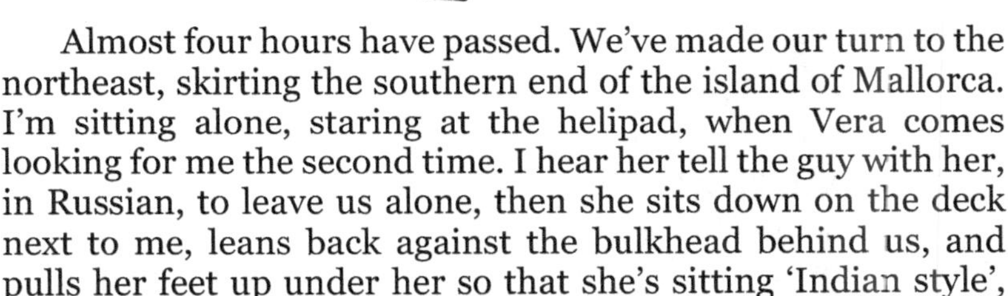

Almost four hours have passed. We've made our turn to the northeast, skirting the southern end of the island of Mallorca. I'm sitting alone, staring at the helipad, when Vera comes looking for me the second time. I hear her tell the guy with her, in Russian, to leave us alone, then she sits down on the deck next to me, leans back against the bulkhead behind us, and pulls her feet up under her so that she's sitting 'Indian style', just as I am. We sit watching the froth of the wake the yacht is making, neither of us speaking.

"How deeply into this, am I?" she finally asks, without looking at me.

"How many of these men are with you, and how many belong to Tarasov?"

She looks completely confused, both by the question, and the speed of my response.

"All but two of them are known to me. I felt that ten would be sufficient – Tarasov insisted I take two others."

"Do you honestly believe his concern was your well-being?"

When she doesn't respond, I continue.

"Do *you* really believe that my sister has $60,000,000?"

"I can only say how much she had when she was 'killed'. Whether that amount remains after so many years is doubtful. But, I would guess at least half of it remains."

"Finally, knowing what you know *now,* do you – in the depths of your soul – believe even for a second, that he has any intentions of 'sharing'?"

Again, silence.

Her tone, continued hesitance, and depressed demeanor tell me she not only checked on her associates but that the results were exactly what I suggested they would be. Seeing a crack, I decide to keep pressing her, in an effort to widen it.

"The man who was with you when you walked up – is he yours, or one of the two?"

"He has been with me for many years."

"Do you still doubt what I am saying about Tarasov?"

"I have become unsure, Miss Paddison – which is why we are having this conversation."

'Gotcha' I think to myself, suppressing a smile.

"So, you are not ready to believe that one of *them*," I nod in the direction of the ship's bridge, "is watching you at all times?"

Again, her only response is silence, as she continues to stare out at the ocean behind us.

"Will your uncertainty support a test of my theory?"

She finally turns to look at me, and the trepidation building in her mind is clearly visible in the depths of her eyes.

"I know you have a weapon, so if you are up for a quick test, simply do this – take it out and lay it on the deck in front of us. I give you my word I will not attempt to take it. I'm betting it will take less than a minute for one of *them* to turn up to ask a question or deliver a message, or some other irrelevant task. You see, Vera, whether you are willing to admit it to yourself or not, *they – the two sent by Leonid – are here to watch you.*"

It's apparent I'm getting to her, cultivating a small seed of doubt. It only takes her seconds to pull a Glock 25 from the small of her back and place it on the steel deck in front of her. Then we sit in silence, watching the never-ending wake behind us.

 

# 30

"So, do you really think you can bluff them?"

"If Alice will let me, yeah, I think I can give Sokolski reason to distance himself from Tarasov. I honestly believe they're probably in on this, in some fashion."

"What's the plan with Kovalenko?"

"I honestly don't know, Melinda. I'm not sure that dying is even a concern to him."

As I'm talking, the co-pilot comes out of the cockpit and walks up to us.

"We'll be on the ground in twenty minutes ladies. There is someone named Simms, waiting for you with a vehicle."

"Thanks, Rick," I reply.

"So, why did you bring me?" Melinda asks.

"Because... your Russian is *fluent,* and mine isn't," I reply with a smirk on my face.

A little over an hour later we're escorted into a hospital room containing a *very* messed up Vadym Kovalenko.

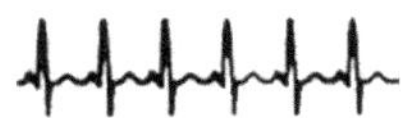

"The whole world is run on a bluff."

Marcus Garvey
National Hero of Jamaica
1887 – 1940

# 31

"Вы хотите жить, Вадим, или предпочтете умереть?" (Do you wish to live or die, Vadym?)

Melinda shows no quarter and starts in on him the second we enter the room.

"Все зависит от того, насколько дорогого мне будет это стоить жить..." (That depends on how high a price living has...) he replies, without opening his eyes.

"В вашем случае, ценой будет всё, что вы знаете о похищении наших агентов. Это информация также сохранит жизнь вашей жены." (In your case, the price will be everything you know about the abduction of our assets. This information will save your wife's life as well).

That gets his attention. His eyes open and he looks first at Melinda, then at me.

"Ваших 'агентов'?" (Your 'assets'?)

"Alexis and Allison Paddison. Ring any bells, Vadym?"

I get him. The look on his face gives him away instantly.

"And you are?" he asks.

"That's irrelevant. It should be enough to know that I am the one who now holds your life in her hands."

"И я настоятельно рекомендую не пытаться ввести ее в заблуждение. Вам вряд ли понравится ее реакция на это..." (And I would urge you not to attempt to mislead her. You will not like her response...) Melinda adds, with a sinister smile.

"What of the others who were with me?" he asks, directing the question at me.

"Do you really need an answer to that question?"

"All of them?"

"Yes. You were moving in the direction of a window, and when the grenade went off behind you, the concussion sent you through it. My people found you in the rubble, two hundred feet from the house."

"The fact you can order such an operation, tells me who you must answer to," he says, a definite sadness seeming to engulf him.

"Сокольский снял с себя ответственность за операцию. Он утверждает, что бы действуете, как жулики." (Sokolski has disavowed your operation. He claims you are operating as rogues).

When I hear his name, I know it's my queue.

"Sokolski says you and Vera are in this on your own – with the help of some of your subordinates. We happen to know someone else is actually in charge of this fiasco, and he doesn't give a shit about you, or your wife."

"Where is my wife? Might I assume she is not dead as yet?"

"She's hijacked a yacht that belongs to us. We know one of our people is aboard with her. Whether your wife lives or dies will be up to her, when we decide we want our ship back."

"Ублюдок лгал нам, с самого начала." (The bastard lied to us, from the very beginning) he says, to no one in particular. Then he looks right at me and asks, "Why did you not leave me with the rest, to die?"

"I need insight into what is going on here, and you were still alive. It was an instance of convenience, nothing more."

"If I cooperate with you, what assurances..." he starts to ask.

"None," I reply, cutting him off mid-sentence. "You know damn well, that in this business, there are no 'assurances'. I will commit here and now to ensuring you and your wife remain alive. That's the limit of my offer."

"And if..."

I again interrupt him. He needs to *believe* that I am deadly serious.

"Everyone even remotely associated with this operation – whether on the SVR payroll or not – will be terminated. Period. That comes from as high up my food chain as Sokolski is up yours. You've managed to piss off some powerful people."

He lays quietly, looking from me to Melinda, and back again, showing little – if any – emotion. At this point, I'm not sure if I have him or not, so I keep pressing.

"So, do we understand each other?"

He nods his understanding, and when he momentarily closes his eyes, I wink at Melinda to indicate to her that it's time to play our bluff. She immediately jumps on it.

"Вы чувствуете, что попались, и задаетесь вопросом: что случится, если вы откажитесь. Пусть тот факт, что вы находитесь на военной базе в присутствии большого количества свидетелей, не занизит вашу оценку ситуации, Вадим – она *убьет* вас. Единственный способ убедиться, что я не лгу…" (You feel you are trapped and wonder what will happen if you decline. Do not let the fact you are here on a US military base with so many witnesses, cloud your judgment Vadym. She *will* kill you. The only way to be certain I am not lying…)

He looks at her for a moment, shifts his eyes to me, takes a breath, and then speaks.

"I am sorry… I cannot…"

Even before he finishes his sentence, and without a word, I reach behind my back, pull out my Px4, pull the slide back and release it, and then take two steps toward the bed. I think the poor guy almost dies from the shock of what he *thinks* I'm about to do. Even as I am doing it, Melinda steps between the bed and me, placing a hand on the Beretta, and pushing it down to my side.

"Let me talk to him, Courtney. I know the orders, but…"

"Five minutes, Melinda. His only options are my way or a box. I don't have the time or the inclination to fuck around at this point. Understand?"

"Yes ma'am," she replies, letting go of my hand.

I turn and go out the door, leaving her alone with him. Once out of view of the room, I walk over to the nurse's station, where a female Captain smiles at me, and flips a switch so we can listen to the conversation in the room.

"You have no idea what Tarasov has gotten you into Vadym. This has gone so far past what you and Vera signed on for, that it can now do nothing but get both of you killed. He told you it was Daria, didn't he?"

There are a few seconds of silence, then Melinda again.

"Do you think I am lying to you – that perhaps this is a ploy of some kind? Let me tell you all about your op so far. Here's what *we* know – the four guys at the hotel in Rabat were his. He didn't trust you and Vera to handle that, so he took care of it himself. He also set up the plane in Tangier, and the boat in Ibiza. You get to ride a ferry to the island – he gets to fly. Oh, and what about *us?* Did he even tell you who you were playing against? And of course, the yacht – I *know* you can't possibly think it just 'showed up' when it did."

There's a momentary silence, and then Melinda continues.

*"For God's sake Vadym, you've all been disposable since this started.* You must see that now."

A few moments of silence pass, and then *he* starts talking.

"He went to Vera and told tell her he found her – found Daria. He showed her photos. He told her that if we helped him, we would each get an even split of whatever money she still had. Vera knew how much was involved – she worked for Daria from the beginning. He told us she is rogue, and that the SVR Directorate wrote the money off as lost, once they killed her. He said she had no cover and no assistance. He said it would be simple. From the beginning, he lied, and we foolishly allowed our greed to control us."

Again, silence – so much silence that I'm able to hear the footsteps behind me, and turn to find Rhyan and Mike walking down the hall toward me.

"What are you guys still doing here? You're supposed to be in the air."

 

"We thought you might... well... need us for something?"

"*'Need you for something'?* Oh, I get it. You two smartasses don't think I am capable of interrogating and killing people on my own? Besides, neither of you thought for a damn second that I was going to simply kill someone."

While neither of them has a comment – other than the silly smirks on their faces – the nurse definitely does.

"Well, Mrs. Whitman, I was convinced you were about to," the captain says, pointing at the gun still in my hand.

The moment she finishes her sentence, the conversation in the room continues. I lay my weapon on the counter, and we turn our attention back to the speakers.

"Perhaps our greed and stupidity are reason enough for us to die."

"If that's what you choose, Vadym," we hear Melinda – who is playing her part to perfection – say.

Then, as the door to the room starts to open, he stops her.

"Wait. Please."

The door again closes.

"Yes?"

"This 'friend' of yours... she is a woman of her word?"

"She isn't a 'friend' Vadym," Melinda says, following it with a snicker, "She's the *Director of Intelligence*. That's how high up the food chain you've managed to piss people off. And to answer your question, she *never* makes statements she can't back up..."

"If I tell you what I know – all of it, will she spare our lives? I do not expect amnesty, but only a chance to find a place to hide and live out what time we have left."

"That's what she's offering you. The two of you walk away, and everyone thinks you're dead."

"Then, I will tell you all that I know..."

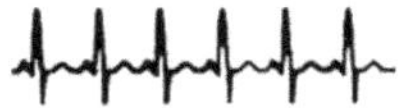

# 32

As I predicted, it takes less than five minutes for us to find ourselves staring at the business end of the MP5 Tarasov's man is holding. Although it isn't pointed at us, I do notice his finger never strays far from the trigger.

"Егор сказало сказать вас он имеет входящий самолет на радиолокаторе. Они кажется, что будут воински." (Egor said to tell you he has incoming aircraft on the radar. They appear to be military)

"Thank you, Yuri. Be certain no one has any weapons visible, in case they decide to have a closer look."

"Very well," he replies. Then, with a nod in the direction of the weapon lying on the deck, he asks, "Проблема?" (Is there a problem?)

"Why do you think there is?" Vera asks, still responding in English, and doing her best to look the part of the 'spy-in-charge'. She manages to hide her fear well.

"Ваше оружие. Оно находится там... на палубе." (Your weapon. It is there... on the deck.)

"And your point is, Yuri?"

"She could..."

"Yuri, do you think so little of me? Do you believe I would leave a loaded," she reaches down and picks up the pistol, the butt of which is hidden by the leg of my jeans, "gun where this woman can get to it?" She finishes by turning the weapon butt up to show him there's no magazine in it, then reaches into the back pocket of her jeans and produces it. "The damn thing was hurting my back, Yuri, so I took it out for a while. As you can see, I *did* remember to *unload* it."

He still looks more than a bit suspicious.

"Go tell them to light the outer decks so those aircraft," she continues, pointing in the direction of the now prominent rotor noise, "can have a good look."

"Yes ma'am" he replies turning back toward the bridge.

"And, Yuri," Vera adds, just before he turns the corner, "если эта женщина хотела мою пушку, то она смогла легко принять ее на любой этап, и мы были бы беспомощно для того чтобы остановить ее." (if this woman wanted my gun, she could have easily taken it at any point, and we would be helpless to stop her.)

The look on his face is priceless.

When he's gone, she turns and once again looks at me.

"Why?"

"Because, if it was loaded, he'd have known we were screwing with him. He isn't stupid."

"And so, even though you are the prisoner, you quickly remove the magazine and hand it to me? You now have my full attention."

"Those aircraft are here for a purpose, not by chance, Vera."

"What has become of my husband, and the others?"

"You attempted to contact them?"

"Yes. None of them answered. I can understand one or two – but not all six of them. They should all be back in Tangier by now, yet none of them answers their phones."

"The fact that Tarasov turned up at the villa, very well may have cost them their lives – I know you saw the explosion..."

I let the comment hang for a moment, to see how she responds. When she remains silent, I continue.

"The people searching for us are very driven to recover us, at any cost, and have the resources to do so. If we were to disappear or turn up dead somewhere, there will be nowhere on this earth that those responsible will be able to hide."

She's once again staring out at the wake behind us, and even though she isn't looking at me, I can still see her eyes well up, and watch one small tear run down her cheek.

"What have we done...?" she says out loud, but not really to me.

I instinctively turn to look in the direction of the rotor noise – which is at a point you can *feel it* – just in time to see two blacked-out UH-72A Lakotas go screaming right over us, not more than two hundred feet off the water. Now, if the thumping noise made by two helicopters going 140 knots just above the water isn't enough to make people pee themselves, the sight of a Black Hawk with M134 6-barreled, mini-guns mounted on the skids will definitely do it.

"Who are they?" Vera asks, standing up.

"Well, whoever they are, I'll bet they aren't on your side."

I have no idea if they're ours or not, but the fact someone is interested in the yacht tells me they *are* tracking us. I find myself wondering if my sister received, and understood, my message.

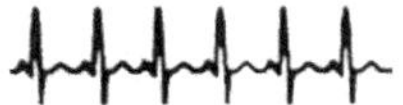

# 33

As we're listening to the conversation in the isolation room, a senior enlisted guy comes down the hall toward us, stopping when he is right in front of me.

"Mrs. Whitman?"

"Yes sir?"

"Chief Master Sergeant Sanchez ma'am, not 'sir'. I'm the SIGINT Chief. I have something I figured you'd want to see – although it's a few hours old."

He hands me a black-and-white photograph. The second I look at it, I know exactly what – *and who* – it is.

"Perfect damn timing, Chief! Excuse me a second."

I turn, walk back into the room, past Melinda, and over to the side of Kovalenko's bed. Without saying a word, I hand him the photograph. For a moment, I think the man is actually going to cry.

"It was taken earlier this morning, and what you see in the background, port side is a fully armed Black Hawk. Need I say anything else?"

"I have told this woman," he points at Melinda, "all I know of Tarasov's operation. Might I ask one last question?"

"Yes?"

"If my wife and I survive all this, will you at least concede to helping us get to a neutral country? I know what you said earlier about no assurances, but I had to ask."

"Mr. Kovalenko, depending on the outcome of all this, it is possible I'll concede that additional point. And for the record, the two women you helped abduct are both *active CIA field assets* – not rogue agents."

I reach out, take the photo from his hands, then turn, and walk toward the door. When I reach it, I hesitate, then turn back to face Kovalenko.

"More importantly, *Vadym*, one of them, *is my sister...*"

The look in his eyes the moment I say it, tells me he fully understands the severity of his situation. I turn and go out the door.

As I walk up to the nurse's station again, my little brother smiles and asks, "So, *Director*, what the hell is that photo of?"

"Our greatest bargaining chip, Rhyan. His wife." I hand him the photo.

He looks at it for a few seconds, then mumbles "...and my sister too, it would appear."

I pick the Beretta up off the desk and am in the process of putting the magazine back into it, when the nurse, who was looking in on a different patient, returns.

"Damn! It wasn't even loaded earlier? *You bluffed him?*"

With a laugh I reply, "I try to refrain from arbitrarily killing people, Captain, but I needed *him* to believe I would. Without bullets, there won't be any 'accidents' – you know?"

I hear Mike and Rhyan laugh behind me. The nurse, who is now shaking her head, turns and walks off, down the hall. We hear her mumble *"...damn sure had me convinced,"* as she disappears around a corner.

"Put on a little show did ya, Court?" Mike asks, grinning.

"In a manner of speaking. Now, why are you guys still here? You never answered me."

"Melinda wasn't sure what you were up to and told us to hang out until she got back to us. Then we heard through the base 'grapevine' that an extremely pissed off, armed, female 'spook' was 'interrogating prisoners' at the hospital."

"And hell, Sis, we *had to* come see that for ourselves," my brother adds.

"Smart ass. I'm surrounded by smartasses."

"Well heck, as long as we're here, Sis, how about we take you and Melinda to lunch, and you can brief us on the op?"

"Deal," I reply, as Melinda comes out of the room, a huge smirk covering her face.

"My God, Courtney, you get the Academy Award for that one!"

"Yeah, yeah. Don't give these two anything else to bug me about, please?"

"Oh, come on, Mindy – if you tell us about Mrs. Whitman's performance, we'll buy you lunch."

"Oh jezzz..."

We turn and together, head for the parking lot.

For some reason, I find Mike and my brother's presence very calming. As we cross the parking lot, the rough plan that formed in my head a day before on Crete is now slowly coalescing into something logical. Howard helped me to see through all the crap that was being presented, and I'm certain there's something else going on here – something deeper than Whitney and Daria being kidnapped by a bunch of renegade operatives.

*Someone has an agenda.*

*And...* you can be damn certain I intend to find out who that 'someone' is.

If the SVR hierarchy is involved in this, God help them.

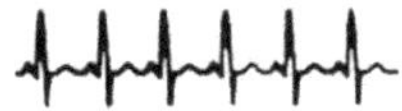

# 34

I wake to the sounds of a helicopter's rotor noise. Wearing only my underwear and a t-shirt, I exit the stateroom I'm in and find my way onto the small observation deck aft of the cabins. I arrive just in time to watch a small helicopter settle onto the ship's helipad.

Seconds after it comes to rest, Fedor Orlov, who I recognize from numerous photos I've seen, climbs out – alone. Orlov, I know, is an *active* SVR asset. Within seconds, Vera passes me, headed in the direction of the chopper.

"Chose your words carefully, Vera," I say, as we watch Orlov approach us. She pauses, glances at me, and her face tells me she understands what I'm trying to tell her. She quickly turns to face Orlov.

"Федор, что ты здесь делаешь? Это не является частью плана." (Fedor, why are you here? This is not part of the plan.)

"Планы меняются, Вира. Кое-что произошло, и Леонид счел что будет лучше, если я скажу тебе об этом лично." (Plans change, Vera. Something has happened and Leonid felt it best if I told you in person.)

"What has happened to Vadym?" Vera responds in English, as the tears begin building in her eyes.

"К сожалению, мы считаем, что вся команда виллы выбыла." (Unfortunately, we believe the entire team at the villa has been eliminated)

"Who did this?"

"We are unsure. It appears that it was a military operation of some kind. Leonid sent me to retrieve her," Orlov replies in English, pointing at me.

"Does he believe the same people will attempt to take her?"

I can see where she's going, even if Orlov can't.

"He did not say. However, if someone attempts to retrieve them, he wants them where he can control things."

*"Someone?"* she hisses, now visibly angry.

She's quickly beginning to understand – and perhaps even believe – what I've been telling her. She, and the rest of them, have always been disposable.

"Go back to your cabin, get dressed, get your bag, and then return here."

She's talking to me but is still staring at Orlov, with murder in her eyes.  I keep my cool and only nod. I don't have a bag, and Vera knows this. Now, I wonder what her plan is. I turn and head back the way I came.

"Stop!" Orlov says to me, as he turns to Vera. "You are sending her alone?'

"Fedor, we are in the middle of the damn ocean. Where is she going to go? *You* may follow her if it makes you feel better," Vera replies, then turns and starts to walk off.

"Where are you going?"

She stops, turns back to face him, and, in a voice seething with malice, says, "I am going to find a way to protect my people from whoever killed my fucking husband, Fedor. Do you have a problem with that?"

His response to her is only a harrowed look. He points at me and says, "Go." I immediately turn and enter the ship with him only steps behind, still wondering what Vera is up to.

I know that whatever she's planning, she will need time, so I lead him down a rather circuitous route, eventually ending up back in my cabin, which I assume is where Vera expected me to go.

Sure enough, the moment I step in, I catch a glimpse of her shadow behind the door. Orlov, of course, doesn't notice her –

but then he doesn't know what I do. I continue toward a small closet on the far side of the room, and poor, foolish, Fedor, thinks I'm going for a weapon.

"Stop! Do not open the door," he says loudly.

I stop, turn to say something and hear the 'pffft-pffft' of a suppressed weapon. I make eye contact with Orlov, just in time to see blood spew from his mouth, and watch him collapse in a heap on the floor. Vera, standing behind him, has a sinister twinkle in her eye, and a still-smoking, pistol in her hand.

"Sorry bastard thought he could leave me here as fodder for whatever was to come. Think again, Fedor."

"Vera... how..."

"I have been around this man for over twenty years, Miss Paddison, so the moment we made eye contact outside – when he asked me where I was going – I knew. His eyes told me. Tarasov told him to get you and screw the rest of us. He needs you – everyone else is baggage."

"You still have two other problems outside Vera, and you can bet your ass they can contact Tarasov in an instant," I say, pulling on my pants.

"So," she replies sticking the Glock into the band on her pants, "I will deal with them in the same fashion. I *will not* be used by the likes of Leonid Tarasov, Miss Paddison."

"What do you want from me?" I ask as I finish dressing.

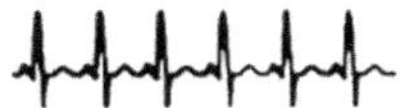

# 35

I've been reading since we left Morón. Mike and Rhyan, who came with us, are sitting in the back of the plane, opting to leave me alone. They can tell my gears are turning.

"How about this?" Melinda asks, handing me a page.

"I saw that, and it doesn't link him to anything. We need something that points *directly to Sokolski.*"

"Why Court? Why are you so sure he's involved?"

I glance at the guys, who seem to be paying no attention to us, then pat the seat next to me to indicate she should move, which takes her only a heartbeat.

"Remember the original photographs Alice gave me?"

I watch her face as she tries to visualize them.

"Two cars – which means *two teams*. At least four guys – more likely six, counting the drivers. Just to snatch *Daria*?"

Her light bulb goes on.

"Next, if you were Tarasov, and you discovered that not only is Daria alive, but where she is, what would be your first move? Go rogue?"

I watch her eyes as she contemplates my question.

"He's still *active* SVR."

"He's a damn *Station Chief,* Melinda."

"Which means he's set when it comes time to retire, or perhaps to move up? Brownie points, Court? Tell Sokolski what you know to get brownie points?"

"And, what if he did this, say, very quietly?"

"No shit – 'dear boss, not only can I get *her*, I can get some of your *money* back.'"

"*And,* I can quietly *dispose* of the problem."

"But wait, she has an accomplice? Who is this person? Covertly recover her prints only to find she's not in any SVR databases. But, according to INTERPOL, her prints belong to someone named Alexis Paddison – which is the same last name Daria is using."

"You're getting there…"

"You do a background check and discover she isn't directly affiliated with Erasmus Shipping – like her sister is."

"What will they discover? What's the sister's connection to the company?"

"Allison Paddison is the company's Chief Operating Officer. She was openly dating someone on the company's board of directors for a while. We made a point of keeping Daria – or '*Allison*' actually – visible, for legitimacy purposes."

"And 'Alexis'?"

"Just a 'little sister' – affiliated with the company only as 'part owner'. Her bio indicates she's a freelance artist."

"Okay, so go back to your original thought process."

"Our mark has a 'sister', which we know is a plant, but we can't discern who planted her, so…"

I can again see her gears turning.

"Oh shit, leverage! Take her, she may or may not cooperate. But, threaten the 'little sister'… Damn, Courtney, that's why they took two teams – *they always intended to take both of them!*"

"Now, assuming Sokolski is in on this, what's the fastest way to get him to hang Tarasov out to dry?"

"Something goes wrong, and it goes public. Realistically, he has nothing to lose. All goes well – he goes public and says that they recovered one of their rogue agents, as well as some of the remaining cash she stole from the State. They return a pittance to the Russian coffers and split the rest."

"But they discover they're wrong – they've snatched the wrong people, there's no money, and it goes public?"

"Jezzz, Courtney, the sorry bastard will be dead in a matter of hours. Sokolski openly denies he was part of it, claims Tarasov was operating on his own and without sanction, and washes his hands of it."

"Okay. What if Alice calls Sokolski and tells him nothing more than, 'release our assets now, or we air everyone's dirty laundry."

"Courtney, what's really going on? What am I missing?"

"What do you mean, Melinda?"

"We can get them back whenever we want. The Sergeant Major and his team proved that. They can easily protect themselves, if there's gunfire. You know this. We don't need to wait until Zürich. When that yacht ports, we can easily take them all and..."

Right in the middle of her sentence, the monitor in front of me buzzes, indicating an incoming call. I push the 'connect' button and instantly, Cassie's face fills the screen.

"Change One, Boss. Once again, Keith is complicating our existence. He was checking the yacht with one of his multitude of satellites when he discovered," the monitor changes to an image of the yacht showing no visible wake, and a helicopter on the aft pad, "not only are they dead in the water, they've got company as well."

"Tarasov's chopper never left the island, Boss. As a matter of fact, it's still there," Keith adds, as again the monitor displays a new image. This one shows the helipad at the end of the short pier, and that damn helicopter, still sitting in the exact same spot.

"Howard!"

"Yeah, Courtney?"

"Every damn commercial aircraft that left Ibiza in the last forty-eight hours – where'd they go, passenger manifests, and as much surveillance footage from the airport as you can come up with. Keith – help him."

"Yes ma'am," they reply at the same time.

"Cassie, they must be using some kind of surveillance at that ferry terminal – get me images."

"I'm on it."

"We're headed back there. I've decided we don't need to take Tarasov before he gets to the bank. I'll explain when we arrive. Talk to you guys in a couple of hours."

I reach down and disconnect the call before any of them can respond.

"Courtney?" Melinda says, looking totally confused.

"I'm convinced we're missing what's really going on here. This has very little – *if anything* – to do with my sister, Daria, or that fucking money. I have an idea, but I need to do more research before I talk. Okay?"

"Yes ma'am. Should I tell Phillip we need to go to Crete?"

"Yeah, if you would? And thanks for giving me some room to maneuver."

"Hey lady," she replies, putting a hand on my shoulder as she stands up, "you're in charge of this virtual mess – I'm just here to do as ordered. But... you have piqued my curiosity."

She winks at me and heads for the cockpit.

Mike and Rhyan give me confused looks when they feel the aircraft go into a sharp bank and change direction. They know something's changed, but neither questions me.

Ninety-six minutes later, the wheels touch the runway at Chania, and twenty minutes after that, we walk back into the safe house.

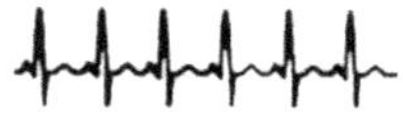



Solution Squared: Recalculation

"I would rather trust a woman's instinct than a man's reason."

Stanley Baldwin
Prime Minister – United Kingdom
1867 – 1947

# 36

"You did very well. How did you know to delay bringing him here?" Vera asks, reaching for the phone on the wall next to her.

"We're in the same business, Vera."

"Of course," she replies, as she starts pushing buttons. It's immediately obvious she's calling the bridge.

"Карл, не задавай вопросов. Просто отвечай. Где Юрий?" (Karl, do not ask questions. Only respond. Where is Yuri?)

She has a plan – I can see it in her eyes.

"А где Егор?" (And what of Egor?)

"Perfect!" she replies in English, turning and looking at me. "Распорядись заглушить моторы, и когда Юрий спросит тебя об этом, скажи что случилась какая-то проблема, и я сейчас разбираюсь в ней." (Tell them to stop the engine, and when Yuri questions you, tell him there is a problem and I am looking into it.)

She hangs the phone up, her face now showing the stress she is under, and says, "Our greed has cost my husband his life. While I have no desire to lose mine, I do not want my team to be massacred, as was my husband's. I will give you my life if it will preserve theirs."

"That's a bit drastic, Vera. How about you all disappear?"

"When they take this vessel, Miss Paddison, I intend for them to find only three bodies – all of which are active assets of the Russian Foreign Intelligence Service. I know there are no guarantees, but do think that a word from you, might stop them from hunting us?"

"I will do my best to ensure that. The problem is, I honestly have no idea what's going on here. Daria is somehow involved in this mess, but to what extent I'm unsure. This all goes far deeper than you and I, Vera, and I think Daria knows how deep. The 'money' you were told about was nothing more than a tool used to manipulate you and the others, by those much more powerful than you and I."

"Well then, perhaps you would like to watch me exact some measure of revenge for the loss of my husband, even though it is our fault we were drawn into this disaster."

"I will tell those that I answer to, what you did here, Vera. I believe you will never have anything to fear from us."

Without warning, the ship becomes eerily quiet. I am quick to realize that the engines have stopped. Vera reaches out and opens the door, waits for me to step over Fedor's body and into the passageway, and then follows me.

She takes a circuitous route – to waste time I'm sure – to the engine room. We enter and find Yuri grilling one of Vera's men. The moment he sees us, he reaches for his MP5.

Vera is infinitely faster.

"Do not attempt that Yuri, for to do so will bring about your end," she says, drawing down on him with her Glock.

"What are you doing, Vera?"

"You are as naive as I am, Yuri. You truly have no idea what Tarasov has done to us, do you?"

When he does nothing but stare at her, she continues.

"They are dead, Yuri – everyone we left at the villa. Those who wish to retrieve Miss Paddison and her sister killed them all. No detention, no questioning. They simply killed them all."

Yuri's eyes give him away, and I wonder if Vera sees it too.

"Vera, are you..." he starts to say.

There is a quick 'pffft-pffft', and I watch him drop to the deck plates in front of us. I turn to look at Vera, who is putting her weapon back in her belt.

"Sorry bastard knew exactly what is going on."

"Yeah, he did. I'm amazed that he thought he could get his weapon up before you could shoot him."

"Not all spies are intelligent, Miss Paddison," she replies, turning to look at the guy still standing there.

"You – take Stephan, go to the galley, and wait for me. Tell no one what you saw, understood?"

"Yes ma'am," he instantly replies, signaling for a second guy to follow him. Once they're gone, Vera rolls Yuri over, pulls a Tokarov from his belt, and sticks it into hers. She also takes two magazines and places them in her pocket.

"Come. Only one remains, and I know where he is. I must assume that if Yuri knew, he knows as well."

"You're certain they couldn't have gotten to any of your people, right?"

"Yes. As is the case, I will bet my life on it."

"Okay. Lead the way."

We make our way through the ship, exiting onto the aft platform where the helicopter is sitting, and sure enough, there's Yuri's partner, standing guard.

"I must retrieve something from the helicopter, Egor," Vera says, making him instantly raise and point his weapon at us.

"No one is allowed to approach the helicopter, Vera," is his stern reply.

It's obviously his ride home and, as one would expect, he's making sure his seat stays available. Vera suddenly stops in front of me, causing me to bump into her.

"What the hell? Whose order is that, Egor? I am in charge on this damn yacht, or have you forgotten that?"

"Vera, I must assume something is wrong, otherwise why would *she*," he points directly at me, "be going with you to the helicopter? Please, do not come any further."

When Vera turns and looks at me, she mouths the word 'back' then as she turns back to face Egor, says, "She is with me, because Fedor, ordered me not to let her out of my sight."

When her back is once again to me, I see it – Yuri's Tokarov stuck in her belt, and assume she wants me to use it.

Without warning, Vera yells something to one of the guys on the upper deck, and when poor Egor lets his eyes move to see who she is talking to, I take appropriate action. In one quick, smooth motion, I pull the weapon from Vera's belt, dive for the deck, roll away from Vera, and fire two, perfectly placed, successive shots.

Egor never sees it coming. He's dead before he falls.

Then, the sound of automatic fire. One of Vera's people is watching, and releases a continuous stream of 9mm rounds in my direction, as I try to make cover. I'm not quite fast enough.

"STOP! *Andrey, stop shooting!*" Vera screams at the guy with the gun, as she runs in my direction.

Although he obliges her, it isn't before I catch two rounds – one that grazes my shoulder and one that ricochets off the deck and ends up an inch deep in my left thigh. It only takes a second before Vera is kneeling next to me.

"Yes, Miss Paddison, you are *definitely* a spy," she offers, rolling me over and looking at the back of my leg. "This one is inside. It must be removed quickly. The other," she touches my shoulder, "is only superficial."

"You know, Vera, under different circumstances, we would have worked well together."

"I believe you are right, Alexis. Can you stand?"

"Yeah, no problem, but who's going to cut on my leg? There isn't a doctor on board," I say, handing the Tokarov back to her.

"Ah, but there is. You just haven't met them yet."

She helps me to my feet, and we hobble back into the ship, leaving a now-deceased Egor, lying on the deck next to the chopper.

As we enter the ship's main passageway, we encounter the pilot who flew the helicopter aboard. Vera instantly lets go of me, pulls the Glock from her belt, and backs him up against the bulkhead. The man looks terrified.

"Unless you have a desire to end up as *Comrade Orlov*, I suggest you do exactly as I tell you."

"Whatever you say, lady. I just fly the helicopter," he replies in English, but with a definite Italian accent.

"Help her," Vera says, pointing to me.

He reaches out, takes my hand, wraps it around his shoulders, and then we make our way to the galley. Once there, Vera sends out one of her guys with orders to get everyone on board to the galley, leaving one person on the bridge to watch the radar.

It takes about five minutes for Vera's team to assemble. I'm sitting at a table making mental notes when the last two come in. To my surprise, they are female. Vera calls them over.

"This is Anna, and this is Irina. Both are nurses and have served with the Russian military."

I nod at them.

"She has a bullet in her thigh. It is a ricochet."

"It must be removed quickly," Anna says.

"Can you two, do it?" Vera asks them.

"Is there a medical facility onboard?" she asks, looking at me.

"Yes. Three doors down, on your left. It's probably very limited in supplies."

"We can easily remove the bullet," Irina says as she feels around where it entered my thigh. "It is the pain involved that is the concern. Even a local anesthetic of any kind will work."

The captain and Jamie walk in during our discussion.

"Jamie, are there any drugs on board this thing?" I ask.

"Jezzz, Alexis, you were on the receiving end of all that gunfire?" the captain asks.

"There's some stuff in the dispensary," Jamie offers, "but it's fairly limited."

"Show me," Anna says, pointing at the passageway.

Jamie looks at me, as if unsure of what to do.

"She's going to get the bullet out of my leg before the lead leaches into my blood, Jamie, so I'd definitely appreciate it if you help her."

The captain laughs and Jamie says, "Follow me."

It takes them an hour to complete their task – and yes, it hurts like hell. In the end, they do manage to get the entire bullet.

While the girls are working on me, Vera explains to the rest of them, what's happened – what Tarasov has done to them. Once she shares the incident at the villa, they all begin to understand. Being fluent in Russian, I get the gist of the mumbled conversations going on around me – *'Where can we hide?'*

Vera explains that, as soon as she comes up with a way out, she will share it with them. She then points at me and tells them that their 'prisoner' is now their best hope of survival. She dismisses them, telling each of them to go back to their positions. She stops the guy who was on the bridge and the guy who kicked Jamie out of her radio room. Then she turns to face the Captain.

"I am returning control of this vessel to you sir, and although an apology isn't worth much at this point, you have mine."

"What became of the rest of my crew?" Captain Bell asks.

"They were bound and gagged and left in a hotel room on Formentera. They were discovered shortly after our departure, and are well and safe."

"Very well. Miss Paddison, any orders?"

"Not yet, Captain. I need to think this through first. Can you make it appear we're moving without actually doing so?"

"For a while, Alexis, but eventually the expensive satellites will tell their owners we're up to something."

"Understood. I'll be quick about it."

He nods and leaves the room, headed for his bridge.

I turn and look at Vera, the stress and pressure of the situation showing in the lines on her face, and say, "So, where and how does one hide nine Russians?"

She exhales heavily, sighs, and sits down next to me.

"I was hoping you would tell me, Alexis."

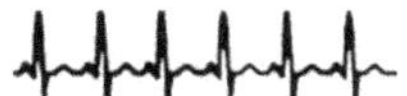

# 37

"It's too damn fishy, Joey – *all of it...*"

"I learned long ago to trust your judgment, Courtney. You say it stinks; I agree even if I don't smell it yet."

"You're *convinced* there is more going on here than just snatching them, getting the money, and turning them over to Sokolski?" Howard asks from across the table, between bites.

Just as I'm about to answer him, my phone rings. I dig it out of my pocket, flip it open, and answer it.

"Whitman."

"Just had another sat pass, and they've disappeared."

"What are you talking about?"

"Well, the last pass was just after 4:00 PM, and they seemed to be doing nothing more than making it appear they're underway. You know, creating a wake."

"And now?"

"Well, what I *can* tell you is that they aren't anywhere they should be, and we're guessing they are running 'cold' so they don't leave a heat signature. Keith says he has no damn idea where they are. SEASTAT, which tracks their transponder, says they're in one place, but a 'hot-shot' from the satellite says they aren't there. That damn Jamie is one tricky young lady."

"Damn..." I mumble, noting that everyone is now paying attention to me. "What the hell is my sister up to?"

"It has to be them, Court. It takes direct access to the radio room, to do what we think has been done, and Jamie is the only person I know of, who could pull it off."

 "Keep trying to find them. Anything new on Tarasov?"

"We're still looking."

"That's the first priority. We'll be back shortly."

"Bye, Boss."

"Bye." I close the phone and glance around the table.

"Something new?"

"They lost the damn yacht. It's not where the satellites say it's supposed to be.

They all sit staring at me, which makes me laugh.

"Oh, never mind. Can we just eat dinner, and worry about all this in say an hour? I'm thinking there won't be any major breakthroughs in the next sixty minutes."

They laugh and go back to eating. I sit poking at my food, looking from one to the next to the next, my mind now lost in thought.

What if we've been drawn into something that isn't what it appears to be? Alice has, after all, done it before. What if the abduction, and the money issues, are all being 'staged' to cover some other op that we aren't being told about? And, if I'm right, what does Alice have to gain this time? What, exactly, is the woman after?

The next question has to be, why did Alice involve the four of us, instead of letting a non-associated team deal with the situation? That's a hard rule – *no emotional ties during ops*. Emotions usually do nothing but create problems so relatives – parents, children, husbands, wives – saving relatives is never allowed. I'm pretty sure that includes *sisters saving sisters*.

*So, what the hell am I doing in charge of this operation?*

Then, Courtney's little light bulb goes on. That's always been my curse through life – logical thought processes. If I play with something long enough, I will inevitably come up with the most logical conclusion, and usually, faster than everyone else. People, and the world in general, function in very specific ways,

     *Solution Squared: Recalculation*

and by specific rules. Properly apply those rules to any specific person or incident, and the final analysis, no matter how absurd, usually turns out to be correct.

Alice pushed this on me because she knows that even after fifteen years, my sister, and I will be on the same wavelength. She knows that once we connect on this – whatever *this* is – they won't be able to get ahead of us. The message Whitney sent telling me they had been separated. The fly-over of the yacht, telling her we're on her. I can put myself where she is, and know exactly what she'll do, and she can stand in my shoes, in front of all those monitors, and know exactly what I'm planning to do. *One mind in two bodies.*

And, *Alice Williamson knows this.*

My sister and I were always Alice's ace-in-the-whole. No one besides the people sitting at the table with me, and Alice, knew about us in the beginning, or know that my sister is still alive. If Whitney and I together are her ace-in-the-whole, Whitney is the ace up her sleeve.

As Joey is so fond of saying, it's *'pure fucking genius'!*

All I have to do is figure out what the hell Alice is up to.

I *could* just ask her. Or, I could do what she told me to do. Analyze, assess, and act.

Mike, who happens to be sitting next to me, interrupts my thought process – which I'm now completely lost in – when he puts a hand on my leg and gently squeezes.

"You ready to take us to wherever you've been for the last ten minutes?" he asks, smiling at me.

"Michael Osborne, you know better than to get into my head."

"Yeah, generally speaking, I'd agree – mostly because it's a seriously scary place..."

Everyone at the table laughs.

"But at the moment, we're a team" he nods at everyone, "and we can't respond with our best if we don't know when, where, and most importantly, why."

I stare at him for a few seconds and then realize it's eerily quiet. They stop eating and turn their full attention to me.

"He's right, Courtney, and you know it." Howard quickly adds. "Everyone at this table, long ago accepted that your damn brain works in far different ways than ours do. Hell, we started trusting your judgment back in Istanbul. You were so far ahead of us on both those ops, that all we could do, was what you told us to."

Although Howard pauses, Cassie picks it right up.

"We drive desks, Court, and we'd like to not only complete this operation successfully but stay alive as well. We'll follow you, *without question,* lady, but it would greatly enhance our performance if you'd let us into your brain, even if only for a short while."

Joey and Rhyan sit there, zoned looks on their faces, staring at me.

"And, what if..."

"Life is a big 'what if', Court," Mike immediately blurts out.

"Yeah, Courtney, 'what if'," Howard continues, pushing his chair back, and standing up. "I've got news for you girl – the five sets of eyes staring at you right now, are willing to bet their lives that your assessment of *any situation* will be the right one. So how about you quit with the silly 'self-doubt' bullshit and tell us where this op is going?  What and who are we really doing battle with here?"

"Yeah," Joey finally says, "who the hell are the bad guys – *the real bad guys?*"

I smile, knowing I couldn't have picked a better team, or group of friends for that matter. I take a deep breath and make eye contact with each of them.

"Okay, you guys want to know what I think, huh? I'm fairly certain that Alice Williamson has us caught up in another one of her 'off the grid' operations, just like the one she used to recover Daria and get Whitney to play with her. Although I haven't sorted it all out just yet, I *will.* I will figure out what the hell the woman is up to."

Then yet another obscure thought pops into my head.

 Solution Squared: Recalculation

"The scary part here guys," I say to no one in particular and yet to everyone at the table, "is that *Alice knows I will...*"

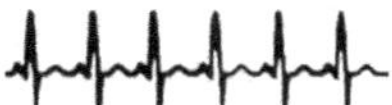

# 38

"Captain, I have a question."

"Yes, Miss Paddison?"

"I need you to punch us up on the SATCHART please."

He turns, walks over to the electronic chart table, punches a few buttons, and gets a real-time triangulated satellite fix on the yacht which, in only seconds, appears on the illuminated map on the table.

"How good are you, Skipper?"

"If I can't do it, Miss Padd..."

I interrupt him.

"Go back to Alexis, please, Skipper."

"Yes ma'am. Anyhow, *Boss,*" he replies with a definite tone, "if I can't pull it off, I'll tell you."

"We need to put these 'hijackers', with the exception of Mrs. Kovalenko, ashore as soon as possible. I need to send a message, without it being intercepted, as well."

"How covert do you want the message to be?"

I turn and find Jamie standing in the doorway to the radio room, looking at us.

"And we are letting them go because?" the captain asks, looking a bit confused, and more than a bit irritated.

"As 'secret' as it was the last time we did it, Jamie," I reply, which is followed by a laugh from the Captain. I turn around and find Vera looking completely dumbfounded. She looks over at Jamie, then at the captain, then back at me.

"It seems I was outclassed, and outperformed, from the very beginning. You were right, Miss Paddison, I truly had no idea who I was up against."

"We're letting them go because I said so, Russ. I'll take the spanking after it's over. I don't kill people just because, and I can't condemn people for following orders – *no matter how damn stupid the orders are.*" I stop talking and glare at Vera.

"Guilty as charged," she says while turning quite red.

"Besides, they'll have enough problems with their people soon enough."

"And I am to remain?" Vera asks, looking apprehensive.

"Yes. Is this a problem, Mrs. Kovalenko?"

"Not in the least, Miss Paddison" she shoots back, her nervousness being replaced by rather a devious smirk.

"I'll need your assistance with a certain matter."

"Well, you're the boss," the captain finally says. "Where do you want me to put them?"

"That's what I need you, to tell me," I reply, leaning on the chart table, which has the Mediterranean displayed on it.

"Well, Alex, the nearest land mass is a hundred nautical miles away. We'll have to cut that in half if you intend to give them one of the excursion boats."

Jamie is now standing next to the captain, listening.

"Can it be done without anyone knowing we're doing it? If someone suspects, they'll start taking pictures immediately."

"Someone?" the captain asks.

"The bad guys, Russ, the bad guys."

"Tarasov has people watching. People who answer only to him. His network is vast," Vera offers.

I turn and look at her, realizing the ramifications of what she said. At that moment I grasp the *why* of Daria's decision. She knows what's actually going on – what the real agenda is. Even more significant, is that she knows *whose* agenda it is.

Her experience told her that, of the two of us, *she'll* have a far better chance of controlling and even manipulating, Tarasov. After all, *they have a history.*

The captain's voice snaps me back.

"Sure, I can do it. They'll think we are having trouble. Catch is, we'll need to let the world know we are in trouble, in order to pull it off."

"That won't work, Captain. The moment you send out a distress call, you'll be boarded. I'm fairly certain the bad guys are listening, and if they discover the Russians aren't aboard before we complete our business, Vera and I walk directly into a trap."

"Got a plan do you, Alex?" Jamie asks.

"If I do, what can you do for me?"

"I can send your message and..."

*"Yes?"* I press her, knowing she's screwing with me.

"Our transponder signal. I have an intimate relationship with SEASTAT, and have the ability to tell it that our signal originates from wherever I want."

With a loud laugh, I interrupt her midsentence.

*"You hacked the damn satellite, Jamie?"*

"Yeah. Sorta. You aren't gonna rat me out, *are you?"*

The captain, Vera, and I break up in hysterical laughter.

*"Anyhow..."* she continues, now bright red, "if I screw up our transponder signal, by the time they – whoever 'they' turns out to be – figure out we aren't where we're supposed to be and start looking for us, the captain will have us back on course. Once it's over, we simply turn off the transponder and send a message that our electronics are screwed up and that we're headed for port."

"Nice," the captain says, turning to the chart table. "I can close to within forty miles, send them off in an excursion boat, and be back on course in about an hour. Should work."

"Where?" I ask, looking at the map. Vera, standing next to me, is looking over my shoulder.

"Ajaccio? It's fairly populated. They should be able to…"

"No," Vera instantly blurts out.

Everyone looks at her, and we find her expression is that of someone who has spoken out of turn. The captain jumps right in.

"If you have some input Vera, please share. They're *your* people."

"I apologize. I forget I am no longer…"

"That was then, Vera, and we're dealing with *now*. What are you thinking?" I ask, again glaring at her.

"They are *Russian*. They will speak and act Russian. If you put all nine of them on an Italian island, *they will be noticed*."

I look at the captain, and he nods his concurrence.

"Suggestion?"

"I assume Corsica is our only option at this point?"

"If we are going to do it without anyone catching us, yes. We are limited by the ship's speed. Although she's fast, there is no way for us to cover an excessive number of miles in two directions and then get back on our original course without *someone* noticing."

"Then I would suggest Tiuccia. It is more remote and is less populated. They can disperse in pairs, in different directions. It is no more than twenty miles to civilization in any direction. They will be able to disappear from there."

"Tuiccia it is then. Do they all know how to swim?"

Vera looks confused.

"I believe so. Will they have to?"

"Yes. They must scuttle the boat. It will stick out like a sore thumb if they beach it. If they drive into a marina somewhere, they will again have the previous problem. Nine Russians in a small boat."

"You will sacrifice one of your boats, to help my people?"

"Russ, sometimes you are too damn dramatic," I blurt out, laughing. "Vera, it's designed to do that. Once this is over, they sail back and recover it. Russ will show whoever is in charge how to do it all."

Vera smiles at me. "I should have guessed."

"Well," the captain says, smiling himself, "it'll be dark in four hours. What say we make this happen?"

"Tell us what you need, Russ," I lay the grease pen I'm holding on the chart table.

It takes us about two hours to get everything in place, during which time Jamie is doing her 'techie' thing, and the captain is covertly moving us towards Corsica.

We give each Russian a pair of overalls, and a watertight bag for their street clothes, to ensure they'll be dry once they get ashore. A bunch of soggy 'tourists' will undoubtedly stick out, which is what we are trying to avoid.

Vera makes sure each of her people knows what has to be done, and assures them that she will meet them at their prearranged point, once she and I complete our task. I give them each a small amount of cash from a stash Daria and I keep in the yacht's safe, suggesting that it's to help facilitate their 'disappearance', and again, I get the 'have you lost your mind?' look from Russ.

The captain spends fifteen minutes showing Anna how to scuttle the boat without doing any damage, and how to activate the high-frequency transponder so that he'll be able to find it again. Once he talks to each of them and discovers they feel comfortable with a mile swim to shore, he tells Anna it's up to her how close she gets, but that she needs to be certain there's at least thirty feet of water under her before she sinks it.

It's two hours after sunset when the captain signals it's time. Running without lights, and depending on Jamie and her radar systems, he manages to get inside the ferry lanes and to within ten miles of the coast, undetected. The small boat can make twelve knots fully loaded and thus, they're looking at a one-hour ride.

Vera and I stand quietly at the railing as they lower the boat into the water. Once all the Russians are aboard, we watch it slowly disappear into the darkness, as the sound of the motor eventually fades. She finally turns and looks at me.

"Each of them asked me to thank you, and the captain, for their lives. They know you have violated many protocols doing what you have done. I have a substantial amount of money put aside that my husband and I saved. I will meet them later and share it with them so that they will be able to fade silently into the world and hopefully, live out their lives in peace. They have all indicated they are finished with the espionage business."

I lay a hand on her shoulder and whisper, "How did you allow yourself to be caught up in all this, Vera?"

"Greed, Miss Paddison. Simple greed. Fortunately for me, the despicable person I have become has been unable to eliminate my conscience."

We stand together on the stern of the yacht, in silence and total darkness, watching the softly twinkling stars above us.

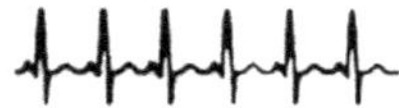

 Solution Squared: Recalculation

# 39

As is usually the case in the Mediterranean, it's a warm Greek night and the clear sky is full of stars. Because of our rural location, there's no ambient light, and I find myself sitting alone, in the dark, on the grass in front of the house, doing what I do best. *Analyzing.*

The players. Who are my players? I have to assume Alice is the main one. Daria and Whitney are on the shortlist as well. Tarasov is, as far as I can tell, the main bad guy unless Sokolski is involved. Mr. and Mrs. Kovalenko are nothing more than foolish, as are the rest of the pawns.

Although I'm convinced this has to be about something more than the money, the money still plays into it. Tarasov is senior enough that he wouldn't risk it all – his career and possibly his life – unless there's a seriously big payoff, that he'll live long enough to enjoy. So, even if he knows about *all the money,* and not just the part Daria and Whitney will admit to having, his part of the prize must be something much bigger. Something far more tempting than just a few million dollars.

I rub my temples and again begin to think out loud.

"Who knows the whole story?"

After a brief period of thought, I answer myself.

"Alice, Daria, and Whitney, for sure. Maybe Amanda, and if Melinda is involved, she's putting on a good act. A total of five people."

I stretch out on the grass, ending up flat on my back, staring up at the star-filled sky.

"Assuming that Tarasov is on the receiving end of the original phone call, what prompts him to even suspect Daria might still be alive?  How did he find out about her?"

My brain is cruising at full speed when, without warning, it slams to a stop.

"If Melinda didn't send them, why in the hell did they go to Rabat in the first place? What the hell could have made them leave in the middle of the night, without a word to her? Is that what really happened, or is Melinda complicit in what's going on? Would she actually do it to me twice?"

Just when I feel the need to talk to him, Howard walks up behind me.

"Hey girl, exercising that brain again, are you?"

"Yeah, but I keep creating more damn questions, and no answers. But it's a bit strange how you respond to my mental requests for your presence," I reply, sitting up.

"Thinking about me, were you?"

"Sorta. I need you to... well, to listen I guess."

"Okay, so give me something to listen to."

"I'm going too fast, Howard, and I'm pretty sure that Alice expected me to. That's why, against standing policies, she chose to involve me. She's no doubt counting on the whole 'sisters' thing."

"And?"

"I have to communicate with my sister, assuming that it is Whitney."

"You now doubt that?"

"No, not really. She's the only person on the planet who could have sent the smiley face message. It has to be Whit. I just can't seem to wrap my brain around her involvement, and it's making me nuts. Do you remember when Alice told us they disappeared in the middle of the night?"

"Yeah."

"Alice indicated that Melinda had no clue either, which creates yet another question. *Why?* She's been their control for over a decade, why would they suddenly start operating outside her knowledge?"

"Any logical ideas?"

"Not really. I do believe the reason, whatever it is, they went to Rabat, is the key."

I pull out the copies of the two black and white photos I keep in the back pocket of my Levi's and carefully unfold each of them. I stare at them for a couple of seconds, then lay them on the grass, and after glancing at Howard, go back to my prone position, this time closing my eyes.

Howard sits quietly, doing nothing more than watching.

I try to turn it all off – clean the slate if you will. With my eyes closed, I make my mind go back to the very beginning.

Less than ten seconds elapse before a single image, stuck for a while, in the recesses of my mind, reemerges. In a single heartbeat, I understand.

*"Holy shit, Howard!"* I blurt out, as I sit up, and snatch the two photos off the grass. After a quick glance, I realize that my revelation is right. It has to be. And, it thoroughly pisses me off.

"Whoa girl, slow down. What did we miss?"

Without answering him, I jump up and rush into the house, freaking out everyone when I burst in through the front door, instead of the side door we've been using. Cassie, who is standing within feet of the door, jumps out of my way, as I zip past, stopping at my briefcase, and quickly opening it. It takes me two heartbeats to find what I want.

"Courtney..." Howard says, closing the door behind him.

"In a second, Howard," I reply, cutting him off.

I turn immediately to face Melinda. The look in her eyes tells me she *expects* what's about to happen. I quickly sort through the photos in my hand, and find the one I want. I pick up the two British passports, flip each one open and do a quick comparison, discovering yet another 'I didn't catch it', which raises my level of 'pissed off' exponentially.

I lay the color 8x10 of the two women leaving the office building, on the table in front of me, then with my left hand hold up the two passports, and with my right the two small photos from my pocket.

"Would you like to explain, Melinda?" I ask with a barely controlled level of irritation in my voice.

She turns ashen, as all the blood rushes from her face.

"I wish I could, Courtney, I swear I do," she replies, as she stands and looks right at me, "but I can't. I, honest to God, don't have an explanation, logical or otherwise."

I'm bordering on furious at this point, and while a part of it is directed at Melinda, the bulk is about Alice. I despise being used, and doing it to me twice is unforgivable. Plus, the fact I overlooked not once, but twice, what I now realize is going on, isn't helping my mood much either.

"You and I need to talk lady. *Right now*. Outside," I say, putting everything into one hand, and motioning toward the door.

The room has gone so quiet, you could hear a pin drop, literally. None of them says a word, and, for a brief moment, I wonder if they'll remember to breathe.

Melinda nods, then turns and heads for the back door, with me close behind. As we pass Howard, he looks for a second as if he's going to say something, then turns and walks across the room, stopping to pick up the photos I put down.

Once outside, I pull the door closed behind me, turn, and head for the front of the house. When I round the corner at the end of the house, I find Melinda standing in the middle of the yard, staring up at the stars.

"Talk to me, M. We can't keep this silly bullshit up and you damn well know it. Although my heart is telling me you wouldn't do it to me twice, I am bordering on rage at the moment."

After a few seconds of silence, she finally turns to face me, and I see the tears in her eyes as they reflect the light of the full moon above us.

"I'm not in on it this time, Courtney, but I believe your suspicions are correct. Alice has us into something. I think Daria is part of it too."

"How?" I ask, holding up the passports.

"Prosthetics. Very high-dollar prosthetics. They had help at first but eventually learned to do it themselves. They've both become quite good at it, as you can see."

"So, we have established that they are *deep cover assets*. Nameless, faceless, and generally invisible. That being said, why in the hell would Daria, go *anywhere,* let alone to a covert meeting, in the middle of the goddamn night," I pause and hold up one of the photos from the abduction, "*looking enough like Daria, that she can easily be recognized?*" I ask, with a tone as caustic as acid.

When she doesn't respond, I quickly and harshly finish my thought. *"Especially considering she's supposed to be fucking dead, damn it!"*

Melinda looks to be on the verge of total panic, which gives me hope, however slim, that she isn't part of whatever is going on.

"Like I said inside, I have no idea, Courtney. *I swear to God.* The last time I saw her," she says, pulling a photograph from her shirt pocket and handing it to me, "she looked like that."

I quickly compared it to the two versions of Daria I still have in my hand – the one of her being kidnapped, and her passport – and it's as if I'm looking at *three completely different women.* I stand, completely speechless, staring at the photos for a few seconds, and to say I'm astounded is an understatement.

*"Who the hell is this?"* I ask, knowing it's Daria.

"Camilla Marie Jones. Erasmus Shipping's Senior Sales Advisor – aka Daria Ladenko, and at least four other aliases. They've both done it, Courtney. We paid an ex-Hollywood type to ensure they knew what they were doing. They've become so adept at the make-up thing that, either of them could make you look like me if we asked them to."

"The question remains, why would Whitney go from 'Alexis Paddison' to 'Alexandra Jaeger' and yet, Daria leaves as Daria? More importantly, why the hell would Whitney not question it?"

"That same question has been driving me nuts for the last three days, Courtney. I know them, *intimately,* and the only way this makes any damn sense is if Alice put them up to it. Off the grid. I'm leaning toward Daria being part of it, but I have to believe that Whitney is just along for the ride. She would never willingly tolerate Alice involving you in anything they did."

I shake my head and laugh.

"Yeah, Melinda – *'off the grid'.*"

I stare at her for a good thirty seconds, before my heart finally gets the better of me, and I have to ask.

"So this," I say, holding up both the photo of Whitney being forced into a car and Alexis' British passport, "isn't permanent? Under all that she still looks like... well..."

"Yes, Courtney, without the make-up she's still one half of a set. And I think, and this is just supposition on my part, that she's beginning to miss that."

"This becomes more convoluted by the damn second. Is there anything else you'd like to share?"

I'm trying to hide the euphoria that sweeps over me the second I realize *I still have a twin sister*. Melinda's voice jerks me right back into the moment.

"Amanda is involved. The message prompting them to leave in the middle of the night originated on her terminal. Being the nosey little shit I am, I did what I do best. I was able to 'decipher' several items I found on Daria's laptop. I'm not sure if Alice realizes..."

"Oh please, Melinda," I blurt out, interrupting her mid-sentence, "if you figured it out, she wanted you to. She is again, manipulating us. But this time, I'm not playing. This bullshit is over."

"Jezzz, Courtney. Are you..."

I again interrupt her mid-sentence.

"Yes goddamnit, *I am.* I'm sick of this crap. Whatever she is into, I would have gladly handled it for her, if she had only *asked* me to. She's done using me. Using us."

"What's the plan then?" she asks, wiping the tears from her eyes, and taking a few steps closer to me.

"She asked me to complete a task, M, and that's exactly what I intend to do. *I will get Daria and Whitney back.* But at this exact moment, I need to know if you're on board. If you need clarification of that question, please say so now."

"None required, Courtney. I answer to you alone, from this point forward, regardless of the consequences. If this plane goes down, I'll go down with it. I know I've violated your trust."

"It has never been about *trusting you*, Melinda. I always have. It did become about you picking *one master* and then sticking with that choice. In this particular game, you can't be on both teams."

Once again, a few tears trickle slowly down her cheeks.

"So, random question. How well do you know Keith?"

"He has been part of our operation since the beginning. Alice purposely placed him where he could serve us best."

"*Alice* placed him, huh? Interesting..."

"Courtney?"

"Oh nothing, M. But now that we are straight, would you like me to tell you what I believe is going on?"

"Oh God, Courtney, more than I can ever explain!"

"Tarasov is on someone's 'removal list', and for whatever reasons, Alice is using us to accomplish the task. She isn't one to be in anyone's 'pocket' so I have to believe it's a setup of some kind. Something she can hang over someone's head later. Also, because of who has so far been involved, like you, I too, have to believe that Daria is in on it as well."

"My God, Courtney. I have been their only control since this started. I know her as well as you know your husband. For her to agree to an op outside of my knowledge, no matter who set it up, is just not within my ability to comprehend. She wouldn't try to off the idiot without orders."

"Maybe not. But, if given the chance, by a higher authority, to run with this, would she say 'no'?"

Melinda stands staring at me, her gears turning, and is about to say something, when the door I burst in through earlier opens.

"Sorry, but the interruption is necessary," Cassie offers.

"What you got, Cass?"

"Tarasov. And the genius says he needs Melinda's help."

My heart rate doubles, instantly.

"Go!" I say, pushing poor Cassie back into the house.

What greets me is a wall full of Leonid Tarasov, Daria, and an unknown female, in a terminal, somewhere.

"Finally!" I blurt out. "Where?"

"Airport in Alicante. They skipped Ibiza altogether. My best guess would be that they took the ferry to Dénia, and then drove the fifty miles to Alicante. That's why it took me so long to find them. And, while you guys were on a 'smoke break', I also found their plane!"

Melinda, being the professional she is, goes right back into character.

"God, I love you, Keith," she says, as she leans over and plants one on his cheek. In seconds, she is back at her keyboard, working on something Keith sent her.

Joey comes over and asks, "Are we good, Courtney?"

That, along with the look Howard gives me, tells me I need to get everyone on the same page.

"Listen up guys. That was the last 'personal conference' that will occur during this operation. From now on, we talk in the open, and to everyone. This is a team, and if we are going to do battle with the powers that be, we need to behave like one."

Then, to my complete surprise, Melinda stops what she's doing, and stands up.

"Guys, I haven't been forthcoming about my knowledge of what is going on, and where I stand in it all. Although what I know isn't very specific, I nonetheless didn't share it with you, or the boss. That's been rectified. Everything I know, Courtney now knows, as well as my reasons for not sharing. I give you all my word, it won't happen again."

Without taking his eyes off what he was doing, Keith suddenly blurts out, "Yeah, okay. And *I'm* 'not who I claim to be'?" following it with a little snicker.

It does what I'm sure he intended. It breaks the tension. As I stand watching him type away, I feel the grin form on my face. *'No Keith'*, I think silently to myself, *'you are definitely not who you want us to believe you are'*.

Everyone laughs, as Melinda returns to her seat and goes back to what she was doing. I reach over and gently poke Joey in the ribs.

"Yeah, Joey, I think we're all pretty much on the same page now, unless, of course, you have an earth-shattering revelation you want to share?"

First, she laughs, and then Howard laughs, which in turn makes Cassie laugh.

"As a matter of fact, Courtney..." Joey replies.

"Oh crap, am I going to be sorry I asked?"

Again laughter, and from the sound of it, I can tell we're once again coalescing into the 'team' we need to be, which is a good thing because, sooner than any of us realize, my original warning that, 'people will be shooting at us', will become a vivid reality.

Unfortunately, however, my analysis of the situation isn't even close to reality. When I do finally reach the 'truth', it will turn out to be far beyond the ability of any normal human being to comprehend.

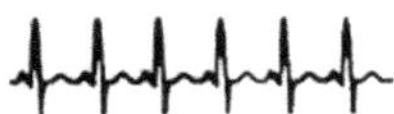

# 40

"You're sure you guys will be okay until someone finds you, right? You aren't going to drift into anything?"

"Yes, Alexis, we'll be fine. The Italian Navy will be on us in a heartbeat once we activate the beacon," the captain replies.

"Yeah," Jamie is quick to add, "especially if there's no radio response."

"Okay then, we're out of here. You'll make sure my message is delivered, right?"

"Of course," Jamie replies.

I smile at them and say, "See you on the other side, guys."

I turn and go out the door, leaving the Captain and Jamie bound and sitting on the deck, which supports their contention of hijacking. It takes me sixty seconds to make it to the helipad, where Vera has the pilot warming up our ride.

"Does he know where we're going?"

"Yes. He is more than willing to comply if it will get him away from us any sooner."

I laugh and say, "Let's go."

Sixty seconds later, we're airborne, headed for Genoa, Italy.

Five minutes into the flight, I nod at Vera and say, "Send it." She pulls out her Blackberry and punches the send key. Five seconds later we hear a single beep, indicating the transmission was successful.

The message she sent?

*'Those loyal to you have been eliminated, just as my husband was. I have the captive. We will see who can get to the money first.'*

I'm thinking *that* will *definitely* get Mr. Tarasov's attention. Although thanks to Vera, I now know what his plan is, I've opted not to tell her it will take both of us being physically at the bank to access the money. Truth is, at this point, she doesn't care about the money any longer. She simply wants to stay alive.

We make the pilot fly us to Massa, rather than Genoa. No one will be expecting us there. Once we're on the ground, I give him an account number, and an authorization code, telling him to use it to refuel his aircraft for his flight back to wherever he's going. I also sternly explain that we were never in his aircraft – he left the yacht empty. He quickly nods his understanding.

Now that I'm not a prisoner, I need to make contact with one specific person. However, to do that, I have to *find* Daria first.

She has never kept anything from me before, and I'm confused as to why she would now. I'm close to convinced that she's gotten us into some kind of 'ultra-covert' op and if that's the case, Alice must know about it. Hell, it's probably her doing.

The only other option is, after more than twenty years, she's gone back to the other side, which I simply refuse to believe.

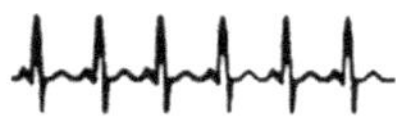

# 41

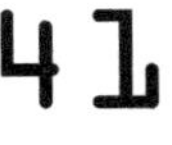

"They used a Gulfstream that is registered to the Russian Embassy in Naples. It apparently flew to Valencia, refueled, and then went to Genoa with our targets onboard."

"Damn it!" I blurt out.

I turn and look at Howard, and the look on his face tells me he understands what I'm thinking.

"Do we have any assets in the area of Genoa?"

"Yes, Courtney, but the targets could be anywhere within a hundred miles by now," Cassie offers.

"Options?" I ask.

"We know where they are going, why not set up there?" Joey asks.

I'm about to share my thoughts when Keith, who has been fairly quiet for a while, speaks up.

"Oh gee, the yacht has been hijacked. Imagine that."

"Huh?" Howard and I say in unison.

"The yacht's duress transmitter is active and has started transmitting the 'hijack' code. That's all, Boss."

"Now just a damn second," I blurt out, walking to Keith's terminal. "It *just* started?"

Before he can respond, Melinda has a comment.

"And, the chopper is gone too."

Instantly, a satellite image fills the main monitor, and although it's totally dark, the yacht is unmistakable – as if they *want* us to see it. I'm concentrating on the now empty, but fully illuminated helipad, and hear both of them typing away behind me.

"Their last four GPS fixes – which now coincide with SEASTAT incidentally – indicate they are adrift, Boss."

"Oh, man. Jamie did it again," Keith says, looking at me.

"She did?" I ask, having no clue what he means.

"A single word, buried in the carrier signal. It repeats every time the transponder pings."

"Which is?"

*"Wait."*

When I feel Howard's hand on my shoulder, I turn to look at him.

"One brain in two bodies, Courtney. She *knows* you are out here. Damned if I know how, but she does. And if she knows you're involved..."

"She's in it up to her ass too," I reply, turning to look back at the image of the yacht on the wall.

I stand staring at the image for at least thirty seconds. Then, without thinking about it, I mumble, *"I am so going to kick your ass, Sis."*

All the snickers in the room make me realize I said it out loud.

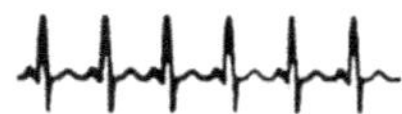

# 42

Tarasov's response to Vera's challenge – *'Why have you done this?'* – tells me that we've tossed a wrench into the machine. But I also know that what I can effectively do is limited, until I talk to Daria. *She* knows what's going on. I'm also hoping Courtney will not only get but will act on, the one-word message I had Jamie send her. I figure that by now, my big sister is ready to kick my ass.

Vera shares her knowledge of Tarasov's plan with me, or at least what he wants her to believe the plan is. I, however, know there's more to it than the money.

Using an Erasmus Shipping credit card and the Alexis Paddison persona, I rent a nice BMW and we waste three and a half hours driving the 125km to Genoa.

Knowing which train Tarasov intends to use, Vera and I make our way to the Piazza Principe, where the main terminal is located. It's close to 5:00 AM, so after purchasing two tickets for the 7:00 AM departure of the #176, which will take us all the way to Zürich, I suggest we find a quiet place in a corner of the terminal and try to relax.

We find a pair of overstuffed chairs stuck behind a row of lockers, that give us a clear view of the station entrance, and drop into them. We end up talking for about an hour as we make note of every person who enters the building. I tell Vera she has her freedom, and that as far as I'm concerned, she's off the hook. She does, however, make it quite clear that for her, payback is a must at this point. The loss of her husband is, as far as she is concerned, Leonid Tarasov's doing. I figure that she probably intends to offer her assistance as a bargaining chip as well.

An hour before the train boards, I have yet another idea. Because I'm still wearing the same clothes I was when Tarasov's people last saw me, a change is a must, just in case. We get up and wander around for about ten minutes until we stumble upon a small store that is just opening. In addition to dressing myself, I outfit Vera as well, just to keep them guessing. I also buy an extra blouse, on the off chance (which I actually expect) I need to change my appearance on the fly.

Now, both clad in jeans and new sneakers, we're sitting at a table outside the station café, drinking coffee and again watching the main entrance. When the video of the yacht turns up on the local news channel, it catches our attention at the same moment. Vera tries to concentrate on what's being said.

"My Italian is very poor, but I think they are saying that a vessel was hijacked by Russian-speaking individuals, who at some point, left by means unknown."

Then, a girl sitting next to us adds, "...and they left three bodies as well. They also mentioned a missing helicopter and pilot."

"Thank you," I say, smiling at her.

Then, Vera's Blackberry signals an incoming message. She glances at me, and when I nod, punches a couple of buttons. Her eye movement tells me she's reading a text message, and the instant smirk on her face tells me who it's from. Without saying a word, she lays the Blackberry on the table, spins it around orienting it so that I can read it, and slides it over in front of me.

*'Это обсуждается?' Is this open for discussion?*

"He has seen the news," she says, as she sips her coffee.

After a few seconds of what appears to be deep thought, and while still looking me right in the eyes, she finally asks the one question that's driving her nuts.

"Can you tell me what is *really* going on here?"

"I honestly have no clue, Vera, and unfortunately for us, the one person who does, is with the head bad guy."

As I finish my sentence, Daria, Tarasov, and a woman come in through the station's main entrance. It appears Daria is in fact, still a 'prisoner', which tells me she probably doesn't know about Tarasov's new problems. I figure she's behaving herself because she's concerned about them killing me.

I kick Vera under the table as I reach for my coffee and nod in the direction, I want her to look. Just as nonchalantly as you please, she manages to glance in the general direction of the bad guys. We watch as they walk directly to the ticket counter.

"He is checking to see if I have picked up my ticket. He will not purchase any as he already has his."

Sure enough, he asks a question, gets an answer, and walks away. I reach over and gently tap Vera on the arm to get her attention.

"It's time to let my sister know I am here. I need you to send him a reply to his last question. Tell him you know something about the money that he as yet does not, and that you will find him on the train. The difficult part will be somehow including the word 'miracle' in your message."

"As you wish," she replies. She takes the Blackberry and quickly types out the message, and hits 'send'. Seconds later, I hear the confirmation tone indicating the message went out.

Tarasov leads Daria into a bar across the station from us, with the new woman right behind. As soon as they're all seated, the woman hands Tarasov the matching Blackberry, saying something to him at the same time. I can tell Tarasov is reading it out loud, because almost instantly Daria's eyes are scanning the entire station. The code word works. She knows I'm here.

I smile at Vera and ask, "What the hell did that message say, girl? It worked almost too well."

"I told him it will be a miracle if we both survive this and that if I were a betting woman, I would bet on myself in the end."

"Well played, Vera, very well played."

"I know I have no right, but may I ask a question."

"Of course."

"You repeatedly refer to her as your 'sister'. Is she *not* Daria Ladenko?"

"She was, once, long ago. Over the years she has become a completely different person. The person you knew as Daria, no longer exists."

"You are not rogues, operating unsanctioned, are you?"

"Not hardly.  Are you truly prepared to know who we are?"

"Am I? You would know that better than I," she replies, her curiosity now piqued.

"Off the grid, black ops, Vera. Know what that means?"

"You are the kind of people that do not exist, and I would guess, have not existed since the two of you were killed, fifteen years ago."

"Uh-huh.  And here's the part that may upset you..."

She smiles and interrupts me.

"Daria has been on your side, all along."

"The thing with the money just happened, Vera, it wasn't planned. The situation presented itself, and she capitalized on it. I believe Daria moved it all so quickly, to keep eyes off of you, because you knew what was going on."

She maintains eye contact with me, and I see something, I'm not sure what, building in her eyes.

"As a team, we've done a lot of good over the years, Vera, I swear to you. It was never about the money."

"Such as?"

"The Zaliv America?"

The look on her face is comical. She sips her coffee a couple of times and does nothing more than stare at me for about a minute, while she regroups.

"The incident in the Afghan desert between Musa Quleh and Sangin, four years ago?"

That one gets her. She turns pale, understanding exactly what I'm talking about.

"Enough said, Alexis.  And thank you."

"For sharing?"

"No. For not killing me – although I probably deserve it. And perhaps, for seeing that I am not the despicable person Tarasov sought to turn me into."

We sit silently again for a few moments, and then Vera slips back into the moment – back into the present.

"So what is it, exactly, that I know about the money, that Leonid does not?"

"Apply some logic and give it a guess."

I fight off a laugh as Vera is again swept up by confusion.

"It has to do with *accessing* it Vera."

"My mind is simply not adept enough, *Miss Paddison*. You are far better at this game we play, than I could ever hope to be. It was perhaps the most foolish mistake of my life, to make you an adversary," she replies, shaking her head and finishing the last bit of her coffee.

"He can't get the money unless *both of us* are there – live and in color, dear. And, not only will we have to sign for the withdrawal *while being watched*, we both have to *supply a thumbprint* as well."

Her eyes double in size instantly, and it's apparent that she's desperately fighting an urge to laugh.

"The silly bastard has no clue. He believes that either of you can withdraw all the cash *alone*. This is the reason he decided to separate you. It appears you and your sister are far smarter than Leonid Tarasov as well!"

"That's how I knew this was about something other than the money. He didn't do his research. And she," I nod in the direction of Daria, "knows what the true agenda is."

"So, do we have a plan?"

"Not much of one. I'm going to make sure my sister sees me, and then get on the train. After that, she will have to make contact with me. For now, that's the best I can do."

"And me?"

"I was quite serious when I said you have your freedom, Vera. You've earned it. I'm certain you have a contingency fund and a couple of passports stashed – we all do. Disappear and I will do my best to ensure that my people don't look for you."

"And should I desire to participate in whatever it is you, and your sister, intend to do?"

"Vera…"

She stops me instantly.

"You have been more than fair with me, considering my stupidity in participating in this mess. I have destroyed my career, lost my husband, and at this point, have absolutely nothing left to lose. Let me help you. It will play far more to your benefit if the asshole *thinks* you are still my captive, will it not?"

"He'll kill you, Vera, without even thinking about it. You know that. He values no one but himself."

"Miss Paddison – *Alexis* – I was dead the moment I let the sorry bastard talk me into this. Please…"

I gently kick her under the table while she's talking and nod to her left. She instantly understands and turns to her right so that Tarasov won't see her as he walks within feet of us, headed for the platforms. It's the perfect opportunity.

"I need a distraction – just a second or two."

"That can be arranged," Vera replies, instantly on her feet and walking away. I too stand and walk a course parallel to the one Tarasov is leading Daria on.

Then, after only seconds, there's a loud crash behind me, which makes almost everyone in the terminal turn to look. Almost everyone. Daria interprets our code word perfectly, and although Tarasov turns all the way around, Daria stops at a quarter turn, and for an instant, we make eye contact.

The only word to describe the expression I see on her face is *'relief'*.

Even as she's looking at me, Daria yells and tries to loosen Tarasov's grip on her upper arm, creating an opening for me to disappear again, without his noticing. It's all automatic, and completely second nature to us. We don't think about it, we just do it. As I cut behind a row of lockers, I hear Tarasov tell her, in Russian, to shut up and not to forget they still have me.

Bingo! The asshole hasn't told her he has lost control of his op. The walls are beginning to collapse around Leonid Tarasov, and as Vera had so eloquently put it, 'the silly bastard has no clue'.

Two minutes later, I'm sitting in a window seat in the coach section of the train. Moments later, a nice Russian woman sits down next to me.

Now, the next move is Daria's.

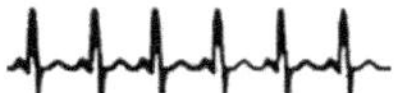

# 43

We all manage a few hours of sleep, with the exception of Keith. He's been awake so long that I'm beginning to wonder when he will finally crash and burn. As I walk across the room, putting my hair back into a ponytail, he is watching me closely, the look on his face one of concern.

"We're going to Zürich. Melinda, I'm sorry but..."

"It's cool, Courtney. I can help you a lot more from here. But, take Keith," she turns and looks at him. "You'll definitely need a communications person on site."

"You guys," I point across the room at Joey, Cassie, and Howard, "are with me. Let's load up. Keith, you heard Mindy — get what you need and be in the truck in ten minutes."

Everyone moves at once, and in less than a minute, Melinda and I are alone.

"Will Keith be mobile again?"

"Yes. The Bern Unit is sending one of their portables to the hotel under seal. Keith can set it up in less than an hour. There are also two satellite-capable laptops — Keith will explain that to you on-site."

"Mike and Rhyan are going too. Can the Gulfstream handle all of us and the weight of all their 'toys'?"

Melinda laughs and says, "I'm thinking that if and when the shooting starts, you want to be able to shoot back."

"Exactly," I reply with a grin.

"I'm going to keep the plane clean – just in case. Besides, I have a better means of getting your toys there," she replies.

"Does it involve the use of a 'Diplomatic' tag? I'd like to keep prying eyes out of them."

"Yes, it does. Only *our people* will be able to lay hands on the container. Just trust me on this one, Boss."

"You got it, lady. As long as you are so willingly handling stuff, I'm going to need some fresh intel on the bank and the neighborhood."

"Keith can download it on the plane, in flight. You will keep him out of the way of the bullets, right?"

"I promise. You'll need to keep me up to speed on Tarasov, Melinda, that's the key. Find him, track him – whatever. But please, please, make damn sure that I can find him when I get there."

"I will. I swear. Good luck. Whatever you need, just call."

"See you on the other side, M." I step up and hug her, then turn toward the bedroom. I hear her fingers on the keys before I'm out of the room.

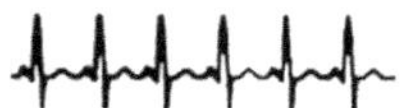

# 44

It takes us close to three hours to reach the Swiss border – and another twenty minutes to clear customs. During the trip, we discover Tarasov has a private berth, and there's no way to watch what he may be up to.

During the customs check in Chiasso, I wander into the station and with my credit card, purchase two pay-as-you-go cell phones – with Swiss phone numbers. I run back, to avoid missing the train.

Once aboard, I program each phone's number into the other and give Vera one of them.

"And this is for?" she asks.

"I don't know at this point, but…"

"I get the idea."

"And," I say, as I power up the one still in my hand, "It's time to check in with the 'good guys'."

Vera quietly watches as I type a short text message.

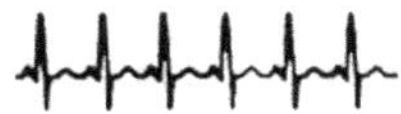

# 4 5

We've been airborne for about an hour when Keith calls for me to join him at the communications console. Once there, I find all his monitors full of news channels – and they all have the yacht on them. Keith turns up the volume, and within seconds, everyone else is standing and watching as well.

The Italian Navy turned out in force when they received the distress beacon from the yacht indicating it had been hijacked. We are watching and listening, in four different languages, when a small secondary window pops up in the corner of Keith's monitor. He immediately turns to me and says, "Mindy says you need to call her right now. Emphasis on 'right now'."

Shaking my head, I mutter, *"what now."* I turn and head toward my seat, reaching down and pushing the button to connect the call when I reach it. Because I punch the 'secure circuit' button it takes a bit longer to connect the call, but I finally hear Melinda's voice.

"Ashton."

"You want me?" I ask, still not taking my eyes off the news.

"Are we secure, Courtney?"

"Of course," I reply, finally taking my seat. "What's up, M?"

"Uh, well... it's an incoming text message, and I think you need to deal with it."

"From whom?"

Silence.

"Melinda, you still there?"

More silence.

"M, talk to me, girl."

"It's encrypted, Courtney. It came to me over TRACECON – *directly*. No bounce, no screening."

"From where? Quit being so cryptic."

"Just trust me on this, Courtney. You need to deal with this. The message has a series of numbers in it, which I determined to be a phone number – 410799226331."

"Okay, Melinda, if you say so. You need to ease up a bit girl, you sound totally stressed."

"Just call it. Now. Please? It's a throw-away, Courtney, and it has only been active for about fifteen minutes."

"Okay, Melinda, right now. I'll talk to you later."

The next thing I hear is the call being disconnected, even before I finish my sentence. Unfortunately, I don't get what she's trying to tell me. My brain is going too fast.

Howard, having lost interest in the news, walks over.

"What's up, lady?"

"Melinda is weirding out on me," I reply, turning toward the front of the plane.

"Hey, Keith!"

"Yeah, Boss?"

"410799226331 – Where does the number originate?"

Howard gives me a quizzical glance as we wait for Keith to answer my question.

"Switzerland, Boss. It's a Swiss cell on a Chiasso circuit."

"O... K... This could prove interesting," I say as I dial."

Although it should have, even Keith's response doesn't flip my 'oh shit' switch.

"What's going on?" Howard asks.

"I don't know. Melinda told me she got a text message with this phone number in it, and says I need to deal with it."

To this day, I still have no idea what makes me pick up the receiver rather than leave it on speaker, but that's what I do.

I'm about to completely understand Melinda's elevated stress levels. The call is answered on the third ring.

"Hey, Sis, took you long enough."

My heart stops, my entire world begins to spin, and yes, I faint.

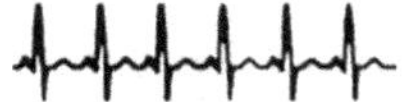

# 4 6

I hear her quit breathing, and then there's a thud, which is followed by some background noise. However, Courtney never says a word.

Seconds later a voice – a male voice.

"Hello?"

*"Holy crap!"* I blurt out, making Vera laugh, and the people across from us glare in our direction.

*"No shit!"* Howard shoots right back at me.

"Where's my sister?"

"She fainted. Your brother is trying to wake her up."

"Strange, I never used to have that effect on her."

Howard breaks up laughing, and after a few seconds, I hear a new male voice.

"Whit?"

"Yes, little brother, it's me. Come to save me, have you?"

"Well yeah, that's the plan. But, if you don't need saving after all, we could just call it a day, and go home."

"Rhyan, you so totally suck – I swear to God. And I love you to death," I reply, feeling myself choking up.

Then, out of nowhere, Vera kicks me hard, stands up, and walks quickly away, in the direction of the restroom at the back of the car. I know there's only one reason she'd do that. I kill the phone, then quickly lay down across two seats and pull my jacket up over my head as if I'm sleeping. After a few seconds,

I hear the approaching sound of heels on the linoleum covered steel floor, walking excessively slowly.

She's looking for us. I force myself to stay perfectly still and listen – which is a task in itself. As the sound of the heels fades, I hear the doors between the cars pneumatically open, and then close. The moment the hissing of the doors stops, I hear the door to the restroom open again, and hear Vera's sneakers squeaking on the floor as she walks right past me. I also feel something land on my legs – something light.

I remain motionless, and as I expected, hear the door between the cars cycle again, and then the same clicking heels – although they are moving much faster this time…

I slowly count to fifty before I move. When I finally sit up, the first thing I find is a wadded-up paper towel lying on the seat next to me. As I reach down and pick it up, I also glance around the car for new faces.

Although unplanned, Vera's ploy worked perfectly. By exposing herself, she drew the female's attention away from everything else, including me.

No new faces, and I don't appear to be the focus of anyone's attention either.

I carefully open up the paper towel and find exactly what I expect – a note. 'Bar. Thirty minutes. Time for our 'bluff.'

I know it's now time to play my hole card – one that not even Vera will be ready for. With a smile, I stand and head for the restroom.

# 47

"Courtney... hey, Sis... Sis... you still with us?"

Rhyan's voice, and I know I'm hearing it, but my mind is still on the phone call. Was it? It sounded like her, but...

"Come on, Courtney, wake up."

It's Howard's voice this time. Then, someone slaps me.

"COURTNEY!"

I hear them... but I can't see... eyes... open my eyes...

"There you go girl, open them up – come on."

Focus... eyes... focus.... Howard... holding my chin... and my hand... and smiling. My head is... cold... water... tricking down my neck...

I reach up and find an ice pack against my head.

"You hit the edge of the desk, Sis."

Rhyan... somewhere. Oh shit! Whitney... it was Whitney on the phone... think... focus...

"It was Whitney... on the phone."

"Yeah, Sis, we know."

Howard cancels my request for a 'shot' of something, saying that the blow to my head was a pretty good one and that alcohol isn't a good idea. It takes another ten minutes to get my head clear enough to think. Although everyone except Howard has gone back to their seats (at Howard's direction), I feel five pairs of eyes diligently watching me.

"It was Whitney, Howard."

"I know. I spoke to her too."

"I need to call her back… I need to…"

"Whoa, Court, slow down."

He motions to Keith, who walks down the aisle toward us.

"Tell her," Howard says.

"She killed the call, Boss – for some reason, she hung up her phone in the middle of a sentence."

"Maybe… she lost the…" I start but am interrupted.

"Come on, Boss, you know I wouldn't tell you something I'm not sure about. It was *disconnected* at her end purposely – I swear."

"That's why we didn't call her back Courtney. I was afraid of compromising her," Howard adds.

"Damn! We have to wait for her to call us, don't we?" I ask, sounding about as pathetic as one can.

"Well, you're running this op, girl."

"Okay Howard, you made your point, you little shit."

In the middle of my comment, Rhyan walks up, squats down directly in front of me, and uses my knee to balance himself.

"The call served one very specific purpose, Sis. It confirmed that the smart-ass at the other end is, without a fuckin' doubt, *our sister.*"

Everyone – including me – starts laughing.

I think back to my sister's one-word message, which Jamie so deftly slipped into the transponder's carrier signal.

*'Wait'*

All we can do is hope the bad guys will wait too.

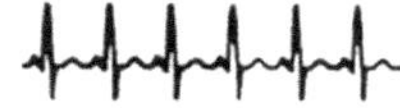

# 48

My ace in the hole over the years had always been the tube of special shampoo I keep stashed in my sneaker. It's totally undetectable unless you know where it is. Realizing I would probably need it at some point, I carefully removed it from my old shoe, and now have it in the front pocket of my jeans.

Poor Vera looked seriously confused when, after we changed clothes, she watched me puncture the soles of both my Nikes repeatedly with a pocketknife I purchased. I think the crunching sound she heard as the knife penetrated, gave away what was going on. She never questioned my need to dispose of them in separate trashcans, on opposite ends of the station.

Our little game has now progressed to the point that I know it's time to play my hole card – the appearance change. At the moment, the bad guys are looking for a redhead with blue eyes who purports to be Daria's sister.

Unfortunately, due to circumstances, this time I have no choice but to go back to being blonde with green eyes. I haven't been this close to being Whitney Bergstrom, in public, in as long as I can remember. This is only the third time, in fifteen years, I've been forced to change my identity on the fly. The last time, I was dodging bullets as I did it.

After twenty minutes in the restroom, I'm now blonde, with a wet ponytail, and have my own bright green eyes. I remove all of the make-up – except the prosthetics – from my face, and now look my age, instead of ten years older. I also change into the extra blouse I bought.

As I pass the seat where we are sitting, I decide to leave my jacket and the bag of clothes there, just on the off-chance Vera leads them back here. It will give her an explanation, or at the very least an excuse, should she need one. I very politely asked the women across from us if they would please keep an eye on it for me, indicating I would return quickly. Although they agree with smiles, it's apparent my change has confused them.

It takes me about three minutes to walk through the four cars ahead of ours and make it to the dining car – which is where the bar is. I spot her instantly, sitting across from the girl we saw with Tarasov earlier.

I walk past them and find an empty stool at the bar that's close enough that I can hear their conversation.

"...и скажи ему, что его план изменился. Отныне, ему больше не придется принимать за меня решения." (...and tell him that his plan has been changed. He does not get to make decisions for me any longer.)

"Она на этом поезде? Или вы ожидаете, что мы просто так вот поверим, что она у вас?" (Is she on this train? Or do you expect we will simply believe you have her?") I hear the girl ask.

"Если вы желаете получить деньги, то у вас нет иного выбора, кроме как верить тому, что я вам говорю." (If you want the money, you have no choice but to believe what I tell you.)

"И причина тому?" (And this is due to?)

"Я знаю наверняка то, чего вы пока не знаете. Тот факт что вы об этом не знаете указывет на то, что тот, кто вами руководит, недостаточно хорошо разобрался в ситуации." (What I know of course – that you do not as yet know. The fact you do not know about it, indicates your 'leader' did not do his research properly.)

"Почему я должна вам верить?" (Why should I believe you?)

I can see them in the big mirror behind the bar, and although I can't see Vera's eyes, I know what's in them when she makes her next comment.

"Мне все равно, во что ВЫ верите. Скажите Леониду, что она у меня и что если он хочет свои деньги, пусть ищет меня в Цюрихе. Я буду в Алден Отель Шплюгешлосс. Он также знает, под каким именем меня искать." (I do not care what YOU believe. Tell Leonid I have her and that if he wants his money, to find me in Zürich. I will be at the Alden Hotel Splügenschloss. He knows where it is. He also knows what name I will be using.)

She's standing even before she finishes her sentence, turning and heading out of the bar, then hesitating after about ten steps.

"И, вы пожалеете о любой попытке поймать меня или попытаться обнаружить, где я держу мисс Паддиссн. Мы ведь поняли друг друга?" (And, you will not like the results of any attempt to take me, or to discover where I have Miss Paddison. Do we understand each other?)

This time I look right at her and find murder in her eyes. She *wants* them to try something. She's seriously pissed off.

Tarasov's associate nods in response, and then Vera turns and leaves. I wonder if Vera recognizes me and plays it off, or if she really has no idea, *it is* me. The moment Vera disappears from view, the woman jumps up and hurries out of the bar. I'm already standing and headed for the door when she rushes past me. I turn ever so nonchalantly to follow her. We go all the way forward to the very first, First Class berthing car, and she never once looks behind her.

Sloppy.

I'm checking doors as we go, and when she finally turns into one of the berths, I slip into one with an unlocked door. The two guys inside both look rather bewildered when they see me. I smile and say, "Ooops, wrong berth," in English, with a forced southern drawl. They spend the next couple of minutes talking to me in Italian, which I don't understand. Eventually, I excuse myself and step into the passageway.

It takes me ten minutes to make my way back to my original seat. On my way, I pull out the cell phone and quickly send a text message to the same number I did before, knowing that Melinda will act on it, just as she did the last time.

At least they'll have a starting point, assuming they can get there before we do.

The look on Vera's face when I walk up and sit down across from her without a word, is hilarious.

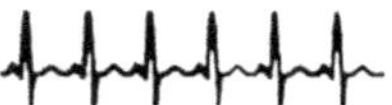

# 49

We have about thirty minutes of flight time remaining when the communications console next to me buzzes. It's an incoming phone call. I reach down and punch the button to make the connection and Melinda's face fills the screen.

"She did it again, Courtney."

Instantly there's a text message filling the monitor:

Alden Hotel - Blonde

"Care to explain?" I ask, as Howard walks up and reads over my shoulder.

"It's a hotel in Zürich. A *seriously* high-end hotel. I think she's also telling us she's back to blonde and not the redhead they originally snatched."

"If she's changed her hair color…" I hear Rhyan start to say.

"She's not a prisoner," I add, finishing his thought.

"That's what I was thinking too," Melinda offers, as her face reappears on the screen. "I also think she told us where the bad guys are going."

"Good possibility, Mindy. Can you get us into a hotel close?"

"I'm ahead of you, Boss — I've already booked four rooms. Two are in the Hyatt, both on the top floor. One suite with a balcony, and a standard double. The other two are in the Alden. A full suite on the third floor, and a double on the ground floor. The suite at the Hyatt is in Keith's name and the double is in Rhyan's name. The big suite in the Alden is reserved in the name of Christine Nelson, and the other one is in Cassie's alter ego. I used the aliases to avoid detection. The hotels are close enough that you can walk between them in only a couple of minutes."

"Back to your disgustingly efficient self, I see."

"Oh, this gets better, Courtney. There are five Russians with reservations during that period, and only one of them has a British 'roommate'."

"Seriously? Can he be that stupid?" I ask as I glance at everyone standing around me.

"I don't know about Tarasov, but *Daria* damn sure knew what she was doing. She gave up her passport, Court. Her name is on the damn room reservation."

"Which name?"

"Allison Paddison. The Chief Operating Officer of Erasmus Shipping. She reserved a suite. And, care to guess who else has a reservation?"

"Honestly, Mindy, I'm fresh out of guesses. This is getting too screwy."

"The guy in the hospital. You know, the one I stopped you from killing twenty-four hours ago."

Her comment makes Michael and Rhyan laugh.

"Hey, computer guy!"

"Yeah, Boss, I'm here," Keith says, from across the aisle.

"High-end hotels are all electronic. I want to know how those two reservations came in, and if possible, who made them."

"I'm on it, Courtney," he replies, his fingers on the keys before he finishes the sentence.

"Okay, he finally used my first name. Everyone make a note of that please."

My comment does exactly what it's supposed to – ease things up a bit. Everyone, including Melinda, laughs.

"Final thing for now, M, and it's important."

"It has been delivered in a sealed container, compliments of Erasmus Shipping, under a Diplomatic Contract. No prying eyes."

"You did have a damn plan."

"Absolutely. *This is what I do.* For security reasons, I was forced to send it together. The container was delivered directly to Rhyan's room, so each of you will have to go by and pick up your 'toys'."

"Or I can just deliver each item where it needs to be. Will make for less traffic," Rhyan replies.

Then, for the first time since we left Crete, Michael has something to say.

"Melinda, when this is over, you and I are going on an extended vacation, and I'm buying."

When I turn to look at him, there's definitely a twinkle in his eyes. One I've never seen before.

"You're on, Osborne! I'll keep you up to date on the rest of this stuff, Courtney. You know how to find me if you need me."

"Later girl," I reply, disconnecting the call.

Once the guys go back to their seats, Cassie and Joey – who's been unusually quiet up to this point – walk over and take seats across from me.

"What's going on in that head?" Cassie asks.

"What makes you ask that?"

"You really want to know?"

"Yes."

"The way you asked Keith about the reservation," Joey says, now looking right at me. "You asked the question with reason."

I laugh. I can't help it. Neither time nor separation can affect our relationship.

"Okay, you each got a dollar? I need to make some lunch money on this one," I offer, pulling a bill out of the pocket of my Levis.

Laughing, they each produce a single dollar bill and lay it on the table separating us.

"Okay. I'm betting someone inside the CIA, no names at this point, made Miss Paddison's reservation. As far as the other one goes, the man never said anything to Melinda or me about going to Zürich himself, so it would stand to reason that someone else made it. My bet is on Whitney's current traveling companion."

"No shit..." Cassie mumbles, looking lost in thought. "Vera Kovalenko made it."

"Amanda," Joey adds, staring intently at me.

"Huh?"

"You think *Amanda* made Daria's reservation."

The accusing tone in Joey's voice along with the burning intensity of her stare gives me goosebumps.

"*And*, you still think Alice is behind all this, don't you?"

"That really bugs the shit out of you, doesn't it, Joey?"

When she doesn't immediately respond, I continue.

"Why?"

"I need to make a secure call, assuming you trust me," she replies, ignoring my question.

Without a word, I stand and offer her my seat at the console, wondering what the hell she's up to. She sits down and starts typing a text message.

"You need privacy?" I ask.

"Nope, not at this point. But try not to faint again," she replies hitting the send button. "This shouldn't take long."

A minute later, a buzzer goes off, indicating an incoming call. The strange thing is, that Joey has to enter an access code to complete the connection.

When Crystal's face suddenly fills the screen, I do damn near faint.

# 50

"So, what's the plan once the train stops?" I ask, causing Vera to finally look right at me.

"Excuse me?"

"Well crap, this worked far better than I anticipated."

Vera's light bulb goes on, she instantly utters a couple of vulgarities in Russian, and then almost laughs herself.

"How?"

"I have a good hair stylist dear, and contact lenses come in a variety of colors."

"Why now?"

"When they see me, they are going to assume you have 'Alexis' somewhere other than aboard this train. They are also going to wonder where you got the 'new' back-up."

Then, she realizes something else.

"You were sitting at the bar!"

"Yes, I was. That isn't a problem, is it?"

"No! It is good that you heard what I told Leonid's new associate. Did you understand it?"

"Yes. The good guys will be onsite before we are. Oh, and very well played too!"

"Thank you. At this point, the plan is to get to the Alden, check in, and then wait for Tarasov to do something stupid, which I feel he will most probably do. I have a room reserved there, in my husband's name. Leonid knows this."

"Well, we have about three more hours, so I'm going to take a nap. Kick me again if anything happens."

She laughs, as I once again lay down across the seat.

I know this adventure is about to get very interesting, which is cool with me. It is, after all, the kind of thing I'm disgustingly efficient at.

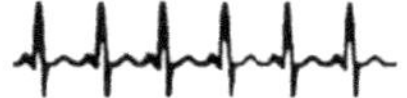

# 51

"*Don't* ask questions, just sit," Joey orders, indicating the chair next to her.

I do as instructed and am instantly greeted by Crystal, who can now see me on her monitor.

"Hello, Director. Hey, Sis."

"Remember what we discussed a while back, Crys?" Joey asks before I can respond.

"Yes, of course. What do you want to know?"

"Give her Alice's number, Courtney," Joey directs.

"No need," Crystal replies, again before I can respond. "I know them all. What time frame are we talking about?"

"The last thirty days, Crys. Can you do that?"

"Sure. Give me a secure deposit point."

"Send it to Melinda's account through TRACECON, and immediately delete all records of the transaction, and don't forget the transaction history file. Understood?"

"Yep. I hope whatever you guys are into, turns out well. If you need anything else, let me know."

"Love ya, Sis. Bye."

Crystal winks at her and disconnects the call.

"What the hell just happened?" Cassie immediately asks.

"Joey's little sister works for IS," I say, with an evil little smirk on my face.

Joey looks at me with a devious little grin of her own.

"By design or by accident?"

"Accident, entirely."

"IS?" Howard asks, walking up behind us. "Who works for Internal Security?"

"Crystal does," I say, looking at him.

"The Crystal we killed, fifteen years ago?"

"Yep, that one. She just agreed to send us the incoming and outgoing call logs from Alice Williamson's phones."

The moment I confirm their suspicions about what they just saw, every one of them has a change in demeanor. They all – well, except for Joey – get very nervous.

"Damn, Courtney! Are you certain about what you are doing here?" Howard asks, doubt and concern embedded into the lines of his face. "Spying on the DCI is a little out there lady – like jumping from a plane with no parachute."

*"You did what?"* Rhyan asks, looking very concerned.

"Okay, listen up! Everyone is clear of this. If it comes back to bite us, it only gets Crystal, Joey, and me. I need the info, and they both know exactly what they've committed to by helping me," I say to everyone while looking directly at Joey.

"You have an incoming from Mindy, Boss. Do you want it on that monitor?" Keith yells at me.

"Yeah," I reply, as Joey punches some buttons.

Melinda's voice fills the cabin before we see her image.

*"Have you lost your fucking mind, Courtney Whitman?"* Where the hell did you get this, and what the hell am I supposed to do with it, for God's sake?"

We all fall out in laughter, including Keith, who's watching on his monitor. Melinda hears them.

"Jezzzz, you *all* know about this?"

"Oh, hell yes!" Cassie blurts out. "We're going to crash and burn together. Wanna come?"

This time Melinda laughs.

"Send it to Keith," I say, knowing this will be the best means of testing my theory. "I assume it's encrypted?"

"Yes, with something that I've never seen before. Do you realize where it originated?"

"Well, yeah?" I reply, as I shake my head and try to fight off another laugh.

"It's on its way. So, Courtney, do I want to know what's in it, or will you have to kill me after you tell me?"

The image on the monitor gives away the big grin on her face.

"I'll tell you if you really want to know. But be warned, you'll probably pee your pants afterward."

Again, laughter.

"Damn! Are there any other 'questionable' tasks I can tend to on your behalf?"

"Yeah, actually there is..."

"Tell Mindy I got it, Boss!" comes from Keith.

"I heard him," she says. "So, what else can I do for you?"

"I need to talk to my husband. Covertly and privately. What can you do for me?"

"I can ensure no one knows you talked to him."

"Perfect. Key words – '*no one*'. I'm certain he, and his team, are being monitored, and what I need to discuss with him is for our ears only. I'm about to draw him into this too."

"Not a problem. He will call your secure cell in about thirty minutes, okay?"

"Thanks, Melinda."

"See ya."

Once I disconnect the call, I stand and walk over to the console Keith is at. My entourage follows closely behind me. Even though the concept of what I've done scares the shit out of all of them, they nonetheless want to know what's in the file.

I drop into an empty chair beside Keith and immediately notice that the file has already been decrypted, and I have to force myself not to smile. Instead, I lay a hand on his shoulder, and keep what I'm thinking – '*interesting that you can decrypt something Mindy has never seen before, and do it in less than a minute no less. Yes, Keith, that's very damn interesting'* – to myself.

"Compare the outgoings from Alice's office on the date the reservation was made. I've already got a dollar on it coming from there."

Without a word, he reaches into his pocket, pulls out four quarters, and stacks them on the desk. If, as I suspect, he's working both sides of the fence, he's learned to hide it well.

"I want in on that action too," he says as he begins furiously typing.

As Keith is doing his thing, I hear a ding indicating the cockpit door is opening, and turn to see Rick – the co-pilot – come out and head toward us.

"We'll be on the ground in Dübendorf in twenty-five minutes, Mrs. Whitman. You may want to secure anything that creates radio signals," he nods in the direction of Keith, "to keep from drawing attention to us.

"What happens if my cell goes off? I've got an incoming I need to answer."

"If it's scrambled, the Swiss military *will identify it.*"

"Keith, shoot a message to Mindy. Tell her to wait forty-five minutes on the call, then shut everything down."

"You got it."

I smile at Rick, who turns and goes back to his 'office', while I find a seat, plop into it, close my eyes, and take a few deep breaths. It only takes a couple of seconds before I feel someone sit down next to me, but I choose to ignore whoever it is. I sit quietly and lose myself in a single recurring thought – *who's on whose side?*

After a few minutes of silence, the person next to me takes hold of my hand.

"You know, Sis," Rhyan says, gently squeezing the hand he's holding, "all these years, and I honest to God, had no idea just how damn good my big sister is, at what she does."

I open my eyes, smile, and then kiss him on the cheek.

"It's also a damn good thing you're on *our* side."

Howard, who's sitting across from us, laughs so hard, that I expect he's going to herniate something.

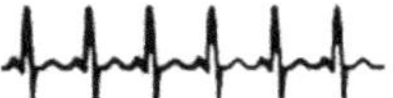

# 52

We wait until the last possible second to get off the train in Zürich, to ensure that Tarasov and his people are ahead of us. Vera leaves first. If there's going to be a tail, it will be on her. I exit onto the platform two minutes later.

As I enter the main terminal, I see the currency exchange booth in the center, exactly where Vera said it would be. I head for it, acting as touristy as one can be. She's standing outside a newsstand next to the currency booth, and when she sees me, *using her left hand she reaches for something hanging on a hook above her head,* another prearranged signal, indicating that she is being followed. I, in turn, change direction, slipping down a hallway leading to some restrooms. Because it affords a means of exit, we know that if Vera goes down it, her tail will have to follow her. A small maintenance door just short of the restrooms, is our ambush site.

On the other side of the door, I find a stairwell going both up and down, as well as a long hallway leading to the exit. If her tail is any good, he or she will automatically push the door *all the way open* which will give away anyone who might be hiding behind it. I opt to go up a half flight of stairs, pushing myself back against the wall on the intermediate landing.

Then, I wait.

Just as we planned, Vera comes through the door, heads immediately down the long hall, and sure enough, her tail comes through seconds after her. I take the stairs two at a time and am behind the new female in the blink of an eye. Because surprise is on my side, I have her face against the wall with her arm twisted up behind her, before she even knows what's happening. When she continues to struggle, I lean in close to her and whisper in her ear.

"Я не хочу вас убивать, но мне придется." (I do not want to kill you, but I will.)

Vera, who turns around as soon as she hears the struggling, walks up and stops next to us.

"Turn her around."

I force the girl around to face us while keeping her arm twisted up behind her back. Then, I almost freak when I see Vera pull the suppressor from her pocket, and the Glock from behind her back.

"Предлагаю вам варианты – они находят вас связанной и дышащей, или мертвой и истекающей кровью. Выбор за вами." (Here are your options – they find you tied up and breathing, or dead and bleeding. The choice is yours.)

The look on her face tells a story – 'rookie'. She's near panic as Vera carefully screws the suppressor onto the Glock, truly believing she's about to die.

The moment she stops twisting the suppressor, there are a few seconds of *very* intense eye contact between them.

"Let her go," Vera finally says.

I do, and the girl relaxes.

"Behind my back or in front?"

I notice she uses English.

"In front will be fine. You may be here awhile."

Vera hands me the Glock and pulls two rolls of medical tape that she found in a store in the station from her pocket.

"Sit," she commands, pointing at the floor.

The girl complies, and once she's seated, Vera kneels next to her and binds her hands and ankles with the tape – using both rolls to do it. She saves one piece, which she uses to cover the girl's mouth.

"Tell Leonid that, as you can see, I do have backup. Also, let him know that Miss Paddison is safely put away where he will not find her without my help. Do you understand?"

She nods.

"I will call station security in half an hour just on the off chance they have not discovered you by then."

Again, she nods her understanding.

"Let's go," Vera says to me.

"Right behind you," I reply using my favorite American accent and handing the Glock back to her.

Fifteen seconds later, we are standing outside in the bright sunshine of a Swiss afternoon in Zürich.

Because Vera knows exactly where we're going, we opt to walk the mile to the hotel. We start down Bahnhofstrasse at a relaxed pace, looking in windows, and watching people. We have time, and while I want to be certain Tarasov is where he's supposed to be, I also want to give the 'good guys' time to get into the game as well.

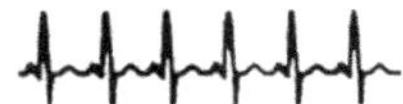

# 53

Because the Swiss are generally suspicious of unidentified aircraft, the twenty-five minutes until landing becomes more like an hour, as they keep us circling for about forty minutes. Moments before the pilot receives landing clearance, I get an unencrypted text message from Alice, via Chuck, indicating she made nice with them.

It's 12:45 PM local time when the tires touch down. When we finally get out of the plane, under the close scrutiny of a couple of Swiss FIS agents, we find Willie at the bottom of the stairs sitting in a new, bright blue, Mercedes GL450. Parked right behind it, is its twin.

"Hey guys! See what Mindy sent?" Willie says, indicating the vehicles. "This was in the truck when I got in," he says, pointing at a silver case on the passenger's seat.

Seconds later the young woman standing next to the second SUV, walks up to us.

"Ms. Nelson?"

"Yep."

"I was told you would be signing for these rentals."

"Show me where," I reply, smiling at her.

As I am signing the contracts, our pilot comes down the stairs and stops next to me. I quickly hold up a hand to him indicating I want him to wait until I'm done. Once the young woman is out of earshot, I turn to face him.

"Sorry about that, Phil. I was signing as 'Miss Nelson' and was afraid you'd call me Whitman."

"Not a problem, Boss," he replies. "We are officially on 'red standby'. Do you need my number?"

"I have it programmed into my phone, Phil. Let's make it 'standby', shall we? I can't see any reason we'll need to get off the ground in a rush. You guys find a hotel close, and hold up."

"Fair enough. I'll need at least thirty to get the engines warm, and file a flight plan when you are ready to go."

I nod, then he turns and goes back into the plane.

"Okay guys, here's the plan," I say, turning to face the rest of them. "Howard is with me on the third floor of the Alden. You two," I point at Cassie and Joey, "get the ground floor."

I stop in the middle of my thought and look around.

"Where the hell is the computer guy?"

Just as I ask, he announces his whereabouts.

"*Holy shit!* This is too damn cool!" we hear him blurt out from the far side of the second vehicle. "Do you guys have any idea what Melinda sent us?"

Joey and Cassie laugh, as he appears between the trucks, with an open laptop in his hands.

"It has dual Xi8 Oct-Core processors. This thing will do as much as, if not more than, all the equipment Mindy has in her little 'compound'. I wonder where the hell she got it."

We all watch him set it on the hood of the truck and start typing. In less than fifteen seconds, he gets excited all over again.

"Crap! The uplink is instantaneous."

With a silly smirk on my face, I continue where I left off.

"Keith, one of the rooms at the Hyatt is in your name. My hope that Melinda set you up, now seems confirmed."

He nods at me and never stops typing.

"Willie," I turn and look at him, "you're in that room too."

Again, a nod of acknowledgment.

"That leaves you two crazies," I laugh and point at Mike and my brother, "in the other room."

I wait for them to acknowledge, and then continue.

"*Stealth* people. *Draw no attention.* Understood? We don't want *them* to know we're here... yet."

Each of them again nods, and then they get into the vehicles for the ride into Zürich. Keith stands watching as I cross the tarmac to a black SUV, its engine running, and two people inside. The driver's window goes down when I'm halfway there.

"Good afternoon, Mrs. Whitman," the driver says.

"Disgustingly efficient as usual, Agent...?"

"Schmid, Director. Carl Schmid. And, we do try. After all, when one of the CIA's *Directors* turns up in Switzerland, unannounced, is not 'business as usual'."

"Nicely done, Carl. So, 'Eidgenössisches Justiz', or FIS?"

"NDB," he quickly replies.

"Black vehicles. Should have guessed."

The two of them laugh at the same time.

"If you will call your boss, and tell him to meet me at the Alden hotel, I'll explain my presence."

"I will do it immediately, Director," he replies, as he pulls a phone from his inside jacket pocket.

"And, as we know you've been tasked with following me, I'll have my guy drive slowly. The second vehicle is going to the Hyatt, just so you know."

The second guy laughs and reaches for a radio.

"As a matter of fact, Director, we were wondering if you would be willing to share the contents of the 'case' that was delivered there late yesterday," the driver says, as he waits for his call to be connected.

As the passenger is telling someone – presumably their second vehicle – in German, where the other truck is going, I smile at the driver and say, "Case? What case?" I follow the comment with a wink, then turn, and head back to my vehicle.

As I approach the truck, a very stern looking Keith, who has been watching me the entire time, I find myself wondering if we beat the bad guys – and my sister – here.

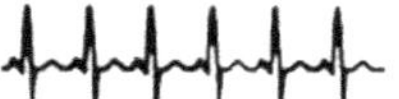



Solution Squared: Recalculation

# 54

We've been walking at a casual pace for about ten minutes when, at the next intersection we reach, I stop. Vera stops a well and watches me as I look down Börsenstrasse, but doesn't say anything. After a few seconds of contemplation, I turn and look at her.

"Come on. Side trip."

As I step off the curb to cross the street, she smiles, nods her agreement, and yet, still says nothing. Three minutes later we're standing on the south side of the street, quietly staring at a rather non-descript building, with a small sign above the door that says 'LB-Swiss'. Vera realizes what it is, and she voices her opinion.

"This is not a good site for what you are considering."

"And what is it you think I'm 'considering'?"

"As you once said, Alex, *we are in the same business.*"

I turn, smile at her and say, "Touché."

"Do you remember your comment about my involvement in this?"

"I do," I reply wondering where she's going.

"I believe you said, *'Tarasov has no regard for life other than his'.* To force a confrontation here, will endanger many lives which are no part of this."

I again smile at her, and after wrapping an arm around her, say, "I know, Vera, I know. I'm just thinking. That's all."

We turn together and head back the way we came.

"So," I ask when we reach the corner, "how much further is this hotel of yours anyhow? My stomach is beginning to make strange noises. I need to feed it."

"A kilometer perhaps, no more" she replies with a laugh, once again relaxing. "There is a wonderful restaurant just at the other end of the street as well. Come, if we walk quickly, we can satisfy that stomach of yours in thirty minutes."

As we turn the corner onto Splügenstrasse, two blocks from the hotel, we pass a small shop full of clothes. Without warning, I grab Vera's arm and drag her inside. We spend the next forty-five minutes trying on this and that, and generally acting like a couple of teenagers with Dad's credit card. The amusing part would be watching us in the dressing room, as we take turns holding the two guns, and the suppressor. Before we leave the dressing room, Vera hands me Yuri's loaded Tokarov, and the three magazines for it.

When we finally leave the store, we're each carrying three bags of stuff. We walk at a casual pace, laughing and giggling as we go. To see us, you wouldn't know we're spies on opposite sides, involved in an active operation no less. A few yards short of the hotel's entrance, Vera stops me.

"I must go in and register alone – for appearances. He *will* have someone watching. You do understand this?"

"Of course. You have the phone. Call me when you are ready for me to come up. I'm going to find a back way into the bar, have a drink, and see if anyone looks familiar. Everyone knows spies are always lurking in hotel bars."

"Okay," she replies with a laugh. "I will see you upstairs."

She takes all of the bags, and once she makes it to the hotel's entrance, hands them to the bellman at the door. I damn near laugh when, as I walk past her, she is explaining to the bellman, "I needed new clothes!'

Inside the bar, I take a stool next to the bartender, and with a smile, order a vodka martini. I hate gin. There are two things I need to do. Make sure he remembers me, and add confusion to whatever information he might share about me. In support of the second task, I choose to go back to my heavy British accent, and never give him a name.

Fifteen minutes later my phone rings, and the Caller ID indicates it's the other cell phone. To increase the confusion, when I answer, I switch to Russian.

"Алло?" (Hello?)

"Номер 326. Почему мы говорим Россию?" (Room 326. Why are we speaking Russian?)

"Сбить с толку, моя дорогая, сбить с толку. Скоро буду у тебя." (To confuse my dear. To confuse. I will be right up.)

"Knock only twice, so I will know it is you."

Without responding, I hang up and finish the remnants of my drink. As I am headed for the elevators, I make a note of two 'interesting' faces I pass on my way out of the bar, for future reference.

Five minutes later I'm lying across Vera's king-sized bed.

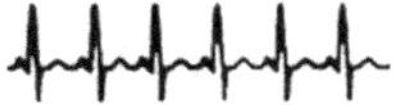

# 55

It takes us about fifteen minutes to cover the eight miles from Dübendorf to downtown Zürich. I'm watching the second SUV turn left off Bleicherweg, onto Beethovenstrasse with the FIS vehicle right behind it, on its way to the Hyatt, when my phone rings.

I know who it is.

"Hey, husband!"

"You sound stressed, babe."

"I'm okay. My brain is working too hard, that's all."

"So, what can I do for my wife today?"

"Tell her how her children are handling all this."

"Your son keeps asking when Mom is coming home, and your daughter is very concerned about you 'dying trying to save her Aunt'. She shared that with your father in a moment of weakness."

I suck in a breath and am overcome by a need to cry.

"But openly, for the benefit of the rest of us, she's her mother's staunchest supporter."

I feel myself smile, ever so slightly, and force back the tears building in my eyes.

"Her grandpa has assured her, however, that her mother is the wiliest agent in the entire CIA."

God, I love this man! And my father too, for that matter.

"So, what did you really want, Director Whitman?"

"Are you secure?"

"Totally – per Melinda's orders."

"I need info, without anyone knowing you gave it to me."

"Will this get me into trouble?" he asks, laughing.

"Well, I *was* told I have access to whatever I need."

Again, Chuck laughs.

"But, to answer your question, where I'm going could very well get us all in trouble."

"You have *all the lunatics* on the short bus with you?"

I laugh so hard that everyone in the car starts laughing too – without even knowing what's so funny.

"I'm going to tell them what you said butthead, but yes, we are a team at this point. You want to join or what?"

"Hell yeah! Is anyone going to be shooting at me?"

"God, I love you, Chuck Whitman!"

I lose the battle with my building tears and feel a few escape my eyes, and slowly trickle down my cheeks. I reach up and quickly wipe them off, hoping no one notices.

"Not that it matters at this point, the voice you asked about, does belong to your favorite Russian. We searched but couldn't identify the other player."

"Yeah, that figures. He's in this up to his damn eyeballs. But right now, I need to know everything *the Russians,* not just *my* bad guys, are up to."

There's a long pause – long enough that I check to see if he's still there.

"Chuck?"

"I'm here, Courtney. Be specific. I know you're looking for something in particular."

"Sokolski."

"I see. More specific, please."

"Everything he's done in the last fourteen days."

"Wow," he replies, as we pull into the hotel parking lot.

"Either you can do it, or you can't, Chuck."

"Silly woman," he says, followed by a muffled laugh. "Who's going to interpret the data once you have it?"

"Me."

"Yeah, right. Tell me what you are looking for and let me help, Courtney. Hell, this is what I do, remember?"

"Communications between him or, anyone close to him, and our target."

It's at this point I notice we're stopped in front of the hotel, and yet everyone is still sitting in the car, apparently listening to me, which makes me laugh again.

"You two go check in," I say to Cassie and Joey. "Howard has to wait for me. Slow down, breathe, and take a long, hot shower. I'll find you when I know something."

Suddenly, Howard speaks up.

"We're," he indicates the girls and himself, "going to the bar and I'm buying. You," he rolls his eyes and continues pointing at me, "I'm guessing, are going to sit here, in this car, and continue being your weird little analytical self for God knows how long. You can call the bar and ask for the 'drunk American' when it's safe to come up."

Then he opens his door, gets out, closes it, and with a very strange grin, waves goodbye to me. Cassie and Joey, both of whom are laughing, are out of the car and standing next to him almost instantly. Seconds later, the hotel's doorman, with two bellmen right behind him, walks up to the car.

Howard makes his point so I concede and get out of the car, the phone still to my ear.

"Ich heisse Christine Nelson, und ich bin mir nicht ganz sicher," (I am Christine Nelson, and I have a reservation).

"Sehr gut – die werden Ihr Gepäck holen" (Very well – they will get your luggage) he replies, indicating the guys following him.

"Bitte sagen Sie der Person am Pult dass ich gleich registrieren werde sobald ich meinen Anruf beendet habe." (Please tell the desk clerk I will be there shortly to register. I must finish this call first.)

"As you wish, Miss Nelson" he replies in English.

"Thank you."

"I gotta go, babe," I say to my husband, as I start toward the hotel's entrance.

"Okay, Courtney. I'll send you some stuff in the next few hours, via Melinda."

"And remember, *someone* is probably watching..."

"Gotcha. Once you get it, let Keith look at it too, okay? He's just like you with this stuff, so listen to him."

"I'll consider that one," I reply to his suggestion.

"Okay wife, you're being cryptic, which usually indicates an *'issue'*. You want to share?"

"Nope. Not until I'm certain. I do need one more favor."

"Sure."

"Tell the 'babysitters' I'm close again. Very close."

"You got it," he replies with a laugh, understanding what I mean.

"Love you. Bye."

I turn to the rest of them, now standing together in front of the hotel's doors, and ask, "Now, who's buying?"

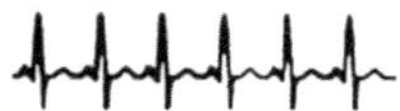

# 56

"I have a question," I hear Vera say, as I finish applying a little make-up to my face.

"Ask away," I reply, putting a band around my ponytail, and then covering it with a white scrunchie.

"Why did you not ask for a weapon?" She crosses the room, stops next to me, and looks at me in the mirror. "You know I have two."

"Because, I believed you would offer one, once you fully trusted me," I reply, as I spray my wrists with some perfume I bought earlier, at Vera's prompting, at the clothing store.

I always find it rather amazing, how simple things like make-up and perfume can adjust one's mindset, when in the middle of stressful situations. Feeling 'girlie', does it for me every time.

"Which I do," she replies grinning, this time handing me the Glock. "Is it time to set the stage?"

"I think so. If you are prepared."

"I am past prepared, Alex."

With an evil smirk, she pulls out her disposable phone and as I watch, she dials. Her call is answered quickly.

"Позвольте мне поговорить с Леонидом. Мне все равно кто вы. Если ему нужны деньги, он станет со мной разговаривать." (Let me talk to Leonid. I do not care who you are. If he wants the money, he will talk to me.)

She winks at me and then sits down on a couch next to the large sliding glass door leading to the balcony.

"Тебе нужны они обе, идиот. Они обе должны поставить свои подписи и предоставить свои отпечатки больших пальцев – лично и одновременно." (You need both of them, you idiot. They must both sign and provide a thumbprint – in person, and at the same time.)

I can see she's fighting the urge to laugh.

"Если не верите мне, спросите вашу пленницу. Я подожду." (If you do not believe me, ask your captive. I will wait.)

She covers the phone and says, "He truly has no clue," then quickly returns her attention to the call.

"Половина всего, что там есть. Это цена за убийство моего мужа. Торг неуместен." (Half of whatever is there. That is what getting my husband killed, will cost you. It is not negotiable.)

"I'll see you there," she replies in English. "One more thing Leonid. I am prepared to die today. Are you?" she adds just before she disconnects the call.

"You were correct, Miss Paddison. He agreed to my terms without hesitation. He *is* up to something."

I just smile at her and say, "Let's get something to eat."

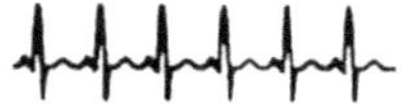

# 57

Once we register, I suggest we check out the rooms, freshen up, then meet in the bar for a before dinner drink, after which we'll decide where to go for dinner.

Everyone except for Howard, who mumbles something about being 'stuck with all the women', readily agrees. Even as he is turning toward the bar's entrance, I grab him and drag him toward the elevator.

"I might need you for something, now come on!"

Inside the room, I go to the bathroom, and Howard goes directly to the mini-bar. I know his increased stress levels are due solely to the impending recovery of the only woman he's ever been totally in love with.

I must admit that ever since I heard her voice, it's been wearing on me as well.

An hour later, Cassie and Joey knock on the door. We spend thirty minutes discussing the op, and another fifteen reading about restaurants in the area. Once we decide on one, we grab Howard and are off to the hotel's bar.

As I take a seat at the bar, my phone rings, making Howard laugh as he walks off toward an empty table, with the girls close behind. I flip the phone open and answer the call, only to find a wildly excited Melinda at the other end.

"Crap, Courtney, you aren't going to believe this!"

"Slow down, M. What is going on?"

"Your 'prisoner' checked into the Alden Hotel. You know, Vadym Kovalenko?"

"What the hell do you mean, he 'checked in'? He's still in the damn hospital at Morón, for God's sake."

"I pinned the reservation in the hotel's computer, Court. I made it appear to be a business request. The hotel's system sent me an email thirty minutes ago indicating the person checked in. I, unfortunately, didn't check it until just now. I was in the middle of something..."

"No shit? I have questions M and no access. Make this easy and help the boss out here."

"Sure! What does the boss need to know?"

"Who were the dead guys on the yacht, and did Captain Bell say anything about the whereabouts of the rest of the Russians? And not what he told the police."

"Hang on."

I nod at the bartender, pick up my drink, then turn toward the table the girls and Howard are at, and find myself face to face with a forty-something guy, in jeans, sneakers, and a dress shirt, grinning at me.

Max Rüegg. Deputy Director of the *Nachrichtendienst des Bundes*, or in English, Swiss Federal Intelligence Service.

"Nice jeans..." he says, still grinning.

"I may have to tell my husband you were checking out my ass, Max," I reply, sipping my drink, and glancing at the others, who are now paying total attention to the two of us. The looks on their faces tell me they realize something's up.

"Welcome to Zürich, Courtney." He turns, pulls out a chair at the nearest table, and motions for me to sit. "Let's chat, shall we."

I smile, and as I turn to sit down, Mindy comes back on the line. Max takes a seat next to me, crosses his legs, and listens.

"Egor Andropov. Active SVR asset attached to the Morocco unit," Mindy says, as I again sip my drink, "was found on the aft deck near the helipad. Yuri Glazkov. Active SVR asset out of the Odessa unit was found on the top deck of the engine room, and you'll like the last one, Boss. Fedor Orlov."

"*Jezzz!* Tarasov's second in command?" I blurt out, noticing the immediate response to the name, not only from Max but everyone at the other table as well.

"Yep. Shot dead in Alex's stateroom from behind."

"Fuck! The sorry bastards are in this up to their asses," I reply, watching Max's face. "What about the rest of them? Did they just disappear?"

"Well, the captain says Alexis, or your sister actually, put them off in an excursion boat in the dark while they were adrift. He also said that she left the yacht with Vera Kovalenko, in the chopper that Orlov arrived in."

My light bulb finally goes on.

"Okay, M, that will work for now. I'll check in once I get Keith's clone powered up. As excited as he got with the first one, I'm a bit concerned that it's going to be beyond my abilities."

"Yeah right, Boss" she replies, laughing. "As soon as Keith comes online, I'll sync with him. Anything else?"

"Actually, there is. What room is *Mrs. Kovalenko* in?"

This time, Max laughs, and mumbles "326..."

Melinda catches on the moment I make the comment.

"*Holy shit!* One sec... She's in room... 326. Do you think?"

I interrupt her mid-sentence.

"I'll bet you another dollar on it. I'll get back to you, M."

I close the phone, lay it on the table, pick up my drink, and take a big gulp.

"Sounds like an interesting story, Director," Max offers.

"You have no idea, Max, no idea..." I suck down the rest of the drink in my hand and then wave at the bartender.

"Can I get another one of these, please?" I say, pointing at the now empty glass.

"Oh, I have a pretty good idea. The Director of Intelligence, two Station Chiefs, and a guy who has been retired for quite some time," he points over his shoulder at the table behind us. "Should be an amazing story."

With a laugh, I go about briefing Max as to what has transpired so far, and what I *think* is going on. It takes the bartender two minutes to bring my drink, and although he didn't order one, the bartender sets a shot of something down in front of Max. Once he turns back toward the bar, I pick up my drink, Max picks up his, and as we touch the glasses in toast, out of the corner of my eye, I see her walk casually past the bar's entrance.

My height. My build. Very little make-up. Quite blonde – with her hair in a ponytail, but... *it isn't my face.*

Without warning, I jump to my feet, race across the bar knocking over two chairs on the way, and freak out the FIS guys sitting at a table on the far side of the bar. I turn the corner just in time to see her go out the front doors of the hotel. Once she disappears, I turn and am about to go back into the bar, when I damn near bump into a second woman standing behind me, watching me it appears.

*Vera Kovalenko.*

I force myself to ignore her, and quickly walk back into, and across the bar, stopping to right the chairs I knocked over.

"You okay, Courtney?" Cassie asks as I approach them.

"It was *her*, wasn't it?"

"Her?" Max asks.

"My sister, Max," I reply, fighting a laugh. I immediately pick up my drink and suck it down all at once.

"But... your sister... is... well..."

"Apparently not, Max," I say, turning to face Joey. "And what makes you think it was Whitney?"

With a grin of her own, she says, "The fact I was forced to turn my back and hide behind Howard, to be certain that *Vera* wouldn't recognize me when she stopped, and watched you walk all the way back over here."

I laugh and kiss Howard right on the lips.

"You guys remember what I told you about people shooting at us, right?"

"*Hopefully*, not in Switzerland," Max adds.

Everyone starts laughing, including Max.

"We're going to dinner, Director," Cassie says, "and you're welcome to join us."

"So, are..." Joey says as she looks around. "Damn! Where did they go?"

I laugh and turn to face Max.

"I assure you, Max, if she doesn't want to be followed..."

I'm interrupted midsentence, by Max's phone ringing. He quickly answers it, and after a few sentences in German, he laughs and hangs up.

"Apparently," he says, grinning, and looking me in the eyes, "you're right. *Neither of them* wants to be followed."

Amidst more laughter, we head out in search of dinner.

*Not* compromising my sister was the most difficult thing I've ever had to do.

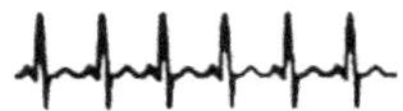

# 58

Sleep is not coming easily, so when my phone rings in the middle of the night, I'm on it immediately.

"Whitman."

"My room, Boss. As quickly as possible."

"Keith?"

"Yes ma'am."

"What time is it?"

"3:02"

"And I need to be *there*?"

"Yes ma'am. Please. I wouldn't be asking unless…"

"I know Keith, I know. I'll be there in fifteen."

"Okay."

I hear the click as he disconnects the call. I crawl out of bed, find my jeans and my sneakers, and slip silently into the bathroom to get dressed. As I'm putting my hair back into a ponytail, instead of my reflection in the mirror, I see my sister – the blonde I saw leaving the hotel earlier. Then, for just a brief second, I see Haleigh and Lyle looking back at me.

It almost freaks me out. Almost.

I shake off the feeling and walk back out into the room, being careful not to wake Howard. I grab my phone, and slip quietly into the hall, carefully closing the door behind me.

It takes me ten minutes to walk a quarter mile to the Hyatt, on nearly empty streets. I smile at the desk clerk as I pass him on my way to the elevators. I push the call button and the set of doors in the middle opens immediately.

When I reach the door marked 406, I knock gently. It takes five seconds before the door opens and I find myself looking at a very grim-faced Keith.

"Hey, Boss."

"Should I be worried, Keith?" I ask as he closes the door.

Five steps in, I understand why Keith has a suite. The place is full of electronics.

"Honestly, Boss? I am. But that's just me," he replies, walking across the room and picking up some stuff off a desk. "Here, look at this."

I take the pages from him, sit down on a couch that's right next to me, and start reading. I find three different lists. The first is a list of all outgoing calls made by Alice Williamson.

"That part gets really interesting on page five."

The second line, on page five, answers my first question. Even as I was grilling Kovalenko at Morón, two days earlier, Alice was talking to Sokolski – directly. Four separate times. By then, she knew we had a 'prisoner'.

We all have reason to be worried. As I suspected, we are in fact, being manipulated. The question is, why?

"This sucks, Keith. It *seriously* sucks."

"Yeah well, it gets weirder. Look at the highlighted entries on page seven of the second stack."

The second stack is a list of communications between a bunch of names I don't recognize, and one that I do. Boris Nikolsky. I do as Keith instructs, and find a list of calls made by Tarasov forty-eight hours earlier, all within minutes of each other, and all to the names I didn't recognize on the first page.

"Who are they, Keith?"

"Nikolsky, as you know, is the lone carryover from the Popkovich regime. As head of the State Security Council, he is the link between Sokolski and the President. The rest of them, as far as I can tell, are members of Tarasov's 'team'. Notice the second to last one."

I quickly scan the page and at the end of the list find what Keith is talking about. A call from Vera Kovalenko was made the evening before, about a minute before they passed me in the hotel lobby. Then I see the last entry.

"Damn. He talked to Nikolsky almost immediately after he talked to Vera. This is plain damn scary. Tarasov, a suspected renegade operative, talking to the head of the State Security Council."

"And," Keith adds, "doing it *very* covertly no less. Chuck – your husband I mean – did a sweep on all incoming calls to the Kremlin from outside the country. That's how they discovered all this. Tarasov used a burner phone with a Moroccan number. The man is either stupid or very sure of himself."

"I'd bet on the latter, Keith," I reply, still reading.

"You need to see the worst of the news, Boss. Last page."

On the last page, there are nine calls, all to the same three numbers over the last two days, all originating from Nikolsky's number.

"And?"

"Izmaylov, Popov, and Borodin are ex-military types who were 'retired' when Sokolski took over."

"And they are talking to Nikolsky because?"

"Very good question, Boss. When you figure it out, the answer *is not* going to be good."

I sit quietly, slowly flipping through the rest of the pages in the pile when something strikes me as strange.

"Keith, what's this number?" I point at a call made at 3:40 AM to a number halfway down the second page.

"I dunno – which stack is that?"

"Alice's."

He does some typing and then says, "It's an incoming to her private cell."

"Here it is again, six hours later."

I start looking for it page by page.

"Holy shit, Courtney," Keith blurts, spinning around to face me. "How could we have missed that?"

"What Keith? What did my favorite technological genius miss?"

"This is getting absurdly weird, I swear to God. That call originated on *Allison Paddison's* personal cell phone, about five hours before they were snatched."

"She was checking in. The second call was a covert 'it's going down' message, lasting eighteen seconds, and wasn't answered. If that isn't a blatant 'signal', I'll kiss your ass."

"Do you have some insight here? I'm confused as hell, Boss."

"No, Keith, we both know you aren't confused. You are far too damn good at what you do, to have missed this. You just chose not to mention it."

He suddenly goes pale and sits silently staring at me.

"How much of what I'm doing are you telling her?" I ask, now ready to call him out. When my phone rings, it makes us both jump. I pull it out, glance at the Caller ID, and then answer it.

"Hey, husband."

"Your problems just grew exponentially girl."

"By a power of what?" I ask.

"Four, at least. Ten minutes ago three aircraft left Moscow, none aware of the others. And, one is about to leave Dulles."

"Four is less detrimental than five I suppose. So, let's see just how smart your wife is. Alice is headed here."

"Yep, but that was a 'gimme'."

"Sokolski is headed here."

"Two for two."

"Nikolsky left just before Sokolski, from some non-descript airport."

"Damn you! How the hell do you do this? And yes, he used a government aircraft and departed from Tushino Airport, in Moskovsky."

"Same way you do what you do, dear, practice. Oh, and the fourth complication is the ex-military types that Nikolsky has been communicating with."

"Yeah. They left last, from Kubink Air Base west of Moscow. The base commander and Borodin served together."

"They're the wild card, Chuck. The thing I can't explain."

"Yet," he replies, finishing my sentence and laughing. "So, what did 'four is less detrimental than five' mean?"

"Hang on a sec and let's see if I need to explain."

I again make eye contact with Keith, realizing that he's far more intelligent than he wants any of us to know.

"You don't."

"Let me get back to this babe, while my brain is running full speed. We'll continue this later, okay?"

"Yes ma'am. And, be careful, wife."

"Always, husband. Always."

I toss the phone on the couch, stand up, walk to the large sliding glass door leading to the balcony, slide it open, and step into the cool air of a Swiss morning. After a couple of seconds, Keith steps up next to me.

"She did say you'd figure me out, I just didn't think it would happen this quickly. Can I ask how?"

"How do you think?"

"Probably AUGER. But then, it had to be done."

"That was the beginning. There were a few other things.

"What now?"

"You pick a side, Keith. Her or me. Based on some of the things you've done so far, like giving up your association with that damn encryption system, I get the feeling you want to be part of this op. I could be wrong though."

"No, you aren't, Boss. As I, *and she,* fully expected, your damn intuition is working just fine."

"Do you know why she's doing this?"

"No. My orders were to report. And well..."

"I know. You weren't given a choice. She does that."

"She did say that if compromise was inevitable, I should solely support you, although I'm thinking this probably isn't the conversation she had in mind. She *was* concerned with my staying involved. I can still help."

"I know you can, and I'd like to keep you. How long have you been working for her?"

"She recruited me out of college, just before the 'incident'. This, however, is only the second time I've been out here, where the real shit happens."

He pauses for a second as if to give me an opportunity to say something, which I take.

"Keith, you can rest assured that she knew exactly how this conversation would end because it's what she does. And, she is the best there is at doing it."

"Yeah well, she has some very capable competition, and the interesting thing is, she knows it."

"If you stay, you work for me. Period."

"Done."

"Does she know about those?" I asked, pointing in the direction of the phone records still lying on the desk.

"Nope, and I had no intention of telling her either. I figured you were testing me when you told Mindy to send them to me. Hell, you *do* have your own secure encryption point. Besides, you have what you believe are legitimate reasons for getting them, just as she feels she has legitimate reasons for her direction in all this. Like you said a moment ago, it's time to pick a side."

"And what about Chuck? Does she know we're talking?"

"If she does, she didn't hear it from me."

"This is all going to get very messy, very quickly, and I need a team, not a group of individuals. This conversation has to stay between us, understood?

"Yes ma'am."

"The others are *field assets,* Keith – they won't understand what I'm about to do. They need to believe we're a team. Right now, they trust you. Howard thinks you're the next best thing to crunchy peanut butter for crying out loud. If they discover your relationship with Alice... it could complicate things."

I stop talking, turn, and look him right in the eyes.

"I have to have the element of surprise on this one, and if trusting you turns out to be the wrong decision, Keith, people will die."

"It isn't. As God is my witness," he almost whispers

Without saying anything else, I turn and step up to the rail of the balcony, gently leaning on it. After a few seconds, I feel a jacket being slipped over my shoulders, and then Keith steps up next to me. We stand together quietly for about twenty minutes, watching Zürich slowly wake up beneath us.

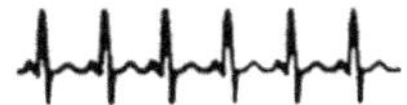

# 59

We're standing on the small balcony, looking out over a still-asleep Zurich, when I make my decision.

"It's time, Vera. We can't do this without some insight. I have to talk to my sister."

"But how can you do that? Leonid will not allow it."

As so many have to this point, her response makes me laugh.

"Not that sister, Vera."

"You have another?"

"Yes. The woman watching me, the one who rushed out of the bar. She's my sister. My twin sister."

"I do not understand. Your *twin*?"

"This," I turn to face her, and at the same time point at my face, "isn't mine."

Silently, and with a strange look in her eyes, she reaches out and gently touches my cheek, then moves her fingers along my jawline. After some brief contemplation, she comments.

"It is too perfect... how..."

"It's a very long and confusing story Vera, but I promise to explain when all this is over. If we are to have the upper hand with Tarasov, I have to talk to her."

She falls back into the moment, forcing aside the apparent confusion that's engulfing her.

"Your *twin sister* is a spy as well?" she asks.

"Actually," I reply, forcing myself not to laugh, "she's the CIA's Director of Intelligence."

Of all the odd things that can occur during an operation, what happens next surprises even me. The burner phone I'm carrying vibrates. When I pull it out and check it, I find an icon indicating there is an incoming text message. Still watching the confusion slowly spilling over Vera's face, I push the required sequence to accept the message, fairly certain I know who it's from.

In a matter of seconds, three words change everything.

### *'I have Kovalenko'*

I take a really deep breath, smile, and hand the phone to Vera. She almost collapses, and I have to help her into a chair, while at the same time, I watch her eyes begin to fill with tears. Seconds later, while she's still holding it in a vice-like grip, the phone vibrates again. She has the most confused and pathetic look on her face, and I find myself trying to understand what she must be feeling at this moment. Little do I know, it's about to get even worse.

"Accept the message," I nod at the phone.

Her hands are shaking badly, as she makes herself push the correct sequence of buttons to download the message. Then, she bursts full out, into tears. Hysterical, sobbing tears. I sit down on the arm of the chair, take the phone from her hands, glance at the screen, and find a close-up of Vadym Kovalenko lying in a hospital bed, apparently asleep, filling it.

I wrap an arm around Vera's shoulders and, with a goofy smirk on my face, mumble, "Damn, Courtney, you just keep getting better with age, woman."

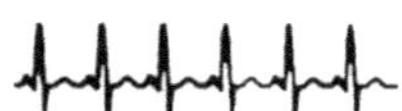

# 60

I think my means of giving Vera Kovalenko and my sister a reason to call me is a bit ingenious. I also know that by making her call me, Melinda will be able to get a trace on the call, and thus give me a location.

Captain Taylor, the nurse at the hospital in Morón, was more than happy to snap a photo of her patient and email it to me.

There are two options at this point. Vera is Whitney's accomplice or her prisoner. The fact that our side laid waste to the people at the villa, which I have to believe Vera knows about, is making me lean toward the former explanation.

There's no way at this point to be certain, so I send the message and the photo to get them to call me, and it works. In less than ten minutes.

"Courtney."

"I'm patching this through to you, Boss."

"Locate it, Melinda. I want to know *where* that phone is, understand?"

"Yes ma'am."

After several clicks and hisses, I hear her voice again.

"Hey, Sis! Nicely done. Very nicely done."

"Yeah, well, I'm still smarter than you," I reply.

"Some things never change, I suppose," she says, following it with a laugh.

"Nope, guess not."

As strange as it will sound, it's as if the last fifteen years never happened. As if we had seen each other the day before. As if we're just working another op…

I get a massive rush of goosebumps.

"So, how did you know?"

"That it's Vera with you? The captain said you left the yacht together. The rest was a gamble. *And,* under the circumstances, I'm pretty damn sure *it wasn't Vadym* who checked into the hotel."

"No shit," Whitney replies, with a deep laugh. "So, is the plan to 'retrieve' us?"

"You tell me."

Realizing that neither end of the conversation is secure, we're purposely being cryptic. Hoping she'll tell me what's really going on, I leave the response to her last question open, knowing she'll understand.

"I'd rather you didn't just yet."

"Your 'sister'?"

"Yeah. I'd at least like to give her a chance. You guys move, she's the first one that takes a vacation."

"And what, exactly, is she up to?"

"God, I wish I knew. I honestly do, Sis."

"I wish you did too. I'd feel better about your request."

"I believe this is about far more than money. It has to be."

"It is little sister. And it goes way up both food chains."

"I *knew* those assholes were involved! The second I saw Orlov get out of that goddamn chopper, I knew it."

She's pissed off. I can tell just by the sound of her voice, even after fifteen years.

"About Mr. Orlov…"

"Not my doing, Sis," Whitney blurts out, trying I assume, to tell me something.

"The Italian Navy is asking questions. They know the three of them are active SVR. The crew claims they were 'sequestered' the entire trip, never heard any gunfire, and were left on the bridge minutes before the chopper left."

I hear Whitney laugh.

"Like I said, not my doing. I was a prisoner, and I have a nice bullet hole in my leg to prove it. Someone else shot them. I swear! Maybe you should ask their bosses who killed them."

I'm not sure how, but I understand what she's trying to tell me, and why she's being so cryptic. She's protecting someone.

"And what about your new 'associate'? She's Russian."

"Yep, that's a fact, Sis."

"So, what are we doing?"

"Your team is watching for now. My team has the ball at the moment. I mean if you are willing to trust me on this."

"Hey, the boss tasked me with recovering *both* our assets by whatever means. The last thing I want to do is screw up and get one – or both – of them killed."

"Zero nine hundred tomorrow, Sis. You know where. All the players will be present. I'll leave the outcome up to you."

"Actually, not *all* the players. I'm still working on who the missing ones are, and who is actually on whose team. Just do me a favor, would you?"

"What's that?"

"Pick your team very carefully. Your niece and nephew really want to meet you."

"I've already met my niece, Sis," she replies, following it with a laugh.

"You did at that. See you on the other side."

I hear her disconnect the call, and realize I'm crying, but I don't care. All I care about at this moment is making this work, and getting my little sister back.

It takes less than fifteen seconds for my phone to ring again.

"Yeah?" I say, not caring who's at the other end.

"She's on the same tower as you Courtney. The tower's GPS said she was less than two hundred yards from you."

"Thanks, Melinda," I reply through my tears and close the phone.

As I suspected, she and Vera *are* in the hotel. Room 326, to be exact.

After a couple of minutes of staring off into space, I wipe my eyes, go inside, and find Keith tapping away at a keyboard, and Willie, who is now awake, sitting next to him watching.

With a grin, I ask, "So, you guys ready to do the spy thing?"

Willie laughs so loudly, that he probably wakes up half the hotel. Then, while Keith and I watch, he reaches behind his back and produces his toy – a shiny Smith and Wesson Model 500ES. Essentially, a portable .50 caliber canon, with a three-inch barrel.

Keith almost chokes on his coffee, making me laugh.

Willie, ever the smart ass, only has one question.

*"When do we start, Boss?"*

 Solution Squared: Recalculation

# 61

It takes Vera about thirty minutes to compose herself after my sister's little revelation. The instant she comes out of the bathroom, she has questions...

"Does she really have Vadym?"

"She wouldn't say she did if she didn't. Courtney isn't one for bluffing," I reply, as I pick up my jacket. It's a lie of course – bluffing is one of the things my sister does unbelievably well.

"And what will become of him – of us – once this is over?"

"My commitment to you remains in place, Vera. You are free to bail at any time, and I will make sure my side doesn't pursue you. As far as your husband goes, that's up to my sister."

"Very well. But whatever she may see fit to do to him, must be done to me as well, for I am every bit as guilty as he is."

"Vera," I take both her hands in mine, "what I need right now is the same girl who an hour ago, was filled with anger and a need for revenge. Let go of your husband for now, please. Savor the fact he is still alive, but go back to being the ruthless spy I met three days ago. Very soon, my friend, people will be shooting at us."

"Do not think for even a moment, Miss Paddison, that my attitude toward this operation or toward Leonid Tarasov has changed. And be very assured that, when the bullets begin to fly, I will be directly next to you, shooting back."

"Just make sure you shoot at the right people," I reply with a smile.

I am still looking at Vera as I open the door, and the stunned look that sweeps over her face, makes me turn and look into the hall. On the floor, directly outside the door, is a medium-sized box, sealed with tape. I hold up my hand to Vera, indicating she should stay back, as I cautiously squat down for a closer look. Seeing a note stuck to the top, I gently pull it off and open it. As weird as it will sound, even after fifteen years, I recognize the chicken scratch handwriting immediately, and let out a small laugh. I pick up the box, realizing that if Rhyan is here, Michael probably is too. I stand and go back into the room, handing Vera the note as I pass her. I put the box on the only table in the room, and carefully slit the tape sealing it, as Vera reads the note, then stands silently, watching. In the box are two subcompact Beretta Px4s, a Glock Model 29, and four loaded magazines for each.

"What does this mean?" Vera asks, waving the note.

"It's an inside joke, Vera. Suffice to say that my brother shot my sister once – a long time ago."

"Your *brother*? Is your *entire family* in this line of work?"

"In a roundabout way, I suppose you can say that. Here…" I smile and hand her one of the Berettas, and the magazines for it.

Looking totally confused, she sticks it into her belt next to her Glock. I put the Glock on my left side – as I'm a much better shot with my left hand, and put the Beretta where I can get to it with my right.

As I zip up my jacket, I look at Vera and ask, "Can you eat at this point? We have about two hours to kill."

"No, probably not, Alexis, but two or three cups of strong coffee cannot hurt."

I laugh.

"So, you noticed the coffee shop too?"

"Yes. It is habit, I suppose. I also noticed that it is on the arrival side of the bank – the street is one-way. He will have to drive past us when he arrives, assuming he comes by car."

"Well then, my friend, let's go have a cup or two of coffee and a bagel. I hate getting shot at on an empty stomach."

She laughs, follows me out the door, and into the elevator. Ten minutes later, we're walking down Dreikönigstrasse, which once we cross the bridge, will become Börsenstrasse – the street our bank is on.

Vera is nervous, I can tell. However, if I changed sides in the middle of an operation, I'd probably be nervous too.

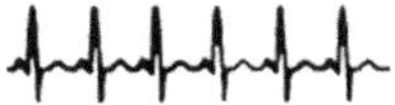

"The two operations of our understanding
are intuition and deduction, on which
alone we have said we must rely, in the
acquisition of knowledge."

René Descartes
French Philosopher
1596 – 1650

# 62

I ask Keith to roust everyone and get them to his room ASAP. While he's busy doing that, I pull Willie aside and give him a little task of his own.

"They will be leaving the Alden sometime within the next few hours. I need you on their asses, without getting made, and without losing them. I have to know where they are, Willie."

"Done, Courtney. How are we talking?"

"With this," I hand him one of the earpiece/microphone set-ups from Keith's collection of toys. "Keith will monitor it constantly. I'll be on in about an hour. If something happens before that, call me."

"Okay. I'm gone in five," he says, heading for the bathroom.

I turn and walk over to Keith, who's still diligently typing away.

"You need to be online with voice in about fifteen minutes. I just wired Willie and he's going to tend to a little task for me."

"I'm there, Boss," Keith replies, waving a headset at me with one hand, and clicking his mouse with the other. "He talks, I hear."

"Good. I need to make a call, and then use your bathroom, as soon as Willie is done. See you in a few."

"Okay, Boss."

I turn, step out onto the small balcony, open my phone, and hit the speed-dial sequence to dial the number of the phone Chuck gave my parents.

I know it's after midnight there, so when it takes four rings for someone to answer, I'm not surprised. The voice I hear at the other end almost freaks me out, however.

"Hey, Mom! Did you find Aunt Whitney yet?" Haleigh asks.

My entire life stops. Although my brain tries, it can't seem to make my mouth speak.

"Mom?"

When I hear her voice the second time, my heart – as well as my brain – engages again.

"*Haleigh Whitman!* What the hell are you doing awake at this hour?

"Jezzz, Mom, gimme a break. *It's Friday night!* There's no school tomorrow, so Gramps asked if I wanted to watch old movies with him. I was closer, so he told me to get the phone."

My own absentmindedness makes me laugh. I'm so lost in all the crap, that I don't even know what day it is.

"I guess your grandparents – specifically your *grandfather* – told you what's going on, huh?"

"Mom, I'm not dumb. I know what you and Dad do for a living. But yeah, Gramps explained what's really going on. Grams didn't want him to, but I kept bugging him. So, did you find her? Is she really still alive?"

"Yes, and yes. I talked to her a half hour ago, and we have a plan. If it works, *we* should be home in a couple of days."

"*Oh, how cool!!* I actually have an aunt!!" she screams. Seconds later, I hear my father's voice.

"She's just like her mother you know. I couldn't help myself. She needed to know, Courtney – she really did."

"Quit apologizing, Dad. You're in charge – and you did what you thought was best."

"And so?" he asks.

"I talked to her – a few minutes ago. It's definitely my damn sister. It was as if the last fifteen years never happened, Dad. It was very strange."

"Seems that weird thing you two always shared never went away, huh?"

"I guess."

"Can you extract her, Courtney?"

"No need to, Dad. This is no longer about what we originally thought – it's gone way past that. Although she's no longer a prisoner, I'm not sure what she's up to. It's a long, convoluted story, but if you wait a couple of days, I'll have her call you."

I hear all the air rush out of my father over the phone. After a couple of seconds, he composes himself.

"Please do. She has the mother of all ass-chewings coming and I fully intend to deliver it – uninterrupted."

"Okay, Dad, I will. Couple of days. Talk to you then. Bye."

"Courtney?"

"Yeah, Dad?"

"I know it's silly to tell you this but, be careful damn it. Do you understand me?"

"Yes sir! Bye."

I close the phone and stand crying, as I watch the sun climb from behind the mountains that surround Zürich. In my heart, I know how all this will end – how it has to end. *How I'm going to make it end.*

I go back inside, past Keith, and into the bathroom, closing the door behind me. I stand staring at my reflection, wiping the tears from my cheeks, wondering.

There's too much going on, and I can't seem to get my brain to work on a single thing. Instead, it's jumping around – from Nikolsky to additional bad guys sneaking around, to Daria and Alice talking secretly.

I wash my face, swish some mouthwash around my teeth, and run a brush through my hair. Finally, I pull my hair into a ponytail and wrap the scrunchie around my wrist, around it.

Time to go back to work. This is, after all, *what I do.*

As I walk back into Keith's little playground of electronics, two things happen. First, there's a loud 'buzz' from something, which I assume is an alert signal of some kind, and at the same moment, there's a knock on the door. While Keith tends to his 'crisis', I go and open the door. Standing in the hall are Cassie, Joey, Howard, Michael, and Rhyan. They all look half-awake.

As they all file in, I go back to Keith's desk. Halfway there I hear my husband's voice.

"Hey, Keith," Chuck says.

"Hey, Boss."

Sitting on the desk is a large monitor with the screen split – my husband on one side, Melinda on the other.

"Mr. Whitman, have you talked to your daughter lately?" I ask, stopping next to Keith.

He looks totally confused by the question.

"Huh?"

"'*Daughter*', Chuck. The damn-near thirteen-year-old girl who lives with you? Blonde hair, blue eyes? Ring any bells?"

*Everyone* starts laughing.

"Well shit, what has she done now, and how the hell would you know about it?"

"She answered the phone you gave my parents."

The look on my husband's face is priceless and completely gives him away. *He knows* – he knows that my father told Haleigh what's going on, and based on his response, I'm willing to bet he had a hand in it himself.

"We – *you and I* – are going to have a very long talk when I get back."

The entire room erupts in laughter a second time.

"So, Mr. Whitman, what do you say we tend to some of the government's business? Whacha got for me?"

He recovers rather nicely and steps right into it.

"Life at your end is about to get very weird. Sokolski will be on the ground there in about four hours. They've called ahead to Jet Aviation's facility for fueling, but insist no one will be required inside the aircraft – which incidentally, belongs to someone else in the Russian government, not to the SVR."

"Why?"

"Unknown at this time. Even our ears inside their system have no clue. He must be hiding from someone or something."

"What else?"

"The ex-military types landed about ten ago, in an older Lear 35 with Russian corporate markings. Interestingly, they landed at the airport in Basel, not Zürich. Melinda managed to bag a few surveillance photos of them picking up a rental car, but you'll have to find a way to get eyes on them again. I'll give Keith a couple of cell numbers that he can use to locate them if they use them again."

"Has Tarasov contacted any of them yet?"

"Not that we can tell."

"Isn't that just a bit interesting..." I mumble while my husband is still talking, but not loud enough he can hear it.

"But if he does, we'll capture his number and location for you."

"What else?"

"This is where I — and everyone here — gets lost. Nikolsky didn't use a government aircraft as we originally thought. He just wanted everyone to think he did. Once we realized our mistake, we did some very intense searching and found him about an hour ago. The plane he actually boarded — a private Lear 31A that belongs to some Russian businessman — is on the ground at Altenrhiein Airfield in St. Gallen, about an hour northeast of you. If he left immediately after he landed, he's probably already in Zürich — somewhere."

"Has he called any of the players yet?"

"Again, not that we can tell. We can't figure out his role in all this. Additionally, *no one* in his office is aware he's in Switzerland. The info we're getting is that he's in Vladivostok — which is where the government jet went — meeting with some members of the Russian Navy."

The moment he finishes talking, my phone rings. I dig it out of my pocket and look at the caller ID — Alice Williamson.

"Hang on guys, and listen in."

"Whitman. Yes, Alice. I believe so. I don't see a problem with the extraction. They're both supposed to be at the bank at 9:00 AM – with Tarasov in tow. Once they clear the bank, it should be simple."

I stand listening for a few seconds, and then again respond.

"Yes ma'am, quite clearly actually. Everyone involved I believe you said. As directed. When? Is there a specific reason why?"

Again, I pause briefly, then give her my final response.

"I see. If it goes as planned, I should have them there shortly after we get them back. Yes ma'am. Goodbye."

I close the phone and turn back to the monitors.

"Okay. You just heard half that conversation. Keith is going to play the entire thing back for you now."

Right after I sent Willie on his mission, I gave Keith very explicit instructions that he was to record every call – *in its entirety* – that comes into my phone, regardless of its origin. He was hesitant at first, but in the end, agreed to do as directed.

He looks at me, I nod, and he pushes the 'play' button.

*"Whitman"*

*"Are we secure, Courtney?"*

*"Yes, Alice."*

*"I've been reading the updates you are sending me. Are we on track?"*

*"I believe so. I don't see a problem with the extraction. They're both supposed to be at the bank at 9:00 AM – with Tarasov in tow. Once they clear the bank, it should be simple."*

*"This has become a very important and delicate situation, Courtney, and I am fairly certain, you must realize that I haven't been completely forthcoming with you about certain things. You do remember my last order to you, do you not?'*

*"Yes ma'am. I believe you said 'everyone involved'."*

*"And I expect you will carry that order out."*

*"As directed."*

*"Okay. I'm coming to get them."*

*"When?"*

*"I'm on my way now."*

*"Is there a specific reason why?"*

*"As I told you, Courtney, I owe them. I will be on the ground at Zürich International at approximately 10:00 AM."*

*"I see. If it goes as planned, I should have them there shortly after we get them back."*

*"I'll be waiting with the engines running, Courtney. Good luck."*

*"Yes ma'am. Goodbye."*

"Okay, there you go. She just blatantly admitted we are, and have been, operating blindfolded. What I need from all of you," I turn to look at Cassie, Joey, Howard, Michael, and Rhyan, all sitting in the living room of the suite, and then back at Keith and the monitors, "are your comments as to how we proceed."

Suddenly Keith starts talking.

"Copy, Ten. Standby."

He turns to me, offers me a headset, and says, "Willie."

I put it on, take the mic, and say, "One. Go ahead, Ten."

"Kovalenko and a blonde are sitting in a coffee shop across the street and roughly fifty yards east of the site. Instructions?"

"The blonde is Target One. Stay with them. We'll be setting up onsite in thirty. Let me know where you are when we get there, understood?"

"Copy that, One."

I pull off the headset and hand it back to Keith, then turn to face my team.

"Well?"

"What do you mean, Courtney?" Howard asks.

"Do we take them at the bank, get Whitney and Daria back, and blow off whatever else is going on here, or do we see this through?"

Joey stands, walks over, and stops right in front of me.

"This isn't the Courtney that saved my ass on a loading dock fifteen years ago."

"I agree," Cassie adds. "She wouldn't ask that question."

"What's going on, Courtney?" Howard asks, followed by a glare that cuts through me.

I stand looking at them and hear Chuck's voice coming from the speakers behind me.

"Talk to them, Court – open up. You're leading this team – and the decisions are on you. If they're going to do what you ask of them, they have every right to know what's going on in your head."

"Damn you, Charles Whitman," I mumble, as I walk over and drop into a chair across from everyone.

My husband knows me so damn well that, even from 4100 miles away, he somehow realizes I'm troubled, and for the benefit of the others involved, he calls me on it. I know it's the right thing for him to do. As I feel the tears coming, I know I have to share what's going on in Courtney's head.

"I'm tired guys. Tired of the stress. Tired of trying to out-think everyone else. Tired of operating in the dark. Tired of ad-libbing. Tired of dodging bullets – and making other people dodge them. *And...* I'm immensely tired of being used by my side."

I'm crying at this point, a line of small tears trickling down my cheeks. Howard picks up a box of tissues and holds it out to me. I take a couple, and after wiping my face, continue talking.

"And, as if all that isn't enough, I have a twelve-year-old daughter at home who just told me she *'isn't dumb and knows what her parents do for a living'. She's twelve, guys* – not twenty. This shit has become so convoluted that, well... I'm actually worried at this point. I'd like to see my kids again..."

"Fair enough, Courtney. You say take them and run – that's exactly what the hell we do. Pretty damn simple," Howard says.

"Yeah," Cassie quickly adds, "none of us want to end up dead either."

"We follow you," Joey says, placing a hand on my shoulder and sitting down on the arm of the chair. "Tell us how to do this, and that's what happens. Then, we all go home."

Then Melinda – being ever vigilant, and very quiet for the last twenty minutes – has a comment.

"Hey, Boss? Not to screw with the moment or anything, but you did say you wanted to know where Tarasov is, right?"

I have no idea why – perhaps it's just the way God designed me – but Melinda's question jerks me out of my funk and back into the insanity. Instantaneously. The mention of Tarasov's name seems to cause a reversion in me, and I switch back to Courtney Whitman, Director of Intelligence. I stand up, walk over to the console, and sit down.

"Yeah, M, I did. Whacha got?"

"Well, Miss Allison Paddison just checked into the Alden Hotel, and she has one 'companion' with her. A Russian whose *diplomatic passport* says he is Leonid Tarasov."

*"What the hell?"* I blurt out, inciting more laughter. "Just now, Melinda?"

"The registration is time-stamped four minutes ago."

"Okay, damn it. This is a huge pile of bullshit, and not only am I not buying any of it, I want to know *what the hell these bastards are really up to.* Did we ever figure out who made her reservation?"

"Yes, Boss," Keith replies, "We were wrong about Amanda. Daria made it herself, from her personal phone, and the call originated on a tower in Valencia, Spain."

The moment he stops talking, I become infuriated.

*"That sorry bitch!* If after fifteen years, she sold my sister out..."

"Now *that* sounds like the Courtney I remember," Joey says, as she walks over and stops behind me. "And she owes me a damn dollar too."

While Joey's comment does what she intended – eases the tension – it also flips one of Courtney's many mental switches.

"Oh shit…" I mumble, as my brain once again takes off.

"What, Courtney? Talk to us, girl."

"Why in God's name would she check into a hotel less than two hours before the meet at the bank, Howard? Think about that."

All of them, with blank looks on their faces, are staring at me, but not a single one speaks.

"It's *a message* Howard – Daria is giving us a heads up. *She's giving us Tarasov's location for God's sake!* That's why she made the damn reservation to begin with! She hasn't sold Whitney out – she's still trying to protect her!"

*"No shit!"* Cassie blurts out. "They could have shown up at the bank at 9:00, picked up the money, and disappeared. She somehow knows we're here, and are watching the hotel!"

"Fucking ingenious!" Joey offers, now excited herself. "And with one simple, innocent move, the lunatic set them up for us!"

"You two," I say, as forcefully as I've said anything in the last four days, pointing directly at Rhyan and Cassie who are sitting next to each other, "are on these idiots. Get downstairs and pick them up on Dreikönigstrasse, when they leave for the bank. Joey, you're on their backup – assuming they even have a backup. They apparently still don't know about us, so they may be operating on the assumption they're safe. Howard, you get to go inside the bank as our passive ears. Wait until they're inside, okay?"

"Gotcha," Howard replies.

"Michael, are you portable?"

"Yes ma'am."

"Find a high spot with an open field of fire that covers the entire street. Remember, we want to *stop the vehicle – not* put rounds inside it, so you need to position on the departure end of the vehicle. If they leave in separate vehicles, stop both."

Mike nods his understanding.

"Now, this is for everyone – *they don't leave the site*. Are we clear on that?"

One at a time, they each acknowledge what I said.

"Melinda, I need to know where the hell the Russians are. *All of the sons-of-bitches!*"

"I'm on it, Courtney."

"Keith, you make *damn sure* our communications stay up. No communications, people get dead – you feeling me?"

"Yes ma'am, like an electrical shock," he quickly replies.

"Get Melinda online with us so I can talk directly to her. She and I will be playing 'director' on this one. Hopefully, we can stay far enough ahead of them..." I let the thought fade into the tension of the room.

"Done," I hear Keith say, even as his fingers are still dancing across his keyboard.

"Okay everyone, the first priority is to retrieve our assets. Then, we are going to find out just exactly what this bunch of assholes is really up to because they have officially succeeded in totally pissing me off."

In the midst of all the rounds being chambered, and jacket zippers going up, I hear Chuck's voice in the background.

"Jeeez... sounds like Courtney's back."

I turn and look at his smiling face on the monitor, and not even knowing why I'm so angry, say, "You bet your ass she is."

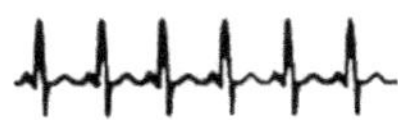

# 63

Unfortunately, for the members of my sister's team, I still recognize most of them. Although they all believe I'm dead, I have in reality, been moving in and out of their lives constantly for well over a decade.

I make Willie the moment I see his reflection in a window we pass. He's fairly stealthy in that he disappears shortly after we enter the coffee shop, but I know he's still here somewhere... watching.

I sip my coffee, watching the street outside, and considering our situation. Although gunfire is inevitable, I hold out hope that my sister and her team will wait until I get a chance to talk to Daria, before they start the 'retrieval' process. This has gone way beyond the money, and I need to know the truth.

Half an hour has passed when an obvious 'bad guy' walks past the big window in the front of the coffee shop, and Vera kicks me... again. Then we see the female – Tarasov's friend from the train – as she walks to the front entrance of the bank, stops, looks around, and then proceeds to the end of the block and turns the corner.

Of course, we both start to get antsy.

I lean over and whisper to her, "The good guys have us covered Vera – since we left the hotel. So, take a deep breath and slow down, okay?"

She starts to say something... then hesitates. She picks up her cup, sips her coffee a couple of times, and then turns to look at me with a goofy grin on her face.

"What?"

"Well, I was about to ask how you know that your people are watching us. Then, in a moment of clarity, the absurdity of the question hit me."

"You really want to know?"

"Yes."

"My sister – the *real* one – is running this operation, and as God is my witness, Vera, *nothing* ever gets past my sister. The woman is frighteningly good at what she does."

"Perhaps," Vera says, turning to look out the window again, "I will get to meet this sister of yours."

I laugh, and say, "Count on it."

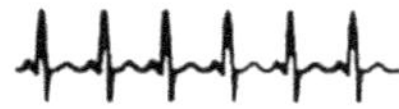

# ᗷᗩ

As I watch each of them go out the door at intervals, my mind is racing – it's in 'analysis over-drive'. I know I'm missing something – something important.

When Rhyan opens the door for Cassie, I feel my heart jump, and knowing I shouldn't, I make a comment.

"Rhyan, do something for me would ya?"

"What's that, Sis?"

"Remember that she's the spy, you're the solider. Please listen to whatever she tells you."

They both get my point and when Rhyan smiles at me, I also notice a quick wink from Cassie. I watch them leave, followed by Joey who smiles at me, before closing the door behind her.

"Sorry, Keith, but you're stuck with the boss. And yes, I'll probably be babbling the entire time." I walk over to Keith's desk and take a seat next to him. "I need someone who'll listen, and speak when they feel the need."

He laughs, never misses a keystroke, and says, "Babble away, Courtney, and if I have a comment, I'll make it."

"I'm missing something, damn it. I know I am. What are these bastards really up to here, and why are we involved?" I mumble to no one in particular, as I reach down and pick up a huge pile of paper from another chair, and begin to sort through it.

Back in Virginia, I'd have sorted out the entire mess by now – but that is a 'sterile' environment, with endless resources.

Now, I find myself thrust back into out-thinking the bad guys under pressure, and on the fly. *And,* just as she's been so many times in the past, my sister is at the center of my problem. 'Damn you, Whitney' I think to myself, and then actually laugh. The audible laugh makes Keith glance at me.

*"What?"* I defiantly blurt out, trying not to laugh again.

"Nuthin', Boss. I have Melinda on communications now."

"Yeah, okay. So, let's do this. Comms check from everyone."

"You got it," he replies, as I turn to face Melinda's image.

"Melinda…"

"Yeah, I'm here."

"I need to know where the Russians are. That's a priority right now."

"I'm looking for them as we speak, Boss."

I turn to the monitor with my husband on it and say, "Chuck, you gorgeous man you, keep us up to speed. You find anything that pertains, even if you only think it might – get it to us ASAP."

"In a heartbeat if not faster, Courtney. Be safe."

I touch Keith on the shoulder and say, "I know you're into the bank's security system, so let me see it on this monitor," tapping the one Chuck is on.

Instantly there's a crisp view of the bank's lobby filling the screen.

"Okay, Sis," I mumble, "tell me something. Anything."

Eight minutes later the ground assets report they are in position – Cassie, Rhyan, and Joey outside the Alden Hotel, and Howard down the street from the coffee shop – waiting.

Three minutes after that, Michael confirms he's found his spot and will have eyes on the bank in less than a minute.

The inevitable insanity starts promptly at 8:45 AM – when Mike announces the arrival of a black SUV at the front door of the bank. As soon as Mike stops talking, Cassie reports Tarasov has cleared the hotel.

For the first time in as long as I can remember, I am truly scared.

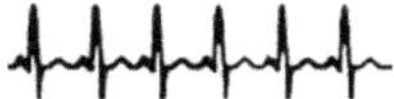

# 65

At a quarter to nine, a black Mercedes SUV pulls up in front of the bank. When, after three minutes, no one gets out, we're fairly sure of what's happening.

It's Tarasov's exit vehicle, and he wants to see if anyone is watching, and will blow themselves.

I smile at Vera, knowing that it's time – time to make our presence known to whoever might be watching. We stand and walk out the door, stopping on the sidewalk. Vera steps up close to my right side, keeping her hand in the pocket of her jacket, to give the impression that, although my appearance has changed, *I'm still a hostage.*

We hesitate for thirty seconds, then slowly cross the street, walking behind the parked Benz, and stopping in front of the bank's main door. Knowing Michael is watching us through his scope, I purposely make sure we're in the clear from above. I find myself hoping Vera's posturing isn't making him nervous.

Vera suddenly nudges me in the back and motions across the street, where Daria and Tarasov are approaching.

This is it...

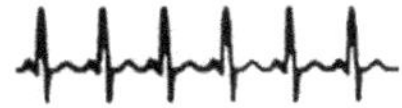

"The eye sees only what the mind is prepared to comprehend."

Henri-Louis Bergson
French Philosopher
1859 – 1941

# 66

"Five – Unit. Our Broker and Target Two are departing the hotel.

"Copy that," I hear Joey say.

It takes less than two minutes for the backup bad guys to clear the front door of the hotel, and Joey announces it.

"Four – Unit. They have back-up, and they look familiar..."

Then, to my complete surprise, a crisp new image of the intersection of Gotthardstrasse and Genferstrasse appears on one of the smaller monitors. Twenty seconds later, Tarasov and Daria appear around a corner.

"Alpha – Unit. I have two probables on the street. One is female, the other male."

The monitor filled with Melinda's face, changes suddenly, to a view of the street in front of the bank – from above.

"Camera on the roof?" I ask.

"Yeah. Let's see who Mike is talking about." I watch quietly as Keith manipulates the camera, and it zooms in on a female at the east end of the block.

"Don't know her."

"Yeah, you do, Boss. Think about it for a second."

So many images have passed through my brain in the last few days that I simply can't pull her face from the mess.

"You're gonna have to tell me, Keith."

He pulls something from a stack on the desk and hands it to me. It's the photo of Tarasov taken just after he left the villa.

"Damn. Nicely done, young man."

He's busily maneuvering the camera again, trying to find the guy, as I key my mic.

"One – Unit. The girl east of the bank is a definite. Repeat she's with our Broker."

Once everyone acknowledges my announcement, Mike has some input.

"Alpha – Unit. A black Benz SUV just pulled up in front of the building. All I am seeing is a driver."

"One – Ten. You're on the vehicle – for obvious reasons."

"Ten copy," Willie replies with a laugh.

Then, on the only big plasma monitor, mounted on a wall next to Keith, the bridge over the Schanzengraben (canal) that flows off of the Limmat river appears.

"What's this?" I ask.

"RF traffic cameras. They have them all over the place. I just had to find the frequency this one was on. They all operate within the same band range, so I can feasibly tap into any of them with some slight adjustments."

As the image comes into focus, I see Tarasov and Daria coming off the east end of the bridge.

"You're a scary man, Keith," I say, never taking my eyes off the monitor.

Next, we see the backup Joey is following as they crest the bridge, and when Keith refocuses the camera, I recognize both of them from the photos of the abduction. Their presence now makes me wonder where the other two are.

We continue watching as one of them crosses the street in the middle of the bridge, and takes up a parallel course, while the second stays behind Tarasov and Daria. The good thing for us – *they have no clue*. They're looking for Vera and Whitney – not us.

"Three – Unit. Our Broker and Target Two are slowing, and checking the area. She doesn't look like she's a prisoner, Boss," Cassie reports.

"Hey, Boss," Keith says, his fingers continuously moving, "look at what Mindy has to say."

A text message pops up on the monitor next to me.

```
I currently have eyes on the airport
via their surveillance system. A
Russian jet just landed, but no one has
exited yet. The really strange thing is
that the Basel group rolled into the
corporate area of the airport seconds
after the Russian jet stopped moving,
but they didn't - repeat didn't -
approach it. For some reason, they're
being very covert. They parked and
quickly dispersed, taking up positions
around the area of Sokolski's aircraft.
```

The military types are at the *Zürich airport?* My brain again begins cycling at full speed.

I turn to a machine next to me and start typing.

```
Intel - what about our third party? Do
you have a position on him?
```

Almost instantly, Melinda replies.

```
Negative at this time.
```

Then, my team goes to work.

"Alpha – Unit. Target One has exited the coffee shop. She appears to again be 'contained', and from my position, it damn sure looks like..." Mike lets the random thought fade.

"Five – Unit. I have eyes on them as well, and confirm Alpha's assessment on both counts," Rhyan says, following it with a muffled snicker.

"Two – Unit. They unlocked the doors – I'm making entry into the bank. I too, have eyes on the male 'probable'. Once inside, I will position on the west side of the lobby."

"Alpha – Two. Keep in mind that we still have a 'probable' bad guy in the Benz. No one has exited since it parked. Use caution when you pass it."

Howard copies Michael's transmission.

"Three – Unit. Tarasov and Target Two are crossing to the north side of the street."

I'm watching Tarasov and Daria as they cross the street at the intersection of Bahnhofstrasse and Börsenstrasse on one monitor, Vera and Whitney cross the street in front of the bank on another, and Howard deftly maneuver past everyone, and slip into the bank unnoticed, on the one in front of me. Even with all that happening, my mind is still on the situation at the airport. My eyes are locked onto one of Tarasov's 'back-ups', as he scans the area, but in my head, I'm hearing Howard's voice.

*'Verbalize it Courtney – it might help'*

I watch Tarasov and Daria approach my sister (who almost looks like my sister again – a fact that would normally excite me) and Vera, but my damn brain won't let go of what's going on at the airport. Although I hear Howard's voice say, 'they are coming in', I'm already talking to myself – out loud – making sure, of course, that my mic isn't keyed.

*"Damn it!"* I say out loud, garnering a very odd look from Keith.

"Boss?"

My brain is going so fast, I don't even acknowledge him…

"The head of the Russian State Security Council is here, and no one – including his superiors – knows about it. *Why?* The head of the Russian SVR is sitting in someone else's plane, at the airport, waiting for something. *Why?* There are three hard-core ex-military types at the airport, and not here at the site of their operation. *Why?"*

After hesitating a moment, I glance at Keith, and although not directing it at him, say, "And, the most bizarre question of all – *why the hell aren't they talking to each other?"*

I'm so caught up in the mess in my head, that I completely miss them entering the bank. I sit, a blank expression covering my face, staring at the small monitor next to me, as one bad guy crosses the street and begins a conversation with the other. I'm watching their reflection in the bank's window, completely lost in all the high-speed confusion filling my head, when I finally



Solution Squared: Recalculation

realize Whitney, and the rest of them, are no longer present. I again look at Keith, and he reads my mind.

"They exchanged some words, then went inside, Courtney. You were in a 'zone' so I figured it best to let you follow your thoughts," he says, with a slight smirk.

Then, something occurs to me – from somewhere I can't define. The thought is simply *there,* and I have no clue why.

"One – Intel."

"Intel – One. I'm here, Boss," she replies but is interrupted by Howard.

"Two – Unit. We're on the clock. The manager told them it would take forty minutes to gather the money together."

Each of the team in turn acknowledges Howard's message, except for me. I have another *'huh?'* moment, making my brain slam to a stop.

*"'The money'?* What the hell? They're getting it *in cash?"* I say out loud, to no one in particular. *"What the hell are they doing?"*

Keith only looks at me and shrugs. Then he shakes his mic with his hand to indicate that Melinda is still waiting for me. With a few blinks of my eyes, my brain reengages.

"One – Intel. Background on the Basel group?"

"Intel – One. I'm bringing it up now. Stand by..."

"One copy. I also need to know where the third player is."

"I'll have that in a second, Courtney," Keith offers. "Chuck's guys at Langley just captured the cell he is using. I'm working on a location fix."

"Alpha – Unit. This is weird. Targets One and Two are standing together, right in front of the window, and appear to be arguing."

"What are the other two doing?" I quickly ask, ignoring the call signs.

"Watching them," Mike replies.

"That's it?"

"Yes ma'am."

"Two – Unit. Target One seems very pissed off. They may be throwing punches shortly. If this is an act, it's a damn good one," Howard adds, in almost a whisper.

"Two, *do not* compromise yourself. Understood?" I pretty much order Howard.

"Two copy."

"Intel – One. You are too damn smart, Boss! They all three have a bone to pick with their ex-boss! So does his second-in-command, over a screwed-up op that he was responsible for. Care to guess who else was involved in the op?"

"DCI just touched down," Keith says.

"Copy that," I say in response to Keith. Then I key my mic and add, "Intel, was it our Broker?"

"Intel – One. Correct!"

"Hey, Boss," Keith blurts out, "the Third Party just called our Broker, and they're talking, via scrambled signals."

"One – Unit. Can you visually confirm that the Broker is on his phone?"

"Alpha – One. Confirm that. He's sitting there, watching our Targets argue, and talking on his cell," Mike responds.

Then yet another of the multitude of irritating switches in my ever-annoying mind flips, and in turn, it makes me start babbling again.

"We have four guys, all of whom have issues with a fifth guy, who turns up at the site of an 'off the grid' operation that one of the four original guys set up. By promising the fifth guy a great reward for his involvement, they lure him – *unprotected* – to the site. And..."

My thought process is suddenly interrupted.

*"Jezzz!"* Mike blurts out. "Target One just slammed her big sister into the damn window!"

*"What?"*

"Standby..." Mike says, followed by an extended silence.

*"She just bounced her head off the fucking glass,"* we hear Howard whisper.

"Three – One. Should we move?" Cassie asks, sounding way too anxious.

I glance at the middle monitor and find the two back-ups rushing toward the bank's entrance, with Joey almost on their heels.

"*No!* No one moves yet."

"*Damn!*" we hear from an excited Mike.

"Alpha – what's going on?"

"They are geniuses – both of them. It was staged, Boss. She sent us a message. I have no clue what it means though."

"Talk to me, Alpha."

"On her right hand at the base of her thumb, in black ink, Target Two has the letters ZRH hyphen YES, all in caps. Mean anything, Boss?"

On a different monitor, I watch Joey suddenly pull up short, acting as though something in a window next to her caught her attention. Once her back is to the bad guys, she keys her mic.

"Four – One. ZRH is the airport code for Zürich. I'm not sure what the other letters mean."

Then, in a moment of crystal clarity, my scarily analytical mind, now running on automatic, begins to put it all together. I know exactly what the hell it means. Although this is probably all an elaborate ruse to cover something else, it is in a way, very much about the money.

Moreover, having sorted through all the presented bullshit, my brain now tells me that the big picture is altogether *not*, what we think it is...

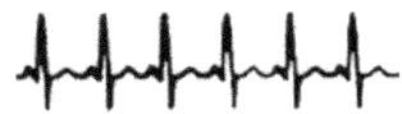

"God, I hope this works," Vera whispers in my ear.

"It will. Just relax and go with it," I reply.

It's then, out of the corner of my eye, I catch movement – it's the woman who scouted the bank earlier, and disappeared around the corner. She's approaching us from behind.

"We meet again, Vera," Tarasov says, releasing Daria's arm.

"Yes, you sorry bastard, we do," Vera defiantly replies.

"Why the hostility? You know that operations can go bad."

"К черту разговоры, Леонид, дай нам закончить наше дело, пока я не разозлилась и не прикончила тебя прямо здесь." (Fuck the discussion Leonid, let us complete our business before I become angry and simply kill you right here.) She jerks my arm violently, and says, "Inside – now," following it with a shove in the direction of the doors. "I wish this to be over quickly – before I find a reason to do something stupid."

Daria's eyes tell me an entire story in only an instant. She has a plan of some kind, even if she can't communicate it to me.

"Hey, Sis," I say with a British accent, forcing a smile.

"He knows," Daria says in English without any accent.

"Knows what, Sis?"

"Everything *Miss Paddison*, including why you are now blonde," Tarasov says. "Now, if you would join us inside, we can complete this difficult business, and you can be on your way." He holds out one hand and motions us toward the door.

"*I* can be on my way?" I ask, maintaining my accent.

"Let it go, Alexis," Daria says, with a quick eye movement in the direction of her hands, which are empty.

With that comment, Tarasov opens the door to the bank, then after glancing at Daria, turns to me and says, "Do I need to tell you the results of non-cooperation? Keep in mind, I have very little to lose at this point."

"No," I reply, stepping through the door and into the bank's lobby. Daria is behind me, followed by Tarasov, the new female, and then Vera.

I'm glad Vera is playing it tight.

Once inside, Daria takes my hand and leads me directly to the Assistant Manager's desk. We identify ourselves, are asked to take a seat, and are told she will be with us as quickly as possible. The others find seats across the lobby from us – Tarasov and the girl together, and Vera near the door.

The moment we're seated, Daria writes the word 'bug' on the desk with her fingertip – with a hesitation between each letter. I know she's trying to tell me Tarasov is listening – which explains why he's allowing the distance between us.

In less than two minutes, a well-dressed female walks up and takes a seat at the desk. Daria tells the Assistant Manager that we intend to withdraw the funds currently in our account in their entirety and that we need it in cash, which immediately gets her attention.

She takes our passports – doing a double take when looking at mine – and then produces a pile of paperwork, which Daria and I diligently sign and return to her. The final step in the process involves a digital fingerprint reader she pulls from a drawer in her desk. We're instructed on how to correctly roll our thumbs across the glass – with her assistance of course.

During the scanning process, I notice a group of letters on Daria's right palm, at the bottom of her thumb. Her earlier 'look' and directional eye movements now make at least some sense. When she sees me looking at them, she gives me a half-smile, then turns her attention back to the Assistant Manager.

Once the woman collects all the paperwork and a memory card from the reader, she turns and walks into the secure area of the bank, leaving Daria and me sitting alone.

"I am sorry that it has come to this, Alexis. But there are developments that you do not know about," Daria says without looking at me, which I assume is for Tarasov's benefit – he is, after all, listening to us.

"You sold us out? Why?"

"I had no choice. It is complicated..."

"Bullshit," I reply, hoping she'll look at me so I can gauge what she's saying, as well as why she's saying it.

When I see the bank's manager walking toward us, I also notice Tarasov's female friend has moved closer and is now within easy earshot of us. Seems she too, wants to listen.

"Ladies," he says, taking a seat where the woman was, "I do hope you realize this will take some time. It can be done, but not very quickly."

"Take your time," Daria says. "There is no rush."

"I hope Swiss Francs will be acceptable. This is quite a large amount, and to do it in another currency will make it difficult at best, to transport."

"With the proper conversion, Francs will be fine. Also, bill denomination is not important, as it is all going to the same place. I do, however, have one additional request if I may?"

"But of course, Miss Paddison," he quickly replies.

"Do not close the account. Please leave only enough to keep it open. The withdrawal is temporary. I will be depositing a larger amount in a few days."

"As you wish. It will take approximately forty-five minutes to complete the transaction," he replies, smiling. "Will you need an escort upon your departure?"

"That's what they," Daria indicates Tarasov and Vera, "are for. They are specially trained security."

"Very well. I will return shortly with your funds." He stands and exits through the same door the Assistant Manager did.

"We need some distance between us – before I lose my temper. I'm going over there," I say, standing and pointing at some chairs near the window on the front of the building. Daria is quick to follow me.

"Alexis... would you please listen to me?"

"Why? What could you possibly have to say at this point, that will justify any of this?"

I stop directly in front of, and only inches away from the huge window, my back still to Daria. I *know* I'm under Mike's crosshairs – I'd bet my life on it.

Without warning, Daria grabs my arm and spins me around to face her – during which time she quickly taps three times on my arm with her forefinger. My heart rate slows a bit in that instant because, by using our private code – one we devised years ago – for duress situations, Daria reaffirms that we're still on the same side.

"Damn it, Alexis. Shut the hell up, and listen to me."

Two taps, a pause, and two more, then she lets go of me.

'Play along'

"Leave me alone, Allison, you can't win this one," I reply.

She reaches out and takes my left hand, with her right. Once again, I notice the letters. Another quick eye movement and a new tapping sequence, tell me it's a message of some kind. She quickly raises her eyes in the direction of the big window – indicating, I assume, that we need to deliver it.

Apparently, *she too,* realizes that Mike's out there.

"What the hell is it going to take..." she starts to say with a raised voice, breaking my train of thought.

In a single beat of my heart, and one smooth continuous movement, I put Daria in the perfect position to deliver her message. I have no idea what the hell it means, but I figure I don't need to. I just hope they understand it...

*"Damn it!"* I yell, grabbing her left wrist, twisting it back, and forcing her to spin around – and right into the window next to us. Just as I knew she instinctively would, she uses her right hand to stop her face from hitting the glass – palm flat out.

*Perfect.*

Tarasov and Vera are on us instantly, as I press into Daria's back, holding her face – *and hand* – against the window.

*"Nothing...* do you hear me! Not a bloody damn thing! And be assured I will find you when this is over." I say loudly enough that it draws the attention of the few people in the bank.

Tarasov and Vera have us separated before the single guard makes his way across the lobby. As Vera spins me around, I see him – sitting on the far side of the lobby, reading something – and my heart stops.

After all this time, and what I'd done to him so many years ago, Howard is here – in Switzerland – apparently to help rescue me. I force myself not to cry, and yet, feel myself slowly slipping. Vera sees my lapse, and although she has no idea what's causing it, she quickly forces me back into the moment.

*"Look, you crazy bitch,"* she says, just above a whisper and with malice in her voice, "I care not about your problems with these animals. I wish only to get my money and be gone. If you do that again, I will kill you myself."

"Fuck you, lady."

Vera, much to the surprise of Tarasov, gets right up into my face and again speaks in the same low, menacing voice.

*"Do not* test me, Miss Paddison. As I have told you, I have nothing more to lose at this point. To simply kill all of you right here, right now, would be a sufficient means of vengeance. Be assured – I have no problem with the consequences of doing so. Now, *sit down and shut up."*

Then she turns to face Tarasov. "You," she glares at him, but points at Daria, "keep *her* on a leash."

I sit down in one chair, Daria finds another a distance from me, and I stare at her with murder in my eyes – or at least try to. It takes her a few seconds to slip in a wink and a small smirk.

At this point, I'd give anything just to know what's going on.

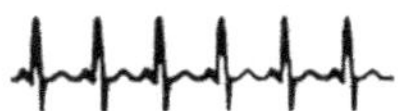

"Sex and beauty are inseparable, like life and consciousness. And the intelligence which goes with sex and beauty, and arises out of sex and beauty, is intuition."

David Herbert Lawrence
English Author and Poet
1885 – 1930

# ᠘᠘

Yakiv Egorovich Sokolski – YES.

I know he's at the airport – we assume to take possession of Daria Ladenko and what remains of his missing millions. What the hell is Daria trying to tell me?

"One – Intel. You still with us?" I ask, looking at the inside of the bank on the center monitor.

"Intel is here."

"What were the military specialties of our Basel group?"

"Stand by."

"Alpha – you still have eyes on the vehicle, correct?"

Before Mike can answer me, Melinda comes back.

"Intel – One. *Spetsnaz.* Two were regular Special Forces. The third was a sniper."

"Why the hell are three ex-members of the Russian Special Forces operating covertly at the site of an unsanctioned op that involves a bunch of active SVR assets? If they're here to support the op, why hasn't the idiot in charge spoken to them – *to any of them*?"

For a brief moment, my mind slips into perfect clarity, and my heart stops.

They're not here to support Tarasov's little adventure! In fact, and more importantly, *he doesn't even know about them!*

They're here for an entirely different reason...

That has to be it! *Nikolsky has his own agenda!*

Alice's presence during what I now *suspect* is going on, almost cements it. If I'm right, the tricky bitch also intends to take credit for it! I have to ask myself, *did Alice set it up, or is she using us to stop it?*

The latter makes far more sense in means of playable chips on the table, in this endless poker game we're all locked into.

"One, are you still with us?" I hear Cassie ask me, as Keith places a hand on my shoulder.

"Where is she, Site?" Joey asks.

When I don't respond to Cassie or Joey, Keith gives my arm a gentle squeeze.

"Talk to us, Courtney – what are they up to?"

"Check something for me," I say turning to look at Keith. "What was Nikolsky's position during the Padorin debacle?"

Although I turn my attention back to the monitors, I can hear him scorching his keyboard behind me. After a few more seconds of quiet contemplation, knowing I need to share my thoughts, I key my mic.

"None of this is what it appears to be. The kidnapping *and* the money are a ruse, people. I believe this entire evolution has been designed to get Sokolski to come here unprotected. *And,* at this point, I'm pretty sure Tarasov isn't running this op."

"He was Boris Alkaev's number two guy, Boss," Keith says, the moment I stop talking. "He has some sketchy, connections to several fairly powerful individuals, most notably, the Deputy Chief of Presidential Administration. He's also on the Prime Minister's shortlist."

"No shit? Get me Chuck, *right now*, Keith – securely."

"Yes ma'am!" he instantly replies. "I thought you might so I kept the connection open."

Less than five seconds later, my husband's face is filling the main monitor.

"You want me gone, Boss?"

"No, you knucklehead – I meant a *secure connection*. Just be quiet." I turn to face my husband's image. "Chuck, I need the secret dirt on Nikolsky and Alkaev. At this point, I know there is some. What can you tell me?"

Chuck laughs and with a matter-of-fact tone says, "Crap, that's easy. Alkaev promised Nikolsky the job Sokolski now has. That one was all over everyone's radar."

No sooner than the words enter my ears, I have a second moment of clarity – this one even sharper than the first – and even Keith notices it.

"No shit... the boss just had an epiphany..." he mumbles.

"Keith, has *anyone* besides Nikolsky been in contact with the ex-military types?" I ask, again turning to face him. At this point, my brain is three steps ahead of the question I just asked.

Keith is once again typing faster than I would have thought humanly possible, as I key my mic.

"Everyone just stand by for a sec. Intel, you here?"

"Intel is online."

"Call me, securely. Now."

It takes less than fifteen seconds for my phone to ring.

"Mindy, I need you to check something, and it has to be done fast – like in the blink of an eye."

"Whacha need, Court?"

"I need you to search those phone files. I need to know if Alice has spoken directly to Nikolsky in the last sixty days."

"I'm on it."

I turn and first look at my husband, then turn to watch Keith, placing a hand on his shoulder.

"Switzerland is neutral. He would have no reason to think anything was amiss. He thinks he is getting his renegade and his money back. No reason to bring his security detail. Hell, he probably won't leave the plane! Besides, if things go south, he was never here."

"Courtney?" I hear Chuck say behind me.

"The only link appears to be between the henchmen and Nikolsky. He has talked to one of them three times in the last twenty-four hours," Keith says, turning to look at me.

"Surveillance. Find me some real-time images of the airport you damn genius! Quickly!"

Then Melinda in my ear.

"Intel – One. The answer to your question is no. Do you need more specifics?"

"Not right now, Intel," I reply, as a huge satellite image of the airport fills the big monitor, and Chuck is just as quickly relegated to one of the lower corners.

Melinda's response answers one of my questions and lets my heart slow down – a lot.

*Alice didn't set him up.* We are in fact, here to be 'saviors'.

The moment I see the complete overhead satellite image of the airport, I know – or at least *think I do.*

*"God help us..."*

I turn and make direct eye contact with Keith.

"Can the stupid bastard actually be *this* crazy?"

"*What?* What's going on, Boss?" Keith asks, his stress level evident in his voice.

"Keith, where's your vehicle?" I ask, ignoring his question.

"It's in lower level parking, space C2. Keys are above the visor."

I lean over and kiss him smack on the lips, with my husband watching and laughing, and then again, I key my mic.

"One – Unit. We're changing sites. Alpha, I need you on the street – quickly."

"Alpha – One. Repeat?"

"*Just fucking do it, Michael. NOW!* Five and Ten – get your butts, to the intersection of Börsenstrasse and Bahnhofstrasse, around the corner and out of sight of the bad guys. I'm going for the truck and will pick you up in five. Do you copy?"

Each of them responds with a sharp "Copy that".

"Girls, you and the old guy are on our original targets. If you think for any reason they are at risk, *take appropriate action.* Copy?" I say as I open the door to the room.

"Copy," I hear Joey say, followed by Howard, then Cassie.

Now standing in the open doorway, I turn to face Keith.

"You sir, are on the second vehicle – which means you need to get your ass over to the other hotel and retrieve it," I say, handing him the valet ticket.

"I'm there, Boss," he replies with a big grin, pulling off his headset and tossing it onto the desk.

"Two things, Keith. First, take a comm set – they need to be able to talk to you. Second – *and very damn important* – stay out of sight until one of them calls for transportation. *Clear?*"

"Crystal clear, Courtney," he replies, clipping a mic to his collar and placing one of the small buds into his left ear.

"Good, let's go."

We get into the elevator together, but he exits on the ground floor while I continue to the basement parking levels.

"Alpha, Ten, Five – where are you guys?" I ask, pulling out into the bright morning sun and making a quick right turn onto Beethovenstrasse, then merging with traffic.

"Five and Ten are on the southeast corner. Alpha is en route to our location," I hear Rhyan say.

"One – Intel. You still with me?"

"Yes ma'am," Melinda replies.

"Surveillance of the airport. Site showed me one good view, but I need eyes on it constantly. Can you do anything for me?"

"I have it up on three monitors, Boss. His plane. Her plane. And a bunch of guys trying to look like they belong there."

"Nicely done M. Be very diligent on this one. Your dinner date could very well be affected. Copy?"

I hear a couple of chuckles following my comment.

"Yeah, Boss, I copy. What, exactly, am I watching for?"

"Anything *any* of those assholes do – got it?"

"Yes ma'am!"

"And find Nikolsky – please?"

"I'm trying Courtney, honest to God, I'm trying."

"One – Unit. Is Alpha on location yet?"

"I'm here," I hear a breathless Michael say.

"I'm crossing the canal. Will be there in thirty."

"Site – One. I'm in the truck."

"Copy that. Move to the area and stand by," I reply, as I pull up next to Rhyan, Michael, and Willie. "One – Two. Your ride is standing by."

"Copy that," Howard whispers.

"Unless the bad guys start shooting, *we don't*. Copy that?"

One at a time, each of them acknowledges my order.

"So, we let them leave, One?" Cassie asks.

"Yes, but stay on them. Say his name, and Site is there with your ride – instantly."

"You and the boys?" Joey asks.

"We're going to the airport, to see if we can't screw up Nikolsky's little plan," I reply as Willie closes the last door.

"Talk to us, Sis," Rhyan says as I step on the gas.

"Let's think about this. *Tarasov is an active asset*. The man has access to numerous untraceable professional back-ups or even killers. Assuming you were to find three Russian Special Forces guys and you were able to convince them to join your 'unsanctioned' op, why do you have a girl and those two idiots," I point back in the direction of the guys leaning up against the Mercedes SUV, "helping you?"

"Good fucking question, Courtney," Willie responds.

"For at least the last hour, my brain has been locked on to one thing – if they aren't here to support Tarasov, why in the hell are *three armed, ex-military types* covertly loitering at the airport."

"She's in her zone, Sarge," my brother says from the back seat, a sinister little smirk covering his face.

"*Nikolsky...*" Michael says. A glance in the mirror gives me a frown on his face. "He's still really tight with Borodin."

"Damn! *Tarasov doesn't know about them!* They're using him and all his people!" Willie says, his brain starting to lock into my theory. While Mike and Rhyan are 'soldiers', Willie is, like me, *a spy,* and his mind easily follows where my thoughts lead him.

I smile at Rhyan in the rearview mirror and continue.

"And, what would be the only other thing you'd need to put your assassination plan in motion?"

*"Assassination?* What the fu..." Michael starts to say, but Willie cuts him off.

"*Cash.* Untraceable cash to pay the assassins. Courtney, you are a goddamn genius, woman! Nikolsky wants the money to pay his bills – he could give a shit less about Tarasov and his team. I'll bet Borodin intends to take all of them out as well..."

"And just who is it he intends to remove, Sis?" Rhyan asks, still looking a bit confused.

"His competition."

Then we hear Howard in our ears.

"Two – Unit. The manager just told them ten minutes."

I key my mic and say, "Copy that. Site, are you in position?"

"Standing by, Boss – with a clear view of the Benz, and the two knuckleheads loitering next to it."

"Keep me up on what's happening, Site."

"Yes ma'am," he replies.

"What are *we* going to do, Sis?"

"You," I look at Michael in the rear-view mirror, "are going to find the highest point you can safely reach. You're looking for your counterpart. Melinda has already confirmed he's here – Spetsnaz no less. You are not only smarter than he is, you're a much better shot Michael, but if he gets even one round off..."

"Won't happen, Court."

"You two," I continue, pointing at Rhyan and Willie, "are now our 'recon'. We need eyes on the other two – and you won't have much time to do it. When you find them, do what it is you do. Neither of them gets to play today. Understood?"

"Yes ma'am."

"I'm going to make sure Tarasov doesn't do anything stupid once he discovers the guy he's working for, sold his sorry ass out to further his career." I give my Px4 – which is lying on the console – a gentle pat. "No matter what else happens, guys, we *do not* let them kill Sokolski."

"Gotcha, Courtney," Willie replies.

Nine minutes later, we pass through the access gate into the general aviation area of the Zürich airport.

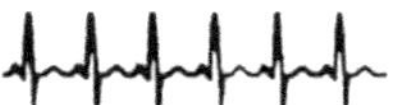

 Solution Squared: Recalculation

# 69

When I see the bank manager approaching the desk with two shiny attaché cases, I quickly glance around the lobby in search of Howard but don't see him.

*What the hell are they doing?*

Daria sees me looking around, and her face tells me she too, wonders what their plan is. She looks close to panic – as if something might happen that will screw up whatever she's up to. The moment Tarasov's associate turns her head away from me, I give Daria a quick wink. She raises her eyebrows as if to say 'are you sure?'

Once we sign on the appropriate lines, the manager takes a second to explain how the high-tech attaché cases work. Being digitally security enabled, they can only be opened with both a nine-digit numeric combination, and our thumbprints – which were downloaded from the card the female took with her. The interesting thing is that it will take both of us, *at the same time*, to do it. The manager calls it 'an added level of security'. We thank the manager, Daria tells him she will return in a few days, and we each pick up one of the cases.

It never occurs to me at the time, to inspect the contents.

Silly me.

As we turn towards the front doors, my eyes find Howard – standing in a corner, with a slight smirk on his face. I make eye contact with him and get a covert nod.

Daria and I cross the lobby and go out the front doors, led by the female and followed closely by Tarasov and Vera. There are two guys leaning against the SUV parked at the curb, and one of them immediately opens the back door.

Tarasov passes us, gets in, and slides across the seat. He then motions for Daria to enter, and I watch as she slides over next to him. The female gets in on the front passenger's side, telling me there must already be a driver, that I can't see.

I feel Vera grab my arm and stop me.

"You can't be serious, you idiot," she blurts out, her hand firmly gripping my arm – the one holding the money.

"Do not draw attention to us, Vera, just get in."

"Like hell, I will! You fully intend to dispose of me and I know it. It is my belief you intend to dispose of these two as well. *I am not going anywhere with you,*" she yells.

When the guy holding the door starts to move, it takes only the blink of an eye for Vera's Glock to appear, pointed directly at Tarasov.

"And if that asshole takes one more step, you die – right here, right now. Am I being clear?"

"Vera, you are in far over your head – trust me on this. This has never been the 'operation' you were led to believe it is. If you do this, you will be signing your death warrant."

Then, Daria gives us some insight – as bizarre as it is.

"Vera, Leonid is my biological brother. He has set in motion a plan to take our country back to its glory of previous years. There is a place for you, if you will trust us."

She's talking to Vera but is looking directly at me, which I take to mean she wants me to react.

"Your *brother?* What the hell is going on?" I blurt out, in clear concise English, with no hint of an accent, trying to agitate the situation.

"Be quiet, Alexis," Daria says, with a quick movement of her eyes, in the direction of the case I'm still holding.

I'm forced to assume, based on available information, that she needs the *money* in the truck.

*"What the hell have you done, Daria?"* I yell, using her real name and trying to get to her inside the truck. Vera violently

jerks me back, which I use as an excuse to drop the case, which in turn lands on the floor of the truck.

Then, for some unexplained reason, when Vera sees me drop the case, she shoves me aside and leans in to retrieve it herself. Her move is apparently exactly what Daria wants – as if she expected that's what Vera would do. She quickly reaches over, and as she jerks the gun from Vera's hand, it discharges a round through the roof of the SUV. At the same time, Tarasov grabs her by the shirt and jerks her partially into the truck. Almost instantly, the truck speeds off, the door still open, and Vera's feet partially hanging out. The guy holding the door, instantly finds himself lying on the sidewalk, and the guy behind it almost hits the pavement as well.

Even as I watch the truck make a wild left turn a block away, onto Stadhausquai, the Glock is in my left hand, pointed at the guy on the ground. My lack of attention almost costs me big time.

When I hear the double report, I automatically assume it's being directed at me. The very next second, Cassie appears from nowhere and is all over the guy on the ground, twisting his arms around behind his back. I quickly turn to look behind me, to see who was shooting, and find myself face to face with Howard Jensen – the only man I've ever truly loved. I feel the tears coming...

Between us, lying face down in the street is the other bad guy – quite dead. In Howard's hand is a .40 caliber Glock.

"I lost you once, Whitney – fuck doing it twice."

I throw my arms around his neck and squeeze him harder than I've ever squeezed anyone in my entire life. Then, the tears come. En masse.

Seconds later I hear Cassie's voice from somewhere behind me – almost screaming.

*"Now Keith! Come get us now!"*

When the shit starts, the bank's lone security guard quickly finds himself outclassed, as well as very out-gunned. He pulls his weapon and takes two steps outside the front doors just as Howard's shots ring out. When he turns around, he discovers the business end of Joey's Beretta. She speaks to him forcefully, and in perfect German.

"Hören Sie genau zu. Wir sind vom amerikanischen CIA. Wir arbeiten an einem Projekt. Legen Sie Ihre Waffe weg und suchen Sie das Bankpersonal. Wenn die Polizei ankommt, erzählen Sie ihr, was ich Ihnen gerade erzählt habe. Haben Sie verstanden?" (Listen carefully. We are American CIA. We are working a project. Put your weapon away and go look after the bank staff. When the police arrive, tell them what I have just told you. Understand?)

His response is instantaneous.

"Ja, ich verstehe Sie." (Yes, I understand) he replies, his face instantly awash with relief – the relief of not having to be involved in any gunplay. He quickly holsters his weapon and steps back into the bank's lobby.

I glance to my left and see Cassie hog-tying the still-breathing bad guy with tie-wraps, and at the same time hear the squealing tires of a bright blue Mercedes SUV as it skids to a stop in the traffic lanes, inches from the guy Howard shot.

"Everyone in – *now!* They have a three-minute lead on us," Joey says, opening the driver's door and all but pushing the guy driving into the passenger's seat and taking the wheel herself.

"What about them?" Howard asks, pointing at the bad guys, as he reaches out and opens the back door of the truck.

"Swiss police are on the way. The bank guard and I came to an understanding," Joey replies with a smirk, pulling her door closed.

The moment everyone is in, Joey starts driving – like a woman possessed.

Forty-five seconds after Cassie yelled for our ride, we're in hot pursuit of the other SUV.

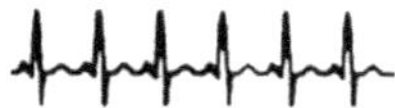

# 70

*"Holy crap!"* Keith blurts out, "All hell just broke loose! The bad guys just bolted."

I find myself hoping one of them will say something, but know better. When the stupidity begins, more often than not, talking isn't part of the procedure.

"Stay put, Keith. *Do not* move until they tell you to. The last thing I need is my computer geek getting killed."

*"Oh shit!!* Two just shot one of the bad guys. He was about to shoot Target One... oh shit..."

Rhyan keys his mic and says, "Easy Site – deep breath man. This is what we do, dude. Relax, okay?"

Then we hear Cassie.

*"Now Keith,* come get us now!"

Having turned onto the access road leading to the General Aviation entrance of the airport, I pull onto the grass beside it and stop.

"We have recovered Target One, and are en route to the airport. Be advised, the bad guys still have Target Two."

The moment I hear Howard say that they have Whitney, my heart stops, my eyes well up, and all the air rushes out of me. All the guys notice my demeanor change, and Rhyan places a hand on my shoulder.

"We aren't finished yet, are we, Sis?"

His words force my brain to reengage, and I wipe a few tears from my cheeks.

*"Oh hell no we aren't.* If I am going to be used, I damn sure will find out by whom, and why."

"One – Two. Let me talk to Target One."

It takes fifteen seconds before I hear my sister's voice.

"Target One. Go ahead, Sis."

"Who's in the truck, Whit?"

"This one or the other one?" she asks, following it with a snicker. All the guys laugh, and I figure everyone in the other truck does as well.

"Still the smartass, I see."

"You grew up, Court, I never did. To answer your question, a female I don't know, and a driver – who was part of the abduction team I think – are up front, Tarasov, Daria, and Vera are in the back. Sis, I swear to you, Vera is a good guy at this point."

"I assumed as much – you can't kill your own team unless you intend to change sides. I'm pretty sure that's a rule."

"HA! You caught that did you? Very impressive."

"Smartass..."

I hear the guys laugh – again.

"I'm putting our intrusion team on the ground at the airport. What's your ETA?"

"They're about two minutes ahead of us, One. We should arrive about the same time they do," Cassie says.

"Copy that. Now, pay attention. *No one starts anything!* We let the intrusion team make the first move. Is everyone clear on that? Alpha has to find their shooter before we do anything."

Then out of nowhere, we hear Melinda. She's been so quiet, I honestly forgot she was on with us.

"Intel – Alpha."

"Alpha – Go Intel."

"I have your shooter."

*"What?"* Mike and I say at the exact same instant.

"Let me draw you a picture, guys. I have three aircraft on the ground. Our boss is on the tarmac outside the Business Aviation center, on the north side of runway two-eight. There is a second Lear there, but it's a private aircraft. Across the runway at the General Aviation center, a Russian Gulfstream – complete with the appropriate government markings on the rudder – is parked, engines idling. No one has entered or exited that aircraft in the eleven minutes I've been watching it."

*"And?"* I ask, prompting her.

"Now, about your bad guys. The shooter has opted for a perch with a totally clear view of the Russian aircraft, rather than the highest point in the area. He is on top of one of the General Aviation buildings at the south end of the runway."

"Damn Melinda, you've been a busy girl!" Michael offers. Until this point, he too, has been unbelievably quiet.

"That's what I get paid for," she replies, laughing. "But, as I was saying, the shooter has a totally clear line of sight to the Russian aircraft and the boss's aircraft as well."

"Satellite stuff, M?"

"Yeah, that's how I found the shooter – and you guys. You're on the grass about fifty yards inside the perimeter gate just off the motorway. I found the other two idiots using the airport's security system. Although they're dressed as airport employees, I'm surprised the Swiss haven't suspected anything yet – based solely on their very questionable behavior."

"Can we get to them?" Rhyan asks.

"Sure," Melinda replies, "where are you sitting?"

"Front passenger."

"Alpha, give him your optics."

"Yes ma'am."

I watch in the rearview mirror as he snaps the scope off his latest 'toy' – an Israeli made M89-SR – and hands it to Rhyan.

"Step out of the truck, Senior Chief, and focus on the two long buildings to the right of the center of the truck."

"Copy. Standby."

We watch Rhyan get out and do as Melinda instructs. After a few seconds of silence, Melinda continues.

"The split in the center of the building – Got it?

"Yep!" Rhyan replies

"Watch the area between the large truck and the luggage transporter for a couple of seconds."

"Well, no shit," we hear Rhyan say. "And the other one?"

"Out of your field of vision. He's between a fuel truck and the end of the freight building. He needs to be the number two priority – he has artillery," Melinda says. "You see the five-story building to the left of your target?"

"Yes ma'am," Rhyan replies.

"That's where your shooter is – northeast corner, currently sighting the Russian aircraft."

Rhyan climbs back into the truck and after looking at me, once again keys his mic.

"What kind of artillery are we talking about here?"

"Size of the case, I'm guessing disposable rocket – probably has two of them. The case is lying on a baggage cart next to his position."

"Copy that."

"Jezzz, they came to start a damn war," I mumble, blankly staring in the direction of a building in front of us.

Finally, the ever-quiet Willie speaks up.

"Time to deliver us, so that we can do our thing. Right over there," he says, his big hand right next to my head with a finger pointing off to our left, "should be good."

"Yep," my brother adds, handing the scope back to Mike, "that will work."

"Uh-huh. I'll get the asshole on the roof; you get the artillery Chief. That leaves the third knucklehead for you Willie. Tell me you have something other than that cannon."

Willie laughs, pulls a subcompact Glock from one pocket and a suppressor from another, then screws them together.

"I don't *always* crave attention guys."

Even Willie's joke can't improve my mood. Although my sister is safe, this has become about far more than just her, and it's about to get very serious. I know I have to let my concerns go and let the guys do what it is they do. I look at each of them, then put the truck in gear and head for the area Willie pointed at.

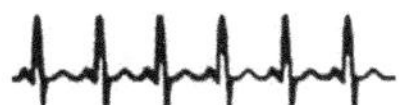

# 71

Joey is driving like a mad woman. The new guy in the front seat – apparently his name is Keith – looks like he might wet his pants at any moment.

"Does he always look that scared?" I ask, looking at Cassie.

Howard laughs and says, "No, just since he's been hanging out with us, actually."

This time Cassie laughs.

"I bet he doesn't even have a gun, does he?"

"He's a computer weenie slash driver, Whit. Give him a gun, he may shoot himself."

"You can take off the 'driver' part," Keith offers, turning to look at me, "because no way can I drive like this lunatic."

Then, without any warning, Joey goes nuts.

"*Oh jezzz!* How lucky can we get? Look... look! There they are!" she yells, slowing slightly and pointing at a black SUV fifty yards ahead of us on the highway.

"Are you sure?" Howard asks.

"Hell yes. I memorized the plate. Some parts of my brain still work just fine."

I lay a hand on Joey's shoulder and ask, "What are the chances you can get us around them, without them noticing?"

"Too easy," she quickly responds.

We watch Joey deftly maneuver across three lanes, ending up on the far right. She allows the Benz to slow, and after a few hundred feet, an irate truck driver behind us swings out to pass. The second we are parallel with the center of his trailer, Joey accelerates, matching his speed. It takes less than a mile before we see the bad guys behind us, two lanes over, and falling back. They're purposely driving in a manner not to draw attention to themselves. We, fortunately, don't have that problem.

"Now what, Whit?" Joey asks, grinning at me in the mirror.

"Get us to the General Aviation Center at the airport," I reply, noticing the intense look on Howard and Cassie's faces.

"You need to be listening to this far more than I do," Keith says, handing me his earbud and mic.

I put the earpiece in and listen to the conversation between Melinda and Courtney's group.

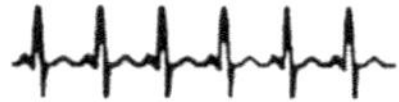

# 72

I pull up behind a food service truck and stop. I look at each of them for a moment, realizing that once again, I'm sending people into harm's way. Rhyan leans forward between the seats, kisses me on the forehead, then opens his door and gets out. Willie just smiles and does the same, followed by Michael, who steps up to my open window.

"Where are you going, lady?"

"I thought about going with you guys but figured one of you would put a foot in my ass if I tried it. So instead, I'm going to go say HI to my fucking boss."

Michael leans in and gives me a kiss – right on the lips.

"Avoid the bullets, girl. See you on the other side."

I smile at him, then he turns and trots off in the direction of the buildings, darting in and out of cover all the way. Seconds later, I hear Melinda in my ear again.

"Intel – Alpha. You're clear for now. Your target is watching the Gulfstream."

I take a deep breath, put the truck in gear again, and head for the Business Aviation building. I know Melinda will guide each of them silently to their targets.

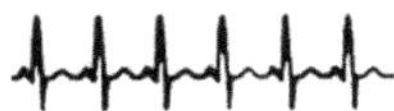

# 73

"Is Target One still wired?" Courtney asks.

"I'm here, One. Whacha need?"

"Whose side is she on, Whit? Do you know for certain?"

"Daria? I have to believe she's on our side. She could have blown this all, on more than one occasion, and chose not to. I mean hell, technically speaking, she can get her hands on far more than twelve million dollars, you know?"

"Uh-huh – I'd already considered that one."

"Did you guys see her message?"

"Yes. And I know what it means."

"How did I know you'd say that?" my sister blurts out.

"They're going to kill Sokolski. Nikolsky wants his job."

That gets her attention.

"Oh my God, Court. Oh shit..."

"What?"

"Something she said, as she pulled Vera into the car..."

"She *pulled* her in?"

"Yeah... and she *said* that Tarasov is her brother."

*"What the hell?"* I hear Cassie blurt out.

Courtney never does reply to my statement.

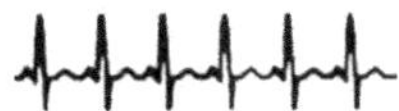

# 74

Without responding to my sister, I jerk the steering wheel and once again come to a stop on the side of the access road leading to the Business Aviation Center. I can see the building and the aircraft parked in front of it from where I'm sitting. A quick glance to my left gives me the Russian aircraft on the tarmac in front of the General Aviation building, heat rising off its still idling engines.

I'm so pissed off, I can feel the blood rushing into my face at an accelerated rate. It's time to call out the one person who has so far managed to remain below the radar and make her cop to whatever she knows, It's blatantly obvious that she damn sure knows *something* about all this shit.

I pull my phone out of my shirt pocket, and dial my boss's office – *at 4 am...*

"Wagner," a groggy voice says.

"Forwarding the office phone? Expecting a call maybe?"

*"Courtney...?"*

"Not who you were expecting, Amanda?"

"Alice is on her way there... to Zürich..."

"I don't want Alice. I want to talk to *you*. This whole fucked up situation has progressed to a point that, I strongly suggest you not only answer my questions but choose your answers very carefully. You know me well enough to realize that isn't a threat."

"Courtney, this is a non-secure line."

"*I don't give a fuck, Amanda!* You're there, tucked safely in your bed, and I just sent three guys to get shot at. You getting my drift here?"

"Yes ma'am."

I can hear the strain in her voice.

"Is he really her brother?"

"On paper, it does appear they are *genetically related.* Alice acquired the information from sources she declined to share with me."

"Verified?"

"Yes. I have all of the documentation. They're products of a secret Russian program…"

"I know about all that. Did *you* send them to Rabat?"

"Yes."

I know she did it under orders from Alice, so I let it go.

"Does Daria have full knowledge of my operation?"

"I don't know for certain, but based on the number of phone calls between the two of them, I'd have to guess that yes, she does. She may have even come up with it. I'm fairly certain your sister is just along for the ride."

"How did Alice know what they were planning?"

"She had ears, Courtney – very secret, very reliable ears – inside Nikolsky's office. She's been watching him very closely, for about six months, and has him as 'suspect' on a number of recent 'issues'".

"*Had ears…?*"

"Once this began, I was told to have the person immediately removed."

Having reached the 'big' question, I find that I'm honestly not sure I want to hear the answer, but I know I have to ask it.

"Only one question left, Amanda."

"She said that if this comes off as planned, it could put an end, for a very long time, to the killing – on both sides."

"She knew I'd call you, didn't she?"

"Yes. Her exact words to me before she left were, 'She's the best in the business, and she will figure it all out – I have no damn doubt of that. When she does, answer her questions honestly, so she will be able to finish her task'."

"Okay. One last thing, Amanda."

"Yes ma'am?"

"Are you expected to check in if I do call you?"

"Yes ma'am."

"Don't. You'll have to trust me on this, Amanda. What we are about to attempt depends on total surprise – *of everyone*. You're in *our* loop now, and what you do next will affect what happens out here. Want a suggestion?"

I hear her sigh heavily.

"Yeah, Courtney, go ahead, suggest."

"Take the day off. Don't go into the office, and cancel the call forwarding the moment you disconnect this call. Disappear for the next twelve hours. I'll cover you if the need arises."

"Okay, I will. One more thing, Courtney. Are we – you and I – okay? I don't really want to spend the rest of my career on your shit list. I only did..."

"Relax Amanda. We're on the same team, even if at times it doesn't appear so. I gotta go."

"Good luck, Courtney."

I close the phone and stare at Alice's Gulfstream, sitting on the tarmac with the stairs down. She figured out what Nikolsky was planning, and opted to be Sokolski's savior, rather than giving him the info and letting him save himself – or perhaps get himself killed. The resulting debt would be unpayable – even in ten life times. It never ceases to amaze me, how damn good at 'poker' my boss is.

After a few seconds of quiet thought, I again key my mic.

"Howard, I need some time. Can you guys slow them down without giving us away?"

*"Oh hell yes!"* I hear Cassie reply, with a few laughs in the background.

One more thing to do. I key my mic again.

"One – Intel. You there?"

"Yep."

"Is Alice *inside* the plane?"

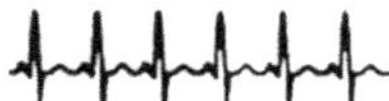

# 75

We're passing under a huge sign over the highway...

*Flughafen Zürich*
*Allgemeiner Flugwesen*
*Nächster Ausgang*
Zürich Airport
General Aviation
Next Exit

...when Courtney asks for help, and Cassie instantly complies.

"Sorry, Joey – we need to be behind them now. I only need one shot dear."

"You got it, lady," Joey replies, as we watch Cassie screw a silencer onto the barrel of a Glock .380, she had on her ankle.

"Keith, you still with me?" Joey asks.

"Yes ma'am," he quickly replies, still looking nervous.

"I need another large vehicle to shadow – what's behind us?"

I duck and let Keith lean over me to look out the heavily tinted rear windows.

"Two in the far right lane behind us, and another one a lane over."

"Which one is closest?"

"The one on your left – he'll catch us first."

"Okay, I'm slowing down. Keep me aware of where the bad guys are. I'm going to use the truck on my left."

"Copy that."

I feel the GLK slow considerably and watch as vehicles begin passing us. In less than thirty seconds, I make the bad guys again, two lanes over, going the posted speed limit. Then, as if it had been planned, a big rig – going faster than both of us – slips between us on our left. Joey momentarily speeds up, and the truck behind us changes lanes and accelerates as well. Then, Joey simply takes her foot off the accelerator, and we're hidden from the view as the bad guys, and the two trucks, shoot past us. In only a few seconds, we find ourselves ten car lengths behind them, and they are none the wiser.

"Give me one clear shot, Joey," Cassie says, as she lowers her window just enough to shoot through.

"This ought to be interesting," I mumble.

"Smart-ass," Cassie replies, as she squats on the seat, with her feet under her, and sights her weapon through the narrow one-inch gap at the top of her window. "Howard, go up on the window quick, once I do this. We're gonna go shooting past them as soon as the tire goes."

"Gotcha," he replies, leaning over and placing a finger on the button.

"How close?" Joey asks as the SUV begins to accelerate.

"Ten yards maybe?"

"You got it."

As I watch Joey and Cassie work, I catch a glimpse of Keith, still looking as if he's going to faint. Fifteen seconds later, I hear the 'pffft' of Cassie's silencer and feel the empty shell casing when it bounces off my knee, as she deftly delivers one round into the treads of the BMW's right rear tire. Simultaneously, there's a short buzz from the electric motor as Howard instantly raises the window. Although the tire doesn't explode as it would if the round hit the sidewall, it's already three-quarters flat, and the driver is slowing and swerving by the time we zip past them.

"Holy crap! *You did it!* You hit a damn tire, at sixty miles an hour, from thirty feet away, through a one-inch gap – with one shot! I don't fucking believe it..."

We're laughing at Keith's hysterics, as Joey keys her mic and reports.

"Five – One. They are officially delayed. What now?"

"Stay with them, without getting caught. Make sure nothing happens to Target Two and her associate. Copy that?" Courtney says, almost before Joey quits talking.

"Copy that," Howard replies.

We're watching out the back window, as the now crippled BMW limps its way onto the shoulder of the highway just short of the exit we are taking.

"Pull up and let me out," Howard says.

I turn instantly and look at him.

"Someone has to watch them, might as well be me."

"What about us?" Cassie asks.

"Get to the airport and get him," he points at Keith, "and his computer online so you can keep up with what's going on. I'll let you know what these guys are up to."

"Are you sure, Howard?" Joey asks as she pulls onto the shoulder about a half mile from the highway exit.

"Yes, Joey, I am. Watching, reporting, and disappearing I can do. You guys are in the loop on this. Go help Courtney and the guys. I'll see you all when it's over."

As he opens the door, I reach for him.

"Thank you..."

He kisses me gently on the lips, in front of everyone, and says, "You're welcome. Don't screw up all my efforts by getting yourself killed."

Then, in an instant, he disappears into the woods alongside the road.

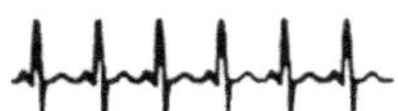

# 76

I'm staring at Alice's plane, trying to shake my mind free of the conversation I had with Amanda, when a new conversation between Mike and Melinda, forces my brain to reengage.

"Intel – Alpha. You have me?"

"Yes, I do."

"And my target?"

"Kind of weird actually. He hasn't moved. At all. Even a little."

"I'm approaching."

I find myself wishing I had a visual.

Then Rhyan's voice joins the discussion.

"I have mine. Stand by."

As I listen, my mind again takes off, which for me, is a curse.

Why the hell did Alice feel the need to come all the way here, if she thought I could handle it? She told Amanda she 'had no doubt I'd figure it out', and yet, there she is, a hundred yards from me.

Then, yet another revelation – *it isn't Alice's Gulfstream.* It's a generic white one, with nothing more than a registration number on the rudder.

Why?

Is she hiding? Again, why? If she's here to step in just in time and save Sokolski, why not do it in the open? Maybe, her presence would tip off the bad guys to the setup?

*Why?* Why would she be hiding? More importantly, *who* is she hiding from?

And, what about Nikolsky? Where's that asshole?

My concentration is again broken by voices in my ear.

"*FUCK!* They're decoys!" I hear a heavily breathing Rhyan say. "Don't shoot him, Alpha – don't shoot him!"

Then Willie.

"Mine too. Definitely *not* ex-military."

"The rocket case is a dummy as well. Apparently, they were expecting someone to be snooping around," Rhyan adds.

But, nothing from Mike. My heart rate increases.

My attention is drawn to movement in my rearview mirror, and I watch the other GLK pull up behind me. I jump out of my truck, and run back to the other one, jerking open the front door on the passenger's side as soon as I touch it.

"Keith, you're with me. Get your 'toy', get in my truck, and get the damn thing online."

He's moving before I finish my sentence.

"Change One, girls. I'm working on the fly here. The decoys mean whoever set this up, is expecting something."

"Are we going to give them *'something'* Court?" Joey asks, with a devious little smirk on her face.

"You bet your cute little Russian ass we are! You guys know how much I *hate* being set up, so if they're going to try it, they better damn well be prepared for the consequences."

Cassie lets out a good laugh.

"You two," I point at Joey and Cassie, "go find somewhere undetectable, within accurate shooting range of the Russian aircraft, to hang out. Sis, I know we just got you back, but you're our bait. *You,*" I say with maximum emphasis while looking her right in the eyes, "are the *very last damn thing* that asshole expects to find in front of that plane. I want you standing right out in the open when he and his band of idiots turn up. You up to that?"

*"Oh, hell yes!"* she replies, the look in her eyes telling me she's more than ready. "But I'll need more ammo."

Her comment is completely hilarious in that, at the exact same moment, we – Cassie, Joey, *and* me – all try to hand her magazines for her Beretta.

"Ladies, the big catch to all this is – *they do not get to kill Sokolski*. Understood?"

Before they respond, we hear Howard, and I instantly realize he isn't in the truck.

"Two – Unit. They're moving again."

*"You guys let him out?"* I ask.

"His idea," Cassie replies.

"Yeah," Whitney says, "and he wasn't going to let us talk him out of it. I think the thing back at the bank got to him."

I key my mic and say, "You're out of the loop, Two. Later."

"Copy that. Go ahead, One, ruin all my fun."

"Ten, you still with me?"

"Yep."

"Five?"

"Here watching," Rhyan replies.

"Alpha, status?"

No response.

"Alpha?"

Still no response. Although I am concerned, I find myself wondering.

"I'll have a new bird overhead in ninety seconds, One," Melinda says.

"Good. I need eyes," I reply. Then I look at the girls. "Get to it, ladies. I'm with the geek – we're going to visit the boss. Be safe girls – I'm still not absolutely certain who will be shooting at us first, so watch your butts."

Once each of them nods at me, I close the door and head for my truck. Halfway there they pass me headed for the General Aviation facility – and the Russians.

As I climb back into the Benz, for some unexplained reason I flashback to a hotel in Istanbul, many years ago, and I'm not sure exactly why, but the thought makes me smile.

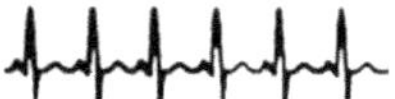

# 77

Although they aren't blatantly obvious about their purpose, I make Alice's security detail as we drive past the Gulfstream, and around the side of the small terminal building that serves the Business Aviation area. I park the GLK between two large trucks in an attempt to partially hide it.

"Are you on M's satellite yet?"

"Ten seconds."

I once again key my mic.

"Intel, you with me?"

"Yes ma'am. Sat is almost online."

"Site is on that, M. I have something else for you."

"Go."

"I need to know where the missing player is."

"Okay, I'm on it."

I sit staring at the rudder of Alice's aircraft, and once again, I start talking out loud, to no one in particular.

"Decoys? Where the hell are Nikolsky's *real* bad guys?"

"Tarasov and his bad guys just rolled in the gate, Courtney," Keith says, never taking his eyes off his monitor.

"Uh-huh," I mumble, still lost in thought. "What if it isn't Nikolsky? What if this goes even higher than him?"

"You might want to tell the girls the bad guys are coming," Keith says as he's typing.

It takes me a second to realize he's no longer wired, which prompts me to key my mic and say, "Three and Four, your target is en route to you. One minute or less."

"Copy that. Our new asset is in place to greet them."

Then, a new thought occurs to me.

"One – Alpha."

Just as before, there's no response. I try again.

"One – Alpha. Do you copy?"

For some strange reason, I know he's up to something, and not 'down' or injured. It was Rhyan's earlier warning that the people in place were decoys that caused him to go silent.

My brain shifts back to the decoys. *Why?* If they don't know about us, why would they have decoys in place? It has to do with Nikolsky covering his tracks.

*Misdirection? Camouflage of some kind?*

"I'm going to talk to our boss, Keith. You keep on that satellite and keep our people up to speed," I say, pulling the bud from my ear, the mic off my collar, and handing both to him.

He looks momentarily shocked.

"What about you, Boss?" he asks.

"I know where to find you," I reply, opening the door and getting out. "And do me a favor, Keith?"

"Sure, Boss."

"When people start shooting, stay in the damn truck."

He laughs and nods at me. I weave my way between a couple of large trucks and find myself standing at the edge of the terminal building, staring at Alice's plane, and thinking. After a brief moment of contemplation, I take off at a brisk pace toward the plane's stairs.

The second I'm in the clear, Chauncey and William – Alice's personal security detail – see me, start moving in my direction, and intercept me at the bottom of the stairs.

# 78

I'm completely dumbfounded to discover only one guy at the bottom of the stairs to Sokolski's jet. *He's* more than a bit dumbfounded, when I sneak up behind him, and put the Glock in his back.

"Don't even breathe," I strongly suggest. "We're going to stand here quietly and wait for your other 'associates' to arrive. I will assume you don't have a problem with that?"

"Я сказал Директору, что было неблагоразумно приходить сюда без охраны..." (I told the Director that it was unwise to come here without security...)

"Меня интересует вовсе не ваш Директор." (It is not your Director I am after)

"Who then?" he asks, relaxing, turning slightly to face me, and looking a bit confused.

"The idiot your boss has placed so much trust in," I say with a sinister smile.

"*Tarasov.*" He's pissed off – it's all over his face.

"Yes. He will be arriving in moments, and the last thing he is expecting is to find me standing here."

"Is he not here for the reason he gave the Director?"

"He thinks so, but he isn't really running this disaster."

"You *must* let me warn the Director." His eyes are pleading with me.

"Relax. Our priority *is* your Director. He is safe."

The man is now totally confused.

"You are armed I assume?"

"Yes," he replies without moving. "It is near your weapon."

"When the shooting starts, please don't shoot me."

"Who *are* the targets then?"

He sees the quizzical look on my face and laughs.

"In our business, trust can easily get one killed. I am also smart enough to realize that if you had intended to kill the Director, I would be dead by now, as would he. Therefore, I will take you at your word, and should I start shooting, I would like to be shooting at the correct targets."

"Okay, but you may not like the answer."

"Perhaps not, but if it protects the Director, I will honor it."

"The woman you know as Daria Ladenko is not a bad guy. Also, Vera Kovalenko is no longer supporting Tarasov. She had a change of heart when her husband was killed."

His eyes get really big.

"You know of this incident?"

"Yes, but we can discuss this later. The people you should be concerned with are Tarasov, his driver, and the woman in the front seat. They are the threat. Oh, and just so you know, Mr. Nikolsky is also in this up to his ass, and I'll bet your boss doesn't know about him either."

"Boris Nikolsky is involved in this matter?"

"Yes. Deeply. As a matter of fact, he's here, somewhere."

We hear the black BMW even before we see it turn onto the apron and head toward us. He glances at me, then at the BMW, then back at me.

"I must tell the Director they are here. It is preplanned," he says, raising a small remote that he's been holding the entire time.

"If you are going to trust me, you'd better take it all the way. Leave Sokolski inside. There is a shooter here as well."

He hesitates for a single heartbeat and then sticks the small device back into his pocket.

"If I have made the wrong choice..."

"You haven't," I reply, giving his shoulder a gentle squeeze, as the BMW skids to a stop within feet of us.

In milliseconds, the doors pop open, and the driver – who I instantly recognized from our kidnapping – steps out. A blink of an eye later, poor Vera is all but pushed out of the back, barely managing to remain on her feet. When I see Tarasov, I point the Glock directly at him. I also draw the Px4 with my right hand and gently stick the barrel into the back of the Russian still standing next to me. The moment Tarasov's driver notices me, I speak up.

"Anyone does *anything* stupid, you die first, Leonid – and there is no way I'll miss at this distance. Are we clear on that?"

Every head snaps in my direction the instant they hear my voice. Daria comes around the back of the truck and freezes the moment we make eye contact. The female who gets out on the passenger's side, starts walking around the front of the truck.

"She takes one more step, Leonid, and you pay for it."

"Делай как она говорит, Кира!" (Do as she says, Kira!)

Once Kira stops, I look directly at Daria, with murder in my eyes.

"And you – you get over here, in the open, where I can keep an eye on your traitorous ass."

I can immediately see she's confused, and not at all sure what's going on. She does, however, comply, walking over, and stopping next to Tarasov.

"Mrs. Kovalenko, would you care to join me?" I ask, with a big smirk covering my face.

"Gladly," she replies, jerking free from Tarasov's grasp, and starting toward me.

"Oh, and would you be so kind as to retrieve *my* money?"

She laughs and says, "But of course, Miss Paddison."

She turns back to the truck, leans in, and retrieves both the attachés containing the money. As she once again starts toward me, Tarasov looks as though he's going to explode.

"Неужели вы действительно полагаете, что сможете уйти отсюда со всеми этими деньгами и, при этом, остаться в живых." (You cannot truly believe that you will get away from here with that money, and remain alive) he says, his voice full of malice and loathing.

"And, *you* can't possibly believe that I came here alone."

"You have no idea what you are involved in."

"And even worse, Leonid, *YOU* have no fucking clue what you are in the middle of. I am, however, prepared to die today. Are you?"

He stands staring at me, a look of death in his eyes.

*Stalemate.*

The amusing thing is that none of them – not a single one – ever notices the two females sitting in the baggage truck, watching.

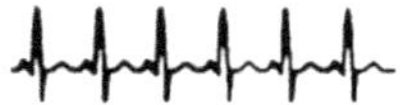

"One deceit needs many others, and so the whole house is built in the air and must soon come to the ground"

Baltasar Gracian
Jesuit Priest and Writer
1601 – 1658

# 79

"Is she aboard?" I ask Chauncey, nodding at the open door.

"Yes ma'am. She said you turn up. Are you armed, Mrs. Whitman?"

"That's a silly question, Chauncey. And no, you can't have it. If that's going to be a problem, I'll just run along."

He's about to stand his ground and refuse to let me board the aircraft when we hear Alice's voice above us.

"Forget it guys. Let her keep her weapon."

We turn, look up, and find her standing in the open door of the jet, smiling.

"Weapon*s* Alice – I'm in the middle of an operation here."

"Come up here, and tell me where we stand – and why your primary targets aren't with you."

I turn and look at William and Chauncey, waiting until they nod their approval, before I turn toward the stairs. The instant my left foot hits the bottom step, I see it – a bright green, high-intensity laser – as it lights up the back of my Adidas, and then disappears just as quickly.

*Michael!* He has eyes on me! But *what the hell is he doing*, I wonder, as I climb the stairs. Inside, Alice points at a console with a lone young girl sitting at it.

"We've been listening."

"I figured you were – Chauncey said you were 'expecting' me. Oh, and I know how you got the key code too."

"You got to him far faster than I thought you would. I will never understand how one mind can be so damn adept at deduction. Every time I ask something of you, Courtney – including the near impossible – you manage to pull it off. How long have you known about Keith?"

"Since the moment he mentioned AUGUR. Like Melinda said at the time – '…only God has access to that system'. Christ, Alice, he had to be a plant. The question was, working for who?"

"How the hell do you know about AUGUR?"

"Come on, Alice. What do I do for a living? I've had access to whatever I've wanted for at least the last nine years. I'm a goddamn spy and *your* Director of Intelligence. Remember?"

She stands, mouth agape, totally shocked at my response.

*"My God!* You are ready to do my job now, not later."

"Quit with the dramatics, Alice. I don't have any interest in your job. Give it to my sister. After this, I'm done. I'm going home to raise my kids and be a wife. This silly little game of yours has become so damn convoluted that I have no fucking idea who's on whose side anymore".

"But Courtney…"

"*Enough,* Alice. I'm tired of all the bullshit. Right now, you need to tell me *what the hell is going on out there,*" I almost yell at her, pointing across the runway toward the other plane.

Then, the young girl speaks up.

"Ms. Williamson?"

"Yes, Samantha?"

"Someone identifying himself as 'Five' is trying to talk to Mrs. Whitman."

"Well, hook her up!"

She hands me a headset, plugs it in, and quickly punches a bunch of buttons. Instantly I hear my team.

"Three – Five. They don't know we're here. Where is Ten?"

"Ten – Unit. Southwest corner of the building. About ten yards max. I have no clue about Alpha."

"Where is One?" I hear Rhyan ask.

Keith responds before I can.

"Off-line at the moment. She's in with the boss," I hear him say without identifying himself.

"I'm here, Five. Status?"

"*Complications*. Do you copy?"

"Yep. Standby," I reply, turning to face Alice.

"I need the space, Alice. Like right now. Please?"

"It's yours. Samantha, let's go get some air," she says, gesturing toward the door, indicating she should go first.

I wait the fifteen seconds it takes them to disappear from sight, then reach down and change the frequency parameters on the communications console. Rhyan and I have always had a fallback over the years – to keep what 'happened' to Whitney from happening to me. He insisted. It's an older channel that no one uses and is so far down the frequency band that it's easy to secure. I flip a couple more switches and then key my mic.

"One – Five. You on?"

"Alpha – One. Listen *very fucking carefully*, Courtney. This is not – I repeat *not* what it appears. Five is, as we speak, about to take out Gregor Borodin, who is trying to sneak up behind Whitney. I haven't found their shooter yet, and I don't believe that the situation I am seeing is what you were planning for. The decoy is still right where he's supposed to be, but he's also talking to someone – appears to be using a handheld of some kind."

"Hold that thought for a sec and let me do something," I quickly pick up the headphones Samantha was wearing and place one side against my free ear. I can again hear the rest of them talking...

"Looks like a stalemate guys. Target One has them standing there, looking at each other."

"One – Unit. I need the circuit. Site, you still with us?"

"Site here, Boss. Whacha need?"

"A frequency that is low powered, associated with handheld LF transmitters, and the users are speaking in Russian. Copy?"

"I'm on it, Boss," he replies.

"Okay guys, no matter what happens, we keep the targets alive. Understood?"

They acknowledge my order, and I switch back to Michael.

"Keith will find him, Alpha. What else?"

"Nikolsky."

*"You finally have eyes on that asshole?"*

"Yes ma'am. And riddle me this big sister – if he *is* after *his boss*, why is he on *your side of the runway?*"

"Fuck!"

"It gets better. Why are Borodin – and all the decoys for that matter – wearing U.S. Army fatigues?"

My brain freezes – solid. The muscles in my neck pull up so tightly, I damn near get an instant migraine. What the hell is going on? *What the hell am I missing?*

"I'll come back in five, Alpha. Keep searching – and keep a damn eye on Nikolsky. I need to talk to the boss."

"Copy," he immediately replies.

Then, out of nowhere, I hear Rhyan.

"Five – Alpha. Target down hard. Next?"

I want to listen but know I need to figure this out – and do it quickly. I twist the dial on the panel and then erase the history file so Samantha can't trace what I did. Then I pull the headset off and run to the door.

"Alice! I need to talk to you – quickly."

Both of them come back up the stairs and while Alice follows me back to the communications station, Samantha, unsure of what is going on, opts to take a seat at one of the small tables. I quickly replace the headset and adjust the volume.

"What's up, Courtney?

"Are they trying to eliminate Sokolski?

"Not 'they' – *he*. I believe Nikolsky is behind this. Info was passed to us by a mole in his office, based on phone taps that were in place. We believe he intends to use Tarasov, to help him move up the food chain. From what we've so far determined,

   

Tarasov is expendable. I assume you've figured all this out, and have assets in place to prevent it?"

"Actually, Alice, that isn't what's going on here. I'm pretty damn sure you've been had."

"What are you..." she starts to say when I raise my hand and stop her mid-sentence. I listen, as all hell breaks loose near the Russian aircraft.

"Ten – Unit. That screwy broad pulled a gun and Whitney took her out! Everyone's shooting. Give her cover!"

We hear the gunfire at the same moment, and Alice's head instantly spins toward the open door. I reach down, jerk the plug from the console, slide the headset down around my neck, and follow Alice as she rushes toward the open door.

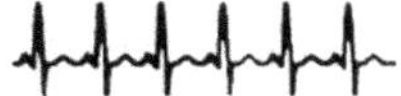

# 80

*"Don't!"* I scream as Tarasov's female accomplice draws her weapon, and attempts to sight on me.

I push my 'hostage' forward and hook his leg with my foot at the same time, causing him to immediately fall to the ground in front of me. With my left hand, I immediately draw a bead on Kira and send two rounds in her direction.

They both catch her in the chest.

The next thing I hear are rounds hitting the steel stairs, as I'm diving under them. At the same time, I catch a glimpse of Daria, trying to take Tarasov down herself, and quickly realize she isn't armed.

As I turn my attention to the driver, I hear the security guy scream, and in my peripheral vision see him roll away from me, toward the cover of the landing gear. In the microseconds that all this occurs, to complicate things even further, rounds start bouncing off the concrete next to me – high-velocity rounds. *Rifle rounds.*

My mind is in a hundred places at once – as is usually the case when one is being shot at. A quick glance to my left gives me Joey and Cassie bailing from the baggage truck, weapons up and firing – but they aren't firing in the right direction.

Next, my brain focuses on the sound of rounds hitting the aluminum body of the plane – almost directly over my head. Someone is shooting at the cabin entrance.

When I hear the automatic weapon, my brain overloads.

I glance at Joey and Cassie – trying to figure out who's on full-auto – just in time to see them flying through the air in the direction of a baggage trailer. I watch the rounds tear through the soft vinyl curtain and aluminum sides, as the shooter tracks their movements. When I look around the Gulfstream's landing gear, there on the other side is a guy in fatigues – *U.S. Army fatigues* – blasting away.

My lapse in priorities is realized about the same time the third bad guy finds his mark – one of his 9mm rounds sets up residence in my upper left thigh, and a second grazes my side. I immediately drop and roll to my right, emptying both the Glock and the Px4 in his direction. The second the slides lock, I drop both magazines and am reloading when I hear Mikey's voice in my ear.

"Alpha – Unit. The decoy isn't a decoy! He's the one putting the rounds into the plane. I'm about to correct that for you."

"Five – Alpha! You'll give away your position!" Rhyan yells.

Next, I hear the distinctive report of a different long gun – but it isn't Michael's Dragunov. It's far quieter. He has a new weapon, or he's a long way off.

Then, a second round. When I don't hear a confirmation, I find myself wondering if he hit his target.

I turn to look for the guy in the fatigues, with the AK, but he's gone. That leaves only Tarasov. I roll up on one knee and am sighting down my Px4, when I find him kneeling, with his gun against Daria's head. I instinctively squeeze off two more rounds...

I have no idea why I don't kill the man. Perhaps it's the way Daria said '*...he's my brother.*' However, with a little effort, I make sure both my shots are non-lethal. The first round hits the grip of the weapon he's holding, only millimeters from his thumb, sending the weapon flying and bouncing off the side of the BMW. My second shot finds his upper thigh. Daria is on him instantly, pinning him to the ground as he screams in pain.

Thinking I've accounted for all the targets, my brain slows and allows my body to catch up. As I am checking my weapons, a thought occurs to me. Vera. Where the hell is Vera *and* where are those damn cases?

I look in every direction, and not only is she nowhere to be seen, but neither are the cases with the money in them. I'm about to get seriously pissed off when I feel the muzzle of a gun being pressed against the back of my head.

My heart stops.

"None of this will matter in a few moments, as our countries will once again be enemies. Deadly enemies."

He starts to laugh, and almost instantly, I hear his demise.

'pffft-pffft-pffft'

Three-round burst from a suppressed automatic weapon.

Thank God for little brothers...

I turn slowly and find a smiling Rhyan standing over the now-dead, momentarily missing, fatigue-clad, bad guy with the AK.

"Hi, Sis! Long time, no see," he blurts out. "Meet Mr. Popov – recently of the Russian Secret Service," he says, using his foot to roll the dead guy over. "His associate, Mr. Borodin, is around the corner of the building in pretty much the same condition."

"You couldn't have shot him *before* he put the gun against my head, and scared the shit out of me?" I ask, gingerly getting back to my feet, and finishing the check of my weapons.

"Now where's the fun and amusement in that?" he replies with a smirk. "You do realize you're bleeding, right?"

"Yes, little brother, I do. Bullets tend to cause that."

That's' when I realize it's quiet. No gunfire. At all. I look directly at my brother, put a finger to my lips, and then point to my ear, knowing that he'll understand. He nods and starts scanning the area, pointing at Cassie and Joey who are coming out from behind the bullet-riddled luggage cart. I glance in the direction of Daria and find she is still pinning a whimpering Leonid Tarasov to the ground, a gun now against his head. A noise behind me causes both Rhyan and me to spin around, our weapons at the ready. Behind us is the bodyguard, leaning back against the front landing gear, trying to cinch his belt up on his thigh in an attempt to stem the flow of blood from a wound. When I start toward him, he raises his hand to indicate he's okay, and that we should finish our task.

Then, I hear a voice, above me. A female voice.

"Alex!"

Rhyan and I spin around simultaneously and take a few steps in the general direction of the jet's stairs.

*"ALEX!"* Vera again screams.

Stepping out from under the plane just far enough to see the top of the stairs, I look in the direction of the cabin door. Rhyan is beside me, his HK at the ready.

Nothing. The stairs and cabin door are empty.

"Whoever is out there, be advised that I have Sokolski and his pilot."

Something – perhaps the trust that's developed between us over the last week – makes me answer her.

"Well, Mrs. Kovalenko, can I ask what, exactly, you intend to do with him?"

She instantly appears at the top of the stairs, and my pulse rate finally begins to drop.

"You appear, for some reason, to be concerned with keeping him alive. That is the whole point of all this, is it not?"

"Yes, it is! And, if you don't mind my asking, *where the hell is my mon...*"

I'm interrupted by another report from what sounds like the same weapon the bad guy was using – a Dragunov SVD – and this time it seems to be further away.

Did Michael *miss*? Impossible – and completely absurd at the same time.

A new Russian shooter?

I'm looking right at Vera when the round lifts her off her feet, and throws her back into the plane, out of my view.

*"SECOND SNIPER! SECOND SNIPER!"* I scream into my mic, as I run for the stairs. Rhyan, realizing I'm about to make

myself a target, tries to grab my shirt, but I pull free and rush up the stairs, taking them two at a time.

Halfway up, God gives me my second break of the day. He again allows me to remain among living, despite my stupidity. As I dive for the cover of the cabin, a second 7.62mm round grazes the back of my head and slams into the body of the plane right next to the open door.

I never hear Michael telling me he can't find the target.

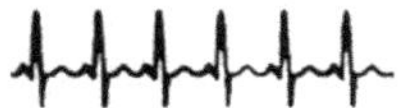

"The intellect has little to do on the road to discovery. There comes a leap in consciousness, call it 'intuition' or what you will, the solution comes to you and you don't know how or why."

Albert Einstein
German Theoretical Physicist
1879 – 1955

# 81

William and Chauncey are in defensive mode instantly. Where they get the MP5s, I have no clue. I turn and run back to the communications console, pick up Samantha's headset, quickly dial in Michael's frequency, and listen. Nothing.

I plug the headset I'm still wearing into the console, just as I hear what has to be a Russian-made Dragunov. Mike has his new Israeli-made M89 – not his Dragunov.

The Russian shooter?

I hear "Five – Alpha! You'll give away your position!"

Seconds later, I hear the report of a different long gun – not as loud as the SVD. I realize if he's shooting unsuppressed, he has to be a distance away. On a distance shot, a suppressor will screw with his accuracy.

Then, a second report, from the same weapon. Two shots? I think, *'you're getting old Mike'*.

My concentration is broken when I hear the automatic weapon. I grab a set of field glasses, toss both headsets onto the console, and again run to the cabin door. The moment the glasses focus, I see Joey and Cassie as they're diving for cover. In the foreground, I watch Tarasov's driver bounce off the front fender of the SUV, and disappear behind it, as someone's rounds find their mark.

Then, I see something strange – Vera Kovalenko, running up the stairs of the aircraft. It only takes four or five seconds for her to disappear inside the Russian jet.

When I look for Whitney, I find not only her but Rhyan as well, standing over a dead guy in fatigues, who still has hold of an AK 47.

Thank God for little brothers.

Then, I realize it's quiet. No more gunfire. I turn, walk back to the communications console, and am about to pick up Samantha's headset, when my brain once again gets away from me.

How was Vera able to simply walk into what should be a secure aircraft? She wouldn't have made it to the second step if she tried it on this plane. It seems I'm correct, and Sokolski doesn't have any of his security. *He didn't feel he needed them.*

Michael's observation creates more questions. What the hell *is* Nikolsky doing on *this* side of the runway, if his target is on the other side? For that matter, why is he here at all? He could have sent the bad guys, and gone to where he's actually supposed to be. He could have stayed 'clean' as they say. And, how in the hell did he expect to get away unnoticed should it all go in the shitter – as it apparently has?

*What the hell is the man up to?*

If things came off as planned, and they were able to make it appear Sokolski had been assassinated, Nikolsky would be in a position to immediately step up and point fingers. Alice's presence would be irrelevant – unless he intended to point the finger at...

*Oh crap!*

What if Alice's 'informant' was a set-up? What if he was planted by Nikolsky? What if the info the informant 'supplied' Alice with, was as bogus as he or she was? That would certainly explain the 'decoys' – *Nikolsky knew we'd be here.* He *was* expecting us!

Why? Why lure the head of the CIA to an off grid operation?

To set her up?

My concentration is broken by yet another report from a long gun – perhaps a second Dragunov. As loud as it is, it has to be damn near next to me.

It would appear that Nikolsky brought more help than we expected. This fact reaffirms my earlier contention that I'm still missing something.

*Something important.*

Something involving the decoys.

Then a second shot. Even as I'm running back toward the cabin door, my brain is still in the 'why' mode. Alice and I arrive at the same moment, and she hands me the field glasses.

I look just in time to see Whitney diving through the cabin door of Sokolski's plane. I turn and look at Samantha.

"Man those headphones girl, and tell me what you hear."

She jumps up, rushes to the console, pulls the headset on, and flips some switches.

"Someone is telling Alex that he doesn't have a target."

"A second sniper? It damn sure sounds like a Dragunov."

Samantha is repeating the communications between the members of my team, but I'm not hearing any of it. I'm a galaxy away mentally – my brain speeding along at warp nine, at least.

*Why?* Why the hell has Nikolsky gone to the trouble to lure Alice here? Pointing fingers at each other is silly bullshit that can be discounted, with little or no effort. Hell, that's what we do. We lie and deceive – especially if there's something to be gained.

And, why hasn't he swooped on that damn plane yet? It's obvious his team is losing.

Then another report from a high-powered weapon. This one is from a different direction. How damn many shooters does he have out here?

What the hell is he up to?

*What in God's name am I missing?*

The decoys! He has them for a reason. Now, it seems there were even more – at least two additional long guns. He's trying to keep our attention away from something.

Then I hear Samantha's voice in the background.

"... and they have at least two long guns. One on each side of the Business Aviation terminal building."

*Huh?* Both of them are on *this side of the runway?* What the hell? That makes absolutely no sense whatsoever. Why put excess distance between your shooters and their target?

I glance down at the bottom of the stairs and notice William *and* Chauncey are gone. Neither would knowingly leave Alice unguarded. Where the hell are they?

As I'm gently pushing Alice back out of the open doorway of the cabin, I again hear Samantha's voice.

"Sokolski is secure. Vera Kovalenko is down, as is Sokolski's only security guard. Alex – I mean your sister – is asking to talk to you, Mrs. Whitman."

I'm so locked into what's happening on the other side of the runway, I don't hear her. Alice lays a hand on my shoulder.

"Courtney, your sister needs to talk to you," she nods in the direction of Samantha.

"Huh? Oh, yeah, okay," I reply, passing the binoculars to her and walking over to the communications console, where Samantha hands me my headset. I'm looking at Alice as she raises the glasses to her eyes when I hear Whitney in my ear.

"Where is One! Damn it, I need to talk to my sister!"

"I'm here, Whit – talk to me," I say, still watching Alice.

"One of the bad guys – Rhyan says his name is Popov – said something very strange to me, just before little brother sent him to meet his maker."

Alice lowers the glasses, and steps out of the plane, onto the stairs, disappearing from my view. My brain is in about a dozen places at that moment, so it never occurs to me to stop her – she's in the open with no cover or security.

Bad move on my part.

Then I hear Chauncey – Alice's security chief – in my ear.

"I have the south shooter! Down hard!"

*What? Why is he on our frequency? Why in the hell did he go after the shooter?*

"What did he say, Sis?" I ask, trying to separate all the shit going on in my head.

Then, Michael is in my ear, before Whitney can answer.

"Nikolsky answered his phone and has started his vehicle. Orders, One?"

A phone call? Who the hell is calling him?

Then Whitney again.

"He said – and this is a rough quote, I was dodging bullets at the time – '...*this will not matter in a few moments, as our countries will once again be enemies.*'"

What the hell? *'Once again'?* Aren't we enemies now?

"Nikolsky is moving – orders?"

"Stop him, Alpha! Don't let him get to the other side of the runway. And, there's still another Russian shooter – Izamaylov is still unaccounted for!" I say into my mic, as I turn and look toward the now empty cabin door.

They aren't in a position to kill Sokolski any longer – we've pretty much screwed that plan up. So how the hell is he going to restart the 'cold war'?

Keith's voice in my ear interrupts my thoughts.

*"Nikolsky is talking to someone within fifty yards of you, Boss!"*

My over-analytical brain processes what he says before he finishes his sentence. In a single microsecond, a crystal clear, high-definition image forms in my mind, and I *finally* wrap my brain around the only logical conclusion, and the concept is so totally insane, it makes my heart stop.

*Izamaylov!*

"Oh shit! *No fucking way!*" I yell, which makes Samantha jump damn near out of her chair.

I have two recurring thoughts as I turn and bolt for the cabin door, tearing the plug from the end of the cable, and snatching the headset off my head.

*'Can Nikolsky really be that damn crazy'?*

*'Have we all lost our goddamn minds'?*

I grab the edge of the cabin doorway and practically swing myself onto the top stair, almost falling as I do.

My eyes lock onto Alice, standing – *in the open* – at the bottom of the stairs looking around, no doubt trying to figure out where her security is. I hear the reports from Michael's first two rounds, and simultaneously hear an explosion somewhere in front of, and to the right of the plane, telling me that Boris Nikolsky has probably just met his maker.

In the few seconds that all this occurs, my initial suspicions are realized the moment I see the dust blow up off the concrete inches from Alice's feet. I'm fairly certain it's the first round from Izamaylov.

That's why Nikolsky is on this side of the fucking runway!

*Their real target is on this side of the runway.*

As I launch myself over the railing of the stairs, a single thought is circling in my mind...

*'Please Michael – be as good right now, as
you were the night you saved me in Odessa'*

I manage to twist myself 180 degrees in mid-air during the twelve-foot drop, and land on my feet in front of, and facing, an unsuspecting Alice Williamson.

As good as this guy is, he must be *Spetsnaz.* He manages to chamber his next round and re-sight his target in the seconds it takes me to leap from the stairs.

During my 'free-fall', I *feel* the second 7.62 round from what I'm certain is Izamaylov's Dragunov. I find myself wondering if his target was me, or Alice. While I'm still in the air, the round hits me in the upper left arm, breaking the humerus. The bullet shatters from the impact, and the remaining pieces come back out the side of my arm, sprinkling the aluminum body of the plane.

Had I not launched myself off the steps at the exact moment I did, the bullet would have hit Alice somewhere in the head. I realize this guy is damn near as good as Michael when his next round arrives in about five seconds.

Alice and I are in a heap on the ground, trying to roll to the cover of the stairs when I feel it hit my left leg from behind. It tears things up on its way through, exiting the front of my thigh and ricocheting off the concrete. It hurts so badly, that I unleash a scream that's probably heard all the way over in the main airport terminal.

He's too accurate! If I wasn't lying prone between Alice and the shooter, his last round would have undoubtedly hit her somewhere in her upper torso, and if by some act of God, the first round hadn't killed her, the last one damn sure would have. I also realize that there was no report from any of the sniper's shots. He's 'suppressed'.

This *has to be* Izamaylov – only a Spetsnaz sniper would be trained this well. The rest are in fact decoys designed to draw Michael's attention away from their best shooter – whose sole and primary target has always been, *the Director of the CIA.*

I'm sobbing uncontrollably when the Russian's next round arrives. I grab hold of Alice's shoulder with the hand that's still working and am still trying to roll us together, under the cover of the jet's stairs, but I'm not quick enough.

The third round that hits me, enters the lower left side of my back, screws up a bunch of stuff inside, and after exiting my stomach on the same side, hits Alice – somewhere.

The pain is more than I can take.

The last thing I remember, before unconsciousness engulfs me, is hearing Alice screaming, and seeing Haleigh and Lyle reaching out to me in the darkness.

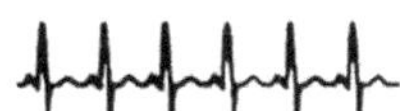

# 82

The moment I hit the floor, I immediately roll toward the main cabin area, coming to a stop against a body lying on the floor.

I open my eyes – which have been closed since I made my leap into the plane – expecting to find a dead Vera Kovalenko, but instead find myself staring down the barrel of a Glock.

My heart stops, and I close my eyes again, wondering if this is it – my very last 'dumb move'.

Then I hear a voice – a female voice.

"Ты чертовски вовремя пришла посмотреть, жива ли я." (It is about damn time you came to see if I am still alive)

"What makes you think I came to check on you?" I ask, a huge smirk covering my face. "I just want to know what you did with my money."

When I stand up, I notice Sokolski and his pilot cowering on the floor, between two seats. I place both my guns into the waistband of my Levis, and then take Vera's hand and help her into one of the seats. Her shirt is covered with blood both front and back.

"I bet that fucking hurts, doesn't it?"

"Kiss my ass, Alex," she replies, trying not to laugh. "And the money is between the tires of the landing gear. When that silly bitch pulled her weapon, I knew what was going to happen so I stashed it."

I turn my attention to Sokolski.

"Bad idea – traveling without security, huh?"

"A decision that will never occur again, Miss…"

"Paddison. Alexis Paddison."

"Although I am unsure of what has happened here, I feel fairly certain you work for Alice Williamson in some capacity. Regardless, however, I thank you for saving me from my own stupidity."

"My pleasure sir," I reply turning back to look at Vera.

"You're bleeding, Alex," she says with a grimace.

"Yeah, I felt the round graze my head. Scalp wounds always make it look like you are dying."

"You should tell someone that we have him," she nods in the direction of Sokolski.

"Yeah, I guess," I reply. "My damn sister did seem rather adamant about keeping him alive."

I glance at the Russians, then key my mic and say, "Unit – Sokolski is secure. Vera Kovalenko is down, as is Sokolski's only security guard. Where is One? I need to talk to…" I start to say, but am interrupted by a male voice I don't recognize.

"I have the south shooter! Down hard!"

Then I hear my sister, who sounds severely stressed.

"I'm here Whit – talk to me."

"One of the bad guys – Rhyan says his name is Popov – said something very strange to me, just before little brother sent him to meet his maker."

"What did he say, Sis?"

Then Michael interrupts us before I can answer her.

"Nikolsky is answering his phone and has started his vehicle. Orders, One?"

It takes every ounce of willpower I have, not to key my mic and tell Mike to kill the sorry bastard. I wait a split second to see if my sister is going to respond, and when she doesn't, I assume she's waiting on me.

     

"He said, and this is a rough quote, I was dodging bullets at the time – '*...all this will not matter because, in a few minutes, our countries will return to being enemies – deadly enemies.*'"

"Nikolsky is moving. Orders?" Michael asks.

This time, Courtney is instantaneous with her response.

"Stop him, Alpha! Don't let him get to the other side of the runway. *And, there is still another Russian shooter!*"

Another shooter? That explains a few things, *and* it makes me realize we aren't as astute about what's happening as we thought. I inch my way back to the door, realizing that if a shooter sees me looking out, it would be an easy task to put a couple of rounds through the side of the plane and possibly take me out. I drop to my knees when I get close, and a quick glance gives me Daria, right where I left her – sitting on Tarasov. I quickly duck back in, and wait for a response.

After about ten seconds, I go for a second look.

Bodies. Motionless bodies. I start to key my mic, and once again hear my sister.

*"Oh shit! No fucking way!"*

Then the circuit goes quiet. I know there's only one person with the ability to see across the runway.

"Alpha, you on?"

"I am," Mike replies to my query.

"Check our boss!" I say, knowing that he, and everyone else, heard Courtney's last outburst.

"Copy that. Stand by."

"Unit – let's count."

"Five is good."

"Three and Four are both good."

"Ten is good."

"Is anyone still being shot at? One suspects there's another Russian shooter out here."

In turn, each of them replies 'Negative' to my question.

Then, we hear Michael go berserk.

*"Oh, Christ!* Someone is targeting Williamson!"

Almost instantly, every one of us breaks from cover, even though we know we're useless from this distance, and stand staring at Williamson's aircraft. We can barely make out the figures at the bottom of the stairs. It only takes a second for Rhyan to appear from under the plane with his spotting scope in his hand.

Again Michael.

"Damn! No report! The bastard is suppressed! I can't find him!"

Then I hear Rhyan call out from below us.

"I have someone down near the rear wheels of the aircraft. Appears to be William."

I take the stairs three at a time, covering the distance to the BMW in the blink of an eye, jerking the driver's door open the second I'm within reach. I'm halfway into the driver's seat when Michael's voice in my ear makes me freeze.

"Oh God. Courtney and Alice are down. She took a round. *Where is the bastard?"*

This is the moment I realize that Sokolski was never the real target, but was instead being set up to be the scapegoat.

I pull the door closed, turn the key and when the engine jumps to life, I simultaneously shove it into gear and stomp on the accelerator. Daria jerks Tarasov clear of the rear wheels just in time to keep him from being run over. Halfway through my u-turn, I hear the door behind me slam shut. A glance in the mirror gives me Willie and Joey's faces.

The speedometer jumps up to 120 KPH in the blink of an eye, and I just keep the pedal to the floor.

Then, out of nowhere, an unfamiliar voice fills my ear.

"Alpha – he's on the roof of the Business Aviation terminal on the east end somewhere. I can hear his suppressor venting," the voice says, almost in a whisper.

"Copy that," I hear Michael reply.

"Who the fuck is that?" I blurt out.

"Keith! It's the damn computer dude for God's sake!" Joey says as I hear her slipping magazines into her weapons behind me.

*"Oh shit... oh shit..."* we hear from Michael.

Ten seconds pass before we hear a report from Michael's rifle. Then instantly, a second shot.

*"Someone get to Courtney! Please!"* Michael all but pleads. It almost sounds as if he's crying, and his plea is followed by another report from his weapon.

I drive through the grass on the opposite side of the runway and am close enough I can see my sister and Alice Williamson lying motionless next to the stairs of Alice's aircraft. My heart stops and I burst into tears.

My mind is still locked on my sister's situation when I hear Joey scream behind me – and I swerve without knowing why. I'm focusing so narrowly, that it takes me a few seconds to notice the big hole now in the front windshield of the SUV. My automatic reaction is to jerk up the emergency brake, push the shifter into neutral, and spin the steering wheel bringing the passenger's side of the truck into the line of sight of the shooter. We need something between him and us.

Then one of the side windows explodes inward, showering us with shattered glass. I'm already out on the tarmac when I see Willie drag a bleeding Joey out of the back, and lean her up against the rear tire.

*"Damnit, Michael! Will you please just kill the bastard?!"* I scream into my mic.

In response to my outburst, I first hear an additional report from Michael's rifle, and then four successive shots from what has to be a handgun, and they are close. Very close.

Then silence.

"Izamaylov is down hard," I hear in my ear, again from the unfamiliar voice. "I'm the movement in your field of fire Mike – please don't shoot me."

"Copy that," Michael replies.

I jump up and run the last two hundred feet to where Courtney is lying motionless. When I see blood, I lose it. Within seconds, I'm sobbing. Moments later, Rhyan comes running up next to me and drops to one knee.

*"She saved me.* Why did she do that? They're trying to kill me and she saved me," Alice says. She too, although conscious, is both crying and bleeding badly.

I pick up my sister's limp head and tenderly lay it in my lap. If God is going to take her, she isn't going to die alone. I carefully push the hair out of her face, kiss her gently on the forehead, and then put my lips right next to her ear.

"This is the toughest battle of your life, Sis – don't concede. You've never conceded – not even once. Fight, Courtney, fight this with every ounce of rebellious indignation inside you. Fight for the three people back in Virginia who desperately need you to come home. Fight Sis, like you've never fought before."

Seconds later, there are Swiss police everywhere, and as if God heard me, a huge Huey helicopter with a big red cross on the side lands within yards of us.

The medics have to force me to let her go.

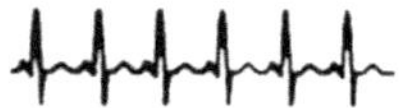

"One cannot plan for the unexpected."

Aaron Klug
British Chemist and Biophysicist
1926 – 2018

# 83

It takes the Swiss military less than five minutes to secure the scene and disarm all of us. The amazing thing is, even with all the gunfire, guys in fatigues, and circling helicopters, only two planes are forced to go around before landing.

Everyone on Sokolski's plane – the two pilots, a steward, and him – as well as his bodyguard, all survive. Tarasov is the only 'bad guy' still functioning – which is my fault. Although I wanted to kill him, being stupid isn't a death penalty offense. Nikolsky, while still alive, is anything but functional.

Alice, William, my sister, and Nikolsky – who is pretty screwed up, even though he was thrown clear when his truck exploded – are immediately airlifted to the trauma unit of a civilian hospital less than a mile away. Tarasov, Vera, and the bodyguard, all go to the hospital in a military ambulance – under guard.

Howard – I have no damn idea what's become of him, which is definitely for the best. Considering he's technically a 'civilian', and yet shot one of the bad guys in broad daylight, in front of a bunch of witnesses, it's probably in everyone's best interest, that the Swiss don't find him. My heart, however, is hoping I'll be able to find him, once all this is over.

Without being told to, Michael and Rhyan did their own 'covert' thing, disappearing quickly and quietly. One thing we can't afford is the discovery of active-duty military personnel involved in a CIA operation in a foreign country.

Oh, and those state-of-the-art steel attaché cases? They too conveniently disappeared.

Once they took Courtney away from me, Keith and I quietly slipped into his truck without anyone noticing, and he drove me back to the Russian Gulfstream, so that I could check on Vera before they took her, and the Russian bodyguard, away. Halfway up the stairs, I notice there's something stuck to one of the plane's tires. I go back down the stairs and am walking toward the landing gear when the Swiss swarm on the plane. The next thing I see is a huge guy in fatigues, sighting his weapon on us, and telling us in German to get down on our knees. Keith grabs me, and pretty much forces me to comply.

Reconnaissance Detachment 10 of the Swiss Special Forces has everyone – including poor Samantha – sitting cross-legged on the concrete, hands secured behind our backs, while their medics tended to those of us who aren't seriously injured. I find it amusing that, although they seem quite concerned about my scalp wound, no one notices the small hole in my jeans – just below the pocket – or the blood trickling down my side and soaking into the waistband of my Levis. Although the bullet is still in my leg, my wounds aren't excessively painful, and I'm not ready to be separated from the others just yet, so I keep my mouth shut.

However, being the elite of the Swiss military, these guys know there's more to what's going on than is visible to the naked eye. Only feet from us, an enlisted guy is reporting, in German, to the captain who seems to be in charge. Fortunately, Samantha speaks fluent German.

"They found a bunch of American made .45 casings – under the Russian aircraft, and around the end of the building," Samantha whispers to me, as we listen to them talking, "along with a note that was held into the treads of the aircraft's tire by another .45 caliber shell casing. None of the weapons they've recovered is .45 caliber,".

*Rhyan.* He was carrying his suppressed HK-UMP, which is .45 caliber. That should make for a multitude of interesting questions, I think to myself. I also find myself wondering what that note said, and after giving it some thought, am fairly certain I know *exactly* what happened to those attaché cases.

Once their conversation is finished, the captain turns and is headed for us, when a black SUV rolls up and comes to a quiet stop within feet of us. Even before it stops completely, the driver's door opens and a pair of new Nikes hit the cement of the apron. When I glance up, I have to force myself not to laugh.

Maxwell Rüegg – Deputy Director, of the Swiss Federal Intelligence Service, closes the door and starts towards us. He stops along the way to speak to the Swiss Captain and to collect what appears to be a stack of passports which he is tapping against one of his thumbs. Max stops in the middle of us and makes eye contact with each of us – Joey, who now has a huge bandage around her upper right arm, Cassie, Willie, Daria, whose shirt is covered with Tarasov's blood, me, Keith, and then finally at Samantha. When she averts her eyes, he shakes his head, then walks over and squats down in front of me.

"I'll bet this..." Max says, gently pulling on the small hole in my jeans, and grinning at me, "hurts like hell."

"Sorta..." I reply, doing my very best not to laugh.

He turns and calls to someone, and in seconds, two medics are standing next to us.

"Miss..." he gives me a look, and then opens my passport, which happens to be on top of the stack, "...*Paddison* seems to have a bullet in her leg." He stands and lets the medics get to me.

The moment Max makes the comment, I realize he knows who I am.

"Courtney ratted me out... didn't she?" I ask, watching the medics as they straighten my leg, and take a pair of scissors to my jeans.

"Yes, yes she did. And let me say, *Whitney*, that you look quite good for someone who has been dead for fifteen years..."

Poor Samantha loses it, and when she laughs, so do the rest of them. Max speaks to the captain, who has been taking all this in, the guy nods, then quickly sets about releasing everyone's hands.

"I should tell you that Director Nyström is quite irritated with the lot of you. He is currently trying to explain this debacle to the General Secretariat.

"Yeah… well… I was just sort of caught up in this one, Max. Courtney and Alice…"

He quickly interrupts me.

"Your sister is in very critical condition, as is Alice…"

"I know. I also know your doctors will do their best."

As the medic finishes taping up my leg and stands to leave, he speaks to Max.

"We have contained the bleeding, sir, but she needs to go to the hospital and have that bullet removed."

"I'll send her along momentarily," he replies, then turns and looks at me again.

"For the record, Claus is still a bit upset that you were able to lose him so handily at the hotel…"

"I've had a few years to practice, Max."

"And it appears your surgery was performed by…" he starts to say, which makes me laugh.

"No surgery involved, Max" I reply. "You want to see?"

His look of total shock makes me laugh – again.

*"That,"* he points at my face, "isn't permanent?"

"Nope," I reply, laughing and glancing at Daria. The smirk covering her face, combined with the look of understanding in her eyes, makes me feel a lot better about what I'm about to do.

I smile, reach around the back of my neck, and after only a couple of tries, find the two tiny Teflon strips just below my collar – one for the left side, one for the right. I know that without applying the solvent, pulling the prosthesis off my face is going to hurt – badly. Regardless, however, I'm going to do it. I take a deep breath and then pull firmly on the right strip. In less than five seconds, about a third of the right side of my face – all the way to my forehead – comes off in a limp rubbery mass, which I lay on the cement in front of me. Needless to say, my eyes water instantly from the pain. I think I even see Daria cringe. I wait a few seconds, then with my eyes closed, I pull the other side off as well, laying it on top of the first one.

The response is instant.

*"Holy shit!"* Cassie and Joey blurt out, simultaneously.

"I agree!" comes from Max just as quickly, *"Holy shit!"*

He again squats down, pokes at the prosthetics with a pen he is holding, and then shakes his head and laughs, as I sit pulling errant pieces of adhesive from my face and neck.

I pull up the left leg of my jeans, under Max's close scrutiny, open the small elastic pouch around my calf, and pull a red diplomatic passport out.

"You're probably going to need that..." I say, as for the first time in fifteen years, I hand my *real* passport to someone. In a matter of seconds, a mass of confused emotions flood into me.

Since my 'death', I've been a bunch of different people at different times, because my life, such that it has been, dictated *I couldn't be myself.* I couldn't be Whitney Bergstrom, *because she's dead.*

This is it. The moment the passport slips from my fingers, I know this is over for me. I've closed yet another chapter, in the story that is my life.

Once the rest of the intelligence world discovers Whitney Bergstrom didn't die on Create, but has instead, been wreaking havoc on the unwary bad guys of the world, my usefulness as a covert asset for the CIA will pretty much be over. Within a matter of hours, I'll have my very own 'personal file' in every intelligence computer on the planet.

So much for being a spy.

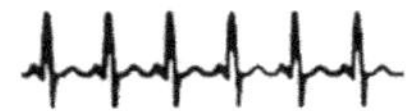

"Every life is a profession of faith, and exercises an inevitable and silent influence."

Henri Frederic Amiel
Swiss Philosopher
1821 – 1881

# 84

We are 'detained' by the Swiss Secret Service for close to forty-eight hours before they eventually cut us loose. Seems that someone in our President's office sent a covert, and off-the-record, request for our release to the Swiss President. The head of the Swiss Secret Service even paid a visit to Alice in her hospital room.

There are tons of questions, and although I want to answer them, I know I can't. How many others were involved? Who did they work for? What became of the individual who shot the Russian at the bank? Who is responsible for the .45 caliber shell casings, and the note found at the airport? And the list goes on. I'm fairly certain they're asking the questions based on protocol – knowing they won't get any real answers. Hell, we are, after all, a bunch of damn spies!

Once they thoroughly grilled everyone involved, they conceded that perhaps, our contention we were simply trying to intervene and stop an assassination, is plausible. Although Sokolski is quick to claim 'diplomatic immunity', even he goes along with our story. I think his concern is what story Tarasov might tell – that could inevitably, implicate him.

What I know that Sokolski doesn't, is that Daria, while she had the Glock against his head on the tarmac, explained *exactly* what he was to tell the Swiss. She also explained the penalty for even the slightest deviation from her instructions.

*"I will help my sister hunt you down."*

When Sokolski eventually goes to see Alice at the hospital, she suggests their conversation about the incident can wait – until they can have it outside the range of prying ears. At this point, the man will comply with any request – or demand – she makes. He knows he's 'clean', only because the CIA has seen fit to sanitize him. Alice's original comment to Daria and Amanda was exactingly correct – a positive outcome of the operation could very well end all the killing between the organizations, at least for a while.

Essentially, the head of the Russian Foreign Intelligence Service is ours.

Because the Swiss want us gone – as in off Swiss soil – we're told to take Alice's Gulfstream back to DC. However, when the Swiss cut us loose, *all of us* go directly to the hospital. At this point, I don't much care what the Swiss want.

We're standing in a line, staring in through a window, watching them working on Courtney when a nurse rolls Alice up.

"I don't unders…" Alice starts to say before I cut her off.

"Because, Alice, it's what we get paid to do. All of us."

I walk around everyone, and through the door into my sister's room, stopping on the right-hand side of the bed. The nurse and doctor are a bit taken aback by the fact I look exactly like their patient. It's obvious they have no idea she has a twin.

After a few seconds, I pick up her right hand with mine, being careful not to dislodge the multitude of IV lines going into her arm. I pull a black felt-tipped pen I borrowed from one of the nurses, from my shirt pocket, and while everyone – including the doctor and nurse – watches, I very carefully draw the one thing my sister needs…

...at the base of her right thumb. I feel my eyes welling up about halfway through and I have to force myself to finish it. Once it's complete, I turn to the doctor and nurse.

"Do you speak English?"

"Yes ma'am," the nurse replies.

"This is not to be removed from her hand for any reason. Is that clear? Tape over it, wrap it in something, if necessary, but do not remove it."

The doctor steps to the end of the bed, picks up the chart from the holder there, flips it open, and begins writing. Once he's done, without a word, he holds it out to me. I take it, and look at what he's written – 'DO NOT REMOVE WHAT IS ON THE PATIENT'S RIGHT HAND FOR ANY REASON' – in both English and German.

"Thank you," I reply. "Now, tell me the truth – what are her chances of surviving this?"

The doctor takes the chart back, and says, "Miss..."

"Bergstrom, Doc. Whitney Bergstrom. This is my sister."

"We figured that out, Miss Bergstrom – the relationship that is."

He makes me blush.

"Realistically speaking," the doctor continues, "she should not be alive now. We – meaning most of the senior staff – are at a loss to explain why she *is* still alive, considering the amount of damage the bullets caused. To be perfectly honest with you, I have absolutely no idea how this will end. I believe it is God, alone, that has the answer to your question, Miss Bergstrom."

I finally lose it, the floodgates open, the tears begin to flow, and there isn't a damn thing I can do about it. In seconds, I'm uncontrollably sobbing. The doctor and nurse smile, then turn and leave me alone with my sister. Once they're gone, I lean over, kiss Courtney's forehead, and whisper in her ear...

*"This little guy is how I am going to keep an eye on you while you are with God for a while, Sis. I'll be here when he sees fit to send you back to us. Be strong and hurry..."*

I kiss her one more time and go back into the hall, where everyone takes a turn hugging me. Eventually, I excuse myself and go to find a quiet place to call my parents.

They need to know.

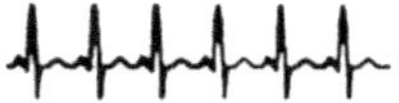

# 85

"So…" I say to the somber faces staring at me. "You guys will send the plane back where it belongs when you're done with it, right?"

Joey and Cassie laugh.

"You mean we can't keep it?" Willie blurts out.

Again, everyone laughs.

"Think we'll ever get to do this again, Whitney?"

"Not likely," I reply. "I'm done. I'm fairly certain Courtney is too. She told Alice she's going to be a mother and wife for a while."

"Good for her. She's earned it, many times over," Joey says.

"Aren't you going back with us?" Samantha asks.

"Nope. I'll see you guys in a couple of days."

"Are you waiting to go back with Courtney?"

"Not exactly. Melinda is taking care of getting them home." I pause for a moment and turn to look right at Samantha. "You will make sure William gets home, right?"

"Yes, ma'am – promise."

"Do you and Daria intend to get into more trouble?" Cassie blurts out, looking way too serious.

"No comment, Cass," I reply, with a smirk on my face. "We have one last thing we need to attend to, and it has to be me and her – the rest of you can't be involved. Besides, it will be easier if you guys are gone – less attention to avoid, if you get my meaning..."

"Fair enough," she replies with a laugh. "Just tell us you have good backup, and we'll let it go."

"We'll have the best backup there is. We've been working together for close to fifteen years," I reply with a wink.

They all understand what I'm insinuating, as well as why they can't be involved.

After we swap hugs, I watch the four of them go out the terminal door, and head for the Gulfstream, which is sitting on the tarmac, with its engines idling. Just for fun, and as an afterthought, I yell at Samantha.

"Hey, Sam!"

"Yes, Whitney?"

"If the plane gets 'lost', you'll have to explain it to Alice!"

I hear them laughing as they climb the plane's stairs. Once the cabin door closes, I head across the building, and out the main doors, to my rental car.

I have one more thing to do before I close the book on this chapter of Whitney's life, and I know right where to find my partner.

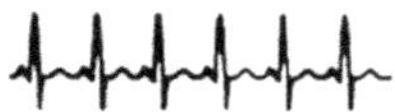

"While all deception requires secrecy, all secrecy is not meant to deceive."

Sissela Bok
Swedish Philosopher and Ethicist
1934 – ?

# 86

I make my tail – the Swiss aren't cutting us any slack – just outside the airport. He stays both visible and right behind me, all the way back to the hotel. He isn't even trying to be stealthy.

I spot Daria sitting at the bar sipping something when I walk in. I carefully steer a path through the tables that brings me up behind her.

"Итак, ты уверена, что хочешь сделать это?" (So, are you certain you want to do this?) I ask, gently placing a hand on her shoulder. She swivels her chair around and I find myself looking at the most solemn face I've ever seen on the woman.

"Будет правильнее спросить, хочешь ли этого ты?" (A better question is, are you?)

"Тот факт, что я его не убивала, должен быть достаточным ответом на данный вопрос. Это важно для тебя и соответственно это важно для меня по умолчанию. Ты стала мне сестрой и навсегда останешься ею." (The fact I did not kill him should be answer enough. It is important to you, and therefore important to me by default. You have become, and will always be, my sister)

She stands up, tears now forming in her eyes, and hugs me tightly. After a few seconds, she steps back and makes a quick eye movement to her left – in the direction of the two Swiss Secret Service guys who've been there the entire time.

"Младший из них позвал кого-то в тот момент, когда ты появилась. Я не думаю, что кто-то из них говорит по-русски." (The younger one called someone the moment you arrived – I don't think either of them speaks Russian) she says, sitting back down.

"Тот, что следовал за мной, сейчас в вестибюле. Он знает, что эти двое здесь." (Mine is manning the lobby. He knows these two are in here.)

"То что мы задумали будет непросто сделать, Алексис, особенно без сторонней помощи." (What we are considering will not be easy, Alexis, especially unaided.)

"А кто сказал, что у нас нет сторонней помощи?" (Who says we are unaided?) I reply.

The totally lost look on Daria's face is priceless.

With a smile, I ask the bartender – in English – for a beer, and take the seat next to Daria.

We sit in silence while the Swiss agents watch us slowly nurse our drinks. It takes about fifteen minutes for the phone in my pocket to ring. Because the Swiss officials 'retained' our weapons and electronics, I borrowed one from Alice's plane when no one was looking. Only one person has the number.

"I'm onsite, and we're a go, Whit," I hear Melinda say.

"Действуете по процедуре?" (Procedure?) I ask.

"Got company, do you?"

"Да, и они сейчас отчаянно пытаются выяснить, где я взяла телефон." (Yes, and they are frantically trying to figure out where I got the phone.)

"Okay. Here's how this will happen. Assets are in place. You need to go for a walk. Go shopping to be specific. Globus, on Bahnhofstrasse. It's a very pricey department store. Women's section. Find something disgustingly expensive and then go to the *attended* changing rooms. They can't follow you in there unless they have a female with them. You're in number six; she's in number twelve – directly opposite. Make sure you each go into the right one. You with me so far?"

"Yes ma'am," I reply in English.

"Good. Once you see the setup, and you are free, come to the Hyatt. I'm in Suite 512. I have everything you asked for."

"Okay, Boss. And thanks for picking up the tab! We promise not to break the bank," I say, then close the phone and lay it on the bar. After a second, Daria looks over at me.

"Boss says we are out of here on a commercial flight in three hours but, we get to go shopping first. How cool is that?"

Poor Daria looks so completely lost, that I actually feel sorry for her.

"Hey! We're *spies*, remember? We simply don't care. They know we're spies. We know that they know. They," I nod in the direction of the two guys watching us, "are gonna follow us. Too bad for them. Now get your damn mood right and let's go." I pick up my glass, drain it, pick up the phone, stick it in my shirt pocket, and stand up. Not knowing what else to do, Daria finishes her drink, throws some money on the bar, and slides off her stool.

Before we go out the door, I stop, look at the surveillance team, and with a smile say, "We're going to Globus to spend some of our government's money before we go home. We can walk slowly if that will make it easier for you. Once we get some new clothes, we're flying home on a commercial flight out of Zürich International. You can verify that if you'd like. Oh, and we promise to speak English from now on."

The younger of the guys is using all his willpower to force back a laugh when he says, "And I hope *you* will not be offended when I say that we, of course, do not believe you," and gives me a really big grin.

I think Daria bites her cheek trying not to laugh – which doesn't work out very well.

Once outside, it takes us twenty minutes to make the casual walk to the Globus department store on the 'most expensive street in the world' – Bahnhofstrasse. It takes a while, but eventually, Daria begins to loosen up and goes back to being the deadly spy she's been for most of her adult life. It's the very first time I've seen her 'concerned' about any operation we've undertaken.

We spend forty minutes pulling this, and that, off racks and then putting it back. We each find two dresses that we like, and giggling like high school girls – under the close scrutiny of our tails of course – we watch the sales girl scan all the items we're going to try on. When she's finished with the clothes, she asks each of us for identification and scans it as well. Seems they like to keep very close track of their expensive clothes.

Once she finishes entering the information into her computer, she leads us to the fitting rooms. We walk down a corridor with doors on both sides, stopping at the end. The girl smiles, then says, "You may use this room, Miss Bergstrom," pointing at a door with a huge '6' on it, "and you may use this one Miss Ladenko," she finishes, pointing at the door directly opposite. I immediately realize she's part of the setup.

"Will it be okay if we decide to wear something out?"

"Of course, Miss Bergstrom. I will be happy to package the clothes you are wearing and send them wherever you would like."

"Cool!" I reply as I open the door to the fitting room.

Inside I find exactly what Melinda said I would. Seconds later, Daria finds hers, and from the muffled scream I hear, it spooks her. But then, walking into a small fitting room and finding *yourself* can be a bit unnerving – especially if you don't know it's going to happen.

Melinda puts in a call to Pierre Fornier, our original make-up teacher, and explains that we are caught up in a 'situation'. Based solely on the insanity of our jobs, he knew it would be prudent to keep ready-to-apply duplicates of all the prosthetics we've ever had to use. Much to our surprise, his collection also includes 'Daria' and 'Whitney'. Once Mindy located two female agents who were a close match to each of us physically, she had everyone flown covertly into Switzerland, and in less than thirty-six hours, Pierre created *exact* duplicates of Daria and me – exact to the point that mine could probably fool even my parents.

Now you know why Melinda is an asset *'specialist'*.

I smile at my double and hold up the dresses I'm carrying. She smiles back and points at the red one, which I promptly hand her. As I'm zipping her up, she whispers to me, "You have excellent taste, Whitney."

"Yeah?"

"Uh-huh."

"Well, how about you keep it when this is over?"

She quickly spins around to face me.

"You're nuts! Did you see the price of this silly dress?"

I laugh as I hand her my documents – my driver's license, two credit cards, and my passport.

"Sure I did, and the boss says it's okay. All I ask is that the two of you get from here, to the airport and on the plane, without incident."

"Promise. You guys be careful as well," she replies, slipping on a pair of expensive heels that were on the chair when I walked in. She runs her fingers through her very blonde hair, and with a smile says, "See ya!" She opens the door, steps out, and pulls it almost closed – leaving just a crack. I step over, peek through, and watch her knock on the other door, then hear her playing her part.

"Come on Daria! Let me see."

After ten seconds or so, the door opens, and 'Daria' steps out in a very short, very tight, blue dress and heels. The likeness is almost scary. I watch the two of them laugh and giggle as they check themselves in the full-length mirror attached to the wall.

Seconds later the young female clerk comes back and starts talking to them. They explain that they intend to wear the new dresses out and that she should send the clothes they left in the dressing rooms to an address in the States. I watch as my double hands the girl my credit card and have to force myself not to laugh.

The doubles follow the clerk out, and after a couple of seconds, I open my door, step over, and tap on Daria's door. She opens it instantly.

"*Damn you*, Whitney Bergstrom. Were you trying to give me a heart attack?" she blurts out in a hushed tone.

"Awww come on, Sis! It got your adrenaline flowing, didn't it? I reply, smiling. "We'll be out of here in just a bit."

It takes three minutes for my phone to ring.

"Yes, M?"

"You have Melinda involved in all this?" Daria whispers.

"You're clear," Melinda says. "All three of the tails are on the decoys. Get changed and get over here."

"Copy that. And thanks!"

"My pleasure, Boss."

I turn, look at Daria, smile, and say, "Yes! Yes, I do. 'Team' – remember? She was all over it by the way. Most of this is her damn idea."

Just as I stop talking, there's a soft knock on the door. I open it to find the clerk standing there with a handful of clothes, a bag that contains two wigs, and a clipboard with a credit card receipt on it. I laugh and sign the receipt, as Daria takes the bag and clothes.

It takes us about fifteen minutes to make our change.

Twenty minutes after that, we're knocking on the door to room 512 at the Hyatt.

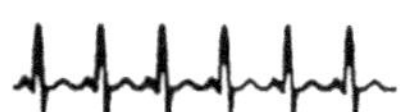

 *Solution Squared: Recalculation*

# 87

Melinda answers the door immediately, and quickly ushers us into the room, closing and locking the door behind us. Inside we find Pierre and his equipment, which in turn causes Daria to stand motionless, looking more than a bit overwhelmed. It only takes a few seconds for Pierre to grab her gently by the shoulders and guide her toward one of his chairs.

Seeing the confused look on Daria's face, Melinda speaks up.

"Oh come on, Daria. Everything about our lives over the last twenty years has been 'off the grid' – why in the hell would this be any different?"

"But..."

"*Team,* Sis," I quickly add. "Off the grid perhaps, but a *team*, nonetheless. His silly ass is apparently important to you, which means we're all in – just like you would be if it was one of us."

She looks at me and smiles, not knowing what else to do.

"Sokolski, and his plane, left two hours ago after they spent three days plugging all the damn holes in it. A different aircraft arrived about ten minutes ago. It will be taking your targets back to Russia," Melinda says, as Daria takes a seat in Pierre's chair, and I begin to undress.

"*Targets?*" Daria asks as Pierre goes to work on her.

"Yeah," I reply, pulling on a bathrobe, and stepping in front of her.

"We have more than one?"

"We are going to retrieve your brother, and Vera as well. I made a promise to her that I intend to keep."

Daria has been exposed to me so closely, and for so long, that she catches even the slightest connotations in my voice – and the look on her face tells me she knows there's more going on in my head.

*"And?"* she asks, with a bit of a glare.

"And... I have unfinished business with Mr. Nikolsky."

As Pierre starts working on her hair, Daria looks directly at me, locks eyes with me, and again glares at me.

"I have never once questioned you, Whitney, but then I have never heard you speak with such a vengeful tone before either."

"Perhaps there's some vengeance involved, Sis, but think about what happens – about the stories that *will* be told – when they get him back to Russia and he wakes up," I say, taking a seat in a second chair and watching Pierre work.

"Well, not to complicate things, Whit, but the bodyguard is going to be with them," Melinda offers.

"I can handle that," I reply with a smirk.

Sitting here, watching Pierre once again turn my partner into someone else, I realize it's the last time we'll be doing this. The strange thing is, it doesn't seem to matter any longer. Inside, I'm completely ready to go back to being Whitney Bergstrom. I've tempted fate far too many times to count, and know it's time for this path to end, and for me to embark on a new one. I also know that in some fashion, Howard is going to be part of my new path.

It takes Pierre about an hour to apply Daria's prosthetics – and she is once again someone else. As she goes about getting her wig on, I take a seat in Pierre's chair. The moment he starts working on me, I'm overcome with an intense feeling of finality, and I think it shows. He stops, places a hand on my shoulder, looks me right in the eyes, and says, "Life, Whitney, does not stop here. It continues and grows. Do not think of this as an ending, but instead, as a beginning. You, young lady, still have many things to do."

Yep.  He makes me cry.

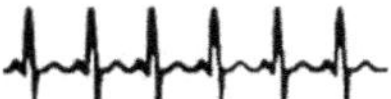

# 88

Snatching the Russians turns out to be far easier than we could have ever imagined. They aren't concerned about us any longer – the Swiss Secret Service *saw* us board a commercial aircraft at the airport.

Melinda monitors all their communications, and with Keith backing us up on the street, our little plan works better than magic.

Because they're now 'traitors to the State', the FSB – or Russian Secret Police – details three internal agents to bring Tarasov, Kovalenko, and Nikolsky back to Russia. Unluckily, for them, they aren't trained as *spies* – and they're just a bit too relaxed, probably because they were told we left the country. They opt to bring their prisoners out the back of the hospital, rather than the emergency entrance, where most ambulances arrive, not wanting to draw undue attention.

Bad move.

Seconds after the lone ambulance pulls up behind the hospital and stops, I walk up to the driver's window and tap on it. When the guy rolls the window down, he's rewarded with a sharp stab in the upper arm, from a small syringe I'm holding, and is immediately unconscious. I have to reach in and keep his head from honking the horn. When the other attendant comes out the rear doors, Daria does the same to her.

We quickly get them into the car we arrived in, which is parked out of sight. When they wake up, they'll have very bad headaches, but that will be it.

Having appropriated the crew's white coats, complete with company logo, I jump in behind the wheel of the ambulance, and Daria goes to report in, just as the real attendants had been instructed. I sit silently watching the rearview mirror for fifteen minutes and finally, a female dressed in white appears, pushing someone in a wheelchair. I open the door, jump out, and after a second look, I recognize her patient – Sokolski's bodyguard, Issak.

As I round the rear of the ambulance, a black Benz pulls up and a single male gets out. I'm opening the rear doors when he walks up to me.

"Sind Sie der Fahrer?" (Are you the driver?) he asks in a very brusque tone.

"Ja." (Yes)

"Wir wollen zum Geschäftsflugterminal am Flughafen. Fahren Sie vorsichtig und beachten Sie alle Verkehrsregeln…. Ich werde direkt hinter Ihnen sein. Verstehen Sie?" (We are going to the Business Aviation Terminal at the airport. You will drive carefully and will obey all driving rules. I will be directly behind you. Do you understand?)

"Ja," I again reply, grinning at him.

The sound of automatic doors opening makes all of us turn and look at the same time. There's a nurse pushing Nikolsky, another pushing Vera, and Daria is pushing Tarasov, followed closely by two guys in high-dollar suits – *definitely FSB*. I know at least one of the suits will be with us, but I need to be certain the nurses won't be. The last thing I need is civilians in the middle of my op.

Daria is helping the bodyguard into the ambulance, and I'm about to help Nikolsky, who is by far, in the worst shape, when I'm suddenly stopped.

"Dieser geht zuletzt," (This one goes in last) the guy driving the Benz says, grabbing Nikolsky's shoulder.

I shrug and turn to help Tarasov into the ambulance. Once Daria has the bodyguard strapped in, she turns and finishes with Tarasov, as I climb out and step toward Vera. I'm about to find out just how astute this woman is.

"Interesting perfume," she says, smiling and gently kicking me in the leg, making it appear to be an accident.

After all the crazy bullshit we've endured to this point, she somehow remembers my preoccupation with the perfume, while in the store we stopped at on the way to the hotel. In fact, it was because of her prodding, that I bought it.

"Thank you," I reply, faking a German accent, and helping her stand up. Her entire upper body is in a temporary cast designed to limit any additional damage to her shoulder until surgery can be performed on it – which the Russians aren't in a big hurry to do.

It's obvious she's not sure, she damn sure suspects. I see it in her eyes – suspicion *and* hope. Hope that she might actually get to see her husband again. Hope that she isn't headed for a Russian prison.

Daria takes her good arm and helps her into the ambulance. I turn and move toward Nikolsky, and again, am immediately stopped.

"Встать, предатель" (Get up traitor) the gruff guy says.

When Nikolsky doesn't immediately respond, one of the other guys grabs him, and forcefully jerks him into a standing position. I think the nurse almost has a heart attack, and when she takes a step toward us, the bad guy stops her.

"Wir werden Ihre Hilfe nicht brauchen. Bitte kehren Sie zum Krankenhaus zurück" (We will not need your assistance. Please return to the hospital) he commands, stepping over and blocking her path to the wheel chair.

When I make eye contact with Nikolsky, as I'm trying to help him into the ambulance, his face tells the story. He knows what his future holds.

It takes Daria and I, working together, to get him onto the cot, which is the only empty seat. As we're laying him down, the gruff guy tries to stop us.

"Er sitzt so wie die anderen. Ihm ist keine bequehmlichkeit erlaubt." (He sits like the others. He is not allowed to be comfortable.) he says, grabbing my wrist.

I jerk my arm free, turn, and glare right at him. As Daria goes about strapping Nikolsky in, I step out of the ambulance and right up to the idiot who is apparently in charge. Fully aware that what I'm about to do is very risky, I do it anyhow.

"Это МОЯ машина скорой помощи, и я тот, кто устанавливает тут правила. Если они вам не нравятся, вы можете везти этих пациентов как-то еще. Вам *это* ясно?" (This is MY ambulance, and I make the rules. If you do not like my rules, you are free to transport these patients by some other means. Is *that* clear?)

Every head, including the nurse who turned back toward the entrance, snaps in our direction. I think Daria, although she hides it well, damn near faints. The Russian's facial response is insanely amusing, to say the least. Nope... definitely *not* spies...

I think it's at this moment, Vera's suspicions are confirmed – I see a huge grin form on her face, that she can't seem to hide.

As angry as the Russian is, he lets it go and turns to one of the other guys, pulling him aside, and talking to him in hushed tones – now that he knows I speak his language. I'm about to close the doors when the second Russian walks up and stops me.

"Я поеду с вами." (I will be riding with you.)

"Как пожелаете. Но тогда вам придется ехать спереди, вместе со мной, поскольку согласно нашим правилам, санитар должен находиться с пациентами сзади." (As you wish. But then you will have to ride in front, with me, since according to our rules, the orderly must be with the patients in the back) I quickly reply, nodding at Daria.

He turns to look at the asshole, and when he gets a nod from him, lets me close the doors. Seconds later, we're on our way. The amusing thing is, just as so many other times in the past, not a single one of them has a damn clue.

We have a nice fifteen-minute drive, and just as we're about to make the turn that will lead us to the expressway heading to the airport, Keith arrives. He comes blasting out of an alley, between two huge buildings and hits the guys in the Benz broadside. Just before the impact, he dives into the back seat, landing on the floor as the cars collide. Seconds later, he's out of the car and halfway down the alley he came out of. It takes the guy sitting next to me about fifteen seconds to realize what's happened. He screams for me to stop, and instantly reaches into his coat for his gun. He's looking at the mirror on his side, so he never sees the syringe. I get him right in the carotid artery, pushing the plunger before the needle is all the way in, and watching his head drop, even before the syringe is empty.

I let go of the syringe – leaving it stuck in his neck – and with my right hand, flip on the lights and siren, jerk the wheel to my right, and stomp on the gas. As I weave my way through traffic and onto the highway, I hear Daria talking in the back – even if I can't make out what she's saying over the siren.

After tearing down the highway for three minutes, I take the exit just before the one to the airport. Halfway up the off-ramp, I turn off the lights and siren. I make a quick right turn, and a mile down the road, see what I'm looking for.

As we roll past the parked van, I glance in the outside mirror and see the headlights flash. Then, it immediately pulls out onto the road behind us. I drive another mile, then turn in behind a large warehouse complex and stop. When the van stops right behind us, I open the door, get out, and as I turn toward the back of the ambulance, see Melinda getting out of the van. We meet at the back doors.

"Damn. You two never cease to amaze me."

"Yeah, yeah," I reply, opening the doors of the ambulance. "So, what's the status?"

"Keith took out the others – the driver is in stable condition, and will survive. A plane is on the runway waiting on them. They weren't expecting any of this, so just as you predicted, they don't have any additional assets on site. But the word is out."

"Cool," I reply, turning to look in the back of the ambulance.

Tarasov, and the bodyguard, are confused, and perhaps a bit nervous. Vera, on the other hand, knows *exactly* what's going on. She has the goofiest smirk covering her face, and now, tears building in her eyes. I glance at her and say, "You sit there, and be quiet."

"You," I say harshly and pointing directly at Tarasov, "are getting your life back – *do not* fuck it up a second time, Leonid."

Tarasov looks at me, then at Daria, and then back at me.

"Blood is thick, Leonid – just ask your sister," I nod at Daria who's now standing next to him. "She's the *only* reason I didn't kill you at the airport. If we find ourselves in the same situation again, I can assure you the results will not be the same. *Do we understand each other*?"

In that instant, I see complete understanding in his eyes, as the realization of who we are, sinks in.

"Yes, I fully understand. From this point in time forward, I am – and will remain – dead to this world. I can assure you, Miss, we will never, *under any circumstances,* meet again."

I nod at him, then look at Daria.

"Get him in the van, Sis."

Once Tarasov and Daria are out, I climb into the ambulance and go about unbuckling Vera.

"You really are going to have to quit kicking me, girl. I think I have a bruise on my leg."

"I only know you as 'Alexis', and I am certain that it is not your true identity."

"My name is Whitney. Whitney Bergstrom," I reply, smiling and helping her stand up, then leading her to the back of the ambulance where Melinda helps her climb down.

"I resigned myself to the fact you would not be able to negotiate my release," she says, as she gingerly makes her way to the ground, "which, in all honesty, I understood."

"I don't make promises I can't keep," I reply, taking the two steps to the pavement, and turning to face her. "You paid your half of the bill, now I'm paying mine. There are some doctors waiting for you at a hospital in Germany. Melinda," I point directly at her, "is going to make sure you get there. Knowing her, I will bet your husband is already there, waiting for you."

"Thank you – for saving me from my own stupidity."

I can't help it – I break up laughing.

"You're the second Russian to say that to me," I reply with a wink. "We will see each other again, eventually. Right now, however, we're on the clock, and you guys need to go."

Daria takes over and leads her in the direction of the van, with Tarasov close behind.

"Get them where they need to go, Mindy," I say, turning back toward the ambulance.

"Whitney..." she starts to say, making me quickly cut her off.

"Not now, M," I respond, turning to face her. "Just get these guys out of here, and let the rest of it go."

"This isn't you, and you damn well know it. Please, don't do this, Whitney. You can't take it back after the fact."

"She's right," Daria adds, leaving Tarasov holding onto Vera, then walking over and putting a hand on my shoulder.

"We have *never* acted based on vengeance – it is not what we do. Besides, *Sis*," she says with a smirk on her face, "what his own people will do to him is far worse than what you have planned. Please, Whitney, let this go. Once it is done, it is done forever."

"I can't let it go," I reply, climbing into the ambulance and sitting down across from Nikolsky. When I turn to look back at them, Vera has hobbled back over and is standing at the open door, staring at me.

"This is not the same woman who so calmly and logically convinced me I was traveling the wrong path – when it would have been far simpler to have killed me. This is not the same woman who has risked her life once again, to ensure my freedom and keep a promise that was made in haste, between adversaries. That woman, would not be doing what you are about to do."

When I don't respond, Daria shrugs, then turns and leads Tarasov toward Melinda's van. After a second, Melinda takes hold of Vera's good arm, and they too head for the van.

I pull a third syringe from my shirt pocket and as I pull the cap from the needle, I hear Daria's voice, yelling…

*"And do not think for a fucking second I will not make a trip to the States to tell your sister just exactly what the hell you did, and why I believe you did it!"*

My heart stops – cold. I turn and look in the direction of the van just in time to see the door slide closed, and in seconds, it's moving across the parking lot, toward the highway.

When I look back at Nikolsky, whose eyes are now open, I realize he's been listening to the entire conversation.

"There is, and always has been, a very fine line in what we do. It separates 'necessity' from 'murder'. Daria is correct – although you want to kill me, your heart will not let you. Although you are quite adept at our game, unfortunately for me, you are not a *murderer*, Miss Bergstrom."

When he stops talking, he once again closes his eyes.

The second I feel the hand on my shoulder I freak, and instinctively pull my Beretta. I spin around, and before I can stop myself, shove it into the face of Sokolski's bodyguard, who is next to me. He immediately raises his hands and leans back away from me.

My heart is racing so fast, I can feel it pounding in my chest. I'm suddenly overcome by an intense feeling that everything is about to get completely out of control – a feeling that I haven't experienced even once, in the fifteen years I've been a spy.

What we do is *always* planned and executed to the detail. Daria and I *never* let things get out of control. *Ever*. People who aren't supposed to die, could, if things get out of control.

"Yes, you are a spy, perhaps even an assassin, Whitney – doing what you are told must be done. But, just as he," the bodyguard points at Nikolsky, "said, you are not a *murderer*. I know and understand what it is that drives you right now, but you must not give in to it. You must be who you are, *not* what it desires to make you."

Without a word, I lay the gun down, and insert the syringe into one of the capped IV lines still in Nikolsky's arm. He never makes any move to stop me, but instead lies motionless, as if he wants me to do it.

Full-on crying, a mass of tears streaming down my cheeks, my heart seems to be beating faster, and faster – if that's even possible – as I place my thumb on the plunger. I'm ready to push it and send Nikolsky on his final journey when for reasons I still don't understand, I turn and again make eye contact with Issak.

I am in fact losing control... *and I know it.*

"You *could have* killed me. You *could have* killed him," he says, nodding at the guy slumped in the passenger's seat, "and you *could have* killed Tarasov. Each time, you knew that it was not *necessary.*"

I suddenly see Courtney looking back at me from the front of the ambulance, and she isn't happy. Although I know she isn't really there, my heart wants her to be. I'm sobbing now, and am one push away from ending Boris Nikolsky's life – not because it's necessary, but because I can... *because I want to...*

Then – *God steps in...* in the form of Keith's voice.

"And what you are about to do, Whitney, isn't even close to necessary. *And you damn well know it.*"

I let the syringe go even before Keith finishes his sentence, and as my hands are shaking uncontrollably, I jump out of the ambulance. Keith half-catches me as my feet hit the ground, and I throw my arms around his neck, squeezing him as tightly as I can.

And I cry. Hysterically.

For a full thirty seconds, I'm in such deep emotional pain, that I truly wonder if recovery is even possible. They're right, of course – all of them. I want *so badly* to kill the bastard, but I can't. I can't just arbitrarily kill him. My heart won't let me.

*And... God knows this....*

I have to believe that's why he made certain Keith turned up, exactly when he did. It's my turn to be saved – from myself.

Once I regain control of my heart, and the sobbing, I realize Issak is now standing, with great effort, next to me.

"I knew it was *necessary* to trust you at the airport," he says, handing my weapon back to me. "You somehow knew that I did, and chose to protect me by pushing me to the ground when the shooting started. I knew then, as I know now, that despite our chosen professions, you are a strong and decent person. Go now and let us deal with this traitor. Be assured he will pay the highest price for all of his treachery – *including what happened to your sister.*"

Just as he finishes talking, we hear the guy in the front seat moaning, as he struggles to regain consciousness.

"We gotta go, Whit. *Now.*"

Then, quite by accident, I see movement inside the ambulance, and my brain instantly switches back on.

*"Oh shit!"* I yell, pushing past Keith, and jumping back into the ambulance. I'm a split second too late. I watch as Nikolsky's eyes roll back in his head, and his hand slips off the syringe. The guy in the front is almost fully conscious, and Keith is getting nervous.

"Damn it, Whitney. *Let's go!*"

"You can let it go, Miss Bergstrom," Issak says, smiling at me. "He has taken care of it for you. Go now, before you are again compromised."

I look at him, then at Keith, and finally at Nikolsky – who is quite dead. Not knowing what else to do, I turn, climb out of the ambulance again, and let Keith lead me to the car he has waiting.

During the ride from the parking lot to the airport, I'm able to remove the wig, and all the prosthetics, this time using the solvent. I even change clothes on the expressway. By the time we pull into the rental car return area, I once again look like Whitney Bergstrom – although I have an alternate ID saying I'm someone else. It takes us an additional forty-five minutes to get through the security checkpoints, and onto our flight. The moment I hit the seat, it all rushes out of me – the entire previous four hours. Keith sees it and reaches out to take my hand.

"You sure you're ready to be plain old Whitney Bergstrom again?" he asks, as the flight attendant hands us each a drink.

"More than I will ever be able to explain, Keith. And thank you – from the deepest part of my being."

I lean over, and with a smile, gently kiss him.

Once we're airborne, I close my eyes and find my sister behind them, smiling back at me. This is over – and I know it. More importantly, I realize that I'm glad it is.

Whitney Bergstrom is now, *CIA, retired.*

It's time for me to quietly fade into the world.

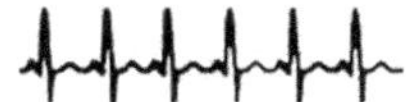

In London, the plan was to continue on to Washington, on a second flight. I change the plan. We're sitting in one of the many bars at Heathrow.

"I've got two things to do while I'm here, Keith, and I know you will understand when I tell you I have to do them alone," I say, between sips of beer.

"Yeah, okay, Whit. Just don't kill anyone here – please?"

I laugh, lean over, and this time, kiss him on the cheek.

"What I have to do here is personal, not business," I reply. "I'm going to change the course of my life. Time for a new path, you know?"

"Yes ma'am. You gave up *your* life and did everything that has been asked of you for fifteen years – without question. I think you've earned a change."

"I'll see you stateside in a couple of days. If you happen to run into my parents, tell them I'm coming.

"Will do. And Alice?"

"Tell her I said to 'shut up and heal'."

"Gotcha."

We finish our beers, then stand, and turn to face each other. I give him a hug, and again, feel a driving need to cry. Although one or two tears escape, I force the rest back as I turn and head for the taxi stand in front of the airport.

An hour later, I'm standing on a sidewalk in Grosvenor Square, staring at the front doors of the U.S. Embassy.

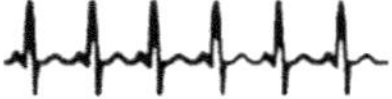

# 90

I damn near jump out of my skin when I hear the voice...

"In days past, I would never have been able to sneak up on you," the female voice says, as she covertly snatches the Beretta from the holster behind my back.

I spin around to find a short, blonde female standing there with a huge grin on her face, and my gun stuck in her belt.

Josephina Masterson – CIA Station Chief, London.

"Jezzz! You must have some good intel people... how'd..."

She interrupts me midsentence.

"Keith."

I laugh.

"He's still looking out for me..."

"Uh-huh. Stood to reason you were headed here, or to find Howard."

"Actually Joey, I'm looking for an old friend. A friend I lost a long time ago. I owe her a huge apology. She works in there," I reply, pointing at the embassy.

"Well, I'm the embassy's Chief of Security, so perhaps I can be of some assistance. Come with me."

She covers the Beretta with her windbreaker, turns, and starts across the street, with me close behind. She shows her ID to a Marine at the gate, tells him I'm with her, and five minutes later, she's closing her office door behind us.

We stand staring at each other for about thirty seconds, neither speaking. Then something very strange happens. For the second time in as many days, Whitney Bergstrom bursts into tears without warning. At this exact moment, everything in my life over the last fifteen years catches up with me all at once, and before I know it, I'm again sobbing.

Joey carefully guides me toward her couch and sits me down.

"God, Joey! I am so damn sorry. Sorry for screwing you then, and for all the years of torment. If I had known..."

"It wouldn't have made any difference, Whit, and you damn well know it. Do you remember when you first found out about me, in that conference room in Istanbul, years ago?"

"Yeah," I reply, trying once again, to get my emotions under control.

"Just before I opened the door and you fell into the room, I told Courtney something. Now I'm going to tell you. It defines who we are – all of us who choose to do what we do. Courtney realized that Howard and Carl had used all of us as a means to an end, and in response, I told her, *it's what they do... what we do, what we agreed to when we signed up. It's very convoluted – but then, it has to be if it's going to work.* "

"You should hate me Joey – if for no other reason, than the internal torment you have suffered over the years. I screwed you and there just isn't any other way to say it."

"When I first saw the photo of you... and realized what was happening, I thought I would. When Courtney looked at me across that table in Gibraltar and asked for my help to recover you, I knew there was no way I could. You did what was asked of you, Whitney, just as we all do in this godforsaken business we are part of. All any of us can do is hope. Hope that some good comes from the daily stupidity we subject ourselves to. That includes you."

"You don't hate me?"

"I hate the world that caused all this to happen. That's why I am still part of all this shit. Every day I pray, that with each new situation I encounter, and with luck am able to resolve, the world might move just a bit closer to some kind of equilibrium between sanity and stupidity. I am smart enough to realize that everything you and Daria have done was in the interest of achieving the same thing. No, Whitney, what I feel for you is not even in the same universe as hate."

"Thank you, Joey, with everything that I am – my entire being. Since the point back on that runway, when I knew this was over for me, I've struggled with how I would try to make you understand – to get you to forgive me. Honestly, I didn't think it would happen."

"Damn! You are still a total nutcase, Whitney Bergstrom. With all the other complications that are about to crop up in your very bizarre life – your parents being at the top of that list – you are worried about me?"

"They are my parents – they sorta have no choice in all this, you know? They'll love me, even if they don't understand. You, on the other hand, are a friend, a partner in crime, someone who covered my ass at the expense of her own. Hell yes, I'm worried about you."

"You did nothing to me, Whitney. I did it to myself. More than once, Courtney tried to make me see that, and I refused..."

She pauses, and strange calmness settles over us at the same time. Again, we stand silently staring at each other, until finally, Joey breaks the stalemate.

"It all stops here and now. I am. You are. And now, 'we' can be again. Move on with your life, Whit, and know that I'm here if you ever need anything. Also, know that should I need anything, your sorry ass is at the top of my list. Sound fair?"

I lean over and hug her as tightly as I can, tears once again trickling down my face. There's now peace, in at least one area of my life. When we break our embrace, I look at her and am about to ask a question, when she arbitrarily answers it.

"She's still in a coma, Whit. I've been checking every few hours, and Melinda promised to call me the moment anything changes."

I only nod in response.

"So," Joey says, walking to her desk and retrieving some papers from it. "You wouldn't know anything about this, would you?" She walks back across the room, stops right in front of me, and hands me the pages. It's a translated signal intercept, and the first few words say it all...

*'...the abduction by unknown individuals, of Leonid Tarasov, and Vera Kovalenko.'*

It takes every ounce of willpower I can muster, to keep a straight face. Doing my very best to look angelic, I lift my head from the pages and look at Joey.

"Now, why would you think I would, Miss Masterson?"

We break up laughing, and after she takes the pages back from me, she continues.

"Alice is seriously pissed off, you know. She's going ream you *and* Daria – because she's convinced you did do it. And to make matters worse, the Russians are seriously pissed off too. You killed their traitor before they could 'interrogate' him. They wanted to know who, exactly, was supporting his insanity..."

"'*We*' didn't kill him. He took his own life. And someone, on their side no less – who was present, knows what happened."

Although she looks quite puzzled, she lets it go at that.

"I have one other thing you can help me with J..."

She again understands. She picks up a piece of paper and scribbles something on it, then hands it to me.

"He was already on a plane headed back here by the time the Swiss collected all of us. His experience, and common sense, told him he needed to get out before shit hit the fan. He knew he'd done what he could – and actually seeing you, got to him. I've tried to get a hold of him three or four times, but he isn't ready to talk to me yet. Personally, I think he needs to hear from you."

"Yeah, another of my major screw-ups, Joey."

"That's his home address, and where he's working," she says, pointing at the piece of paper I'm holding. "He's teaching and lives just across the river, a short distance from the school. Whatever you do, Whitney, *don't* approach him the same way you did me. He was, and I believe probably still is, very much in love with you. Approach him with that in mind, okay?"

"Yes ma'am," I reply, wiping my face for the hundredth time.

"Do you need a place to spend the night?"

"No, I'll find a hotel in the area and hold up."

"The Crowne Plaza is a mile away, on New Bridge Street, or the Holiday Inn in Southwalk."

I'll go with the Plaza – I know how to get there. Figures he'd end up at one of the best schools in London. I'll come by before I leave for the States, okay?"

"You'd better," she replies, handing the Beretta to me. "I want to know how this all works out. *And...* if you chicken out and run, I *will* hunt you down. Understood?"

*"Yes,"* I reply, laughing and putting the gun back into its holster. "I'll see you later. And thanks, Joey."

We exchange another hug and then I'm off to find Howard – at the London School of Economics no less.

As I'm descending into the Underground Station a couple of blocks from the Embassy, I realize I'm more afraid of facing Howard than I am of facing my parents.

This, I think to myself as I board the train that will take me to Blackfriars Station, should prove quite interesting.

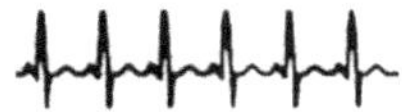

# 91

It isn't at all difficult finding Howard's class – he's teaching Political Science. After only a couple of tries (using my now perfect British accent of course) I encounter someone who's headed for one of his lectures. I find it amusing that his students refer to him as 'the Yank who teaches PolySci'.

With very little effort, I sneak into the lecture hall and find an empty seat at the back of the room. I will, however, discover I'm not as stealthy as I think.

It takes less than an hour for me to realize that Howard is an amazing teacher – as if it's what he always should have been doing. I watch, completely enthralled, as his students open one debate after another on a host of subjects related to Political Science, and Howard is right in the middle of each one.

After almost ninety minutes of 'class', Howard suddenly raises a hand, and the entire hall goes silent. What happens next, I would have never expected in a million years.

"Okay guys, you recall I explained my recent absence by telling you I was off saving some friends of mine who are in the 'spy' business, right?'

The moment he says it, I know I'm in trouble, and for a split second even consider getting up, and leaving. There's the general whooping and hollering that one expects from college students, and then someone in the front of the class speaks up.

"Professor Jensen, we are still waiting for you to provide us with sufficient evidence to support your claim of a life in the CIA."

"Well, Martin," Howard says, stopping in front of the young man who spoke up, "today I happen to have that proof – right here in this room." Then he looks directly at me, and it's as if he read my mind.

"Don't even think about it," he says, loudly enough he's certain I hear him, then quickly returns his attention to the kid in front of him.

"Are you prepared to determine validity, should I present it?"

Dead silence. The place is suddenly quieter than a church – which probably isn't possible. It seems as if they have all quit breathing. I also notice a few looking in my general direction. Then my damn 'light bulb' goes on, and I realize what he's about to do.

"Martin?" Howard says, prompting the kid.

When he doesn't respond, Howard addresses the entire class.

"This, just like every other debate in any of my classes, is an open one. Every opinion – whether it sucks or not – must be offered."

"Professor, no offense intended..."

"And none will be taken, Nikki. Please, state your position."

"Assuming, you were associated with the CIA, is it not reasonable to assume that you could fabricate any information or 'proof' you wanted? I mean, that's the kind of thing that intelligence organizations do, isn't it?"

"A point has been presented. Are there any comments?"

A young girl in the middle of the room – who appears to be oriental – stands up, just as a horn sounds marking the end of the class. The amazing thing is, not a single one of them moves.

"Professor, I offer this. Remove the speculation. Present this 'evidence' so that we might prove, or disprove, your claim."

"Very well put, Miss Soong. Perhaps that is what I will do. Any objections, Martin?"

"None, sir."

"Very well. Whitney, come down here please."

My damn heart stops as he turns and again looks directly up at me, with the most sinister smirk on his face. It's in this moment that true understanding floods into me. This is his way of making sure I don't get away from him a second time. Silly Howard thinks he's compromising me!

"Come on, Whit. They're innocent college kids. I promise not to let them hurt you – not physically anyhow."

That draws several laughs and snickers from the room. I know I have to make a decision – even if Howard has no clue. I stand, and the second I do, every pair of eyes in the room is on me. When I glance again at Howard, the biggest smile I've ever seen on the man covers his face. After thinking about it for a moment, I step out into the aisle and start toward the front of the auditorium.

"Ladies and gentlemen, please allow me to introduce, Miss Whitney Bergstrom – most recently a member of the Black Ops arm of the Central Intelligence Agency. And of course, my fiancé."

The entire place erupts in applause, and I know I'm brighter red than I've ever been in my entire life. As I'm going up the stairs at the front of the room, Martin has a new comment.

"Professor, no insult intended to the lady, but if she were a true covert operative, involved in 'questionable' proceedings no less, why would you tell us that? Seems more than a bit far-fetched, sir."

As Howard holds out his hand to me at the top of the stairs, the applause dies down, and he leads me to the middle of the raised platform. Then, in my usual Whitney manner, I make a comment – without thought one to the consequences.

"Howard Jensen, you are such a bloody wanker at times," comes out of my mouth, in a thoroughly British manner.

Again, an eruption of laughter and hooting, during which I walk over and stop in the vicinity where 'Martin' should be. Howard never says a word, but instead only watches.

"And which of you fine, young, gentleman is Martin?'

A rather cute guy in the third row back reluctantly raises his hand, and at least four pairs of eyes in the vicinity lock on to him, giving him away anyhow.

"What form of 'proof' will you require to substantiate the claims of my boyfriend?" I ask, a sinister glare on my face, and my hands on my hips.

"I intend no disrespect, Miss Bergstrom," he replies, a very anxious look now covering his face.

As I glance around the room, I realize that every single one of them is still here – not a single one left when the class ended.

"And none is taken, Martin. I simply wish to corroborate the professor's claims. I am here in your class and so, I too, am bound by his," I stop, turn, and give Howard a really dirty look, "rules of engagement. If this is truly an 'open debate', then let us proceed."

The young Chinese girl speaks next.

"Should we assume your position is that the Professor's claims are true? He *was* a member of the CIA, and you are as well?"

"Correct. Howard told you the truth."

Then a new girl stands and joins in. It seems the entire room is again buzzing with activity and hushed conversations.

"If you are a spy, Miss, is it safe to assume you are armed?

"Of course. I am in search of my counterparts working for other governments, and they are in search of me. It would be a bit foolish for me to run around chasing other spies unarmed."

Again, the room falls silent. The girl who posed the question is now a pale white and even poor Martin looks a bit spooked. I turn around, look right at Howard and when our eyes lock, all I see in his is, 'I dare you' – which of course is the wrong thing to say to me, but then, Howard has always known that.

I turn back to the students, all of whom are still silently staring. Up to this point, I've been doing my Alexis Paddison persona – right down to sounding thoroughly British.

Time to change up on them.

"Okay then, I'm getting the distinct impression that my word isn't gonna cut it in this situation," I say, now sounding completely American, and evidently confusing the crap out of most of them. I reach behind my back, pull the Px4 out of a holster on my belt, which is very conveniently hidden by the oversized windbreaker I'm wearing, drop the clip out of it, pull the slide back ensuring it's clear, and then lay it on a small desk at the front of the room where they can all see it.

The result is priceless.

"Next question?"

It immediately comes from a completely confused Martin.

*"You aren't British?"*

"Nope. I was born in Virginia – which I'm pretty sure you know, is in the States."

Then, the Chinese girl again.

"You really are a member of the CIA? Like a 'secret agent'?"

"Yes. I'm part of the CIA's Clandestine Services Division and have been since I was twenty-three. That's where I met this jerk," I reply, laughing and pointing at Howard. I reach into the back pocket of my jeans and pull out *my* passport which, along with the Px4, was delivered to me at the gate when we deplaned at Heathrow.

"Just remember, you started this," I say to Howard, without looking at him.

He breaks up laughing as I step off the end of the platform and then, in a very unladylike fashion, over the first two rows of seats, coming to rest in the chair right next to Martin, who at this point looks petrified.

"Here. Let me know if this is sufficient proof. Oh, and if I don't get it back..."

Again, the room is filled with laughter – this time a bit more subdued, however. I'm halfway to where Howard is standing, my gun in his hand when we hear poor Martin.

*"BLOODY HELL!"*

"You do realize what you've just done, don't you?"

"No, I don't. Tell me."

"Oh, come on, Whitney," Howard replies, handing me the Beretta.

"If you're thinking I just compromised myself, think again, buster," I reply. As I release the slide, the metallic 'click' as it slides forward echoes through the room. I'm still looking at Howard with a smirk, as I slide the clip into the weapon, and then replace it in the holster.

"Meaning?"

"I was compromised – on purpose, I might add – four days ago on a runway in Switzerland. Had you not disappeared so damn quickly, and had given me a chance to explain things..."

Again, Howard gets my attention with nothing more than the look in his eyes. When I quit talking for a second, I realize it's once again deadly quiet in the room, and that all eyes – and ears – are on us.

Oh well. The cat's out of the bag anyhow, I think to myself.

"Why'd you vanish so damn fast anyhow? Me or the op?"

"Both," Howard replies.

This is the moment my epiphany occurs – and I realize that having this discussion with the audience is making it easier for him for some reason, which is fine with me.

"I compromised myself when I pulled the prosthetics off my face in front of everyone. I knew then I was done, Howard, and I'm okay with it. That's why I'm here. My sister gave everything to give me another chance and..."

Howard goes pale when I say it, and I instantly regret the choice of words.

"Is Courtney...?"

"No, Howard, she isn't. She's still out, but she's in the best hands she could be. "

"Thank God."

"I have numerous times. Now, about your disappearance from Switzerland..."

"Uhh, excuse me, Miss. *Switzerland?* Are you talking about the airport in Zürich?" asks a different young woman in the second row.

I turn my attention away from Howard for a moment – which seems to relieve him a bit and face the young woman.

"Yes ma'am. Three days ago, Professor Jensen and I were there – together."

"*Oh my God!* You were the ones on the news! *You were in the shootout at the Zürich airport!*"

Howard starts laughing, as I take a step toward the front of the room and start talking – again.

"I was. Howard wasn't. He was there but departed prior to the big fiasco you saw on the news," I reply, walking around the table and then sliding up onto it from the front.

"Were the news reports true, or accurate?" someone asks.

Suddenly I have their attention, and it's as if I've become the teacher. And their interest is genuine. They all want to know – they want to know *the truth*. I think this is the moment I finally understand that, if she wants one, Whitney Bergstrom can perhaps, find a new path. I also know it's Howard's fault. He did this – put on this 'performance' – purposely.

I spend the next hour and a half – time that's valuable to a student working on their Master's Degree – answering their questions. When I can't give them an answer, they simply move on, and don't question my reasons. They're getting an inside look at a world they all suspect exists, but feel they'll never know the truth about. This is the deepest any Political Science graduate could ever hope to get into the world of espionage – short of joining up. And, they make the most of every second.

It's easily the most incredible ninety minutes of Whitney Bergstrom's entire thirty-seven years of life.

Then, my brain arbitrarily resets itself, right in the middle of our discussion. Out of nowhere, my means of retaliation – for being set up – manifests itself. It's something Howard said earlier. I stop a young man, right in the middle of a sentence.

"Uh, guys... can I have just one minute please. I need to address something," I say, sliding off the table. "Hang around and I'll be glad to continue, but this is sort of important."

They once again fall silent and watch as I turn and walk to the desk Howard has been sitting at since I started running my mouth. He realizes something's up when the room goes quiet again.

"Excuse me, Professor Jensen. I have a question if I may?"

His face tells the story – he knows he's in trouble.

"Yes, Miss Bergstrom?"

"What was the deal with the whole 'my fiancé' thing back when you put me on the spot?" I ask, placing both hands on his desk, and leaning about halfway over it.

"Excuse me?"

"You did say that, Professor!" I hear Martin yell out behind me. He's quickly followed by at least ten other students, all agreeing with him.

"Do you intend to make good on that comment, Howard? Do you intend to marry me? I mean hell, you just went halfway around the damn world to find me."

I want so badly to finish that sentence, but know saying 'and killed the sorry bastard who was about to shoot me' would be taking it too far. Besides, I have him, right where I want him. I can see the little beads of sweat forming on his forehead as he squirms a bit in his chair.

"Come on, *Professor*, we aren't getting any damn younger, and I would like to have a couple of kids, while Mother Nature will still let me."

Suddenly that same childish-sounding voice, the Chinese girl with the very British accent, fills the room.

*"You bloody well better marry her, Professor lest you have twenty-six extremely cheesed-off students on your hands!"* she yells from her seat, which she's now standing on.

The room once again erupts in laughter, howling, applause, and whistling – to the point that students in the hall are coming in to see what's going on. What started as twenty-six Master's students has, in only seconds, grown to well over fifty who are now filling the aisles.

I never break eye contact with Howard, and at the moment it happens, I know. His eyes give him away. He stands, raises a hand, and draws the room to silence.

"Okay guys, would any of you say that I – Howard Jensen – am a complete and utter fool?"

They all yell *'NO'* so loudly that the entire room shakes.

"Well then," he says, locking eyes with me, "the decision is made. Only a *complete and utter fool* would say 'no' to such a beautiful proposal. Tell me when, and where, Miss Bergstrom."

I lose it – completely. I launch myself over his desk and land in his waiting arms. My world is perfect, the instant his big arms close around me. I can't stop the hysterical sobbing that follows, even if I want to.

It takes twenty minutes for two Deans, and two campus security guards, to quell the ensuing 'riot'. It gets so loud at one point, I can hardly stand it. In the aftermath, Howard is called away by the Deans, and I take the opportunity to slow down before I blow a circuit.

Once the students have been dispersed, I sit down on the wooden platform and cross my legs under me. I sit rubbing my temples, and trying to think. It's almost back to being quiet when I feel a presence behind me. The 'spy' in me takes over, and I speak without opening my eyes.

"Come around here. I'm not moving."

I hear their footsteps on the creaking wood, as they come around my right side and stop in front of me. It's Martin and the young Miss Xiao Soong.

"I wanted to return this personally, Miss Bergstrom. I think that having you hunt me down would not be a pleasant event," Martin says as he hands me my passport, with my bright red CIA ID still securely inside.

"Thank you, Martin. I'm sorry if I freaked you guys out, but I'm hoping you will thank everyone here for their acceptance and understanding. It meant a lot to me," I reply, taking the documents from him, and sticking them back in my pocket.

They stand staring at me quite intently – as if they have some kind of burning questions loitering behind the intensity of their eyes. It takes a second, but I figure it out. All I have to do is think back to Courtney and me, and our first conversation with Carl, so many years ago.

"Okay, sit down and ask. And thanks for being diplomatic enough not to ask in front of everyone."

Their eyes light up and both instantly drop to the floor in front of me. At almost the same instant, one of the security guards comes back in.

"You two! Let's go!"

*"HEY!"* I pretty much scream without so much as a glance in his direction, and scaring the crap out of the two kids. "Can't you see we're talking here?"

"And you are?"

"…about to become your worst fucking nightmare! I swear to God, some of you British males are about rude! Here are your options – go find Professor Jensen, and ask him that question, or watch carefully as in about fifteen seconds I…"

He doesn't wait long enough for me to finish the thought.

"Sorry. Where were we?" I ask after he disappears out the door.

Poor Martin is as white as a ghost, but the girl has a devious smirk on her face.

"Wow," Martin mumbles.

"Is it worth it, doing what you do? Do you feel that you serve an important purpose?" the girl asks, bringing Martin back from wherever he momentarily went.

"Yes. Since I began this journey, I've saved a number of lives – innocent lives that have nothing to do with the daily stupidity of governments or those who promote terror. Ask any of them if my existence serves a purpose."

Martin's turn.

"Have you ever… well…"

I save him from having to say it.

"Yes, I have. People everywhere have a problem with the taking of a life, Martin. Even I have a problem with it. But in this world we live in, sometimes, unfortunately, there just isn't any logical way to avoid it. Let me put it to you this way. If you're standing in a line in the supermarket and the guy behind you pulls out a gun, puts it to someone's head, and shoots them, would that not anger you?"

"Of course," the girl replies. Martin too nods his agreement.

"But, if the same scenario occurs and I happen to be in the next line over and am able to shoot the silly bastard *before* he can kill anyone, then how do you feel?"

I can see the gears turning behind both sets of eyes.

"I would shake your hand, and thank you," Martin offers.

"As would I," the girl adds.

"I just took someone's life. I coldly shot and killed another human being. That's bad, isn't it?"

Again, they're both lost in thought. It makes me smile – Whitney the teacher. I see the glint in their eyes as their little light bulbs go on about the same time.

Unbeknownst to me, Howard returned only moments after I scared the shit out of the security guard, and has been sitting at a desk in the very back of the room – listening.

"It's not, and can't be, cut and dry – or black and white. It must exist in the gray area of life. What it is you do, I mean," the girl says, a big grin covering her face.

"Exactly. Yes, I have taken lives, but never once was it done out of anger, vengeance, or just because I could. I *always* look for an alternative means of completing an operation. Killing is – *and should always be* – a means of last resort."

"Was it hard? Was it difficult to... to...?"

Again, I save poor Martin.

"Shoot and or kill someone? For me, the truthful answer would be no. It isn't. I hope that doesn't make me appear to be some kind of monster."

"Not at all," the girl says, smiling. "Any other answer would not have been truthful, Miss Bergstrom, for if it was not easy – or perhaps 'just a job' – you would not be able to do the things they ask of you. It is called human nature ma'am – the thing God came up with, to make each of us unique."

"Since I started this journey, over fifteen years ago, I have always operated on a single principle, shared with my mother many years before I was born. She too, took a life once, and in an effort to understand what she did, she went and talked to a very close friend of hers who lived a life of solitude in the mountains of Colorado. With one short, simple statement, Mr. Cromwell took the moral factor out of the equation."

"What did he tell her?" the girl asks.

*"Some people… just need killing."*

"If one looks at the world today – *our world*," Miss Soong offers glancing at Martin, "it's obvious that sadly, Mr. Cromwell is correct."

"And, it's time for me to quit. It's become *too* second nature to me, and that means I need to let it all go. It's time for me to find another path to travel, and to quit tempting death as well. As you just said, it's *your world*, and therefore it's time for your generation to take over."

They sit staring at me for a few seconds, and then without any further comments, stand and collect their books.

"Thank you, for talking with us," Martin says. "I've learned more in the last three hours than I have in the entire rest of my life. I hope things with you and Professor Jensen work out."

"Me too!" the girl says as she turns to follow Martin out of the room. As they step off the platform, I call out to her.

"Xiao. Come here a moment, please?"

She stops and turns back to face me.

"She'll catch up with you in a minute, Martin."

He nods and continues toward the door. The girl walks back and stops in front of me. As I get up, I notice Howard coming down the aisle.

"No one could have talked me out of it, and I wouldn't presume to think it would be my job to do that to you. All I will say is this – be *absolutely damn certain* before you decided to travel this path."

She suddenly becomes serious, as if I peeked into her diary or something. She stares at me for a moment, and after some silent contemplation, speaks.

"How did you know?"

"That you might be considering this as a career?"

"Yes."

"I see myself, fifteen years ago, reflecting in your eyes. That's how. I just hope you realize that this is by far the most dangerous and destructive path you could possibly choose. In the end, the price of participation will be far higher than you can ever imagine at this point in your life. Do you understand?"

"Yes ma'am," she replies, a devious little glint returning to her eyes. "And thank you, for being concerned enough to warn me."

"Okay then, get out of here, and do your damn homework."

She laughs and heads toward the doors, passing Howard as she steps off the platform. She suddenly hesitates and spins back around as Howard walks up to me.

"You should teach. You would be a brilliant professor, Miss Bergstrom. Honestly."

Then with a smile, she disappears, leaving Howard and me alone in the now quiet, and empty lecture hall.

"I'm sorry Howard. I will make the necessary apologies — even to the asshole if I have to."

"You mean to Randolph? Forget him. He's just our resident pain in the ass. No one — least of all the students — like him. Besides, a couple of people who heard it from the hall were quick to tell the Dean, he had it coming. You're quite popular around here already."

"Thank you. Thank you for the most awesome day of my life. I don't think I ever felt as alive as I have for the last three hours."

"Not my doing. That, my dear, was all Whitney."

I step up and plant a kiss on him, then with my lips to his ear, whisper, "Take me home with you Howard. We have a lot of catching up to do."

The next twenty-four hours of Whitney's life are amazing, extraordinary, miraculous, unbelievable, phenomenal, and a million other adjectives that I can't think of right now.

I know God is giving me a second chance.

I also know I intend to use it to its fullest.

I spend two more days with Howard, doing a lot of catching up, and of course, a lot of explaining. In those few days, Howard manages to recapture my heart – entirely.

By the time I leave London, it's as if the last fifteen years never happened – well, where Howard and I are concerned at least.

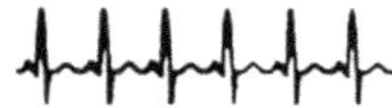

# 92

It's a five-hour flight, going in the opposite direction of home, but it's something else that *has* to be done.

When my plane lands in Istanbul, I go in search of a taxi, and instead, find my favorite ex-Marine standing next to a black Benz limo just outside the baggage claim area. Without the slightest hesitation, I run over and jump into his arms as he opens them. I'm giggling when I plant one right smack on his lips. The girl, who I assume is the embassy's driver, has the most amusing look of confusion on her face.

"Welcome to Istanbul, Mrs. Whitman," she says.

I can't help myself – I break up laughing, and not knowing what else to do, Willie follows suit.

"Wrong person, Lily," Willie says, as he puts me down.

"Excuse me?"

"My name is Bergstrom young lady. Mrs. Whitman would be my sister."

"But..."

"Let it go, Lily, it will just give you a headache. Trust me," Willie says, once again laughing.

"Okay, Will... I mean, Mr. Ramirez," the girl replies, turning an interesting shade of red as she does.

*"Oh my god!"* I blurt out. "I'm kissing your boyfriend!"

"Jezzzz, Whitney – just tell everyone why don't you?"

This time, even Lily breaks up laughing.

We get into the limo for the ride to the embassy, and along the way, I try to explain to poor Lily how it is that Whitney Bergstrom is still alive.

Over the next two days, I try to explain and beg forgiveness – from Cassie and the rest of them. Much to my amazement, all of them willingly accommodated me.

It seems that all is fair in love, war, and espionage.

The totally amusing thing about the visit is, Cassie *and* Willie hound me relentlessly until I finally crack, and tell them what *really* happened to the two 'abducted' Russians...

Once a spy... forever a spy.

On the day I'm preparing to go home, Cassie pulls me aside and quietly delivers a message.

"Melinda said to tell you they're home. The docs said they were stable enough to be moved, so last night she put them in an air ambulance and sent them back to Virginia. Courtney is in the ICU at VHC."

"Okay," I reply, trying once again, not to cry. "That will be my first stop. Wish me luck."

"No luck necessary, Whit – this is about family..."

I give her a hug, and ten minutes later am in the back of the limo again, on my way to the airport.

As I board the British Airways 747 for the flight back to the States, I know that the last two people in my life that I have to make peace with are diligently watching over my sister, who damn near died getting me back.

It seems I should be terrified of what awaits me in Virginia, but I'm not.

It's just one more thing that has to be done, on my road back to being Whitney Bergstrom.

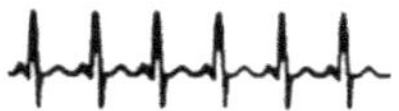

# 93

I choose not to tell anyone I'm coming – it just seems easier. I figure I'll just show up at the hospital – that way, I can face them one at a time.

My plan backfires when, by sheer chance, I find both of my parent's *cars* in the parking lot of the Virginia Hospital Center, in Arlington, where Alice insisted the Agency put Courtney.

So, knowing they aren't home, I instead head for their house, for no reason other than I really have nowhere else to go. And no, the absurdity of being thirty-seven years old and having 'nowhere to go' in the area where I was born, isn't lost on me.

My parents live on forty acres just south of Manassas at the very end of Applewood Lane. Because of what they chose to do for a living, this was the ideal spot for them – less than an hour to any of the 'facilities' they might need to access quickly.

After I was 'killed' in Greece, and Courtney married Chuck, they offered them part of the property just to keep my sister close. When my sister gave birth to Haleigh, she and Chuck quickly built a house less than two miles from my parents.

It takes me about forty-five minutes to get from the hospital to the house. My house. My past. It's beyond strange, to say the very least.

The first thing I do is walk around looking, and thinking. It's all exactly as I remember it, and when I see that damn tire swing hanging there, I can't help myself.

As I sit, lost in thoughts of my past, I begin to wonder where my niece and nephew are. Then, as my brain catches up with what's going on, I realize they're probably in school – where a twelve and ten-year-old are supposed to be.

I've become so far removed from 'normal', I have to laugh at myself.

I get up and head for the back deck of the house (I know where the key is hidden or was at one time in my life), when something catches my eye, next to the small barn my father built. Although it's covered with a tarp, as I turn and head toward it, I begin to suspect what it is, based solely on its shape, and the shock of the entire concept almost gives me a headache.

"Why in the hell would Dad do it?" I say out loud, to no one but the trees and birds.

The moment I jerk the tarp off, my heart stops – and I find myself face-to-face with *my damn Jeep!* My father kept the silly thing for *over fifteen years!*

I open the door, lean inside, and look at the now dust-covered odometer – 13,559. It has about forty more miles on it than it did when I parked it, a week before Courtney and I went to England. I'm not only astounded but speechless as well.

After a couple of seconds, I start unzipping and removing things, and in less than ten minutes, the top is in a pile on the ground next to me. Another two minutes, and I have all the support bars off as well. I walk around to the back, lean over, carefully reach under the rear bumper, and as if by magic, my fingers land right on it.

The secret key I left in a magnetic box.

I break up laughing – almost hysterically. I am, however, about to get the shit scared out of me. As I straighten up, and turn back toward the driver's side of the Jeep, I hear a shrill voice – *a female voice* – screaming at me.

*"YOU BETTER GET THE HELL AWAY FROM MY AUNT'S JEEP!"*

I look just in time to see first, my niece (who has her mom all over her!) dialing away on a cell phone, and second, my nephew, racing toward me with, of all things, a *baseball bat!*

The instant I clear the Jeep and they see me, that's pretty much it. Of course, their confusion is understandable.

*"MOM!"* they scream simultaneously. Funny thing is, Lyle forgets to stop his swing. Fortunately, subconsciously I'm still a spy, and I sidestep him, catch the barrel of the bat in mid-air, and jerk it out of his hands.

"Damn, kid! You trying to kill me, or what?"

Haleigh drops the phone, and the two of them rush over and grab hold of me so tightly, that I know I'm going to lose it. My heart is racing and I can feel the tears as they start trickling down my face. After a few seconds, I pull them loose and squat down between the two of them.

"No guys, I'm not your mom. I know that's confusing but," I say, reaching out with one hand and putting my fingers on the side of the jeep, "it's actually, *my Jeep.*"

My niece shows me how much like her mother she is.

"Oh my gosh! *Aunt Whitney?* Oh... ohhh.... ohhhh...."

I'm full-on crying at this point, and half-expect the child to explode right there on the spot. Lyle, who has one arm wrapped tightly around me, keeps staring at me, looking as confused as anyone I've ever seen.

"But... how come you look *just like* my mom?"

"We're twins, Lyle – we are supposed to look the same."

I can see small tears on Haleigh's cheeks as she struggles to understand what's going on. I know in this instant, what needs to be done.

"Who are you calling, Haleigh?" I ask, standing and walking toward her phone.

"911 – like Mom always tells us to do," she replies.

"You might want to tell them everything is okay before they send a deputy out here to check," I say, leaning over and picking up the phone from the dirt of the driveway.

"I never pushed the send button, Aunt Whitney – I was too freaked out."

I laugh as I first look at her, then at my nephew who still has a death grip on my hand.

"Come on, let's go sit on the swing and discuss this. We'll see just how good 'Aunt Whitney' is at explaining things to kids."

*'Aunt Whitney'* – in my mind the entire concept is not only foreign but seriously bizarre as well.

I spend the next hour, sitting on a tire swing in my parent's backyard, with my niece and nephew, trying to make sense of the fact their aunt, whom they've been told their entire lives is dead – isn't.

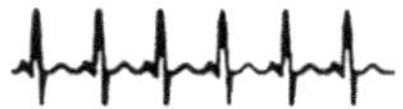

# ⊓4

It takes eight days, but God does finally send me back. It simply isn't my time.

It's a repeat of the weirdest sensation I've ever experienced – one from many years back in my life – that forces me back to consciousness. The last time I felt it, I was standing on the aft deck of a Greek freighter, in the Mediterranean Sea.

Whitney's here, somewhere. Doing something. *I feel her.*

My father's voice is the first recognizable thing that reaches out to me from the real world. Seems he's been having a running conversation with God, the entire time he's been in my room – which has apparently been nonstop since I arrived. It's the latest installment of his conversation that causes my mental reemergence into reality, but even as I struggle to make my brain reboot, I do it silently – not letting him know I'm awake.

I need to feel the calm I've always found in his voice...

"...and forgive us our trespasses, as we forgive those who trespass against us. And lead us not into temptation, but deliver us from evil. Amen."

I realize my father is reciting the Lord's Prayer, and knowing HE is the only reason I'm still among the living, I decide I too should thank Him, with a quick prayer of my own.

Once I finish, and the fog in my mind begins to lift, I'm about to open my eyes, when that same chill and intense rush sweeps over me. The moment it happens, my heart rate spikes, and damn near all the monitors in the room go crazy.

My father is on the right side of the bed, sitting in a chair, his eyes closed and a rosary in his hands, talking to God when all hell breaks loose.

"...and you kept her alive – for whatever reasons. You could have taken her the moment the first bullet hit her, but you didn't. She took three bullets – bullets that should have killed her – but she's still here. Please, Father, just let her open her eyes, please give me back my first born..."

The moment the monitor alarms begin to sound, he jumps up and reaches for my hand. The look on his face when I open my eyes is beautiful, but when I try to speak to him – and damn near choke – I realize there's a tube down my throat. The more I try to say something, the more I choke.

I start crying – I can't help it. I try to move something, an arm, a leg, anything – but it all seems to weigh a ton. Seconds later a nurse and a doctor come rushing into the room, and as I begin to choke again, the doctor cuts the tape holding the tube, then very quickly, and carefully, pulls it out.

*'Thank God!'* I think to myself, turning my head slightly and again looking at my father. I wait a second, try to get a full breath, and again try to talk, but no words will come out. I squeeze (or think I do) my father's hand with the one he's holding. This time I barely eke out the word 'water'. When my father reaches for a glass next to the bed, the doctor stops him.

"Slowly, Mr. Bergstrom. Very slowly. Just a few drops, do you understand?"

"Yes sir," my father replies, as he sticks his fingers into the cup, and then gently wets my lips. I will never be able to explain to anyone just how good that felt.

As he's making his third pass over my lips, it happens again – the intense rush of my sister's presence. And again, the monitors go berserk. For just a brief second, I have a flash in my mind... of my kids... sitting on the tire swing... smiling... and talking to someone. I force the word 'Whitney' out of my mouth in barely an audible whisper. My father, understanding what I'm doing, quickly leans over and puts his ear next to my lips.

"Whitney..."

He pulls back, looks at me with a ton of guilt in his eyes, and says, "We haven't heard from her yet, baby."

This time I smile at him. I mouth the word 'no' and he again leans over where he can hear me.

"She's with the kids... on the swing..."

When my father straightens up and looks at me, we hear what could be a glass-shattering scream from somewhere out in the hall, and moments later, my mother bursts into the room.

The moment she takes my free hand and I look at her, she falls completely apart. While she's crying, I turn my attention back to my father, giving him a look with a specific message in it.

*You can't be angry with her.*

Seconds later, he breaks into tears himself. He reaches up, gently touches my cheek, and with a smile says, "Welcome back young lady." He leans over the bed, kisses me on the forehead, and then kisses the rosary, which is still in his hand. After he carefully places it in his shirt pocket, he looks straight up and boldly says, *"Thank you!"*

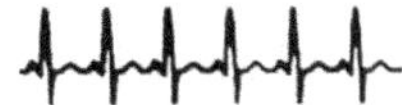

# ٩5

Throughout our lives my sister and I operated pretty much 'in unison' – with the exception of one thing.

On a sunny afternoon, on the tire swing in my parent's yard, Courtney and I are about to become 'complete'. The one thing that my sister and I have never shared – Courtney's strange ability to 'sense me' – is about to cross the conduit that has forever connected us.

The last time it happened to her, was during the operation that I 'lost my life' in. Joey's exact words when she told me about it, after Courtney and I switched places on the freighter, were "... *it was just plain fuckin' spooky.*"

Now, in just a single heartbeat, I understand.

It's a sensation of being cold – freezing almost. Although it's a balmy 77° at the moment, I'm suddenly covered with goosebumps, and for just a second, my body shudders. I realize it's happening exactly the way Courtney explained it, so many times.

Even my niece and nephew sense something is amiss.

"Are you okay, Aunt Whitney?" Haleigh asks as she lays her hand on my thigh.

"I don't know Haleigh. Something very weird..."

My sentence is interrupted by a second cold flash, and a rush that again makes me shudder. Then, as I'm trying to stand up, I have a... well, a 'visual flash' I guess would be the best way to describe it. Although I know I'm in my parent's backyard, my mind tells me that I'm in a hospital room – Courtney's hospital room, and she's struggling…

"Oh crap," I blurt out.

"What's the matter, Aunt Whitney?" my niece asks as she too finds her way off the tire.

Her voice brings me back, and as the visual image dissolves, I understand what's happening. It would seem I've joined my big sister. For the first time, I 'sense' her. I sense that she has regained consciousness.

"We gotta go kids, *now*. Come on!" I say, picking Lyle up off the tire, and setting him on the grass. Haleigh is already standing next to me.

"What's the matter, Aunt Whitney – is something wrong?"

"Your mom just woke up kid, and I think you need to be there. I think we *all* need to be there."

"But… how…"

"Not now, Haleigh. Just go get in the truck, and put on your seatbelt," I say, taking Lyle's hand and starting toward the rented SUV parked in front of the house. When Haleigh doesn't move, I turn to look at her. 'Confused' is an understatement.

*"Please?"* I ask, looking as pathetic as possible. "I'll explain as we go, I promise."

Ninety seconds later, we hit the pavement on Old Auburn Road, and I make a left without stopping. It takes me twelve minutes to get to US 29, and another ten to get to the interstate.

In total, it takes forty-seven minutes from the time I started the truck, until I turn it off in the parking lot of the hospital. I'm shaking like a leaf in a high breeze, as I pull the keys from the ignition. I'm so lost in what's going on, that before I know it, my niece has gotten out of the truck, opened my door, and is standing next to me.

"Come on, Aunt Whitney. It will all be okay, I promise. Let's go see my mom," she says with a big smile.

The kid is 100% her mother — there's no disputing that.

# 96

I've been awake for close to an hour. All the doctors are baffled by the fact I seem to be completely functional, although talking is still a bit of a task. My mother has been in tears most of the time, and my father just keeps smiling and refuses to let go of my hand.

It takes less than thirty minutes for Alice Williamson to show up – she gets here, even before Chuck does. Benefits of being at the top of the food chain, I suppose.

An endless stream of doctors asks questions one after another – which I understand is important. After all, I really shouldn't be here to answer them. I am in fact, a medical miracle. Because my vocal cords are still struggling to operate, I limit my responses to nods of my head. To be completely honest with you, as serious as I know it is, I still find the entire situation totally comical.

I know it's just Courtney – being Courtney.

When a cold chill and rush hit me a third time, I know why.

Whitney is close. *Very close.*

I quickly turn to my mother, and with much effort, place my hand on one of hers. When she looks at me, she understands what I want, and leans over close so she can hear me. Everyone else in the room goes silent the moment they see her do it.

"No matter what she did, Mom, she is still and will always be your daughter, and my twin sister," I force myself to say.

When my mother raises her head and we make eye contact, I see the confusion in her eyes.

"I know, Courtney, I know. At this point, I just want her to come home," she says, reaching out and gently touching my cheek.

If she isn't confused enough, the smile that spreads across my face amplifies it exponentially.

Thing is – I know my mother is about to get her wish.

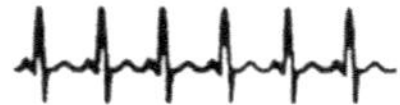

# 97

The moment the doors of the elevator open, the 'sensation' repeats itself – so intensely, it makes me shudder, again. Being connected to my sister is one thing, but this is getting silly.

"Come on, Aunt Whitney, it's this way," my niece says, as she pulls on my hand, and leads me down the hall. When we pass the nurse's station on the ward my sister is on, the woman sitting at the desk looks as if she's going to faint. I guess no one told them Courtney has a twin.

My heart is racing – to the point that it can probably pump fluid to the roof of the building if necessary. When Lyle lets go of my hand and runs toward a door at the end of the hall, I know this is it. I watch as the two of them burst through the door into their mother's room, and hear my nephew scream *'MOM'* as the door closes.

I hesitate for close to a minute, watching through a window, as my niece and nephew are all over their mother. It's only a matter of seconds before the three of them are crying. I begin to tear up myself and think for a brief moment, about how close we came to screwing all this up.

When I see my father headed toward the door, I step back out of the way so he can open it. He comes out, stops, and when the door closes, sees me. His tears are instantaneous.

*"It's about goddamn time, Whitney* – were you waiting for a personal invitation, or what?" he forces out, as he steps over and wraps me up in a tremendously emotional hug, lifting me off the floor.

*God, I love my father.* He's so... *perfect!*

"Sorry, Dad. I had to work up to the inevitable ass-chewing I have coming," I reply.

Eventually, he puts me down, I kiss him on the cheek and squeeze him as hard as I can, and then we stand staring at each other – neither knowing what to say. After a few seconds, we turn together and stand quietly watching what's happening in my sister's room.

"Well... once your mother finds out..."

"Yeah, Dad, I know," I reply in the middle of his sentence.

After another thirty seconds of silence, I make myself do what I know has to be done. I pull the door open and go in, with my father close behind. Two steps into the room, I see my sister pull on the sleeve of one of the doctors, and he leans down as if to listen to her. When he straightens up, he turns and looks in my direction – his expression tells me that apparently, none of them know about the 'twins' thing.

"Mrs. Whitman would like a moment alone with her sister – let's all step out for a few minutes, please."

Even before he finishes the sentence, my mother – who's sitting on the edge of Courtney's bed – spins around, and the very second our eyes meet, she faints. Luckily, a nurse is close by and catches her as she damn near falls off the bed. We stand and watch as they put my mother into a wheelchair, and take her out of the room, still only semi-conscious.

"Come get me when you and your sister are done with your 'reminiscing'. And thank you, Whitney – for calling me when you did. It made it a lot easier for your mother and me. Haleigh, Lyle, come on – let's give your mom and aunt a few minutes to talk."

"Let them stay, Dad, they just got their mother back."

He kisses me gently on the forehead, then follows the last doctor out of the room. I walk over, sit on the edge of my sister's bed, and just look at her. For the very first time in my life, I honestly don't know what to say.

"Является ли ваша жизнь прямо? (Did you get your life straight?)" Courtney finally asks, in just above a whisper.

"Что вы имеете в виду?" (What do you mean?)

"I swear I going to learn to speak Russian, so you guys can't do this..." my niece interjects, making both of us look at her.

"Do what?" her mother asks.

"Have secret conversations – that's what."

My sister and I look at each other, then laugh.

"You know exactly what the hell I mean," Courtney says, in English, again, just above a whisper.

"We can do this later, Court. I can see..."

"Oh, bullshit! Don't you dare pull that crap."

"Yes ma'am. I talked to all of them, and apologized my silly ass off to each of them."

I see poor Lyle's eyes get really big.

"Sorry, Lyle. I haven't been around kids a lot, and well..."

"They're just words, Aunt Whitney. Mom says sometimes, you just gotta use them. The trick is to know when – but mostly, *when not to,*" my niece says, smiling at me.

I reach over, gently touch her cheek, and smile.

"And, did the operation end the way it was supposed to?"

My damn big sister, ever the diligent spy, is worried about *her* operation.

"Do you mean did the good guys win? Heck yeah!"

"Отлично. И, что о вас? (Excellent. And, what about you?) You look like me, which in your business, can't be a good thing."

"You sure do!" Lyle blurts out. "Look like my mom I mean."

"And will you *please* quit that?" Haleigh adds, sounding totally exasperated.

I look at her, reach over, and gently jab her in the side.

"Well, Sis..." I offer, turning and looking at Lyle and trying sincerely to suppress a laugh, but failing miserably. "You can't get any more compromised than I am now. Computer systems around the world are updating files on me as we speak. The only 'business' I can possibly be in at this point would be the 'unemployment' business. You may have to fire me..."

My sister finally smiles. I know that's what she wanted to hear. That I'm done, and I'm ready to go back to being her sister again.

"I've seen the photos, Whit – we both know it's only over if *Whitney* wants it to be over. You know I will support whatever *you* want to do like I always have, but it has to be what *you* want – not what me, or Mom and Dad, or anyone else wants. I think you know that. We look the same, but we're different people – and we have different paths to travel."

"Honestly, Sis, I want to marry Howard and have kids. Hanging out with yours all afternoon, kind of cinched it up for me," I reply, glancing at my niece and nephew.

I watch the tears form in her eyes and realize I've reached the end of this particular path.

I've reached a juncture – I have to choose a new path and a new destination. It's time for me to be 'normal' – assuming that's even a possibility.

Fate... destiny... karma. Seems my mother wasn't as full of crap as I always thought.

When my sister lifts her arm, I lean over and let her wrap it – with great effort – around me and I hug her back.

"I love you, Whitney."

"And I love you too, Sis – forever and always."

In a matter of seconds, we're both softly sobbing.

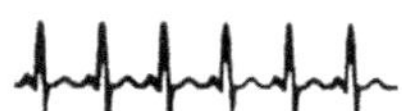

# ꟿ8

I do finally make my peace with all the people in my life who are important to me, including my parents, but then blood is thick, and family outweighs all else.

Of course, the fact my sister stood up for me, didn't hurt either.

Even though Courtney sided with me, I have to 'accept' where my mother is concerned. She conceded to 'accepting' what I did – although she says she'll never 'understand' it. I cried when, in private, she told me that regardless of all the insanity, she does and always will, love me, but simply can't find a way to 'forgive' me. I know, under the circumstances, it's probably more than I deserve. At least I have parents and a family again, which for me at this point, is more than enough.

So… about the story. What the hell actually happened?

Here's not only how it all started, but also, how convoluted it eventually became…

Boris Nikolsky, it turns out, silently held a lot of pent-up anger toward most of his superiors, partly because they commandeered his appointment as Director of the SVR, but also because of their movements away from the old-school politics. As far as he was concerned, the United States – in whatever form it took – was the mortal enemy of Russia, and nothing should invalidate that. The current regime found it more effective to trust us – within reason – than to go back to the ways of the 'cold war'.

Nikolsky was convinced that if he could somehow position himself properly, he could be there to pick up the pieces after he created a disaster for Sokolski. He knew that Tarasov bore a good amount of resentment over the loss of his brother all those years ago and that he felt the same way about the changing politics of their country. A perfect patsy. To this end, he was able to convince Tarasov to join him.

Even as he planned his coup, the revelation of a 'mole' in his office, gave him his first moment of realization. His need to force a change in his government's political stance – perhaps even cause a shift back to the 'old ways' – could be coupled with his ingenious plan to bring down Sokolski. All he had to do was pull the CIA into the mix, and he was certain his little plot would succeed.

The problem was, Alice Williamson had a plan of her own.

Even as it began, and the information trickled in from her source, she knew she could use the whole situation to her – but more importantly, to the Agency's – benefit. The instant she saw Tarasov's name on a document that crossed her desk, her heart raced, and her brain ran rampant. She knew she had the single thing on the entire planet that Tarasov wouldn't be able to resist.

The traitor to Mother Russia – who it now appeared, was in fact, his biological sister as well. And, she was alive no less!

So, the game began, each of them dangling bait, and waiting for the rats to take it.

Alice took hers – hook line and sinker. She was all over the 'alleged' assassination attempt immediately, and with a single phone call, set her plan in motion.

Tarasov was on his just as quickly – the moment he heard that Daria Ladenko was still alive, he was on a phone to Nikolsky.

From that point on, all one could do was sit back and watch the ballet.

Daria? Oh yes, she definitely knew what was going on from the beginning. Alice talked to her at least five times in the days prior to our abduction, and she knew what Alice predicted was going to happen – which in the end turned out to be quite far from reality. Although Alice didn't have to tell her that she had documents indicating Tarasov is her biological brother, doing so only created a more urgent incentive for her to see the whole thing through to completion. Once again, it was a case of Alice demonstrating her ability to manipulate people.

As you can see, the head bad guy – knowing about Alice's informant – played his cards well when leaking information. The day the whole drama began with our abduction, our assets snatched Alice's informant only minutes before Nikolsky's people turned up looking for her.

Two points for the good guys.

Alice and Daria kept the information loop closed – meaning left me in the dark – so that it would appear to be a random incident. Courtney's avid pursuit of a bunch of 'unsanctioned' kidnappers would lend far more credence to the story that we 'just happened to be there' when the attempt was made on Sokolski's life, than would a bunch of CIA assets loitering around the site, for no apparent reason.

I didn't know about any of this, so when Amanda called and told me we had a 'more covert than usual' meeting in Rabat with a 'highly placed Arab informant', I wrote down the details and acknowledged the assignment. And of course, the moment I realized Daria intended to go to the meeting without any make-up and looking *very much* like herself – neither of us had been in public as ourselves in over fifteen years – I knew there was more to what was going on.

However, I trusted her implicitly for those same fifteen years and saw no reason to suddenly start questioning her. If I needed to know, she'd tell me. So off we went to the airport, at 3:00 AM, no less – and without a word to Melinda.

Yep, something was going on.

Although Alice's trap was being opened in clear view of her 'prey', she never gave a thought to the possibility that Nikolsky was leading her into one of his own. The two great spiders had begun to spin their webs, and neither side was, at that point, willing to admit it might be wandering into the other side's trap.

Nikolsky's real plan didn't involve assassinating Sokolski, it just gave that appearance. From the moment he learned of the existence of the mole, his plan had been to kill the Director of the CIA and make it appear that Sokolski had masterminded it. What better way to turn our countries back against each other, and to 'restart the cold war'? Once shit hit the fan, he would simply step into Sokolski's position, assuring both the Security Council and the Prime Minister that he would do a thorough housecleaning of the SVR, and would bring the Russian intelligence machine back to its glory of old. That of course meant carefully placing individuals on his 'trusted' list into various key positions, thus assuring his continued reign over the SVR.

Now, all that being said, the one truly amusing thing here is, that *not one of them* – not Alice, not Sokolski, certainly not Nikolsky or Tarasov – took the time to factor in the tenacity of my big sister.

But then, my sister is *the best in the business.*

Checkmate.

Courtney out-screwed them all, and the whole absurd mess ended the way she wanted it to, on her terms, and by her direction. In a roundabout way, she'd told them not only is she smarter than they are, but that they could all kiss her ass as well.

Courtney = 1. Idiots = 0.

God, I love my big sister.

Now, let's talk a bit about my 'adopted sister' and her role in our little escapade.

As I mentioned before, Daria knew from the very beginning what was going on – to a point. She knew that Alice's plan involved unleashing Courtney and that given enough time, my sister would, 'crack the case'. She was responsible for my being on the yacht, opting to get me loose, rather than stuck with Tarasov. She knew I would easily be able to break free of Vera if I put my mind to it. Even when it came to the incident at the bank, she knew that once Courtney and I connected on what was happening, we'd be unstoppable, which is why Vera ended up in the truck with them, instead of me. She did eventually admit to me, that by getting Vera to change sides, I'd screwed up her original plan, and forced her to ad-lib.

And the message on her hand? Genius. She managed to hide it from Tarasov the entire day, knowing that once she got close to me, I would understand. Once she gleaned enough information from Tarasov – playing on his feelings for his new-found sibling – she devised a way to let us know exactly what was going on. She knew that if she could get the message to Michael, who was undoubtedly watching the whole scene, he'd deliver it to my sister who would decipher it. *And...* the very second Courtney discovered *where* on her *right* hand the message was written, she knew it was legitimate. Daria is the only person on earth other than my sister and I, that knows about the smiley face – because I told her about it, right after the incident at the daycare center.

After fifteen years of constant exposure, Daria knows my sister and me, at least as well as we know each other.

And finally, there is the small matter of some missing money – 12.3 million dollars to be exact.

Well, *it's not actually missing*.

For that matter, it never even left the bank. Daria, while not the 'analyst' my sister has become, is nonetheless quite the devious and deceptive spy. Knowing what would be the driving force behind Tarasov's thought processes – the missing money – she arranged with the bank for just such a situation.

A duress code that she had set up directly with the bank's manager, and assistant manager, at a private meeting. She told them that if we ever came in on the premise we were going to empty the account, and she used 'I' instead of 'we' (it was after all a joint account) in any sentence, things were not what they appeared. Her early statement *'I will be re-depositing within a few days'*, was all it took.

With the code delivered, the bank's assistant manager took the predetermined amount of time to fill the cases with pieces of paper equal to the weight of the correct amount of money. It never once occurred to me – *or to anyone else for that matter* – to check the cases! I just assumed there was money in them.

And conveniently, so did everyone else.

Two more points for Daria.

What became of those two high-tech, seriously expensive, attaché cases you ask? Why didn't Daria, who was within feet of them the entire time, see what happened to them?

Because of my stealthy little brother.

Although Daria also heard the conversation that Samantha translated for me back on that tarmac, she didn't care. You see, she was the only one who knew that the cases were irrelevant to everything. She knew that they were full of paper!

Rhyan didn't realize it either, when he covertly absconded with both of them, just before the Swiss arrived. While the rest of us were concerned about what was happening on the opposite side of the runway, he and Mike were talking – on a 'secret' frequency. Mike happened to be looking in the direction of the Russian aircraft when the shooting started and he saw – through his scope – Vera stuff the cases between the tires of the landing gear. He told Rhyan what he saw – although none of us heard him.

The moment everyone's attention had shifted to Alice and Courtney's dilemma, Rhyan had – with Daria and a screaming Tarasov ten yards away – quite deftly removed the cases and stashed them for later retrieval, leaving a handwritten note that said 'TAG – You're it!'

Boy, was he ticked off when, a few days later, Daria told him they were full of paper.

My comment was, "Welcome to our world, little brother – where nothing is ever what it appears to be".

So, there you have it – the reality of my last operation as an active field asset of the Central Intelligence Agency.

And no, I'm not going to miss it.
Not even a little.

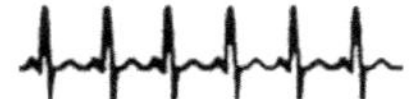

# 99

As it turns out, I'm actually 'pretty shot up' as spies are so fond of saying. Although my broken arm isn't a 'compound fracture', it still took a piece of stainless steel and six stainless steel screws to reassemble it. The doctors say that with proper rehabilitation, I will eventually regain 'full use'.

My thigh wound is the same, although at the time it hurt so badly, that I thought it was going to kill me. Seems that muscle, tendon, and soft tissue damage can, in fact, hurt like hell! The round that hit me in the back, and then hit Alice in the chest caused the real damage.

It first left a nice 'ding' in my pelvic (or hip) bone right near the top. The glancing ricochet was just enough to deflect the bullet up and slightly to the left, where it first severed the renal artery on the left side of my body, and punctured my left kidney, before trashing my spleen, and then nicking the edge of my stomach, leaving a nice tear in it. Finally, still intact and moving at damn near full velocity, it grazed one of my ribs and exited just under and to the left of my left breast. The fact it managed to completely miss both my heart *and* my lungs, baffled all the doctors involved. The Swiss surgeons spent just short of twelve hours trying to clean up the mess and plug all the leaks in my internal organs. Fortunately for me, they were both very skilled and in this case, quite successful.

After the bullet was done with me, it moved on to Alice, entering her chest on the right side, just below her armpit. By then it had slowed enough, that her lung was able to stop it, but not without a good bit of damage. Alice almost broke into tears when the doctors told her that, had the damn thing not traveled through me first, it would have probably been able to cover the half-inch it came up short, on its trip towards her heart.

There is nothing quite as bizarre as the trajectory of a high-velocity bullet.

I suppose that God isn't finished with either of us.

Although being shot anywhere isn't exactly a picnic, the rest of them had what spies like to call 'pocket change' wounds – meaning not all that serious. Whitney is missing a small piece of her scalp and they removed a 9mm round from her thigh. Joey caught the remnants of a 7.62 round that came in through the windshield of the BMW, in her upper left arm. Both are quite painful, but not what a spy would consider serious.

Vera Kovalenko wasn't quite as lucky. She caught the full force of one of the sniper rounds in her left shoulder, and it did some fairly serious damage. In the end, the doctors in Germany decided it was best to replace her entire shoulder – joint and all. She'll have to endure at least a full year of rehab, to get back to where she can use it reasonably well. Vera's comment to my sister when she went to visit her was, "You gave me back my husband and my life – screw the shoulder".

Leonid Tarasov – one seriously lucky son-of-a-bitch. My sister managed – for reasons totally beyond my comprehension – not to kill him. Seems that with time, he too will regain complete use of his left hand and left leg – which is where my sister shot him.

Isaak Eltsin – Sokolski's lone bodyguard. The bullet he took in his leg right after Whitney pushed him to the ground, was a ricochet, fired by the sniper that Chauncey eliminated minutes later. He too had minor injuries and was expected to recover fully.

And finally, the only negative result of the whole mess.

William Carl Wright. The most senior member of Alice's personal security detail. He was the only good guy we lost.

When I looked for him and Chauncey that day and didn't see them, it was because William was down by Izamaylov's first shot. You see, Izamaylov needed to be certain that Alice would exit the aircraft completely. Shooting her in the entrance or on the stairs allowed for the possibility that someone could drag her back into the aircraft, and thus remove his ability to ensure the 'kill'. So, the moment he saw Chauncey move away towards one of his decoys, he killed William – knowing that *no security* would immediately draw attention. Especially from Alice.

His devious little plan damn near worked.

If Alice had looked behind her at any point and had seen William lying there, she would have inevitably gone to his rescue – and wouldn't have been standing there when I leaped the railing and landed in front of her. My appearance was what made Izamaylov fire when he did – he was afraid he was about to lose his 'window'.

Fate. Destiny. Whatever you want to call it. So many things, all needing to happen in a very specific manner.

I often wonder if William's death somehow contributed to someone else still being alive. Although he was put into the medical chopper with Alice and me (at Alice's insistence), in reality, William died the moment the bullet hit him. His job now finished, he now rests in God's capable hands.

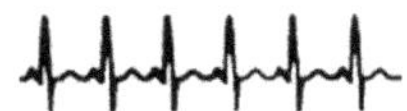

# 100

After sixty-seven days of hospital food, I tell the doctor I'm going home. Although he's not at all happy with my decision, he somehow knows better than to argue with me about it. I'm given a particularly regimented schedule for rehabilitation, and give my word I will strictly adhere to it.

The amusing part comes when my daughter takes the papers from my hand, and after looking at them for a moment, tells the two doctors and the nurse, "Don't even worry. Mom will stick to this – word for word – I promise!" As everyone in the room laughs, I know I'm in the best hands I can be.

Over the next few months, I have several talks with those around me – Chuck, Mom and Dad, my sister, my brother, Mikey, and finally, with my children. Life slows way down and becomes physically grueling for me, but because everyone around me pushes, encourages, and helps me survive each day, I refuse to give in to my injuries.

It takes me nineteen months to get back to 'normal'. Well, as normal as I will ever be. In the end, it's the tenacity of a thirteen-year-old girl who simply won't let her mother quit, that gets me through it all. I never saw the true incongruity of my daily life until that morning on the phone, when my daughter – with just a single sentence – opened my eyes...

*"Mom, I'm not dumb. I know what you and Dad do for a living."*

It's on one of my early morning two-mile jaunts (in support of my 'rehab'), that my daughter and I finally have our long talk.

"Just what, exactly, is it you think your father and I 'do for a living' Haleigh?"

"You're spies, Mom. *Sheeesh...*"

"Excuse me? I'm *certain* my job description says 'analyst' young lady, not 'spy'."

"Yeah, right, Mom. So, I'm supposed to believe that when you signed up and they gave you the gun, they left off the part about being a spy?"

She makes me break up laughing.

"And what, exactly, do 'spies' do?"

"Oh, come on, Mom. I'm thirteen – not five," my daughter responds, without missing a stride or slowing the pace, "My father and mother are the ones who make sure that everyone in this country gets to stay free."

"I see..."

After about twenty yards, I slow to a walk and watch as my daughter does the same. We walk together silently for about a quarter mile when without any prompting, Haleigh restarts the conversation.

"Seeing that the whole mother-daughter conversation thing is hard for you, Mom, I'll help you out. Yes, I know that you have probably killed some people. How I know isn't important, so if you are cool with it, we'll just leave the source out of this."

"My daughter is a little smart-ass!" I say, following it with a laugh. "But yes dear, I can guess your sources. Does what you just said, bother you?

"That you have killed some people? Oh *please*, Mom – look around us. Watch the news sometime. The world – *my world* – is full of assholes, and..." she pauses, as if deeply considering something. Then in almost a whisper, she finishes her thought, "*...некоторые из них, вероятно, должны быть убиты.*"

It takes about a heartbeat for her to realize what she said, and she instantly blushes – bright red. The fact she said *'some of them probably need to be killed'* in grammatically correct Russian, for some reason, doesn't seem to be of any concern to me.

"Sorry, Mom. That just sorta slipped out, honest."

"Which part?" I ask, struggling to fight off a laugh. I change directions, walk over, and take a seat on the steps of the small structure used by kids waiting for their buses in the morning. After a moment of hesitation, my daughter joins me.

"Mom? It really did slip."

"Oh relax. I'm just thinking, Haleigh – just thinking. It's not every day that a daughter tells her mother that she knows she's killed people. I'm trying to absorb that one."

"Yeah, well, I think that makes us even, Mom. It's not every daughter who has TWO parents in the CIA either."

I put an arm around my daughter's shoulders and squeeze. Then, I kiss her gently on the forehead.

"And how many, exactly, do you know, Haleigh?"

"Actually... just one."

We both laugh.

"Can I ask something else, Mom?"

"Young lady, you are allowed to ask your mother anything you feel the need to. There's no logical reason to hide anything from you any longer."

"Aunt Whitney – did she *really* do all those things that..."

"Your father and uncle are both blabber-mouths, but yes, Haleigh, she damn sure did. My sister, and her 'associate', were responsible for saving more lives, of all nationalities, than any ten people on the planet combined."

"Wowzers. That's like totally cool, Mom."

"What? That your aunt is a hero or that I told you she is?"

"Yep," she replies with a smile.

"I assume I should blame your aunt for what appears to be your near-perfect Russian?"

"Uh... well..." she pretty much forces out, definitely unsure how to answer my question.

I laugh and say, "Come on kid, we still have a mile to go."

She jumps up and then pulls me to my feet as well. As we are about to take off running again, I reach out and grab her by the shoulder.

"Haleigh, would you do your mother a favor?"

"Sure, Mom, what?"

"Would you promise me that you'll never..."

My wonderful daughter, who amidst all the madness that my life is, turned thirteen a month earlier, gives me a devious little smile and interrupts me.

"Did *you* promise Grams? Or, did you just do it?"

I've been put in my place, by a thirteen-year-old.

"GO!" I yell, giving her a gentle shove. As she takes off in the direction of home, I add, *"God help you, if I catch up with you, young lady!"*

And yes, she makes certain she gets home before I do.

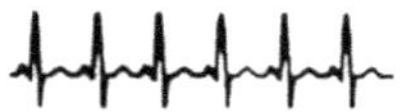

 Solution Squared: Recalculation

# 101

During the time I'm recovering, I do a lot of soul-searching – as does my sister. I, however, have more to consider than she does – the two main things are Haleigh and Lyle. The slightest change in any of several things that happened in Switzerland and Chuck would be raising them by himself.

Although I try to have the same conversation with my son that I had with my daughter, he's far less receptive. Pretty much all I get is, 'Yeah, Mom, okay, whatever'.

Yes, the child drives me nuts.

My husband, however, is a different story. He *knows* me.

"You'll have to quit Court – and you know it. There's no way you can be around the daily insanity, and not end up back in the field."

"Excuse me? I most definitely can, Charles Whitman! In the last six weeks, I've managed to stay quietly behind my desk, and push paper."

"I think not. Some crisis or another will eventually arise, and you will be out from behind that desk, gun in hand, and in the middle of it in a heartbeat – if not faster. It's who you are, babe."

"He's probably right, Courtney," my sister says from behind me. "Genetics – you know?"

That gets a laugh from everyone.

When I turn away from Chuck and glance into the kitchen, I see her standing at the stove cooking, and experience another of my 'intense rushes'. It's a repeat of the one I had back on Crete when Melinda confirmed that there's still someone who looks *exactly* like me.

"But, what else can I do?"

"Teach," Howard says.

"Yeah, okay. But I'll still be exposed daily, to the goings on of the Agency."

"Not at the Agency. At a university somewhere. Together. That could be interesting, if not amusing..."

"Yeah, I guess," I reply, as I walk over and stand staring out into the woods through the sliding glass door on our patio.

A couple of seconds pass before my sister walks up behind me, lays a hand on my shoulder, and puts a glass of wine in my hand.

"Come on. It's time for one of those 'sister' talks, I can tell."

She slides the door open, leads me across our back deck, and out into the yard. When we approach the big oak tree, she points at it, says 'Sit down," and takes a seat right beside me.

"Flashing back to a conversation on the tire swing, aren't ya?"

"Yeah, that, and other things. If we'd known what the hell we were getting into, the day Natalie sat down at our table, do you think we'd have done it anyway?"

"Yes."

I turn to look at her, as I sip my wine. She has the cutest little smirk on her face.

"That's it? Just 'yes'?"

"Oh, come on, Courtney. Even with – or maybe especially with – foreknowledge of all the shit we have *both* been through, there is no way you can convince me you'd go back and make any different decision. You said it to Mom yourself..."

"I know – *it's our path and we have to travel it.*"

I raise the glass to my lips and take a sip of wine, staring off into the distance. She's right of course, and I even admitted it to myself, an entire lifetime ago, when she and I were sitting on that damn tire swing.

"What's really on your mind, Sis?"

"Something your husband said to me – back when we first started looking for you. We were talking about Tarasov and I made the comment that the silly bastard needed killing – which at the time, of course, seemed a reasonable position."

Whitney laughs.

"In the middle of my rant, Howard looked me right in the eyes and told me that *'perhaps he did, but it was the speed with which I was willing to do it'* that really bugged him."

Whitney takes my glass, takes a sip, and sits staring at it.

"It's what we do, Sis," she finally says, handing me the glass.

"Yeah, I know. But, has being shot at and killing, become *too* ordinary for us? Crap, Whitney, I'm a damn soccer mom for crying out loud. I'm a forty-year-old woman, whose daily life involves keeping up with a husband, and two parents, raising her kids, and when necessary, running around with spies, being shot at, and shooting back while trying to save the damn world! Sorry, but you can't convince me that's even remotely close to normal."

"I never claimed to be normal, Sis. No way would a 'normal' person involve themselves in *this* world. You have no idea of the things I've done…"

She stops, again takes my glass, and sips it, all the while staring off into the trees.

"I snuck onto a Russian flagged oil tanker, and then killed – with help of course – sixteen guys who intended to turn it into a floating bomb, and use it to kill God only knows how many innocent people, just to make a 'statement'. I let a very warped lunatic use me – *for whatever he wanted, Sis* – just so I could get close enough to him to make his death appear to be suicide so there wouldn't be any questions or repercussions. I helped my partner modify a bomb that not only destroyed a munitions supply but also killed about two hundred people, who were in the immediate area. I even killed a fanatical female on a train, up close and personal, while she was sitting next to a ten-year-old child…"

She stares at the wine glass the entire time she's talking, and when she stops, she almost drains it before handing it back to me.

"No, Courtney," she continues, now looking directly at me, "none of that would qualify as 'even close to normal', but it's what I do. And you know what? Not only am I *very fucking good at it*, but *some good comes from it*. Even if this sounds cold and callous, it's far better that I kill a hundred, than they should use the weapons and bombs and terror to kill a thousand. The bottom line is, if you can find a way to rid the world of lunatic assholes, I'll promise to quit killing people." A couple of tears have already escaped her eyes, and are slowly trickling down her cheeks when I lean over and hug her.

"She won't give in until she talks one of us into it, you do realize that, right? Short of retiring, I don't know what else to do."

"And why are you trying so hard *not* to retire, Sis? I mean, considering what you've been through."

"Smartass…"

"You aren't done, are you? You need to keep doing this… God knows why, but you honestly need to keep dealing with the insanity of what we do."

"I'm afraid, Whit – afraid that if I get off the path, I'll never discover or fulfill my destiny," I reply, letting my head come to rest on her shoulder. "HE kept me alive for a reason, and I somehow feel like I have to keep going until I reach the end. I need to understand the 'why' of all this…"

"Well, big sister, we are individually, *the best* at what we do. Alice knows it, everyone in that building knows it, and even the damn bad guys know it. It's the logical progression of things if you think about it."

"Do *you* want the job?"

"We both know you'll be far better at it. You're the expert at 'comprehension' and 'strategy'. It's like Howard and Carl, and Alice too for that matter, have been constantly telling you since

Istanbul – *your damn brain works in far different ways than the rest of ours do,"* my sister replies with a laugh.

She returns her gaze to the woods in front of us, now lit by the setting sun, and as an afterthought she adds, "I, on the other hand, am quite adept at *'facilitation'*."

As the words leave her lips, the brain my sister is talking about gets away from me – again.

"Holy shit, Sis! I just had the most bizarre idea!"

"So, share."

"I need to ask my daughter a question first."

"Let me help you with that."

My sister sticks her fingers in her mouth and lets out a whistle that damn near deafens me. Seconds later the sliding glass door opens and Howard sticks his head out.

*"What!?"* he yells across the yard at us.

"Send my niece out here, would ya?"

He nods and seconds later my daughter comes out, closes the door behind her, and crosses the yard to where we are sitting.

"Sit, Haleigh."

"Yes ma'am," she replies, taking a spot on the grass facing us and tucking her feet up under her, Indian style.

"How would you feel about your mother keeping her job?"

My daughter laughs at me – the kind of laugh that usually indicates the total absurdity of a question.

"Heck Mom, I'd rather have you happy and sane, than what being a 'stay-at-home-mom' would turn you into. You always tell me and Lyle, *'do what makes you happy'* – so maybe you should practice what you preach?"

My sister responds to her niece's comment with a rather loud laugh of her own.

"Mom, none of my friends have a clue about what you and Dad do. They all think you're some kind of secretary and that Dad is just a computer geek of some kind who works for the government. I'll bet you have noticed that Marie and Justin and

Melanie and all the rest of my friends are always hanging out over here, at our house, haven't you?

"Now that you mention it..."

"Do you even know why, Mom?"

"Even if she does, I don't – so tell me," Whitney blurts out.

"Because *my mom* is the coolest mom around. They're all jealous of me, that's why," my daughter replies.

Then she turns and looks me right in the eyes.

"You *always* seem to be there, Mom, when me or Lyle – or whoever – needs you. Even when Aunt Whitney was in trouble on the other side of the world, you didn't even hesitate. You just went and got her."

"Well now, can't argue with that logic," Whitney says, leaning over and hugging my daughter.

"You need to do whatever *makes you happy,* Mom, and if being a 'spy' – God that sounds so completely goofy, I swear – is what you," she stops talking for a second and looks at Whitney, "and you too – want to do, you guys should definitely keep doing it."

When she stops to breathe, I lean over and hug her.

"Besides," she continues, glancing at Whitney and smiling ever so deviously, "the rumor is that my mom and my aunt *are the best in the business.*"

Whitney and I break up laughing at the same time.

"I guess I'll have to ask your bro..."

"Mom, he's a boy. He doesn't care – trust me. If it's not about football or video games, Lyle doesn't care."

"Well, it seems my niece has just decided our futures for us, Sis. You ready to implement this 'idea' of yours?"

"Whitney, you have no idea how much trouble we are about to get into here..."

So here we sit – my sister, my daughter, and I – on a warm spring day in Virginia, laughing like a bunch of fools.

"Every man has his own destiny; the only imperative is to follow it, to accept it, no matter where it leads him."

Henry Miller
American Novelist and Painter.
1891 – 1980

# 102

It's 2:30 PM on a warm summer day in July, on the patio of the O Nosso bar, on Rua da Carreira, in the town of Funchal, on the Portuguese island of Madeira.

As they say in the 'spy' business – *neutral ground*.

A casually dressed older woman walks up and sits down at a table occupied by a lone older gentleman.

"Welcome, Alice. It is good to see you again. You appear to have healed properly. Were there any complications?"

"No, no complications medically, Yakiv. Business, however, was a completely different animal. How are things for you? It appears Isaak is back in operating condition."

"Yes, he healed quite well, and as I am sure you know, your Miss Bergstrom called to check on him a few months after the 'incident'."

Sokolski's verbal tap-dancing draws a healthy laugh from Alice Williamson. Moments later, a waiter walks up, and with a friendly smile, Alice orders a glass of red wine.

"Are you prepared to take this meeting completely off the record, Yakiv?" Alice asks as the waiter disappears back into the bar.

"Are you, Alice? Over the last few months, I have come to understand that our ongoing untrusting nature must be placed behind us and left conveniently, at the end of an airport runway in Switzerland. Frankly, I feel that our current circumstances dictate that it has been left to us – *you and I* – to change the way our business is done."

"I couldn't agree more," Alice replies with a huge smile, as she pulls the bud from her ear, and then removes the small mic under the collar of her shirt. Just before she lays them both on the table, she holds the mic in front of her mouth and says, "It's time. Come over here please."

With a laugh, Yakiv Sokolski does the same thing, speaking in Russian to whoever is monitoring him.

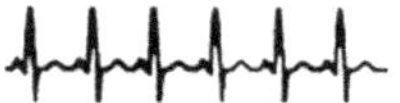

# 103

The moment I hear Alice call for me over the circuit, I step out of a car that's parked across from the bar, and take a moment to straighten the wrinkles in my dress. As I'm closing the car door, a casually dressed, rather handsome guy, who appears to be about the same age as me, comes out the front entrance of the bar, looks directly at me, then turns and walks toward the side of the building. I immediately cross the street and we arrive at the small gate into the patio area of the bar about the same time. With a smile, he opens it, allowing me to enter first. As we approach their table, Alice speaks first.

"Both of you sit down over there, and be quiet."

With a devious smirk, I head for the table Alice points at. The Russian, however, turns immediately to his boss.

"Директор?" (Director?)

With a hearty laugh, Sokolski replies, "Do as she suggests, Andrei, and learn about your opponent, for as I have come to discover, she is quite adept at what it is she does. And just so you know, both speak our language – fluently."

The poor guy looks totally confused but does as instructed, taking a seat directly across from me.

"Andrei Gryzlov," he says, extending his hand to me.

"Whitney Jensen," I reply, shaking his hand.

"Свободно?" he almost whispers.

"Да, весьма свободно" (Yes, quite fluently) I reply.

He returns my smile and we turn our attention to our bosses – who many consider to be the two greatest minds in the world of espionage – and sit listening.

"The untimely death of Comrade Nikolsky did, as I am sure you expected, greatly complicate the political atmosphere in Moscow. However, with the help of the President, we have identified a few remaining hardliners in the Federal Assembly."

"I completely understand. My Commander-in-Chief took the time to personally rake me over the coals numerous times. It seems the Swiss were *very* unhappy with the mess we made in their yard. It took my office three months of continuous and intensive 'damage control' to explain, and smooth over that little debacle."

"Because of that failure, I have come to understand this has become a game for those far younger than you and I," Sokolski offers, using a handkerchief to wipe sweat from his forehead. "I fear we are too old, and too set in our ways, Alice, to keep up any longer."

"I too, am quickly learning that, Yakiv."

"Well then, to that end, I suggest you and I take a walk, and allow younger minds to deal with the absurd politics of our respective governments. I think we deserve an opportunity to do nothing more than enjoy a hot summer's afternoon."

For a microsecond, Alice Williamson truly looks confused. When Sokolski nods in our direction, Alice turns and looks, and the moment her eyes find us sitting across from one another, the reality of the situation sinks in.

"Damn... How did you know, Yakiv?"

"We are so very much alike, Alice, from days past. Because *I* understand the inevitable, I must assume *you* too understand it. The Switzerland debacle served to confirm my suspicions. It is time – *for both of us*."

With a deep, hearty laugh, Alice turns to face us again, and says, "Okay, you two can talk now. While Yakiv and I take a walk, you two sort out this mess. When we sit down together for dinner, we will expect positive results. Understood?"

As totally comical as it is, we both say, "Yes ma'am," at the same time. We watch quietly as they stand, and then go out the same gate we entered through, disappearing from view, in only a matter of seconds. We sit staring at each other for at least a full sixty seconds – both quite unsure of the situation we've just been thrust into.

"Well, that was totally weird."

"Yes, Miss Jensen, I would have to agree."

"Let's go with Whitney, and start on a positive note?"

"As you wish, *Whitney*. Before we start, I wish to inquire as to your sister's recovery. Has she healed?"

I have to bite the inside of my cheek, trying not to laugh. My mind quickly drifts back to a time in our youth, when my sister and I perfected the art of being each other.

"Yes, she has.  It was difficult, but she has fully recovered."

"As severe as her injuries were, I believe that it is God who is responsible for her survival. I hope to meet her someday."

His comment makes me smile – I can't help it. I also realize there's something about him... something... 'comfortable'.

"So, Mr. Gryzlov, when dealing with difficult issues, I prefer to just step off the cliff and see where I land. Wouldn't you agree that we need to step right into the 'shit' and go from there?"

He laughs – a true and honest laugh. A laugh that allows me to relax, ever so slightly.

"I think we will do well as 'opponents', Whitney."

"Okay," I reply, as I stand and walk to the other table, "I'll start." I pick up Alice's almost full glass of wine, then turn and walk back to our table. "Yes, I do know what has become of your missing 'assets' – all of them," I say, taking a sip of the wine, smiling, and then taking my seat again. "And no, I'm not going to tell you."

"I see. I have only one question on this subject, and in the interest of fairness and our new 'negotiations', I hope you will be willing to answer it."

"And that would be?"

"Can you give me your *personal assurance* that none of them will ever again, be involved in our daily business?"

"That depends. Can *you* assure me that your 'superiors' are no longer interested in finding them?"

"I can."

"In that case, you have *my personal assurance.* In fact, I intend to make damn certain they *all* remain *retired.* And just for the record, no, they haven't joined the other side."

"Well, thank you for sharing that. In the interest of our new 'understanding', the Russian government now considers this a closed subject. I will, however, hold you to your word."

"That works both ways," I retort. "Next issue?"

"The small – or perhaps large – matter of certain 'missing' Russian funds."

"You play this game very well, Andy. Can I call you Andy?"

With a genuine smile on his face, he instantly replies, "You may use whatever name or nickname makes you comfortable, Whitney. However, the new issue remains unaddressed."

"I assume you'd like to open negotiations on the possible reacquisition of these funds, you claim belong to the Russian government?"

"No, nothing quite that formal I am afraid. I am thinking more along the lines of 'we want our money back'."

I laugh – loudly. He played it perfectly.

"Yes, Andrei, I do believe you and I are going to become good friends, and in the process, we may do some interesting things for our governments as well."

"I agree. I suggest we start immediately. Will you walk with me? he replies. Then, with a big smile, he stands, walks around the table, pulls out my chair, and helps me to my feet. As we head for the gate, we each reach down and pick up the items left behind by Alice and Yakiv, stick them in our pockets, and then exit onto the street.

We turn opposite the direction our bosses went, and over the next few hours, the current Director of the Russian SVR and the new Director of the American CIA become not only new adversaries but more importantly, new friends. Sure, we'll still play the games that our countries have been playing for over a hundred years, but we – Andrei and I – are about to rewrite the rulebook.

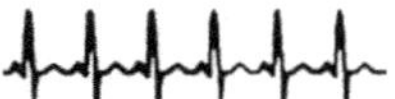

"The torment of precautions often exceeds the dangers to be avoided. It is sometimes better to abandon one's self to destiny."

Napoleon Bonaparte
Emperor of the First French Empire
1769 – 1821

# 104

It's 2:55 PM on a hot summer day in July, and across the street from the O Nosso bar on Rua da Carreira, in the town of Funchal, on the Portuguese island of Madeira, a green-eyed blonde, with a long ponytail, steps out of a small store, stops momentarily and looks around, then slides a pair of designer sunglasses over her eyes. Seconds later, she crosses the street and falls in a fair distance behind the *new* Director of the SVR and the *new* Director of the CIA.

The first thing one notices about her, besides her striking good looks, is that she looks *exactly* like the new Director of the Central Intelligence Agency.

As seems to be usual of late, perhaps because I've been dead for quite a while, no one took the time to factor my existence into their silly games. Well, no one except the current DCI — who happens to be my big sister.

Go figure.

After fifteen years, you'd think they'd learn, wouldn't you?

I mean, hell, how can you miss *two* good-looking blondes, with bright green eyes, who just happen to be...

### Identical twins...

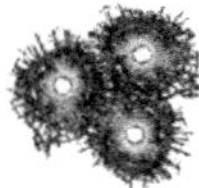 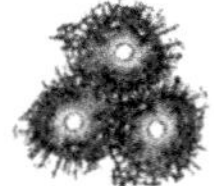

www.ingramcontent.com/pod-product-compliance
Lightning Source LLC
Chambersburg PA
CBHW071422190726
48292CB00001B/82